A Night With No Stars

A Night With No Stars
SALLY SPEDDING

First published in Great Britain in 2004 by
Allison & Busby Limited
Bon Marche Centre
241-251 Ferndale Road
London SW9 8BJ
http://www.allisonandbusby.com

A catalogue record for this book is available from
the British Library.

10 9 8 7 6 5 4 3 2 1

ISBN 0 7490 8312 3

Printed and bound in Wales by
Creative Print & Design, Ebbw Vale

Born in Wales, Sally studied sculpture in Manchester and at St. Martin's, London. She is still a practising and exhibiting artist. Having won an international Short Story competition, she began writing seriously whilst teaching full time and her work has won many awards, including the HE Bates Short Story Prize and the Anne Tibble Award for Poetry. She regularly adjudicates national writing competitions and teaches Creative Writing for Leicester University. She finds both Wales and France complex and fascinating countries – full of unfinished business – and has a house in the Pyrenees where most of her writing and dreaming is done.

For Rebecca and Hannah

What is blacker than a raven?
                    – Death

From the Wooding of Ailbe

It is the "no time" when the thin veils between the two worlds of the earthly year – the Samhain and the Beltane – are at their most fragile. When cosmic order is suspended and the ancient dead rise up to stir the souls of the living.

The seven Pleiades are also rising in the north-east sky and Beltane dawns as if the first in all creation. While the sun slides upwards into the acid blue, licking away the night's sharp frost, the young inhabitants of Rhayadr-gwy wake up to the prospect of a day without school. A Baker Day of empty classrooms, silent playgrounds, yet nevertheless a day full of possibilities. When anything can happen.

For those on farms there's winter silage to cut and stock to primp and preen for tomorrow's Gamallt Show. For those without land but possessing boots and bikes, there are hills and valleys with stones glistening under laughing river water.

There's laughter too on the Ravenstone estate, but by the time the ravens have left the alders' branches to make a single rogue cloud against the blue, that laughter dies to a silence of fear. The killing room won't know the sun until late afternoon but its damp shade is the perfect home for slaughter; its dimness the only blessing for those who must watch...

Footsteps now. The drag of steel-tipped heels on stone, enough to cause sparks. The scratch of fingernails against bone as a knife's dull glow appears. Do those lads on the hills who are downing their beer or the girls undressing in the grass hear the scream which follows? Does anyone stop from their pleasures to wonder what crime has deserved such punishment? No, because the air already sings with suffering and in those ancient rural parts, familiarity has bred not compassion but contempt.

And in the aftermath, while the sun clears the high bank with its scalp of scrubby trees and the chimney's smoke dwindles and dies, one thing is certain. A reign of madness has begun.

Chapter One

Sacred land. Sigh of my soul with its springs
Of eternal youth. Whose waters return the stars'
Gaze, whose mirror traps the Glory of the Day
And turns His eye to gold...
RFJ 1986

At six o'clock on a mid-June evening in London's Covent Garden, and so hot that even the pavements seemed to be sweating, Lucy Mitchell, twenty-nine year old assistant editor with the literary publishers Hellebore, passed through the hotel's automatic door and into its Art Deco-tiled foyer.

Everyone knew the Chandos because its function suites were regular backdrops for celeb parties reported in the gossip magazines, and on this occasion, the basement Tabard Room had been booked for a signing by Hellebore's most distinguished author, James Benn.

After her ID had been processed, she clacked her way on three inch heels down a flight of stairs and into a large basement room of leather sofas, marble bistro tables turned pink by their red shaded lights and a trio of morning-suited musicians beginning to tune up. But to her, it was the giant-sized photographs of a greying middle-aged man filling every available inch of wall space which made her catch her breath. James Benn, no less. The biggest jewel in Hellebore's crown. Arguably the most successful writer of literary fiction since the mid-nineties, and here she was, in lieu of the man's absent editor, to pay homage to his latest book – a biography of his wife.

Having set out four stacks of the bulky hardback on a table ready for signing, she turned her attention to the display, glancing from one portrait photograph to the other, feeling the author's steely gaze on her from wherever she placed herself. He was hypnotic, larger than life, and, more importantly, through his recent Booker shortlist successes, extremely influential. It was vital therefore that on meeting him face to face for the first time, she look her best and make a lasting impression, because up to now her six-year career had slipped to being merely Keeper of the Slush Pile, and he might just be the one to help turn all that around.

However, right now, she felt too hot, too nervous to do herself justice.

'Where's the loo?' she asked one of the waitresses with some urgency, and within seconds was standing in an orgy of gold and granite where floor-to-ceiling mirrors had the unnerving effect of adding extra inches to her hips. She removed her black peep-toe shoes and placed them next to one of the sculpted washbasins, feeling the pleasure of cool tiles against the hot bare soles of her feet. In fact, these Manolos belonged to her best friend Anna, who'd been given them by one of her wealthy exes. Now she was settled near Lambourn with, according to her, a well-hung horse vet. Freelancing as a Sayer Price editor from home, doing all the things Lucy could only dream about...

'They're not called Fuck-Me shoes for nothing,' Anna had joked, before handing them over the day before. 'And you wear air hose with them, okay? So keep your knees together.'

Lucy snatched a paper towel from a stone-shaped dispenser, dampening it under the tap then working it between her purple varnished toes. She recalled the moment she'd unravelled the fabulous pair from their silvery tissue-paper beds to slip them on her feet, and the word wicked had also come to mind.

She could hear other voices now. The strains of classical music. The nerves in her stomach began to kick in. It had been a rush that afternoon, with a screen full of emails still to open and a pile of manuscripts waiting to be read, but everyone had orders to get to the Chandos on the dot of six. Benn must be kept sweet or else. There were plenty of other publishers waiting for him to slip out of Hellebore's net.

She re-entered the now busy room and mentally prepared herself for her encounter with the man she'd not yet met. The man who probably didn't even know she existed. This Dorset millionaire had featured in either every Booker longlist or shortlist since 1994 and been narrowly beaten for the prize itself last October. Now *Tribe* was tipped to make the longlist in two months' time. She'd read it of course, and could hold her own should he deign to speak to her. He certainly knew his stuff, she thought. How the other half live, or rather, survive. How one family member's betrayal brings a lifelong fall-out. But what had puzzled her was how an archetypal Tory and ex-army major living in a part of the country where a car port would set you back a hundred grand, could write so convincingly about sink estates and the dispossessed. She'd dipped into the biography too, and been struck by his obvious devotion to a woman who now clearly needed a lot of care. Elizabeth was both his inspiration and soulmate.

She watched the Publisher and his Sales Director hover near the door. She'd been told to ensure that Benn started signing at 6.45 after the welcoming address, and to keep a good supply of books at the ready. There'd also been the instruction not to drink too much, when a drink was what she needed most. And now the room was beginning to fill up.

A tremor passed through her body. Why so nervous? She knew she looked good. Her thick fair hair gathered in a neat bun at the nape of her neck – the way Jon, her boyfriend, had always liked it – her black chiffon slip dress crease-free, showing off the smooth skin of her arms. The newly manicured and varnished nails...

She was just wishing that Anna was here to give her some moral support when the room's open door suddenly revealed a tall white-suited man, accompanied by a tiny grey-haired woman walking with the aid of a zimmer frame. The discreet applause became a buzz of interest as admirers and well-wishers gravitated towards them.

She knew Benn was forty-eight and his wife ten years older, but the black-shawled figure with the strained white face looked more like his grandmother. And as for him... She stared hard, comparing reality with the photographs. Unsurprisingly, the photographs won, because his skin – a mix of ruddy and tan – was sun-damaged around his nose, and his hair seemed altogether more grey. He introduced his wife to the Publisher and his team, then, having snapped his fingers for the crab canapés, began feeding her as if she was still a baby.

Lucy stared at this strange scene until those alarming blue eyes of his immediately went into roam mode as if he was out on manoeuvres somewhere. She quickly lowered her gaze when they turned her way. He was also more jowly in real life, she thought, but otherwise in good nick like a typical gym junkie; immaculately groomed with a maroon shirt tucked into an expensive-looking belt.

Then those eyes again. On her. She looked down at her wine, embarrassed, aware of his whiteness drawing closer. When she looked up again she saw that he'd abandoned his wife to a posse of journalists and was now alongside. He took a glass of red wine from the Italian waiter's tray and, to her surprise, clinked it against hers. He then stared down at her Hellebore ID badge pinned above her left breast as if he'd never heard of her before. As if he'd no idea she was his editor's assistant.

She was right. This was typical Hellebore.

'Here's to whatever it is you want, Miss Mitchell,' he smiled. His eyes still on her breasts.

'To the Booker, then,' she replied, aware of a sudden blush hitting her cheeks. What kind of naff comment was that? she scolded herself inwardly as Nick Merrill, the Publisher, approached and pointedly ignored her.

'Signing in half an hour. Will that suit you?' he asked Benn, lifting yet another full wine glass from the proffered tray then surveying the almost full room. 'I must say, it's looking good.'

'Sure.' The author finished his drink in two gulps and moved in even closer towards her, his linen arm brushing her skin. Boss aftershave, she decided. The same as Merrill. Who was influencing who? she wondered, aware of Elizabeth Benn's silvery head turned her way. However, the author's wife was soon swamped by yet more media people. Not family, she noticed. Not a one.

But he was asking about hers with what seemed like a genuine interest. Then he began talking shop. How *Tribe's* paperback cover was proving tricky and the American market tightening. How hardbacks published in January were losers before they were even unpacked from their boxes. Nothing she didn't already know, but that still didn't alter her rapt focus on his every syllable.

'So, how's the new novel coming along?' she ventured, having heard through the grapevine that *Kingdom Come* was almost finished and was, if anything, even better than *Tribe*.

'Thirty chapters done so far,' he caught his publisher's eye and gave a quasi-military salute. 'Should be ready by the end of this month. Would you like a sneak preview? You'd be the first.'

But before she could reply, his hand was on her bare arm. Warm, slightly moist fingers, squeezing, relaxing in turn on her skin. The Haydn was in full swing now and when it seemed to her that the combination of talk and music had reached its climax, he took her glass from her hand, laid it on the drinks table and led her towards the door.

This was sleep-walking all over again. Something she'd often done as a kid, especially whenever staying over in a strange house. Not only that, but she was suddenly blind, hearing not just the cello sawing out the melody as they left the reception room behind, but also her own heels mark out her walk to the lift, until muffled by its rubber-matted floor.

What the hell was she doing? She didn't know the man, didn't even fancy him. And yet the flattering enticement to read his manuscript had wrong-footed her at a time when no one at Hellebore was asking her for anything more than cobbling showcards together or schlepping through the mountains of hopeful manuscripts. But why the lift? And then she twigged. This was an hotel. With bedrooms...

'Let me out at the next floor, please,' she said as evenly as possible, despite seeing his tanned finger press three.

'This won't take long. Just a quick skim. A few suggestions...'

'I can't impinge on your editor's territory, Mr Benn. We don't do that at Hellebore.' She felt the lift judder to a halt and the doors slid apart to reveal a waiter poised to enter, bearing an empty tray.

'Bollinger and ice for room sixteen in fifteen minutes,' he ordered the man, guiding her out on to the dimly lit corridor. 'After all, thirty chapters is something to celebrate.'

'I want to go. Now.'

'In a moment, please.' His grip tightened. 'You see, I've got a problem. Manda Jeffery's coming from a totally different viewpoint. She's too New World biased, whereas me, I'm...'

'She's done you alright up to now,' she protested. 'You've made the Booker shortlist umpteen times and now there's *Tribe*...'

'You don't seem to understand, Miss Mitchell. I want to work with *you*. So, let's go and take a look, shall we?'

She tried to escape, to kick out with her sharp heels but his grip firmed up.

'And it's no good making a noise,' he warned, heading for a room marked 16. 'This place has twenty-first century sound-proofing. No one will hear you. Not even someone next door. So you see, you'd better conserve yourself.'

Those words sent fear into every small corner of her. Her feet slipped around inside Anna's shoes, her dress rucked up under her breasts. It no longer felt like a dress, but a trap as he pulled her towards the bedroom door. With one swift movement his key was in the lock and the door pushed open.

Everything was white. Obscenely white, it seemed, with the blinds already drawn on the late daylight behind, the carpet, the embossed swirls which pressed into her back once he'd pushed her down on to the bedspread. His suit a malevolent spectre from which powered that reddened face and hands pushing her dress up to her chin then ripping her briefs over her shoeless feet.

'I've got my period,' she lied, still looking for a chance to put him off.

'Liar.' His breath rank and sour.

She screamed as a pulpy palm swamped her mouth and then something else, forcing her lips apart. She began to retch, unable to shift his thrusting weight and for a moment he withdrew, still straddling her with his iron thighs. Still keeping control. She shut her eyes and bit her lips as he forced her legs open. She smelt latex and something else. He was big, rough. Noisy. She was just meat, a space to be filled, to be devoured until his grunting climax, and when he'd finished she realised she was still alive.

He pulled out and rolled to her left, and immediately she wriggled free, grabbed her bag, her shoes and what was left of her pants and ran towards the locked door and turned the key. In that instant she turned round and saw him advancing, zipping up his fly.

'You come here.'

'Fuck off.'

Within three minutes, she'd reached the corridor, the empty lift, and after what seemed like an eternity, was once more outside the crowded racket of the reception where that same waiter seen earlier was on his way to the lift bearing a bottle of champagne tilting in its ice bucket. A white cloth neatly draped over his arm.

'Are you alright, Signorina?' he asked.

How could she answer that one? Bruised and burning, she just wanted to be sick again. To vanish forever with her own private shame. For how could she tell anyone, let alone her own mother? The one person she needed right now, and with the frantic music, and Nick Merrill's bark filling her ears, she reached the stairs then the automatic door, which sighed open, releasing her out into the hot city.

Chapter Two

TINA TWILIGHT

TONIGHT! SAT. APRIL 25TH 1987, AT THE CAE IESTYN WORKING MENS' CLUB, BRIDGE STREET, RHAYADER.

A Cole Porter miscellany from our favourite lady of song.
I've Got You Under My Skin & many, many more!
Doors open 7p.m.

While Lucy was back in her Tooting flat, sluicing away Benn's legacy under her antediluvian shower, some ten hours ahead of GMT and 12,000 miles away in Sydney, former bank clerk Robert Ferris Barker clamped a nervy hand on his alarm clock the moment its wake-up call began. He'd set it for 11 p.m. the night before, knowing he wouldn't sleep a wink with the racket going on in the unit next door. He decided it wasn't worth having a blue over it. Not with what he'd got planned for the next 24 hours.

He blinked out at the eerie night sky which cast his old roller blind a strange silvery colour, and if he moved his head just a little, could see the ivory disc of a full moon hover over Redfern's tenement blocks. There was something about it which stirred his memory and made him swing his tanned legs off the mattress with more vigour than anything he'd recently done at work. He switched on the shadeless bulb which hung from the ceiling by a knotted black flex, peed into the small cracked hand basin, then washed himself thoroughly all over with the tepid water which came one-paced from the single lime-scaled tap.

He checked himself in the mirror nailed over the sink. He looked okay, he thought, considering, and decided to leave the three days' stubble on his chin. In fact, every guy who was someone in Sydney was doing the same. Besides, it made him look older which was no bad thing.

Having doused himself with Urgent, a leaving present from the sheilas at the bank, he dressed in his work clothes and the expensive trenchcoat which he always kept in a dry clean wrap behind the door. That way he'd come over as a guy on business or a lawyer even, especially with his briefcase and matching luggage kindly donated by his boss and the Senior Team.

He checked his travel documents yet again. He'd been systematic about all of that, but at some cost to his recent social life. However, it was worth it and nothing was now more pleasurable than to safely re-tuck the white-smile photos, the proof of his dual nationality and return visa into their special pale pigskin wallet. Next he counted out all the pounds sterling he'd saved since last March; since his decision to shake off a life of forever looking over his shoulder; suspicious of strangers and the secrets behind their eyes. Why he'd shacked up in Redfern in the first place. It was a cesspit, but had suited his need for anonymity. He'd lived cheap, walked to the bank on Upper Street which kept him fit and where he could shower, and now it was time to say adios.

'See you, mate,' he said to the Abo crashed out by the stairs, careful not to let the man's liquid laugh reach his shoes. Its smell stuck in his throat as he hefted his suitcase over the Aborigine's legs, noting how his flies were undone and a hint of purple cock showed through the gap in his jeans.

Within five minutes, he was in Elizabeth Street and stopping a cab. As he closed its door behind him he glanced back at the dark screen of squats and, forgetting he was in the presence of a stranger – the driver – let out a burst of laughter. Part relief, part triumph because his mission was underway, and in two hours from now, he'd be in the air, leaving winter behind.

'Had a good night, mate?' asked the driver, a redneck in a quilted jacket. 'Or shouldn't I ask?'

'Ace, yeah.' He enjoyed, even encouraged this kind of banter. He knew he looked like the kind of spunk any half-decent sheila would drop her grundies for. So where was the harm in perpetuating the myth? It made him feel a real man, especially after the sexual humiliations he'd endured in The Lucky Country.

'Does she have a name?' The driver persisted, following airport signs and fiddling with his radio.

'Eve.'

'But not the first, eh?'

'Shit, no,' he laughed again, letting the man have his delusions. Then he stopped abruptly as the midnight news delivered by a woman newsreader's clipped, educated voice filtered into the cab. Each syllable she spoke made his breath tighten. Made the kilometres between him and his plane too many.

'Hey, get an ear on this,' the other man turned up the volume and leaned forwards as if to miss nothing. 'Nasty stuff.'

'Sydney police report that a sand cleaner on Bondi near The Pavilion has discovered the partially decomposed body of a young white Caucasian woman. So far there's been no formal identification and in the meantime the public are requested to keep away from the area until forensic teams have completed their investigation of the site. Meanwhile, Police Chief Bill Shaw has stated that it's possible the body has lain there undetected for at least five months and that records of all females missing around that time are being checked...'

'Never fancied there,' Robert lied. Yet as the moon continued to illumine the city's southern suburbs, and party-goers making their way home, he recalled lonely summer evenings with just other people's yabbering and the roar of the waves climaxing against the shore for company. 'Poor cow.'

'Yeah. I've got a kid sister,' said the driver, reducing the radio's volume as the latest on the UK's foot-and-mouth crisis hit the airwaves. 'Was just imagining how my folks'd be taking this news if it was her...'

His fare was thinking how imagination seemed the least of his attributes, when a surprise question threw him yet again.

'You from Redfern, then?'

'No. King's Cross.

'Right. Pukka place.'

'Yeah. But a guy can't stay in the chicken coop all his life. Got to see the world before he snuffs it.'

'No Nasho then?'

He hesitated. Being turned down for a digger in the army was not something written in bold capitals on his CV, and only he and his doctor back in Darwin knew that an uncorrectable medical problem had been the reason.

Uncorrectable? I don't *think so...*

With relief, he saw the airport lights beckoning. He just wanted this cockroach to shut the fuck up and get him there.

'Plenty of world in our house, if you want to look at it that way.'

He didn't, but the man went on regardless.

'My kid's just had grandchild number four. Got a unit on our second floor and pays us ninety dollars a month. Works out fine.'

'Sounds cosy.'

'Yeah. Company for the wife. Means I don't have to work Fridays.'

'By the way, I've been thinking,' Robert blinked as a booze bus overtook them and sped off along the dual carriageway. 'That girl in the sand. I reckon she's been dumped there recently from somewhere else. So she *would* be found.'

'Why do that? Sounds risky to me.'

'Must be a crook playing Hare and Hounds. Remember getting high being chased at school?'

'Yeah, I do, come to think of it.' He winked into his driving mirror. 'How I met the wife. In the playground.'

'I didn't major in Psychology for nothing,' Robert grinned back, sensing his pulse quicken as the cab slid into a designated bay near the

QF International Terminal building.

'Paid your departure tax, by the way?'

'With my ticket.'

He added a generous tip to the fare and collected his luggage from the boot.

'Good luck wherever it is you're going,' the cabbie called out as he unrolled yesterday's paper for a re-read.

'I'll need it. Cheers.'

He stood there in the chilly night and shivered. The well-wisher had caught him off guard and for a split second he considered changing his mind and hopping back into the warm cab. Then he heard the oncoming rumble of a plane coming in and visualised again as he'd done so often, what would be waiting for him once *he'd* landed, and knew that turning back was simply not an option.

Twenty-four hours later Robert collected his Vuitton luggage from the flight's crowded carousel in London Heathrow's Terminal 2 and made his way through the cattle-market crush of travellers towards the escalator.

Once through the exit gates he noticed two things. Firstly, that everyone seemed to have a cling-on who welcomed them with the kind of noises made during sex. Weird that, he thought. Secondly the clothes these overweight Poms were wearing were not a good omen. Was the economy so bad here that they could only afford shell-suits and polyester trackies? he asked himself trying to push his way through as quickly as possible. Hardly, judging by what he'd heard in the bank and a thorough perusal of the *Australian Times* on his non-stop flight.

The scene before him was like no one could be arsed any more. But was that really such a bad thing given his forthcoming agenda? Nor should he complain that the Bondi business wasn't mentioned in yesterday's *Sydney Morning Herald*. There'd been enough time to look for it during the flight, dammit, so he binned it as he made his way towards the nearest cafe and when he reached the counter, ordered an espresso.

The Chinese girl handed him his heavy little cup and saucer with that kind of inscrutable look he'd never got used to, even at school. Yet her lips, soft and bud-like, looked as if they could give good head. Yeah, he'd been there and had that done in the Chinatown clubs more times than he cared to remember. Just so far and no further. Always the same deal – accepted and paid for. Beyond that, well… That was his personal business. No one else's.

He finished his coffee and made for the sunlit tarmac outside the automatic doors. The few visibly armed cops prowling around didn't bother him nor the dark-skinned dero who harangued for change. Normally, in a more private place, he'd have kicked him in the nuts and told him about the boats his country used, bobbing around for ever in the Indian Ocean. But not now. Because here was evening sun on his skin, warming his blood and as he strode away with black shoes shining, and gelled hair glistening towards the nearby Novotel building, he knew that for him, the crucial transition from darkness into light was just beginning.

Chapter Three

𝕿𝖍𝖊 𝖗𝖆𝖛𝖊𝖓𝖘 𝖆𝖓𝖘𝖜𝖊𝖗 𝖙𝖔 𝖒𝖞 𝖈𝖆𝖑𝖑,
𝕿𝖍𝖊𝖞 𝖎𝖒𝖎𝖙𝖆𝖙𝖊 𝖆𝖓𝖉 𝖗𝖊𝖆𝖉 𝖒𝖞 𝖒𝖎𝖓𝖉,
𝕸𝖞 𝖇𝖗𝖔𝖙𝖍𝖊𝖗𝖘 𝖆𝖑𝖑, 𝖎𝖓 𝖇𝖑𝖆𝖈𝖐 𝖘𝖔 𝖋𝖎𝖓𝖊,
𝕬𝖗𝖊 𝖓𝖊𝖛𝖊𝖗 𝖈𝖗𝖚𝖊𝖑, 𝖆𝖑𝖜𝖆𝖞𝖘 𝖐𝖎𝖓𝖉.
𝕰𝖓𝖌𝖑𝖞𝖓𝖎𝖔𝖓. 𝖈 𝕽𝕵𝕵 1986

If only she, Lucinda Caroline Mitchell, had been able to share this terrible secret with her one surviving parent, it might have made all the difference to her post-June life and helped her get the work setbacks more
in perspective. But how could a convent-educated girl confess to her
serial church-going mother that a man like Benn had so easily flattered
her? The answer was, she couldn't.

Nor could she have told Jon Sadler, trainee partner with a firm of
solicitors in Clerkenwell. They'd been an item since her first year at
Warwick, and both had sensed parents increasingly impatient for the
engagement ring, the wedding and their chance to be eventual grandparents. Now in mid-August, free of her job, her grungy flat, with the
prospect of a new era opening up, he too, was past tense and she had-
n't seen him or his parents since a trip to Kew the weekend before her
attack. If she'd happened to be Jewish and married, divorce would
inevitably have followed such a disgrace whether it had been her fault
or not. Such was the shame of rape...

Perhaps she'd have finished with him anyhow. Safe and steady
should have been his middle names and more than once she'd reminded him he was twenty-nine, like her, and not eighty-nine. Especially
since his precious fridge magnet collection was growing apace and his
father's old brown Volvo had landed in his eager lap. Cruel? Yes, of
course she was, but after the subtle and not-so-subtle humiliations
meted out to her at Hellebore and then by James Benn, she'd grown
cynical and suspicious. The opposite of the kind of daughter she'd once
been. The woman she really wanted to be.

Now badly burnt after a failed interview for promotion, then getting the sack for impulsively shoving some slush pile manuscripts into
a tart's hands outside the Hellebore office, she was beating a retreat.
But her conscience was clear. For six years she'd worked her nuts off
for pants pay and no recognition, and that surely was enough out of
anyone's life.

Her late father's gift of forty thousands pounds would be hers on
her imminent thirtieth birthday, and this had spurred her into not only
sending for the details of a promising looking property near Rhayader

in rural mid-Wales, but also dipping into her meagre bank balance for the second-hand blue metallic 4 x 4 she'd just bought from a Balham garage.

Survival, definitely. Reckless, maybe, but more and more she'd felt her future somehow inextricably woven into a past where strands of her childhood were already disintegrating and would be lost altogether if she didn't act. And one of these lay on the seat beside her. *Magical Tales from Magical Wales.*

She glanced down at the treasured childhood book lying on top of the Ordnance Survey map for Radnorshire and Griffiths Brothers Estate Agents letter confirming her appointment to view a house called Wern Goch at 3 p.m.. The cover depicted what had once been a luminous rainbow arching away towards green sheep-strewn hills, and although now faded, its symbolism remained as strong as ever. Because here she was, on the road, heading west towards that promised pot of gold.

Another glance and a deft flick of the first few pages, seemed to make the past twenty years of her trying too hard, notching up all the conventional goals of life slip away. She was back once more in her old bedroom in Rusholme, sharing with her beloved father the treasure trove of exotic fables and their intricate and colourful illustrations. For despite his gruelling regime as an inner-city GP, Dr William Mitchell had always made time to enjoy with her, his only child, this mythical aspect of his favourite part of the world. A world so far removed from the one which was daily sapping his energy and, unbeknown to either her or her mother, straining his too-generous heart.

She knew off by heart the sequence of double-spread paintings showing deep blue lakes edged by majestic forests and beyond these, wild uplands rugged against the blue sky. Next came snow-dusted peaks and lush, shady groves inhabited by gods and goddesses too beautiful to be ever human, she'd thought at the time. A long-haired Epona astride her horse, Blodeuwedd in a sunny flowery glade and the handsome Dagda with his sun-burnt skin, his tunic of feathers set against a sky full of twinkling stars. How in the mystical time between Beltaine and Samhain, the Queen of the Faeries rides out on her white horse and its tinkling bells can be heard through the night for miles around. How if you hide your face she will ride by, but look at her and she might choose you.

Lucy smiled to herself despite the slow-moving traffic. How often had she'd dreamt of being "chosen" and taken away to an enchanted land? Every day of her life, it seemed. And what about the glossary of Welsh words at the end of the book? That particular list had soon subverted the compulsory bedtime prayer into a string of glistening jewels.

arian = silver
baban = baby
cofio = remember...

Yes, she remembered every single word, even now, and as she recited them while nudging her way through clogged-up Balham, they delivered a fresh conviction that this is what her father would have wanted not just for her, but himself. Even after death? Who could say?

Stuck behind an unloading van on Trinity Road, she focused again on the cover, which the sun now mercilessly highlighted. Its corners worn bare over the years, its creator's name, long rubbed away, while inside, these same details had been smothered by an Ex Libris sticker and forgotten. But not so the opening poem inside, framed by elaborate Celtic knots. This too, she knew off by heart.

'O King of the Tree of Life,
The blossoms on the branches are your people,
The singing birds are your angels,
The whispering breeze is your Spirit.'

Each syllable spurred her on to put miles between not only that job which had sapped *her* spirit, but also the man who'd nearly destroyed her. Who'd caught her unawares at her desk only four days ago to whisper that she was looking lovelier than ever. Bastard.

She was going too fast. Had to brake hard at traffic lights as she tried to erase his image from her mind. To dwell instead upon what today might have in store. The most important day in her life. Besides, wasn't the notion of regeneration the very core of Celtic belief? she asked herself, setting off again. She only had to think of the forty pages beside her to realise that the hot grimy streets around her now represented a kind of birth canal and she'd soon be coming out the other side into a brighter, better world. The world the book had shown her, but this time instead of the ancient willow dwelling nestling beneath a gentle hill on page twenty-four, it would be Wern Goch on the Ravenstone estate. She'd already decided that the moment the Llandrindod estate agent's email and various attachments about it had landed on her desk at work.

The grainy photos showed a substantial Victorian house, which although in need of total modernisation, boasted three acres of land, bordered in part by the river Mellte. The agent, Lloyd Griffiths, had also waxed lyrical about what she could do with such productive pasture and informed her that the owner, a retired police officer from

Cardiff CID, was looking for a quick cash sale.

A mixture of excitement and alarm fuelled her journey towards the A40, because although Anna was backing her all the way in this scheme and promising to pass on some manuscripts for her to read once she was settled, her mother, still up in Manchester, was bound to be another matter altogether. This was why, so far, she'd been told nothing.

With a full petrol tank Lucy headed west towards Wandsworth and the river, but roadworks meant a static half hour listening to Nelly Furtado with the day's new sun on her face. So as not to get lost and waste time she pulled out her old A-to-Z and before she could access SW London, the pages opened on to Piccadilly where the site of Hellebore's office lay under a blob of fluorescent marker. At the time, fresh from university and into a work experience placement, it had represented the sun in her universe. Her one big future, and seeing it now brought everything back into painfully clear focus.

The road drilling ended only to be replaced by a massive dumper truck nudging out of a nearby side street. It was then, in the added wait, that she finally plucked up the courage to reach for her mobile and punch in her mother's number.

The one-sided conversation which had followed lingered in her mind like a hangover all the way to Oxford and then along the A40 towards Cheltenham where the sun finally succumbed to thick grey cloud moving in from the west.

Damn the woman, she thought, snatching her sunglasses from her face and leaving them on the map in the vague hope they'd be needed again. *Don't the ones we love know just which buttons to press?* Then a quieter, more insistent inner voice retaliated, *but don't they generally speak a truth we can't bear to hear?*

She shook her head as if to shift this surreal dispute from her brain and sounded the car's raucous horn at a dithering moped rider ahead. She felt instantly better, for Barbara Mitchell had been in a rush to get to some teachers' union meeting and had needed answers fast. Answers which Lucy couldn't give. Such as, what will happen to your pension contributions? To Jon? Why choose to live somewhere you barely know? And, as I'm your mother without your father to help, it's a bit rich you've so far not said one word to me about this crazy project of yours...

After a strained silence which Lucy had broken by stating that in the interim, the Rusholme address had to be on both her driving licence and insurance certificate, the line had died. ending in a final non-negotiable click. Barbara Mitchell had put the phone down on her.

With the petrol tank half full, Lucy pulled in at a Little Chef outside

Gloucester and felt the light kiss of rain on her skin as she locked the car. Then suddenly a chill seemed to envelope her whole body and, for a moment she stalled outside the cafe's welcoming entrance, truly aware for the first time since she'd left London of the enormity of what she was about to do. Ignoring at least two warning voices, she was cutting the cord which had connected her to the past twenty-nine years of her life, while overhead the light disappeared from the sky. In its place came those huge rolling clouds she'd noticed earlier. But this time ominously bruised, laden with water, descending low over the summer trees. And still the temperature stayed cool.

She crossed both arms and slapped her body to generate some warmth... Was this some kind of portent? she asked herself. Some divine signal sent courtesy of Barbara Mitchell? She shivered once more as she held the cafe door open for a woman even younger than herself to emerge, struggling with a double pushchair. Her twins' eyes also focused on the sky then closed simultaneously as if to shut it out.

At Ross-on-Wye, instead of taking the A44 north to Hereford, Lucy chose a B route south which would take her past the Black Mountains and eventually on to the A470 to Builth Wells. Having crossed the swirling Wye at Hay where, during her first year with Hellebore, her invitation to take part in a literary panel had been swiftly transferred to her editor, she set her wipers to full speed. The rain wasn't the only obvious and visible change since leaving Gloucestershire. The foliage too was different. Here oak and beech crowns glistened darkly against the gunmetal sky and the surrounding landscape grew starker, with firs cresting the odd bare hillside like so many Mohican spines.

Here too, a tractor slewed into the middle of the road in front of her leaving thick ochre tracks in its wake. There a bullock cavorted on the wrong side of a shorn hedge and at Hinton dirt-brown sheep of no particular breed picked their way across the tarmac while a few yards further on she saw one lying upturned by the roadside, its legs stuck in the air. She was tempted to stop and see if the creature was still alive, but one glance at those blind eyes, that grimace of tiny teeth told her to keep going.

That sixth form trip from the Ursuline Convent had brought her to Rhayader and the Elan Valley from the north, via Oswestry and Welshpool through summer fields and pretty villages. Her little book come to life, she'd thought at the time. However, here was clearly another country and by the time she'd re-crossed the now overflowing Wye at Glasbury, she was cocooned by the downpour and a gradually thickening vapour rising from the earth.

She switched the de-mister to maximum and leant forwards to clear the inside of her windscreen with a free hand, only to see what looked like giant burial mounds rearing up on either side of the Tarmac. She also noticed with an anxious lurch of her heart that the road's reassuring white lines had vanished, so that when some vast *thing* with no lights loomed up in front of her, she skewered the Rav into the soft spongy verge, and sat there watching the mud it had flung slowly slide down her newly valeted windows.

Having checked her open map again and after some tortuous mental arithmetic, she realised that with 5 miles to the inch or 3.2 kilometres to 1 centimetre, Rhayader was still over half an hour's drive away. And that didn't include Wern Goch which, according to the agents' map could only be reached by a long twisting minor road. What state was that likely to be in after all the heavy rain? she asked herself as she moved off, casually glancing at the petrol gauge before settling the Rav on the road's steep camber.

Damn.

The needle had mysteriously slipped a whole section and now lay perilously near the red slash meaning empty. No. It was impossible! She peered again as her pulse moved into overdrive, but nothing had changed.

Builth wells was a good fifteen miles away and the time between now and her crucial appointment was shrinking by the minute. None of the hamlets or small straggly villages which she passed through at a steady 30 mph possessed anything resembling a garage and it was with a numb dread of being stranded in the middle of nowhere that she arrived at Builth's outskirts. However, even the bright Texaco sign which had instantly lured her onwards was a con, for both the garage's entrance and exit was blocked to all vehicles by a double row of orange and white traffic cones.

What now?

She swung the car alongside the nearest cone barrier and switched off the engine. Within ten seconds she'd sprinted around an oil tanker parked alongside the pumps and was inside the vivid strip-lighted shop facing a young Asian lad who sat behind the counter flicking through a Play Station catalogue.

'I've got to get some petrol,' she began, trying to keep hysteria out of her voice. 'My tank's empty. Dead.'

That last word made the boy look up.

'Sorry, but you'll have to wait until our new supply's in.'

She remembered her father with his lawnmower and the full red petrol can he always brought back from the local garage.

'Can't I have some in a can, then?'

'Not for half an hour at least.'

She bit her lip hard as she stared out at the damp scene beyond the shop's widow where nothing was happening. Nothing that is, except more rain and a deep conversation taking place near the air pump between the Texaco driver and an adult version of the lad by the till.

'Does it always rain so much here?' she asked no one in particular.

'Water Break Its Neck.'

She spun round to face him.

'*What?*'

'My best mate from school drowned there last year.'

'I don't understand...'

'Up near New Radnor. It's one hell of a waterfall.'

'What a weird name.'

'There's a lot weird round here, I'm telling you. I keep asking me dad if we can all go back to Small Heath but he goes deaf on me.'

'Perhaps this is his dream.'

'You must be kidding.'

'Well, just be patient,' was all she could say. She'd absorbed enough gloom and doom already and for a brief moment, thought almost longingly of Curlew Road and Albion Villa with its blackened London brick, the chipped windowsills. And then her mother's recent comments flooded her mind.

'I give it three weeks at the most,' she'd said. 'You'll have seen sense by then, my girl. You mark my words. And don't forget how hard your father worked so he could leave you something...'

She paid the lad for a packet of Orbit gum and six second-class stamps, knowing in the marrow of her bones that after just two hours her mother and another Hellebore author who'd also uttered warning words, being proved right.

'Which way you goin'?' the tanker driver asked as she left the shop.

'A470 Rhayader. Why?'

'There's a Murco garage on the left after the main roundabout out of town. Shouldn't be telling you that, mind,' he smiled.

'Thanks.'

Aware of both men's curious stares as she returned to the Rav, praying the engine would start. It did, and in her urge to get away she crashed first gear and took off as if the devil was on her tail. Ten minutes later on yet another damp forecourt surrounded by gloomy dripping pines, the 95 Unleaded nozzle was throbbing reassuringly in her hand to the tune of £28 and still rising. When she paid, using her card, she asked the girl at the till if there was anyone around who could take a look at the car and explain the strangely malfunctioning gauge.

'Ain't no one here at the moment, only me,' the girl replied. 'Me uncle's not back till five. Where ye from, anyway?'

'London.'

'Join the club.' Her ruddy cheeks widened in a smile, then to Lucy's surprise she lifted an old anorak off a nearby hook and pulled its hood up over her head. She locked the till and came round from behind the mountain range of travel sweets and snacks to lead the way outside. 'Me and me mum used to live in Streatham. Hey, this is mad.'

'Small world.' She followed her to her car where the girl promptly squatted down near its tank and sniffed for petrol.

'Definitely a leak,' the girl announced, straightening up. 'Just drive her over the pit in the Service Bay and I'll take a proper look.'

'Thanks, but what about your shop?' She'd spotted a middle-aged couple heading towards it, grey heads bent against the rain.

'This won't take a mo.'

Lucy positioned the wheels on to the tracks either side of the pit then watched as her saviour descended into the black oblong beneath the Rav.

'Who sold you this pile of shite then?' she called up a few moments later. Lucy's heart sank recalling the helpful salesman at the Battersea garage and the three-month guarantee.

'Private sale. Camden,' she lied.

'Well, whatever. You've been 'ad. Unless a stone or summat's hit you underneath.' She emerged from the darkness up the pit's corner steps, uncoiled two lengths of flex and dragged them down with her.

'What are you going to do?' She got out and peered after her.

'Put my GNVQ metalwork into practice, ain't I? Soldering over the 'ole in the fuel pump. Might need proper welding later on, mind.'

Lucy thought of her insurance cover, less than a day old.

'Surely there'll be sparks?'

'Nah. You're thinking arc or oxy-acetylene.'

Suddenly a man's cough echoed in the Service Bay. Lucy looked up, startled by the grey-haired customers' sudden proximity.

'Isn't anyone serving in the shop over there?' he grumbled. 'We're late already for our next appointment.'

Next appointment? She eyed them both up and down. What did that mean? she asked herself. Were they house-hunting as well? And if so, was it possible they were going to see Wern Goch?

'Won't be a sec,' muttered the girl as the smell of sizzling solder filled the shed. 'Got an urgent repair to do 'ere first.'

'Forget it.' The man took his companion's arm and turned to go. 'However, I'm sure Murco will be pleased to hear about your attitude.'

With that both scuttled away towards their car and slammed its doors shut as loud as they could.

'Miserable old crusts,' said the girl. 'Always the same with the grey brigade. Fuck-all to do all day but hassle everyone else trying to do a job of work. They're ten a penny round 'ere now, I'm afraid. And tight as fishes' arseholes. So,' she grinned mischievously, 'welcome to God's waiting room.'

'Don't any younger people move in, to say, start new businesses etcetera?'

The girl re-appeared, winding up the soldering iron's wires.

'Nah. It's too bloody quiet. Besides, the locals don't want no one takin' work from 'em. Was bad enough getting this place. My uncle's had dog shit through the letterbox and a death threat. Anyway, where you off to?'

'Rhayader.'

'Right. You livin', workin' there, or what?'

'Just looking around.' She climbed back into the Rav and reversed it out into the forecourt.

'Bit too quiet, that place an' all,' the girl went on, securing her anorak hood under her chin. 'Gives me the willies.'

Lucy tried not to listen. Instead she fumbled in her wallet. 'Anyhow, what do I owe you? You've saved my life.'

'Nothing. But p'raps we can keep in touch. I ain't got many friends, specially round 'ere. My name's Hazel. Hazel Dobbs.'

'And I'm Lucy. Short for Lucinda.'

'That's posh. Got an address?'

'I will have after next week.'

'Least you know where I am.'

She left her picking up a damp newspaper from the outside rack and, as she drove away with the petrol gauge steady on full, wondered why she'd not heard any stone or any other object hit her car underneath. It was a total mystery, yet she had a gut feeling that this wouldn't be the first to contend with.

A distant thunder murmured over the Cambrian Hills to the west and a now night-black sky released bigger, heavier drops of rain. Not angled or driven by any wind, but straight and to the point, battering the Rav's soft top, casting what felt like yet another curse on her future plans.

Chapter Four

'Ev'ry time we say goodbye, I die a little,
Ev'ry time we say goodbye, I wonder why a little,
Why the gods above me, who must be in the know
Think so little of me they allow you to go...'
Cole Porter

Although her watch showed barely three o'clock, as Lucy reached Rhayader's southern outskirts, the afternoon could easily have been mistaken for a November evening, and the fog lamp of the driver in front led the way like the Devil's eye through the wet dark streets lined with lit-up houses.

When she reached the town centre's prominent white clock tower, she suddenly found herself on her own. The place was completely deserted, eerily quiet as if the locals had guessed that worse weather was to follow. This wasn't what she'd remembered at all from her sixth form trip or even visualised from her glassed-in sixth floor office at Hellebore. The very name Rhayader had promised quaint shops from another era, friendly folk only to happy to reassure her, a peaceful sky folded between fir-clad hills.

But this was different. As if some cosmic artist had peevishly chosen this one spot to overdo the black and finally tip his dirty water out. And dirty it was too because most of her screen wash was already used up and its last-gasp spurts effected no change to her visibility at all.

Just when she needed it most. Just when the expected turning to Ravenstone Hall was imminent.

She parked on the main road's verge and, having been drenched by a speeding coach and nearly run over by a latter-day Hell's Angel doing a ton, she ran over to where, according to her map, the minor road should be.

This can't be right...

But it was.

The unmade track in front of her was barely wide enough for a car let alone anything bigger and, once she'd manoeuvred the Rav into its tight confines, she could hear the scraping of hawthorn against her paintwork. No way could she stop to check the damage because there wasn't enough room to get out. A wave of panic hit her. She must keep going, because the longer she was there, the greater the risk of something else meeting her head on and wanting to pass.

She took in everything of her surroundings. Here a squalid hamlet lining the verge, there a solitary cloaked figure with a sheepdog staring after her. She said a silent prayer because there was still no way any other vehicle could get by, nor could she turn the car round. But after three more miles with no widening of the track, that prayer soon multiplied.

Her face felt on fire while her fingers gripped the steering wheel to keep the car from veering into the unending hedgerows. What the hell was she doing here? she asked herself. Supposing it was some kind of trap? All this and worse coursed through her mind as yet another mile went by with still no sign for Ravenstone Hall. It was as though the place didn't exist. As if the plans she'd been sent and the blurred picture of Wern Goch were part of some sick joke and someone somewhere was laughing themselves stupid.

Chapter Five

I am shadow of another
I am guardian of this place
I am a wind of the sea
I am a tree of the forest
I am a teardrop in the sun.
M J J 1987

Mark Jones pulled his old parka hood up over his wet head and waded purposefully through the slipping mud towards what had been his treasured den for as long as he could remember. He'd borne the brunt of yet another angry exchange with his father up at the Hall over its forthcoming sale, and endured yet more hurtful remarks from that inebriated mouth. There was only so much grief he could take…

'I hate him. I *fucking* hate him,' he chanted, turning his face away from the lowering clouds for today was Gethsemane all over again, only this time two thousand and one years later. This creeping gloom signified not only the end of *his* world, but also yet again, the end of his will to live.

As the tall young man slithered further down the track which levelled out to bisect the waterlogged marsh, his curses at Hector Jones's betrayal grew. He stopped for a moment to take in the scene around him as if for the last time. Then he checked his watch. Last year's Christmas present from his father, when the best gift he'd offered had been a promise never ever to sell his special refuge. Now that promise was broken and there was just half an hour to go before the first viewing. His head felt ready to explode. It was stress. He didn't need a doctor to tell him why or to suggest he give up chainsawing the firs in the Coed-y-Bryn Forestry. No, it was because he'd been harnessing all the psychic energies brewing in his head, to effect a change on a certain inanimate object.

Her car.

Yesterday, having finished an early shift and after his mission in Hereford, he'd called in to the estate agency in Llandrindod Wells where Lloyd Griffiths had told him of Miss Mitchell's change of plan. Instead of next weekend, the young woman was coming to view at 3 p.m. today. 'Keen as mustard she is,' he'd added. 'Driving all the way from London.'

'M4 or M40?'

'Now why d'you need to know that?' Griffiths had surveyed him with a look of suspicion and pity. Just like everyone else had done for the past fourteen years, whenever he'd stuck his head above the parapet.

'I just do, OK?'

But there was no budging the agent on her name or her whereabouts, and Mark knew it was because people talked. He was the object of their gossip, the young man from Ravenstone Hall, who trod too slender a tightrope between sanity and madness.

But the new office girl there hadn't been quite so circumspect. For when he, the sawyer, had first called in and seen Lucy Mitchell's email enquiry about Wern Goch abandoned in full view on the counter, this was just the very information he'd needed. And his anonymous reply to her at her London workplace had been swift and to the point.

'*Young woman,*' *Lloyd Griffiths had said…*

Mark's own mother had been a young woman too. A wild blend of beauty and laughter, her hair the colour of the copper beech which still flourished close to the Hall and which every autumn covered the ground around it with gold. He'd think of her and touch its bark every time he passed by. Another reason why he'd never been able to leave the area and explore a wider world. This was her place. And where he must be too. He could recall everything about her as if it was just yesterday. Her skin, always as soft and white as Bryn Evans's goats' milk. Her wide grey eyes and delicate fingers with their always perfectly varnished nails. The musky after-scent of her clothes when she'd kissed him goodnight…

He slipped and quickly righted himself. He was almost there, where the one tall chimney stood almost defiantly from the little house's roof. Where the glassless sash window on that north side beckoned him on, as if into harbour. But just then, the prospect of someone else following this very path, of taking possession of what was rightfully his, was unbearable and it took all his concentration not to let the blackness overhead enter his being and strike him down.

However, this imminent stranger wasn't the first who'd shown interest in the property. A couple from Birmingham who should have come to view last Monday afternoon, hadn't shown up because their brakes had failed near Kidderminster. No one had been hurt in the incident, but Lloyd Griffiths had informed his father they'd lost their nerve to proceed to Rhayader.

At least that was something.

He approached the ancient scullery door always kept half-open to the weave of the wind and the blowing rain. It provided a passing shelter for the Evans family's Welsh mules which had successively grazed the land since the death of Queen Victoria. The year the Hall had been built. But this time the door was fully open. His pulse rate jumped. Someone or something must have moved the thing since he'd been there yesterday afternoon. Maybe Bryn Evans, maybe one of his sheep, spared the latest cull. But in his heart he knew somebody else had been there. An intruder with evil on their mind.

He entered the gap with room to spare and noted the wet flagstones and a trail of sheep's droppings like mini-grenades glistening in the dull light. Then he ran his fingers down the door's edge to check if any fleece had scagged on the old splintered wood, only stopping when a distinctive coppery smell reached his nostrils. He sniffed the scullery's damp air before two more urgent steps brought him into the kitchen space where an old salting slab which had once served as a homework desk lay under the one sash window.

His chest tightened, his breath trapped in his lungs as the dim light revealed a large black bird slumped across the stone. Rhaca his pet raven. Was he dead or just stunned? Two more paces gave the answer.

Jesus wept...

As he studied the rigid corpse more closely, the past fourteen years seemed to be slipping away. Except that now, instead of trickling darkly down human skin to that same salting slab, the bird's blood had congealed against its own skin and bone, because most of its feathers had been brutally torn off.

He felt himself go pale. His stomach suddenly leaden as a mix of rage and terror bubbled up inside and seemed to concentrate in his head. Rhaca was his only friend. His one true mate.

This was no normal killing. So who had done it? And why? Surely brave old Rhaca would have tried to guard Wern Goch from intruders? His eyesight the keenest of all the other ravens, his trust not easily won. Yet there was no sign of any struggle. Maybe he'd been tricked into a false sense of security. Whatever the reason – guilt at taming him in the first place, perhaps – bloomed and mingled with the other shit in his mind like night smoke from the recent foot-and-mouth pyres.

He stroked the bird's denuded wings, aware of summer flies beginning to muster as yet more unanswered questions tumbled around in his mind in the same way the river Mellte swirls around the rocks beyond the alders. Could his own father have thrown a freaky? No way. The old tosser never came near the house any more, too pissed for a start. The drink of oblivion had seen to that. But Bryn Evans sometimes turned up, if only to chase his sheep out of the scullery. Could it be that the farmer was getting greedy, wanting yet more land and another house for himself? Especially as he'd just lost his goats and prize flock of Beulahs. Was this act of savagery some kind of message? A warning?

It was clearly time for questions, he thought, trying to gently prise apart his raven's claws. But both lay locked together like the kind of quick-fix sculpture now littering Cardiff's public spaces. Junk, that's all it was. Art for the punters. It was all crap.

'Rhaca?' He whispered, touching the creature's open beak, as if this simple movement might draw some delayed response from the bird. 'Who's been in here? Who did this to you?'

When no answer came, he quickly cast a wary eye over the rest of the kitchen and beyond to the dark parlour and hallway barred from the marsh by a front door which had never been used for as long as he could remember. He thundered up the short flight of woodwormy stairs and ran from window to window in the two upper rooms in case the killer should be still hanging around outside. But there was no living thing. Only the scraggy mules foraging among the reeds.

When he returned to the scullery he stared deep into those dead amber eyes, realising with an overwhelming sense of loss that they were already elsewhere, scanning the Otherworld, borne by those same two outspread wings.

He cradled the lifeless body in his calloused hands and carried it outside to the tumbledown barn which lay just beyond the house's eastern wall. Here he found a piece of dry sacking and tenderly set down his only real friend amongst its stiff folds.

'I won't be long,' he said as if the creature was still alive and listening. 'Wait here.' Then he ran back up the waterlogged track towards the Hall. His headache seemed worse, thumping out those same questions *who?* and *why?* into his brain with each footfall but, by the time he'd reached his father's study, once the grandparents' Chapel of Rest, and opened its door, he knew the answers to both. And that knowing re-kindled a deep paralysing fear which he'd suppressed for so long. Someone wanted to drive him mad, and that someone knew just what to do...

He gripped the door handle to steady himself as blood again deserted his face and his first intended question for his father died in his throat.

'That you, son?' Hector Jones's voice rose above the gloomy chime of an antique sidereal clock which stood against the room's end wall. He looked up from inside the tatty gold-quilted corner bar; a half-empty gin bottle in one hand, a glass tumbler in the other.

'Has that scullery door got a key?' Mark wrinkled his nose at the thick mix of booze and fags. Fags and booze. Every hour Happy Hour. This is what his father, once an able Detective Inspector in Cardiff's CID had come to. He stank like a wino and he damned well looked like one. Under normal circumstances, he'd have felt some pity for the man who'd once lovingly ironed his grey trousers and packed his daily lunch-box for the school he'd hated, but nothing had been normal since 1st May 1987. And if he searched his heart, his father hadn't been the only victim.

'What scullery door?'

'At the house.' He nearly added 'twpsin' but thought better of it.

'That Bryn friend of yours had it years ago. And for the front.'

The way he said 'friend' made him catch his breath. What was he implying? Because although there'd been whispers about Bryn being gay, it was the one thing *he* wasn't nor ever could be.

Women were like the moon. Lustrously inviting on the one side, but on the other, dark and treacherous. Why at twenty-six years of age he was still a virgin.

'But surely the cops locked it straight after...' His voice trailed off. Even now, he couldn't bring himself to refer to the events of that May morning in 1987 when all the neighbouring farms were whitening their stock's fleece with talcum powder and boot blacking hooves for the local show. His father shook his grizzled head.

'No. They never did do that. You wouldn't let them. Remember?'

Mark used the silence to refocus on that one important question. To regain his courage to ask it.

'Has Richard been in touch at all?' As casually as he could, but Hector looked as if an electric current had just passed through him. He reached for the bar in front of him like a drowning man to a lifebelt.

'No. And long may it stay that way.'

'Are you sure?'

'Of course I'm bloody sure. Jesus Christ, give me strength,' he sighed, regained his former position then added more gin to his glass.

'Well, someone's been in the place – yesterday sometime, I reckon. Rhaca's dead. Stabbed in the neck.'

The ex-copper stared at this son who'd seemed to have inhabited a different world since the day he'd left his mother's womb. He poured out a further generous amount of gin from the Gordon's bottle and stood it next to his glass on the ring-marked mahogany bar. 'Look, son, some old bird's not exactly what we've been missing all these years, is it? Get real, I say. Get a life, eh?'

'Just like you, huh?'

Hector took a drink and wiped his lips with a dirty pullover sleeve. The old scar on his right wrist still visible. Still raw after all this time. Mark waited with a suddenly dry mouth for a reaction but his father was clearly full of surprises. 'I heard they're looking for army recruits over at Sennybridge,' he said. 'You'd have a decent wage there. The chance to see the world...'

'I don't want to see the fucking world.'

'You should.'

'So what I'm bringing in here isn't enough?'

Hector laughed. A great gaping roar which showed a throat as deeply red as the dead raven's flesh.

'You must be bloody joking.'

Mark drew closer. His head pulsing. If he'd had a weapon on him then his dad, who was disposing of his whole world for peanuts, would be breathing his last. Instead, he backed away because with that much drink inside him, Hector Jones was capable of anything and he didn't want his head messed up any more. To the Celts, this soul home contained the most potent source of power, and that fact was as real to him as his late mother's smile.

Hector Jones recovered his composure and emitted a loud burp. He then pointed to the ceiling over his head where Mark's official bedroom lay. 'Oh, and by the way,' he began, 'if and when our viewer comes a-calling, you steer clear. I don't want her put off the place. Understood? And if there's any mess down at the house, get rid. Pronto.'

Fuck you.

He slipped out to the tiled hallway and found the bunch of keys he was looking for in his father's old duffle-coat pocket. It took him just five seconds to extract the one he wanted from the keyring, knowing that in the hour it would take to get a replica made at Kwiklock in Newbridge the old git wouldn't notice it was missing.

He heard the study clock chime three as he leapt up the shallow stairs three at a time and reached the locked door he wanted. Upon it hung a dusty ceramic rose whose petals were the colour of blood. He hated the thing, but even after fourteen years still hadn't yet plucked up the courage to shift it. However it was the key to his mother's room which mattered.

At last.

As a pub and club singer originally from Bute Town, Cardiff, Sonia Jones had kept her working shoes and dresses strewn everywhere, often spending days altering hems and necklines on a venerable old Singer sewing machine which always stood on its own table in the window bay. For him growing up, the room had been a real Aladdin's cave, with bright pink stoles, glitzy baubles covering every surface and cottons of cobalt emerald and scarlet which he'd rewound for her, pretending they were temples from some far-off land...

That's what he'd remembered.

He held his breath as he turned the key in the lock and entered, as if this still musky-scented air which met his nose wasn't his to breathe. Then he stopped in his tracks wondering for a moment if he'd got it wrong because apart from two unfamiliar wardrobes, the room was bare. Even the sewing machine had gone. He felt numb as he looked around in vain for some remnant of his childhood there when the afternoon sun had turned the floorboards the colour of sand and the noise of her feet working the treadle had been the most soothing he'd ever heard. But now, not one single coloured thread remained and soon his numbness changed to anger. There could have been only one person who'd done this, and he was downstairs, probably comatose by now.

Then he remembered the object of his mission. To find something of hers to wrap Rhaca in, and surely she'd have forgiven him that? The bird who'd stayed constant during the worst years of his life. The one living creature who'd kept him sane, so it was important that this latest burial and the shroud itself – the racholl – represented both loss and love. He glanced at the two matching wardobes ranged against the far wall, chose the nearest then pulled opened one of its doors.

Nocturne…

He gripped the door knob to steady himself, wondering how come that scent was still so powerful after all these years?

Suddenly he heard his father clomping around in the study. Time was short. He must find something for his raven before his chance was lost, and when he peered inside the wardrobe, saw his mother's clothes pressed tight together on their rusty iron hangers; the toes of her stilettos and leopard-skin ankle boots protruding beneath the dress hems, as if ready to move. But in fact going nowhere.

A bolt of pain seemed to hit his heart as he prised the hangers apart. Finally he chose a pink silk blouse with a scalloped collar, and having hidden it hidden inside his parka, re-traced his steps. At the sight of his father shuffling around downstairs he kept his clenched fists in his pockets. If he hadn't, there'd have been more blood. More misery.

Chapter Six

𝔍 𝔥𝔞𝔟𝔢 𝔣𝔩𝔢𝔡 𝔞𝔰 𝔞 𝔴𝔬𝔩𝔣 𝔠𝔲𝔟, 𝔍 𝔥𝔞𝔟𝔢 𝔣𝔩𝔢𝔡 𝔞𝔰 𝔞 𝔴𝔬𝔩𝔣 𝔦𝔫
𝔱𝔥𝔢 𝔴𝔦𝔩𝔡𝔢𝔯𝔫𝔢𝔰𝔰...
𝔗𝔞𝔩𝔦𝔢𝔰𝔦𝔫

The now deeply rutted track abruptly turned downhill – its gradient as vertiginous as a Big Dipper run, except that this particular route was awash with surplus water and large loose stones which lifted her wheels, made the car lurch perilously from side to side, and sent her book flying to the floor.

At last Lucy reached the bottom which was under at least a foot of mud and saw a further track lead off on the right. At its corner stood a washed-out sign saying RAVENSTONE.

Thank God.

And, without realising, she began to breathe normally again.

But her relief was short-lived. She peered through the filthy windscreen and noticed with dismay a high ridge of grass between the ruts. Almost too high, she thought, slipping into first gear, just in case. The Rav stalled, again and again, trapped on this unkempt island until with a surge of power, she pressed onwards as the track opened out on to a weed-strewn hardcore driveway.

She stared in amazement at what lay at the end of it. Was this huge Gothic pile real or was she hallucinating? Anything was possible after what she'd just endured. She blinked, switched the smeary wipers to top speed for a better view, without success, and the longer she stared at the building's forbidding bleakness, so did thoughts of Transylvania stay stubbornly in her mind.

While the visitor waited, the rain strengthened and drove down mercilessly on both man, beast and the boggy land they shared while the forestry worker made his way round to the blind western side of the Hall. Mark knelt down next to the unmarked spot where his mother now lay and used his bare hands to gouge out a small hollow alongside her. Just as he was smoothing the top layer of soil over the pink silk bundle, he heard an unfamiliar car's engine close by.

He sat back on his haunches and stared in the direction of the access track beyond the drive, convinced that neither Bryn Evans's Defender nor Dai Fish's Transit was paying a call. For a start, there was some hesitation going on with the engine idling then revving. His pulse quickened; the carotid pumped in his neck. Maybe Miss Mitchell had arrived and was changing her mind after all. And why not? He'd worked hard enough to prevent her getting there, but, if she still insisted on viewing his den, at least that blood on the salting slab would be sure to put her off. No way was he going to clean up and sanitise the place as he'd been instructed. Those souvenirs were all he had.

His wait was soon rewarded, for a muddy metallic blue poser's car appeared at the end of the track and struggled up the last few yards to the turning area in front of the Hall. After a few moments he saw the slim figure of a young woman wearing jeans and a white T-shirt under a denim jacket emerge from the driver's side door and, having checked the car's bodywork on both sides, began making her way towards the Hall. He saw several sheets of printed matter in her hand and with a lurch of his heart recognised the estate agency's distinctive logo on the top page. So, here she was. At last.

Chapter Seven

The Samhain's passed and in the sky
The moon so bright it blinds my eye,
While all around, Dark Mother sleeps,
And binds my soul to hers for keeps.
Englynion, MJJ 1987

Lucy felt the sodden ground leech into her trainers, but other things were now more important than wet feet and the few scratches which had spoilt the Rav's blue metallic paint. Namely Ravenstone Hall. It was evident from the building's lichen-covered stone to the crumbling window sills that the place had been neglected and unloved for years. Equally, a palpable aura of sadness clung to it despite the presence of a huge copper beech tree whose colourful crown nudged against its end wall. Here also a rusted truck and a battered old Renault van were parked together near a wheelie bin, camouflaged by a premature fall of golden leaves from above.

That wasn't all, because as she stared at the row of stained steps leading to the Hall's main door, a tall good-looking young man appeared from beyond the beech tree, his two red clay hands dangling at his sides and both knees of his jeans stained the same colour. Without any word of greeting, he fixed her with a brooding stare, while every nuance of his body language spelt out "You, trespasser. Get lost."

'Hi,' she began, despite her nerves kicking in, as an older greyer man tottered with the aid of a stick down the Hall's steps. Either he was disabled, she thought, or had been hitting the bottle big time. Her instinct was to go and help him, but the dark stranger now stood firmly in her way. 'I'm Lucy Mitchell,' she volunteered brightly, already judging how far she was from her car and a possible escape. 'Has the estate agent arrived yet?'

'He's coming straight from Cae Harris and the river's flooded up by Gaufron,' said the other man whom she assumed must be the ex-copper, in his late fifties. He gripped the end of the iron balustrade and announced, 'I'm Hector Jones, and this is my son Mark. I must say, young lady, I'm damned pleased to see you. Now then,' he moved forwards and tapped his son with the stick on his wet shoulder. 'What did I tell you, eh? Get that bloody muck off your hands and leave us be.'

'He won't be coming.'

'Who won't?'

'Griffiths. I told him Wern Goch was off the market. Didn't want to waste his time, see.'

She looked from one man to the other as her stomach turned over. She'd been in dodgy pubs before now and knew a bad atmosphere when she saw one.

'Indoors you and no messing.' Hector Jones ordered, his unshaven face the colour of the sky, every inch of his long-abandoned body trembling. With a backward glance at her, Mark advanced towards his father and prodded a muddy finger into his chest, leaving a noticeable smear on his already shabby donkey jacket.

'I've got a witness. Miss Mitchell,' he pointed at her. 'Wern Goch is *not* for fucking sale.' With that he disappeared round the side of the Hall and, in the ensuing silence she recognised that same weird croaking sound which she'd heard on the phone only yesterday.

'Corax…corax…corax…'

She looked towards the old beech tree and realised that the soil underneath matched that on the son's hands and knees. Something very odd was going on, yet she felt as if an unseen force was drawing her inexorably into these two people's lives. People she'd only known for a matter of minutes. Was this to be her new start? The place of her renaissance? She hardly thought so now…

'Ravens,' the man suddenly interrupted her thoughts. 'Damned things. For a start, they shit everywhere. He encourages them, I'm afraid.'

'Who?'

'Mark.'

'Is that why this Hall's called Ravenstone?'

'Ten out of ten to you, my dear. Right,' he eased himself away from his support and without further ado, took her arm. His sudden weight nearly made her topple over. 'Let's go.' Together this unlikely couple reached the point where the hardcore ended and the muddy track began. Hector Jones looked at her trainers and tutted. 'Didn't that Griffith idiot tell you to bring boots?'

She cursed inwardly that she'd forgotten that particular suggestion, aware that all the while they were being watched from the Hall.

'I just forgot. It was such a rush getting away…'

'Getting away?'

'I mean, getting a car, all my gear organised.' She glanced sideways at her companion who, although clearly the worse for wear and reeking of gin, wasn't stupid. He kept his head lowered, taking care not to slip on any of the loose stones partially hidden under the mud. 'Look, Mr Jones,' she paused, blocking his way, reluctant to go any further without some questions answered. 'Mark obviously doesn't want you to sell Wern Goch. He could make things difficult, surely?'

'The Deeds are in my name, not his. Besides, I don't intend starving in my old age.'

Or dying of thirst, she thought, smelling his breath.

'I know what you're thinking,' he said suddenly, looking at her out of the corner of a liverish eye. 'But let me tell you, he's all mouth and no trousers that one. Harmless as a puppy. Just so long as he can dream, he's happy.'

'We all need to do that,' she said with feeling.

'Indeed we do.' Then Hector Jones looked away. It was clearly time for a change of subject. 'So, you want to grow organic fruit and veg here? That's what Griffiths said.'

'I'd give it a try, anyhow,' she replied. Except that as she scoured the bleak surroundings and saw how the land sloped down to a lake of standing water she realised this was more like cloud-cuckoo land. Barbara Mitchell was right again. And what would her father be saying? She dared not think. 'Would there be someone round here to help me sort things out?' she asked finally.

'No problem. Lots of folks I know'd be glad of some extra cash in their pockets.'

She remembered the tiny run-down cottages along the first track she'd taken off the A44. The collapsed barns and piles of corrugated junk. What was she to believe? The teacher's warning words or his?

'Is that the truth, Mr Jones?'

'I am an ex-copper you know. In my book, lies are like moles. They hide for a while then up they pop and God help you. Get my meaning? Which is why nothing's been tarted up here. What you see is what you get.'

Indeed it seemed so.

The rain slowed up and the smell of lanolin from the sheep hung in the air. There were hordes of them, not taking the slightest bit of notice as she and the drunk progressed downhill. This lot didn't resemble the creatures she'd once pored over in *Magical Tales* – white and fluffy with cute black noses. These were ugly. Brown-faced with larger than usual ears and where they'd been scouring beneath their tails, the fleece hung black and reeking. What had RS Thomas written about the fluke, the foot-rot and the fat maggot being too far to see? Here, reality was far too close.

She stopped again to consult the land plan and frowned. So where was the actual boundary to the three acres? Because up to now, there was no demarcation visible, never mind the house itself.

'I can't see any fencing,' she peered ahead into the gloomy afternoon.

'You'd have to put it in.'

Her heart sank, and not for the first time that day.

'That'll cost an arm and a leg. Why didn't these particulars say none existed?'

'Wood is everywhere,' Hector Jones let go of her arm to wave his stick at their surroundings. 'Anyway, Mark can knock you up posts and pig wire in an afternoon.'

Doubts about the whole project were multiplying apace, but asking Hector Jones's surly son for help wouldn't be her priority. 'So, where's Wern Goch?' her finger rested on the Hall's familiar oblong on the map. 'It should be here.'

'It is. Follow me.'

She let him slither and slide ahead of her until the watery track which they were on opened out into sheer mud which in turn led down to a clot of red-brown mire upon which stood a tiny tumbledown house. She held her breath as she registered the glassless windows, the decrepit roof and how the building was totally dwarfed by its surroundings. Her one wish was slipping away...

'My God. Is that it?' she gasped.

'A gem and a bargain, all rolled into one.'

She felt her already queasy stomach take a wrong turn inside her. This was nothing like the photographs which had shown a normal-sized dwelling. She stood stock still for a moment, her thoughts awash with the nearby sounds of running water, then she showed Hector Jones the agent's pictures.

'That Lloyd Griffiths is a bloody liar,' she said, as tears welled up. 'This is more like a doll's house.' She crumpled the offending sheets into a ball and hurled it into the air, whereupon it fell into the mulch. 'What did the couple from Birmingham say about it?'

'They're keen. Mentioned getting planning for an extension. Main thing though was somewhere for the kid to have a pony. Never mind one, I told them. They could have ten here.'

'Have they made you an offer yet?'

Hector nodded and, although at the moment, this was the last place she'd consider, she nevertheless sensed a stab of disappointment.

'Fifty. Ten over the asking.'

'Fifty? You're joking!'

'Honest to God I'm not. Anything with land's on the up and up. I'm frigging giving this away at forty, excuse my language.'

She turned in the direction of the running water and saw spray leave the nearby bank in a silver arc and add itself to the rising pool in which both she and Hector Jones were standing.

'Surely it all needs draining. I mean, the whole lot'll be under water if this keeps up.'

'Bad summer, that's all. Usually dry as a camel's arse, believe me.' The former policeman waded towards the old barn, using his stick to prod for hidden stones. 'And here's some perfect storage space.'

She followed, her mind in turmoil. Was the house too small or wasn't it? Maybe it *could* be quite snug, she thought, as long as there was room enough for a spare bed. At least it would be cheaper to heat than some rambling pile. At least it was suitably old.

Soon all cautionary thoughts on the costs of new pipework and re-roofing were sabotaged by the notion that with goodwill and determination it all might just work, and this imagined scenario propelled her onwards with a growing sense of inevitable loss. Why should someone else enjoy the peacefulness of this spot? The closeness to real nature? Why shouldn't she, after all she'd gone through? And the more she dwelt upon this nameless faceless couple from the Midlands and their offer, the more possessive of Wern Goch she grew.

Hector Jones pushed open the barn's old stable door into a dank darkness – a distillation of wildlife smells and rotting organic matter, where ancient farm machinery and layer upon layer of iron wheels lay against its sagging walls. Heaps of sacking and empty feed bags vied with every kind of detritus imaginable. There was scarcely room to move.

'Will all this be cleared if I decide to go ahead?' she asked hopefully. 'Because it could be an ideal area for seedlings.'

'So what are you offering me?'

'Hey, I've not seen inside the house yet.'

'*Suivez-moi.*'

Out of the barn where the curtain of indigo cloud had finally parted to reveal a shaft of iridescent brightness, Hector Jones stumbled towards the scullery door and let her enter first.

She gasped again. That barn was like the Ritz next to this squalor. There wasn't one level flagstone or one dry wall and she stubbed her toe several times as she went over to the one kitchen window, under which lay a crude granite block perched on two large stones. It not only exuded the smell of stale liver, but also bore what could be fresh bloodstains. Added to this was an inexplicably overpowering malevolence. A housefly landed on her hair, then another. She swiped them both away, whereupon they promptly settled on the stone.

'What on earth's *that* thing?' she asked, pointing at it yet at the same time recoiling from the growing smell.

'A salting slab. Where the meat used to be preserved.' Hector replied from the doorway deliberately keeping his distance.

'What meat?'

'Pork mostly. My folks kept a few pigs around the place and every Easter, Bryn Evans's father would bring his knife for the slaughter. Clean but slow. Quite a performance.'

'So what's this blood doing here now? I mean, it's foul.'

Hector stepped forwards then stopped in his tracks when he saw the stains. A hand went to his head in despair. 'I told him to clean up here. He promised.'

'Mark?'

'Yes. He's been tending an injured bird. Look,' he dipped a finger into a patch of dark liquid and sniffed it.

'No thanks.' She shivered before moving towards the inglenook and its old hobs and bread oven, blackened by age and a million flames. She fingered the dusty iron cauldron suspended from a rugged beam over where the original fire must have been and found herself wondering who else had lived in the house, died here...

She peered into the vessel's mysterious heart and saw a night with no stars.

'They say never buy where people have been poor or unhappy,' she announced, making her way to the one glazed window at the front which had a northerly aspect overlooking the marsh.

Hector snorted his contempt.

'That would mean a lot of empty houses, now, wouldn't it? No, this place hasn't been lived in since the Hall was built and even when a certain Frau Muller took it all over just before the end of the last war.'

'Muller?' Lucy frowned as she repeated it. The name rang a faint bell from somewhere.

'Was she German, then?'

'Yes. And I don't think she ever bothered putting furniture in here, mind. Probably too busy. She was into all kinds of things, so I heard. Philology – especially the Celtic language, oh, and ravens. Which explains her renaming the Hall.'

'What name did she give it?'

'Rabenstein.'

'That's strange.'

'The locals thought so too. In fact they didn't like it. Apparently it means – and I quote – the old stone gibbet of Germany, so called from the ravens, damned souls which were wont to perch on it...'

'Ugh.' She shivered again. 'So, what became of her? Did she ever return to Germany?'

Hector Jones hesitated, his red hand rubbing his rough chin.

'You'll find out soon enough, I suppose. Something truly terrible happened. Right out of the blue.' He turned to her. 'I really don't want to put you off any more...'

'Please go on.'

'Well, she was shot, then left for the birds to eat.'

Lucy gulped. 'That's totally disgusting. Where? In here?'

'Up by the ruined Abbey over there.' He pointed in a vague easterly direction. 'Bryn Evans's grandfather was part of a local militia. A Dad's Army kind of outfit. Anyone with a German name round here fell under suspicion and although there was no proof, to them she was a traitor.'

'Poor woman. So no refuge for her, then?'

'She wasn't the only one in this county. Zealous lot, those bunion breeders. Trouble is, give a man a gun and a uniform...'

'But *you* were a policeman? Lloyd Griffiths told me.'

'I was indeed.' Then Hector asked in a darker tone, 'what else did he say?'

'Nothing. Why?'

She drew aside the rag which passed for a curtain and saw the woodworm damage to the window frame and its sill. Orange dust trickled from every tiny hole.

'Go upstairs if you like,' he said, clearly glad of a diversion.

But on reaching the top step, her heart seemed to sink inside her chest. Here was worse. A real and tangible melancholy where layers of floral wallpapers scrolled from the two bedrooms' walls leaving patches of soot-black plaster from which sprouted clusters of fungi. Where a grate set in a once pretty fireplace lay stuffed with twigs and assorted feathers.

'Any bathroom?' she called out from the landing.

'Bucket and chuck it. Always has been, though God knows where...'

She laughed and the sound seemed almost sacrilegious. Yet she couldn't stop till she noted Hector looking anxiously towards the Hall as if something was bugging him. Then she remembered Mark.

'We'd better go,' he said. 'Talk on the way back, eh?'

The old stairs sighed under each of her descending steps and soon she was heading outside, convinced that the smell of stale blood still followed her. By the time she and Hector Jones had re-convened by the scullery door, the sun's brightness had widened and lengthened to cast the house's old bricks, the rotten wood and fractured guttering in a haunting uneasy glow.

Suddenly, as he shielded his eyes, a body of ravens lifted from the alders by the river Mellte and drew nearer, hovering for a moment before encircling the one chimney until perching in an ominous row above the scullery door. *Unkindness* came to mind. The collective noun for these birds which she'd read in a recent Hellebore book. Now that and the rest of the literary world – in fact any world – seemed aeons away. Even Anna.

'See. This is what he does.' Hector interrupted her thoughts with a mood change. 'Encourages the fuckers. Normally they're solitary, but not this lot. Oh no. This a bloody war cabinet.' He bent down to pick up a wet stone and none too steadily positioned himself to throw it at them. However, she put a restraining hand on his arm.

'Don't,' she said, unnerved by his words, wary of their stillness, their intense gaze. 'I think they're here for a reason.'

'Thank you.' Another voice sabotaged Hector's planned riposte. She spun round and heard the intended stone drop into the mud, whereupon Mark Jones raised both freshly washed hands in the air. He then made a strange but familiar noise in his throat, whereupon all the ravens left their perches and briefly touched his fingertips with their beaks before winging away once more towards the river. His smile was the strangest she had ever seen. A mixture of triumph and sadness. But now wasn't the time to quiz him about this or the blood-red email and the weird croaking phone call to Hellebore just before she'd walked out of her job. For who else could it have been? And for God's sake, why?

'I told you to stay out of the way,' barked Hector to his son. 'this is *my* business with Miss Mitchell.'

'I think she knows already that it's *mine*.' Mark's dark eyes met hers. 'So why don't we see if we can come to some arrangement?'

'What?' Hector looked nonplussed. But I thought you didn't want me to sell...'

'What can you offer the grasping old git, eh?' Mark turned to her, still ignoring him. 'Thirty, thirty-five...?'

'There's already been an offer for fifty,' said Lucy, 'so that's me out of the frame.'

'Who said?'

'Your father. Just now.'

Mark advanced towards him and grasped the lapels of his old donkey jacket in both hands.

Hector's face ballooned above his grip. Incoherent with surprise and rage.

'You liar,' snarled the forestry worker. 'She's the first to view Wern Goch and there's been no fucking offer.' He let go of his father and began striding away through the wet and into his domain. 'Just get something right in the whole of your rotten life, eh?'

Both she and Hector stared after him, but neither moved as the scullery door was dragged open, squealing against the old flags, and with that dark oblong of the tiny room behind him, Mark Jones stood waiting for both a man he despised more than any other, and a total stranger, to decide his future.

Within just a few moments that implosion of sunlight had shrunk between the clouds once more and it was as if some grimly downturned mouth now inhabited the sky overhead. More and more was that decorative world of her picture book being eroded by a different reality, by undertones she couldn't ignore, and the more Lucy stared at those celestial white-blonde lips as she accompanied Hector Jones back to the Hall, the more confused she became.

She knew the ex-copper was expecting her to make an offer and so too, in a strange way, was that son of his. But the few pleasurable sensations such as watching the sheep, imagining a restored and cosy Wern Goch, were drowned – yes, drowned *was* the word, by a definite atmosphere. This wasn't simply to do with the alarming amount of water everywhere, nor the presence of so many ravens. No. It was an overwhelming sense of hopelessness. Of lives blighted by a deep and secret sadness. Was this what she wanted to take on? Did she really have the will to turn things around and make this little corner of the world a better more productive place? She didn't know, because there were still too many unanswered questions of both a practical and personal nature.

She was just about to broach the first of many, when all at once her ears picked up an eerie wail which seemed at first to originate from the direction of Wern Goch. Whether animal or human she wasn't sure, but when she spun round she saw a shadow of ravens silently circling the one chimney. Were those the same ones that she'd seen earlier? She couldn't tell, but she did notice that the scullery doorway was now empty, yet that same chilling sound was still audible.

'What on earth's that?' she caught up with Hector and tapped the back of his old donkey jacket. 'Listen.'

'Someone getting the sheep in, most likely,' he grunted without stopping. His head and stick stuck out as if he was aiming for some imagined winning tape, except that here, she thought, glancing round again, there were only losers.

'It was a scream, I'm telling you. And I can't see anyone moving any sheep.'

'Not here you won't. Up at Bwlch Ddu it is. The next farm. They use a whistle, see.'

But she wasn't convinced by this explanation and when they both reached the drive once more, she positioned herself in front of him, trying to ignore the sudden appearance of wetness around his eyes.

'It was from the house,' she insisted. 'I don't imagine things.'

'Look, young lady. Let's be honest. This isn't the kind of place you're used to, coming from London. I mean, here is full of mystery. It's Pagan, for a start. Always has been. Which is why you'll not find many churches round here.'

'Pagan? You mean Druids?' Her eyes widened. She saw that the hand resting on his stick was trembling.

'Possibly. Now then,' his tone lightened. 'Mr Griffiths at Llandrindod told me quite a lot about your big dream for Wern Goch. And which of us hasn't lived on dreams, eh? Who doesn't need some kind of future to look forward to?' His damp eyes took on the colour of the darkening sky as he angled his stick at the Hall's forbidding shape, its black curtainless windows. 'The truth is, I can't afford to go on living here and subsidising Mark, without some reserves in the bank. Selling the little house and a bit of land is my only option. But I still need to have the place near. To still see it from time to time. D'you understand?'

She nodded, but that was the easy part.

'Doesn't Mark work at all, then?' she asked.

'Oh yes. He's a sawyer over in the forestry, but his wage packet's not nearly enough. I mean, what if he had a family, not just me?' He blinked back tears the same time as big raindrops began to fall from above. She didn't push it. Clearly Wern Goch was more than just a pile of old bricks and a ragged roof to these Joneses and she resolved one day to find out why. For now, she must weigh everything up and make a decision because by this time tomorrow Hector Jones could be shaking hands on it with someone else. She took a deep breath to steady her nerves.

'I'll give you thirty-two,' she announced, avoiding eye contact. 'I know it's not forty, but so much needs doing, I won't have enough left over for anything else.'

'Thirty-four.'

Lucy paused, wishing with all her heart that her own dad was there to advise her. Hector Jones's rough cheeks were now glistening with unchecked tears. He was a wreck, all washed up. In many ways, just like her. But right now, she'd never had so much power in her whole life. Not even with those slush-pile authors at Hellebore. And it was his obvious desperation for a reasonable sale which weakened her resolve.

'OK. Thirty-four it is.' In retrospect, those words had fallen like stones from her mouth as Hector's free hand gripped hers and his first smile appeared.

'Let's drink to that, eh? Come on, Miss Mitchell. This way. I've not had anything to celebrate for years.'

Chapter Eight

𝔈𝔦𝔤𝔥𝔱𝔭 𝔫𝔦𝔤𝔥𝔱𝔰 𝔥𝔞𝔳𝔢 𝔍 𝔩𝔦𝔳𝔢𝔡 𝔰𝔦𝔫𝔠𝔢 𝔱𝔥𝔢𝔫, 𝔱𝔥𝔢 𝔟𝔩𝔲𝔢, 𝔱𝔥𝔢 𝔯𝔢𝔡
𝔗𝔥𝔢 𝔪𝔬𝔪𝔢𝔫𝔱 𝔴𝔥𝔢𝔫...𝔄𝔫𝔡 𝔥𝔬𝔴 𝔱𝔥𝔦𝔰 𝔭𝔢𝔩𝔩𝔬𝔴 𝔢𝔞𝔯𝔱𝔥
𝔅𝔲𝔯𝔫𝔰 𝔪𝔭 𝔰𝔨𝔦𝔫, 𝔪𝔭 𝔟𝔩𝔬𝔬𝔡, 𝔪𝔭 𝔱𝔬𝔫𝔤𝔲𝔢 𝔱𝔲𝔯𝔫𝔢𝔡 𝔪𝔲𝔱𝔢
𝔅𝔲𝔱 𝔫𝔬𝔱 𝔪𝔭 𝔪𝔦𝔫𝔡, 𝔰𝔱𝔦𝔩𝔩 𝔰𝔥𝔞𝔯𝔭, 𝔞𝔰𝔱𝔲𝔱𝔢, 𝔴𝔥𝔦𝔩𝔢
𝔉𝔲𝔱𝔲𝔯𝔢 𝔇𝔢𝔞𝔱𝔥 𝔞𝔴𝔞𝔦𝔱𝔰...
𝔎𝔍𝔅 1987

So far, so good, Robert conceded to himself as he sprinkled two sachets of sweeteners into his coffee at The Blackamoor just off the A40 near Ross-on-Wye. A classy pub, this, which matched his newly-acquired Maverick, now full of walking and camping gear, instead of his earlier more formal luggage. The handsome 4WD dominated the car park. The name of his wheels too, was pretty neat, considering.

He was taking his time. Doing things in stages, and after his stay at the Novotel it was as if one night had folded into another in a kind of molten blur. Just like when he'd been at Uni in Sydney and used his study time to hang around Potts Point and Garden Island in a kind of amnesiac dreaming...

So, yes, apart from some cretin cutting him up near Cirencester on his journey west, it would seem that things were generally looking up. Not that everything could be achieved at the drop of a hat, mind. Far from it, and his search for the more profound meanings of life – *his* life – was like crossing one of the many streams in the Botanical Gardens back in Oz. Each stepping stone different from the last, sometimes tilting underfoot, yet still taking his weight, furthering his purpose...

He looked out through the pub's leaded window at a hill where sheep toiled along its green flank, silhouetted against the afternoon sky. He felt a sudden pang of longing. For green and more green. The sound of rain on the bedroom window, the scent of a certain woman's skin...

Suddenly the pub door opened and six middle-aged men wearing cycling gear and each clutching a melon-shaped yellow crash helmet, hovered for a moment, then ignoring his death-stare chose the closest table to him. He eyed them in turn as he downed the last of his coffee. What a load of fucking whackers, he thought. Besides, they made the place smell like a dunny. At one point, a gnarled knee actually prodded his thigh.

'Sorry, mate,' the guy said, but Robert knew he didn't give a monkeys.

'Plenty of space over there,' he said pointedly, gesturing towards a deserted area beyond a brick archway.

'Dinners only,' the man said. 'We just want a snack.'

Just then a mini-skirted girl whom he he'd not noticed before, came over from the bar to take the cyclists' orders. She wrinkled her nose before rattling off the bar snacks menu, then jotting down that they all wanted tuna and coleslaw jacket potatoes. Finally she turned her attention to him and he blinked in disbelief.

Her musky scent, the way she stood in that ridiculous skirt. Jesus Christ, she was Liza Docherty all over again. Bondi's cheapest, stupidest piece of meat. He gulped inwardly, tempted to leave, but knew he couldn't without drawing attention to himself. Was it possible that the fashion student from Paddington had an identical twin sister who'd emigrated, just like him?

'Would you like another coffee?' the girl asked.

He felt her saucer-like eyes fixed on him expectantly.

'Yeah.' He tried to pull himself together. 'Cheers.'

'Espresso or Cappuccino?' She shifted her weight on to her other leg and Robert spotted a couple of the cyclists eyeing her butt. He also saw an engagement ring on her finger and found himself wondering on a scale of one to ten what kind of wife and mother *she'd* make. His own experience told him zero.

'Espresso. Thanks.'

She strutted away, and with each step her buttocks pressed in turn against the black fabric wound tight round her hips. Liza had done exactly the same after he'd picked her up. Flaunting her sex, bringing him to that same old cul de sac. Except, on that sunset evening with the College barbecues being lit further down the beach, she'd humiliated him. Said he'd 'got no toothpaste in the tube,' and then begun to get dressed without a care in the world, until he'd pulled her down into the sand...

No one had seen anything. Why should they? They'd just been passing strangers with too much sun on the brain. One minute she'd been there, straddling him, goading him, the next, she was down with the other buried rubbish and bits of broken shells which are no use to anyone.

'Thanks,' he acknowledged the girl's return with his fresh coffee then quizzed her as he slipped his tanned fingers round the cup's handle. 'Who's the lucky guy? Or is that too personal?'

'Hey, course not.' She flashed him a smile then put out her hand for him to inspect her trophy more closely. 'It's a Topaz. Nice innit? My birthstone. And his name's Darren.'

Pity for Darren, then...

'So, when's the big day?'

'Next June. Got to save up first.'

'Right.'

She moved on to the cyclists who by now were silently disembowelling their potatoes as if they'd not eaten for a year. The odour of oily fish reached his nose – Farm Cove on a hot day – while strands of coleslaw dangled from their lips and in that moment, in that overcrowded place in an overcrowded country, he had to get out.

In the car park, the midday sun caught the chained-up cycles, the open-topped BMW and a silver Mégane, and to his relief, showed up every vital dust mote on his four-wheel-drive. Even the cleared arc of glass in the rear window made this look like a country vehicle, not some prissy school run job. Exactly the effect he wanted. Perfect, in fact. Until he saw the mud.

He used the Gents and topped up with petrol in a one-horse place south of Hereford. So far the weather had been on his side and with the onset of evening beginning to change the light he knew that in an hour's time he'd be back at the planned B&B in time for a shower and a wander round the handily placed town of Hay.

'Smart wheels, sir,' the guy said, handing over his change and two plastic coins for the jet wash. 'Odd it's so mucky, that. Black usually keeps pretty pukka.'

'Why I chose it,' Robert gripped the discs between his teeth then dropped the last of his loose change into a nearby chilled drinks dispenser and seconds later pulled out a can of Coke.

'Yours then?' asked the man.

'Sure.' He'd picked up on this particular piece of pond life's envy and, to quell any more questions, pinged back the Coke can's lid. 'Just had a bonus from work if that's okay with you.'

'No tax disc, I see.'

'My boss has got it.'

'Pity if you got stopped.'

'Yeah. But it'll be on there in half an hour.'

'Half an hour's a long time round here.'

'I guess.'

He selected Power Shampoo then Laser Rinse, but afterwards not only was this mud resolutely clinging to the Maverick's sills but was also drying like old blood in unsightly patches on his jeans. A moment's panic. Spit wouldn't be enough to shift it and a trip to the Gents would mean going past his inquisitor again.

However the cashier had left his post and was approaching at speed as if he had something important to add, but Robert was already in the driver's seat and had fastened his belt just as those unwashed fingers rapped on his closed window.

'I've had a thought,' the man mouthed, and Robert noticed the wet flesh inside his bottom lip. He wanted to drive off but the fucker's hand was still on the car's hood. 'Can you hear me?'

'Sure.' His window opened enough to let a previously unseen line of jet wash foam slide down the glass. His engine idled silently.

'Why not get some valeters on the job? They'd clean inside an' all, and give a turtle wax. My brother'd do it cut price for you. He's only a mile away at King's Thorn.'

Robert shook his head, his normally equable features tightening. 'Sorry mate. No offence, but I'll decide what I do with my wheels.' He then heeled the throttle and, deliberately exceeding the 10 mph speed limit of the forecourt, left the dill standing in a pall of exhaust, and headed west for the second time that week.

Chapter Nine

Sacred land, Sidh of my soul, with its silver oaks
At moonlight, whose waters return the stars' gaze,
Whose sprits rise to stir the sleep of the Damned
That they too may know Death...
MJJ (with a little help)

At five o'clock, with the taste of Hector Jones's almost neat gin still in her mouth, Lucy sat in the front parlour of Horeb House B&B in Rhayader's West Street, with a so far untouched milky cup of tea on a chipped occasional table next to her armchair.

She felt drained, so tired she could sleep for ever and, if there hadn't been that Vacancy notice in the front bay window, would have probably kipped in the car. But she'd been lucky. The landlady, Mrs Evans had just received a cancellation which meant that the tiny back bedroom overlooking a neglected vegetable garden and further on a Griffiths & Sons Meat Processing plant, was all hers for the next fortnight.

Was *everyone* round here related? She'd asked herself, once the woman had finally bustled away with a deposit of £50 in her pocket, clearly miffed by her guest's reticence as to her life history. Were Jones, Griffiths and Evans the only names to be had? Normally, that quaint notion would have made Lucy smile, but not now. For too much at Ravenstone Hall was still unexplained and too little volunteered. What was that weird scream all about and why had Hector Jones's eyes filled with tears upon hearing it? Why was Mark still hanging around? What exactly was holding him there amongst those random water springs, the spongy saturated land? Maybe she would never know. Maybe she wouldn't *want* to know...

But she couldn't help thinking about him all the same. His toned body, his skin which all weathers had turned the colour of dark oak. Those eyes which to her seemed as bottomless as a still lake at night and which sometimes caught her unawares. By comparison, Jon looked as if he came from a totally different planet. Pale from an indoor City job, a body which hadn't seen the inside of a gym or played any sport since Uni. Yet a man who, she had to admit, had been as steadfast as the rising and setting of the sun. Until she'd turned him away without any explanation when he'd phoned as she'd left her flat. Maybe he was chatting up someone from work by now. How could she blame him? Maybe they'd already made it to a bed, and that imagined scenario sent more than a prick of jealousy through her system. In fact, it felt more like an electric shock. But she'd needed time to heal, to cope with Benn's violation on her own, because even now it was like an open wound, too easily damaged, still hurting too much. One day, *if* there was a one day she'd tell him and perhaps he'd understand.

Perhaps...

'Will you be needing food?' Mrs Evans' dyed black head had popped round the parlour door. 'You never said.'

'Yes please. I'm starving,' was her automatic reply.

'Half an hour then. It's lamb chops.'

The woman disappeared attended by the distinctive smell of sprouts. Lucy's appetite suddenly waned and she found herself wondering if Rhayader did take-aways or pizzas. She stared at the glass-fronted display cabinet filled with fancy porcelain from another age. Hideous mostly, but there was something touching about the pride in which these particular heirlooms had been preserved and displayed. How in this one room with its sepia studies of haymaking at Pontsian, or fishing on the Afon Gwy, the past seamlessly interlocked with the present. The same for Wern Goch, and the contrast between the day's discoveries and Hellebore's slick surroundings couldn't be greater.

As if to reassure herself that what she was doing was right, Lucy dug out her wallet from her shoulder bag and found yet another little piece of her own past kept next to her driving licence in its own windowed pocket. A photo of her mum and dad which she'd taken on that last on holiday as a family near Caernarfon. Another place he'd loved. Yet she didn't really need to see it again for, like *Magical Tales*, each tiny detail was ineradicably imprinted in her mind. Their hair interlocked in the breeze; their eyes only for each other while William Mitchell rested his weary doctor's hands on his wife's shoulders. The isle of Ynys Mon sleeping in the sea where his ashes had briefly lightened the waves then disappeared...

She returned the print to her wallet with a fresh determination that she musn't waver now.

On Monday morning she'd have fixed a bank loan to put down the ten per cent for Wern Goch after exchange of contracts, and by the same afternoon located a hopefully trustworthy solicitor. Meanwhile, in the intervening week until her father's money came through she'd spend every waking moment working out an action plan for her project and finding the right local tradespeople to help her turn it all around.

'No survey, then?' quizzed Mrs Evans as she hovered with the mint sauce over Lucy's table in the overdecorated dining room where an elderly couple sat pecking at their meal in the far corner. 'Now I'd say that was taking a big risk. None of my business, mind.'

'I've had a good look round.' Lucy unravelled her intricately folded napkin and let the woman pour some of the green minty liquid over her chop. 'I mean it's been standing since the Rebecca Riots and at least the brickwork's in good nick.'

Mrs Evans seemed impressed by this reference to Welsh history but nevertheless still lingered with as yet unspoken opinions.

'Who's to say what another bad winter will do?' she said. 'No harm in my Bryn taking a look for you, is there? Being my own flesh and blood he calls a spade a shovel.'

Flesh and blood...

Lucy stopped chewing. The pink meat in her mouth suddenly not very appetising. Neither was the sense that her business was quickly becoming everybody else's. Besides, this Bryn Evans might be a rustic rip-off merchant. She'd not yet met him, or even glimpsed him.

'It's okay, really. Thanks.'

Mrs Evans's moustachioed mouth drooped at each corner, like that one which Lucy had spotted earlier in the sky. Her small black eyes narrowed to pinpricks and Lucy remembered that same Hellebore author's comments about the Welsh. Maybe she wasn't reading the landlady's script...

'But he knows plumbers, decorators,' insisted the woman. 'Fair hand at building, himself, mind,' she added. 'Didn't Mr Jones at the Hall tell you?'

'No.' She laid her knife and fork together, her meal barely touched. Her dream had to start somewhere, and at least this Bryn Evans probably knew the old house inside out. Refusing help at this stage wasn't really an option. 'Perhaps we can meet up tomorrow sometime?' She said. 'He could then give me a quote.'

Mrs Evans shook her head.

'My Bryn's chapel. Twice on Sundays without fail. He's a Deacon, see.' Then she brightened. 'Shall I tell him Monday. Say eleven?'

'Where? Wern Goch?'

'Why not here?' She smiled. 'Then you both can have some of my Welsh cakes. As it's quiet at the moment, I'll do a special batch.'

'Thanks.' Yet there was something about the way she'd said 'you both' which set alarm bells ringing again, because her Bryn might well be a bachelor on the look-out. She looked at her meal, all hunger gone. She didn't want to be on anyone's agenda at the moment. There was enough to do, to think about and for some reason a ripple of panic passed through her because she was poised to involve someone else in her scheme, and the deeper she went, the harder it would be to climb out.

For some reason the vision of a freshly dug grave came to mind.

Damp, lined with seeping red soil. The same as she'd seen on Mark Jones's rough hands. Lucy shivered, pushing her plate away then reassured herself that an offer on a property for sale was verbal, nothing more. Not binding in any way. She therefore had thirty-six hours until Monday morning to weigh up all the pros and cons of her venture and finally decide whether to proceed or not. Meanwhile her priority was to find out as much as she could about the two men she'd just met. Never mind her mum, her dad would have expected nothing less.

'You look tired, my girl,' Mrs Evans interrupted her meditation. She removed her plate and presented her with a hand-written dessert menu. 'Why not try a nice piece of my apple pie and cream? The way I see it, you'll be needing your strength.'

'What do you mean?'

The woman tapped her nose in a way she found strangely unnerving.

'So, pie it is,' she said.

'Fine. But please tell me something.'

'Depends what it is. I'll try, of course.'

'How well do you know the Joneses at Ravenstone Hall? I mean Hector and Mark.'

Mrs Evans checked the old pair in the corner weren't within earshot and leant towards Lucy, her moustache now quite pronounced.

'You'll need to keep your wits about you. Get my meaning?' She resumed her former position and picked up the cruet. 'That's all I'm saying.'

'Please don't talk in riddles, Mrs Evans. Imagine I was your daughter...'

That was all it took. The woman pulled out an adjoining chair and sat down.

'That estate goes back a long way, as you probably know. Just as the drovers were beginning to take their stock by rail and a lot of labourers were made idle. The tolls had been torn down and there was a lot of grievance against the English government so when the Tory Lord Howells of New Radnor decided to build on it, you can imagine, no one wanted to give him their sweat. He had to get foreigners over to do his dirty work. Just think of that.'

'Foreigners?'

'I mean the English.'

Lucy blinked, but Mrs Evans was leaning closer, whispering in her ear. 'It's cursed, that place. I know I shouldn't say, but it's as if the Morrigan's made it her home...'

'The Morrigan? Who on earth is she?'

'The Goddess of Death.'

A brief but potent silence hung between them in which Lucy felt the blood leave her face. Then Mrs Evans resumed her account.

'My Bryn calls me a heathen for believing it,' she said. 'But what else is one supposed to think? I mean, first Lord Howells was murdered in his bed with his eyes taken out, and from then on there was always one in his family who met a bad end there.'

She remembered that terrible scream. How could she ever forget it? 'And Frau Muller?' she asked, then realised her mistake.

Mrs Evans looked shocked. 'Who told you about that?'

'Can't remember now. Someone in the cafe here, I think.'

'Well, whatever, it's all lies. That woman dabbled in things she shouldn't have, and that's the end of it.' Mrs Evans's mouth had pursed into a tight line. Clearly that particular avenue was closed. At least for the time being.

'And then?' She encouraged her, seeing the old couple leave their table and struggle to the door. They exchanged farewells in Welsh with her companion then were gone. 'What happened next?'

'The Joneses took over. Mary and John they were. Funeral directors from Hereford. Did well there. I mean, it was quite a thing for folks round here to go to Ravenstone to sort out a death. Nice driveway then it was. Big chapel of rest too. Bit more special-like than Beynon's in the High Street.'

'I see.' But with so many unquiet spirits lurking there, Lucy thought it the last place for any rest. 'And how did they end their days?' she asked.

'They both went sudden, like. One after the other. Nothing suspicious – at least that was the talk. Then Hector who'd had enough of being a copper moved up from Cardiff with his wife and the boys.'

Lucy frowned. This wasn't making sense.

'Boys? Are you sure?' she asked.

'I should be. Used to mind them most Saturday nights. When Mr and Mrs were off round the clubs.'

'How many were there?'

'Just the two. Richard and Mark.' She caught Lucy's puzzled look and was just about to add more information when the telephone in the hall began to ring. While she was gone, Lucy mentally raked over everything that had happened so far since her arrival at the Hall. Not once had another son or brother to Mark been mentioned.

'Sorry about that,' said Mrs Evans upon her return, setting herself once more next to her guest. 'Another cancellation. Couple from Bristol have just had a burglary. Pity for them. Now then, where was I?'

'Richard and Mark.'

'Yes. Lovely kids they were. Like two peas in a pod. Mark used to say he always knew what Richard was thinking. Bit of a dreamer he was even then. Mind you, I think after what happened there, he should have left, joined the navy or something. Got himself well away. Just like Richard did.'

Lucy's empty stomach felt leaden as if some of the stones from Wern Goch had settled there. Nevertheless, she had to find out more.

'Why? What happened?'

But Mrs Evans seemed to have lost her nerve. Her flow came to a halt as she fidgeted with the plastic menu holder and got up from her chair.

'It's not my place to say. But you'll be alright there, I'm sure. Hector Jones isn't a bad man underneath, and Mark...' Here she paused and Lucy held her breath. She had to trust this woman therefore what she was about to reveal would decide whether or not she would go to the bank tomorrow morning.

'Go on, please.' The wait was agonising.

'He's mending, if you get my meaning. But you won't see any scars. Oh no. They're all up here.' She tapped her black permed curls, then added 'tlawd cariad,' with feeling.

'Does that mean you think he's mad?'

Mrs Evans looked affronted.

'Du du, no. He's got the brain of five people, despite what folk say. Sometimes though, I tell my Bryn it's best to be a bit simple in this life and then you don't take things so hard. But between you and me, that Mark needs someone like you to cheer him up. Make him laugh sometimes, and forget about his woes for a while, because as God's my witness, I've not seen a proper smile on that face of his for fourteen years.'

Chapter Ten

Hi you,

Just to say I'm around and still on this planet. Only just, mind, the way things are going.

Got a new name would you believe? Takes some getting used to. Are you seeing anyone else now?

Not that I can do much about it if you are. It's like everything's come to a stop. Even the poetry.

I'll send you some when I get going again. No one must know I've written, OK?

Our big secret.

Your Numero Uno fan. xx

The following evening while Lucy Mitchell lay in the small back bedroom in West Street, Rhayader, listening to fresh rain hit the window and wondering about the Joneses, James Montague Benn turned up the tension on his Pulsar X exercise bike to maximum and spent the last ten minutes before the TV news panting his way to fitness.

His red neck had thickened in the process, bringing oxygenated blood from his head to the already strong erection which strained the front of his nylon shorts. It was the same every time. The friction of his balls against the saddle; the sheer sense of power firming up his whole body. But what spoilt it was *her*, staring from her position in the archway to what used to be their shared bedroom. She'd bought the bike for him in the first place, what else did she expect? That he'd snatch her from her recliner and lie her on the bed just in time for his climax? Never in a million years. Those days had long melted into the mists of time, before the move to The Manor House in Burton Minster and her tumble into the ornamental pond after a well-lubricated dinner party. Before Manda Jeffery and the one-night stands had become an addiction.

He grimaced, trying to ignore his wife and those eyes still fixed on his groin. If she wasn't careful, he thought to himself, another "accident" would soon be forthcoming. But not until *Tribe* was in the bag. Not until his literary future was secure…

Just as his mind briefly wandered to tomorrow, Monday, and the announcement of the Booker Prize longlist, his mobile suddenly rang from its perch on the nearby chest of drawers. He saw his wife push her frame towards it with little sign of her limp. My God, she could be quick when it suited her, but an even quicker exit from his bike soon put the phone out of reach.

'Who is it this time?' she demanded, looking pig sick.

'Mind your own damned business.'

His cock was subsiding. Sweat smeared his vision, but not enough to see that the number on the mobile's display was Hellebore's. Someone working late, he thought, and on a Saturday too. He listened hard, striding all the while towards the landing and down the stairs to the privacy of his lockable study.

'It's me. Are you horny?' The editor's familiar drawl insinuated its way into his ear. Benn slid the bolt across his sanctuary door and slumped into his swivel chair.

'I was. And you?'

'Of course.'

But it was Monday, not Manda that mattered.

'Look, are there any whispers I need to know about?' He asked, aware of the zimmer frame on the move, the squeak of her shoes on the parquet floor. She'd be outside his door now, ears flapping. Suspicion cramping her features.

'None, so when can we fuck? You coming up here tomorrow?'

'Naturellement.'

'Great. Everyone's expecting a result. Champagne's in the fridge already. Nothing but the best, according to Nick.'

He smiled to himself, slipping a hot hand down inside his shorts. However, it was Vikki Tate, design assistant, with the neat arse and a nice line in flattery who was firing more than his imagination. 'By the way,' he added, holding himself back, enjoying the moment. 'Your assistant won't be around, will she?'

'I checked with her landlord on Friday evening. Apparently she's gone.'

He stopped working himself. A spasm of unease had interrupted his pleasure.

'Where?'

'How do I know. Gone's enough, surely?'

'You're right. See you soon. No panties, right?'

He pressed END and, having brought himself to a sudden and jerking climax then cleaned up with a wad of pastel-coloured tissues, sat staring at his blank PC screen. That Lucy Mitchell could be trouble. He knew it the moment she'd run from the bedroom at the Chandos Hotel over two months ago. He could see it in her eyes when he'd attracted her attention at Hellebore last Tuesday when he'd called in about his paperback cover. But at least she was a class act, unlike those other dogs, Sarah Dyson and the Filipinos from the Embassy, and once the editing of *Kingdom Come* was finished, he might be tempted to make contact again.

He smiled to himself because at the moment, everything he was touching was turning to gold and, barring an asteroid hitting the planet or Hellebore going bust, 2002 would see him evens favourite to lift the really big one. And his publisher hadn't been the only member of the literati with that opinion.

He re-adjusted his shorts and, to catch his wife unawares, swiftly unbolted his study door. Predictably, there she was, up to her tricks again, blocking his way. It was time to chuck the walking frame, he thought. Time to clip her wings.

'For God's sake...' he began, then gulped. For between her hands lay an item he'd not seen for years. His old army knife. Its blade glinting in the light from the chandelier above.

I have been a blue salmon
I have been a wild hound
I have been a cautious stag,
And a stump of a tree on the shovel.
MJJ and Taliesin 1989

On Monday afternoon, with the sun beginning its downward journey behind the Cambrian Hills, yet still managing to shine obstinately in her face, Lucy drove back from the estate agency in Llandrindod Wells towards Rhayader.

Hector Jones had convinced Lloyd Griffiths that the sale was indeed still on. He'd accepted her offer, and withdrawn the property from the market. So far, then, everything had gone to plan. Her ten per cent deposit on Wern Goch had been transferred in readiness, from Barclays to a Martyn Harries, solicitor in Gamallt Street and her mid-morning meeting with Bryn Evans at the B&B had been equally productive. So much so, that he'd promised to be at the estate that afternoon at 4.30 p.m. to start his "survey" and give her a list of possible trade contacts.

He'd seemed surprisingly positive and encouraging about her business project, even suggesting how she might best make a living in the wake of foot-and-mouth. She could either sell her organic produce direct from Wern Goch, join a co-operative or rent a regular market stall, because in his opinion, enough fussy Saesnegs were moving into Radnorshire from urban England to make her crops a profitable enterprise. Besides, there were European aid grants she could apply for, particularly to help with getting the ground ready for sowing.

The meeting in Enid Evans's cluttered kitchen had also been revelatory in other ways, for although Bryn Evans was a grown man in his mid-forties, prematurely bald with a complexion as red as Wern Goch's soil itself, his mother had treated him as if he was still a hungry schoolboy. Plied him with one Welsh cake after another before his last mouthful was finished. Completed his sentences for him, apparently even reading his thoughts...

Soon only the doily remained on the cake plate and the coffee jug emptied to a trickle, but when Lucy had asked again about Hector Jones's other son, Richard, and then Frau Muller, both mother and son had stopped chewing and exchanged uneasy glances. Mrs Evans had then exited to the kitchen for more supplies and when she'd returned, the conversation had turned to the paltry compensation he'd received for the loss of his prize Beulahs and whether or not he'd have anything to exhibit at next year's Royal Welsh Show.

Now she turned on to the A470 towards Ravenstone Hall, praying that the next hour would not only totally vindicate her having cajoled £3,200 pounds from the bank manager for her deposit until repayment next Monday, but also delete the few but persistent doubts which wouldn't leave her alone.

As she left the main trunk road and entered the now-familiar confines of the unnamed lane, her mobile suddenly rang from the seat beside her.

'Damn.' She'd meant to switch the thing off in case her mother was up for some more negativity, but no, it wasn't her number which appeared, but an unknown one. She dropped down to second gear as she let it ring until her voicemail took over and a female voice echoed into the car. She felt her stomach tighten as she passed Carreglas Farm, but there was no sign of either Bryn Evans's Defender, or his collie dog which had sat upright in the passenger seat outside the B&B while his master was inside.

'Your friend,' the woman began. 'In case you've not heard the news. He's on the Booker longlist.' That was all.

Your friend? The Booker longlist? Who else but Benn?

Her grip on the steering wheel loosened and in that split second, the Rav veered to the right, its bonnet suddenly buried in the hawthorn hedge. Her blood had already chilled despite the moist warm day not just because of that call but because she'd spotted a much bigger vehicle looming up behind.

She then revved the throttle so that plumes of blue smoke obscured her view through the rear window. It's power was oddly satisfying and just what she needed. Then fifty, sixty, far too fast, not just to lose the huge piece of farm machinery which seemed to be gaining on her but symbolically putting more distance between herself and the world of lies and betrayal she'd just left behind. Of people who, like fishermen, draw in their drift nets ever closer to the boat until life within is reduced to a twisting struggle, a last painful gasp.

'Who are you?' she yelled. 'And how the hell did you get my number?' But only the roar of the following vehicle answered, making her glance round again. If she slowed up, she'd be mulch.

She careered down the watery hill and then a sharp swerve into the track for Ravenstone. With her pulse thudding in her neck, she stalled to watch through her rear view mirror as the yellow combine harvester with its giant beak stuck out at the front, bowled along behind her and vanished beyond the untrimmed hedge which bordered the estate.

She was shaking all over. Whichever maniac had been driving that contraption surely wasn't some local yokel in a hurry. They'd *wanted* to frighten her. Maybe worse. Maybe, this was just the appetiser, and if so, she'd better get some allies behind her. Better get a survival plan up and running, she told herself, setting off again to reach Wern Goch, because later might be too late.

So. If this longlist news was true then the monster was halfway to winning. She felt sick imagining the Holy Trinity at Hellebore swanning around, champagne glasses in hand. Just like last year and the year before... Of course, it had been Manda who'd just called her with the Booker news. Who else had her number? And no problem for her to borrow someone else's phone. She must have heard something about June 15th at the Chandos, and that would explain her subsequent *froideur* in the office. QED. Lucy punched RECALL but nothing came up.

Her legs felt boneless as she emerged from the Rav and, despite the sun's residual warmth on her back as she faced the Hall, it was as if all the blood in her body had turned to ice. She shivered then fetched her denim jacket from the boot. It didn't help much and she was still trembling with rage and fear as Mark Jones appeared, sawdust in his black hair and a shy smile on his face.

'Are you OK?' he asked. 'You look as if you've just seen a ghost.'

'I'm fine, thanks,' she lied. 'Except some bloody great combine harvester thing seemed to want me out of the way. I thought life was supposed to be a bit gentler out in the sticks.'

'It should be,' he said knowingly, brushing the bits of wood from his hair with a few swift movements. 'But where two or three are gathered together – same old story, I'm afraid.'

'Is Bryn Evans around?' she asked to fill the slightly strained silence which followed.

'In there.' Mark indicated the Hall. 'Why d'you want to know?'

'He's offered to do a kind of survey for me. Work out what needs doing first.'

'I bet he has.' A look of concern came and went on his sunburnt face, but not before Lucy had noticed. 'So where did you come across him, then?'

'Met his mother in the Morfa tea rooms in town. She suggested it, and I thought, why not? Hey, is anything wrong?' she challenged, wondering why so many questions, but not yet prepared to tell him where she was staying.

'No. Not at all. It's just that I know a guy at work whose brother's a surveyor. Got the right letters after his name and the rest. You should have asked me...'

'How could I?' she retorted. 'You were hardly putting out a welcome mat.'

'True.' This time a wry smile moved his lips then he glanced again at the Hall. 'But at least with him there'd be no vested interest problems.'

Her look of puzzlement made him explain further.

'The Evanses have rented the land off us even before my grandparents moved here...'

'You mean, when Frau Muller was around?'

'She was called Irmgard. Anyway, how did you know about her?'

'It seems to be common knowledge.'

Mark closed his eyes for the briefest moment against the sun and she noticed how long his eyelashes were. How they curved like a blackbird's wing against his cheek. They were beautiful, but now wasn't the time to suggest he put himself forward for some Calvin Klein modelling.

'Anyway, as I was saying, Lloyd Griffiths let slip that Evans was trying to get some money together to buy the whole acreage. Bloody cheek.'

'I know that foot-and-mouth's been bad round here, but I thought farmers were basically rich,' she said. 'Don't they get huge subsidies and that sort of thing?'

'Carreglas isn't high enough. Not like Bwlch Ddu. And put yourself in his boots. If he can't have the twenty-eight acres then three will do. It's a start.' He glanced at her. 'I could paint an even nastier picture to put you off, but I won't.'

'You mean that poor German woman?'

'We've got our theories. So,' his tone changed as he held her gaze with a fierce intensity, 'you're definitely going ahead with Wern Goch?'

'Of course,' she nodded and was surprised to see a faint look of relief pass over his face. Then she spotted the top of that same yellow harvester skimming the top of the distant hedgerow on a return journey along the lane. This time it was crawling along, but just to see it again made her catch her breath.

'Look,' she pointed in the direction of the growling engine. 'That bloody thing's coming back now.'

'Sad bastard.'

'Who?'

'Hughes, Bwlch Ddu. Always showing off his latest gear. Don't know where he gets the dough from. People smuggling, I bet.'

'Why pick on me, then?'

Mark shrugged and she wasn't entirely convinced by this show of nonchalance.

'They're the Odd Squad alright. We just give them a wide berth.' He squinted into the sun until the noise and flashes of yellow steel had all gone, leaving the taint of diesel in the air. 'By the way, Miss Mitchell,' he turned to her once more, looking sheepish. She decided it didn't suit him. 'I've an apology to make.'

'What for?'

'It was me who sent you that email to your work. I'm sorry.'

'You?'

'Yup.'

Was the hangdog look genuine, or was he acting? She wasn't sure.

'I was scared stiff if you must know, what with that blood colour filling the screen. Our IT bloke at Hellebore reckoned it had come from an internet cafe in Hereford. So, you went all that way just to bug me?' She continued, deliberately avoiding his eyes. 'And why call its subject SPEAR? That was so creepy.'

'I am spear that roars for blood.'

'Oh, come on.' But she shivered, nevertheless.

'Seriously, I couldn't help it. You see, it was the thought of someone, anyone, having that house. One day you'll get the whole story. I promise.'

She wondered if this revelation might include anything about his brother Richard, some plausible reason for that haunting scream and the blood on the salting slab, but sensed that snow in July was more likely.

'So, how did you get my email address?' she asked instead.

'Easy. On the Hellebore website. But there's something else I need to know.' He raised a hand to shield his eyes from the now orange sun. 'Did anything go wrong with your car on the way here on Saturday? Think.'

'I don't have to. I was in the middle of nowhere and my petrol gauge suddenly slipped to empty. I had to pay for a fuel pipe repair at Builth. Thank God I managed to get there.'

'My fault, sorry.'

'*What?*' She stared at him and then recalled what Mrs Evans had said about local opinion. He didn't look like some weirdo with a swollen head or bulbous eyes. There was nothing blatantly odd about any part of him. Intense, yes. Fit, certainly, with an ease of movement which came from an outdoor life. 'You?'

'Yes. I was desperate.' He dug in his jeans pocket and produced two folded ten pound notes. They still felt warm from his body. 'Take these, please. It's the least I can do. I've been a total idiot.'

She put out her hand to stop him and tried not to smile.

'Some fencing might be a better penance.'

'You're on then. Thanks. And I'll write you a poem. I'm not exactly Dylan Thomas, but Truth is the Word. Will give it a shot anyhow.'

'I'm impressed. "Do not go gently" was my dad's favourite.' She blinked away a tear just to think of it.

'Mine too, if you must know. Oh, and Taliesin.'

'You'll have to excuse my ignorance as far as he's concerned.'

'I won't just excuse you. I'll forgive you.'

Was he joking? No. He was deadly serious.

'Thanks.'

Just then, the Hall's front door begin to open.

'Someone's coming.'

Mark spun round as Bryn Evans came down the steps with surprising agility for a man his size. He jogged over towards them both clutching an old clipboard and piece of paper held together with a rusty clasp, while a fat pencil lay wedged in the greying curls above his right ear.

'United we stand,' whispered Mark in her ear. He smelt of pine sap and the forest. 'Trust me.'

'Afternoon, both.' The farmer gave him a strange look then led the way proprietorially towards Wern Goch, his gimlet eyes missing nothing of his sheep-strewn surroundings and after several stops and measurements with an extra long steel rule he jotted down some figures on the top sheet, smudged them out and began again. 'Let's say four hundred for two layers of hardcore over this track and three drains,' he announced. 'Then you'd get your car down the house no problem.'

She and Mark exchanged glances.

'OK,' she said. 'But what about the land? Surely that needs some drainage too? I mean, look at it.'

'I'm not going to pull the wool, Miss Mitchell, but that's a big job. You'd need a ditch at the bottom end of that field and an outflow under the lane into the Mellte.'

'That would need planning, surely?' she queried.

Mark tapped the farmer's boiler-suited shoulder.

'I can easily sort it out. Leave that to me, eh?'

'And what about my grazing?' The other man's eyes had narrowed and suddenly, the little bonhomie which had existed between the two men evaporated. Lucy looked from one to the other, wishing now that she'd not fallen so easily for Mrs Evans's idea.

'That'll be up to Miss Mitchell now. But I'm sure any manure will be useful.'

Bryn Evans didn't pursue the matter but walked on ahead, probing the early evening air with a length of his steel rule. Like a fine sword blade, it caught the light and, when he'd reached the bottom of the track, he tapped its end against the red-brown bank where that same jet of water still flowed from the soil.

'We can get your water supply from here,' he announced as she and Mark joined him. 'Then run the pipe under these.' He stamped the ground with his big black wellingtons and bent down to prise up one of the thick stone slabs buried under the mud. 'Say five hundred quid.' He let it drop and, because Mark was closest, the mud copiously splattered his jeans. He looked down at his legs in dismay.

'Shit, man. Did you have to?'

'Accident, beg your pardon.' He turned to her, unrepentant. 'Now then, what about fuel? The choice is oil, electric or LPG.'

She tried to defuse the situation by asking him which would be best.

'Take your pick. If you go for oil, mind, remember the tanker'll need access and you need to ask yourself, do you really want to depend on the bloody Arabs for your warmth and comfort?'

'So what's LPG?' she asked, wondering if all Chapel Deacons were really bigots in disguise.

'Expensive and it stinks.' Mark piped up before Evans could reply. 'Besides, who wants to see loads of canisters hanging around the place? I reckon electric's best. I've got a mate who can get you a generator in. Then you can heat your poly tunnels, run a computer, the lot. That's all you need, plus wiring of course. It can go by the barn – nice and discreet.'

'Thanks for that, squire.' Evans was bristling now, spittle whitening the corners of his mouth. His pencil fell into the mud and he didn't even bother to retrieve it. 'You see, Miss Mitchell, your friend here knows damn well I'm the local LPG dealer round here.' He tucked his clipperboard under his arm and turned to leave. 'And if you've half a whit of sense, you'll put your money back in the bank and look for somewhere else to invest it in.' He then wagged a blackened forefinger at her. 'Don't say I didn't warn you.'

With that he headed back up the wet path, but Mark ran to catch him up and in the stillness of the day's ending, she heard every word.

'Rhaca's been killed,' said Mark. 'Was anyone hanging around here on Saturday morning?'

'You accusing me, then?'

'Should I?'

'You're bitter enough.'

She watched Mark draw nearer to the older man. For a moment she thought he was going to hit him, but when he spoke, his voice was clear and controlled.

'By the way, Mr Preacher, we'll have those two keys back if you don't mind. You've been hanging on to them long enough. They're Miss Mitchell's now.'

'What keys is that, then?'

'You know damn well. Front door, scullery door. You've till midday tomorrow. Got it? And by the way, tell that little Hughes nonce of yours not to go round scaring the shit out of other road users. It isn't very clever. And whatever you're paying him for intimidation, it's not worth it.'

She sneaked up closer to the two figures to hear their voices more distinctly, but nothing prepared her for what came next. And when Bryn Evans had stopped shouting, Mark pushed him aside so he stumbled on to all fours, then ran back past her, into Wern Goch. His whole face resembled an angry mask, and for the first time since they'd met, she saw murder in his eyes.

Hi, you again. Been nearly a year. My fault. How slow time passes in hell. I've stopped eating, only you won't want to know about stuff like that. Not very sexy is it? But the only way I can get the f——s to listen. Remember Bobby Sands? Well, this is my Troscad. I had a nightmare last night and some woman's voice told me a scream always brings a death.

Your one. x

ps Now for the Biggest Secret ever. In invisible ink. Read then hide safely.

On that same dry Monday afternoon, the small Dorset village of Burton Minster seemed to have coiled itself into an invincible shell of quietude. Even the ancient beech trees which lined the Wimborne Road out of the village, and normally home to a multitude of singing birds, were eerily silent.

Elizabeth Benn found herself longing for their cheerful chorus, indeed *any* sound other than the mind-numbing tick tick tick of the alarm clock placed just out of reach on her bedside table. She was being punished alright. That small show of defiance with the army knife last night had meant that today her hands and feet were bound by a pair of stockings apiece and her bedroom door had been locked from the outside.

She also noticed that the blinds in her ground floor room had been cleverly half-closed to deter any stray visitor from peering in, and now the late sunlight brightened their white slats bringing memories of Paphos where twenty-seven years ago she and James had honeymooned in the height of a perfect summer. This detail was typical of the man who never left anything to chance. Whose novel plotting read like a novella itself and whose characters were strictly caged within its limits. Under his strict control. However, no less than Tom Sachs of the Literary Review had already deemed this to be one of *Tribe*'s main flaws. And he was on the Booker judging Committee.

Despite her growing discomfort, she smiled to herself that maybe after all, justice would be done and by autumn, James Montague Benn would have slid away from the public gaze he so craved. That would, for her at least, be some consolation.

Tick tick tick…

No one would be calling. She knew that. Forget the once-chatty bread man, the fruit and veg husband and wife team, or anyone else from church or the village. The author had deterred them all by his disdain for those who worked with their hands, not the right side of the brain as he did. Those who'd never learnt Latin nor knew what a thesaurus was. And as for any carer or family…

She swivelled her tired eyes to the two photographs of her only daughter, which stood on her dressing table. Not even Katherine was around any more. The dear sweet child born from a short affair with Oxford history professor Lance Hewitt, had died of leukaemia, while Benn, her step-father was still with the Queen's Own Regiment in the Falklands. Before the books had spilled out of his head and fiction had usurped any truth. While there'd still been some love between them.

She stared at the schoolgirl's happy smile and felt such a surge of longing to hold her again that a small cry escaped her parched lips and tears lurked, ready to fall behind her eyes. For this house had been Katherine's too, and its large meandering garden had fired her young imagination, provided the centrepiece to her world. There'd been the treehouse cradled by branches of the massive chestnut tree, the pond full of newts and water boatmen to which she'd given names and made up stories about their watery lives...

Now all that remained were a few splintered planks of wood scattered on the unmown grass, while the once glistening pond bore a skin of green algae. Elizabeth forced herself to recall that July evening three years after Katherine had died and James had come home for his last leave. There'd been too much drink at the Manor House, too much careless dancing on the uneven brick terrace just yards away from the water. Yes, she knew all about newts too. Hadn't they slithered between her breasts inside her cocktail dress after she'd hit the pond's murky depths? And then, just before her near-death experience hadn't he been the first to plunge in and keep her face clear of the water? To ring for an ambulance because she hadn't seemed able to move? Major James Benn, brave and loving for all the world to see.

And then, there'd been Hellebore and the biography. All 530 pages of it dedicated *To Elizabeth, My Darling Wife*, complete with a dark core of monochrome photographs from herself as bonneted baby to consenting adult with her eyes ever watchful and wary. Strange how this particular feature never seems to alter with age, she thought, looking at Katherine again and wondering for the millionth time what the rest of her would look like now as an adult...

Suddenly she flinched as a phone began to ring somewhere in the house, followed by another, and another. To alleviate the pain of her stiffening joints, she tried to imagine who was calling. Not Manda Jeffrey, because she'd already rung yesterday. Besides she and the ex-Major were probably busy fucking in between photo shoots. Nor could it be the publisher again, for The Reptile, as she called him, had already made contact at midday and his glowing longlist news had turned James's hateful face the colour of a red pepper. After all, *Tribe* had been given the biggest print run and the most publicity that year, so the mutual backslapping she overheard was predictably, and to her mind, obscenely over the top.

She strained to hear if any messages were being left, but all she could discern was her husband's answerphone voice. Abrupt as always.

So now here she was. Like those other times when she'd upset him. A prisoner in the very house bought and paid for with her late parents' inheritance. A house worth over a million, the only real equity she possessed, and while Katherine was alive, lovingly nurtured. Every room a delight with her glossy-leaved plants, and Amelia Bowerley's charming watercolours. Things which had sustained her during her daughter's last illness. And which even now, gave her some comfort.

She should have outwitted him with that little knife. Kept it hidden until he was vulnerable, but hindsight is a wonderful thing, she thought, aware of her bladder now beginning to ache. Next time, if there was a next time, she'd find a less obvious weapon. A bodkin, perhaps or a fine-pointed bradawl which could be tucked away up her cardigan sleeve.

Whatever. Being secretive and careful was the only recourse she had. Hence her call to Miss Mitchell just before James had played his usual game by tying her up and leaving the house. She'd been given the young woman's mobile number by yet another new temp at Hellebore's front desk and had explained that as the author's wife, she wanted to thank the assistant editor personally for all her help with her husband's books. Clearly regulations on confidentiality hadn't been drummed in there because the temp had also let slip that Miss Mitchell had left work last Tuesday and couldn't be traced.

Still, at least she, Elizabeth, had her number and could keep in touch. Luck at last. And that luck held out while James was busy showering before driving to the station for the London train.

His *Conquests 2001* list had lain snug in his wallet between his Coutts Bank card and a recent receipt from a visit to The Ivy. Such carelessness. Such arrogance, she thought, but those two female names and two work numbers had been all she needed. Last year's soiled goods, the three Filipino girls hadn't wanted to hear her proposition. Jobs at the Embassy were hard to get and hard to keep, they'd said, so she'd not pursued it.

But things had proved more fruitful with Kingsdown Travel in Shaftesbury and, having dialled 141 beforehand, Elizabeth was able to anonymously probe young Sarah Dyson who worked there as a booking clerk as to what exactly had happened to her on New Year's Day eight months before. Fortunately the office was quiet and she was temporarily in sole charge while her boss had gone to the bank next door, so that having listened to Elizabeth's accurate description of her assailant, Sarah had whimpered then begun to cry as she recalled the ordeal. No, none of her family or friends knew anything about the rape in that frosty field after work when she'd had a lift home in the N reg black Fiesta. Elizabeth's car before her pond "accident".

Nobody knew that Sarah had been made pregnant and undergone an abortion. She'd been dumb enough to trust the smooth talker, she'd sobbed. It had been all her fault. However, when Elizabeth had gently informed her that her attacker had been none other than famous author James Benn, then asked if she'd be interested in £2,000 cash to tell the newspapers all about it, the girl had brightened. She was planning to move from the area anyhow, get a better job and buy a place of her own. Besides, her parents were going through a shitty divorce so they'd got enough to think about. Yes, Sarah Dyson had told her. She was very interested indeed.

Elizabeth smiled again despite feeling warm urine drizzle from between her legs and dampen her grey pleated skirt and the bedspread beneath her. She would play fair with both young women. That identical carrot would be offered to Miss Mitchell as well, provided she showed the same spirit as Miss Dyson. Provided she was prepared to knock yet another hefty nail into James Benn's coffin.

She felt dirty. Could smell her pee more distinctly now as the afternoon progressed. Wetting herself had been a childhood thing, hardly befitting a normally fastidious fifty-eight year old. But it was thirst which concerned her most. When she'd given in to this pathetic little ploy of his, she'd not taken into account the air's dryness. The sun's warmth still heating her bedroom's west-facing wall. She spread what little saliva there was around inside her mouth. Her breath felt stale, her lips like old leaves. She must keep control and not let her imagination run away with her. She must be stronger than she'd ever been in her life.

He wasn't planning on staying in London overnight – she'd overheard that much, so it was a question of waiting as calmly as possible, flexing her mind and planning her next move once he'd returned.

She heard the kitchen phone ring again and for some reason found herself thinking back to that June reception for the biography. How James had proudly introduced her to the Hellebore big-wigs. How he'd spooned the succulent little canapés into her mouth as if she couldn't feed herself. She winced at the recollection. But how convincing he'd been. Every movement, each expression of concern on his flushed face a bravura performance.

And the Haydn, her favourite. He'd even chosen that for her, however, as the piano trio had reached its climax, she'd suddenly spotted him in close conversation with Hellebore's blonde assistant editor wearing a natty little black dress and peep-toe shoes.

She'd looked like that once, in the days when she'd been Lance Hewitt's secretary at Balliol, moving amongst the cream of academe, until her one big mistake which was imagining he'd loved her. Just then, in the Chandos Hotel, she'd stared as if at herself all those years ago. The intimacy of James's hand on the girl's arm, the eye to eye contact which never wavered.

Once the Haydn had ended to sporadic applause, and Elizabeth had been briefly side-tracked by some feminist literary critic, she'd realised that both James and the girl had disappeared. While the musicians were taking a break, she'd moved as best she could towards the lift sited outside the reception room. It had taken what seemed like an eternity to come down to her level and when its doors had finally slid open, a young Italian waiter attempted to push past her and out on to the marble landing. Although clearly in a hurry, he'd paused when she'd asked him if he'd seen James Benn anywhere.

'Si, Signora. Third floor. Room 16. I've just taken up some champagne.'

'Was he with anyone or on his own?'

The young man had smiled knowingly at her, then hurried away.

'Grazie,' she'd mumbled, unsure what to do next. Supposing James were to catch sight of her hanging around listening? For that's what she'd intended to do. Supposing another guest raised the alarm about a stray middle-aged woman loitering with intent?

Instead, she'd rejoined the reception where already a sizeable queue waited by the signing table for the handsome flourish of his gold-sheathed pen.

'Such an honour for you,' someone had said.

'What a writer he is…'

'This book will give people hope. It's *so* inspiring.'

'Indeed.' Elizabeth had gracefully acknowledged them all then noticed The Reptile nearby impatiently downing yet another glass of red and plainly annoyed at having to fob the punters off with excuses about the men's room and non-existent crucial phone calls.

'Where's our man, then?' he'd barked to the room in general.

'I'll get a Desk message out,' someone said. 'I'm sure that'll do the trick.'

'And *I'm* sure he'll be along once he's finished consulting with Miss Mitchell,' she'd added, savouring the moment. 'I believe it was an urgent matter.'

She now smiled again to herself as the rest of that eventful evening had unravelled in her mind. The clatter of the young woman's heels on the stairs up to the street. James's creased white suit and ugly flush to his cheeks as he'd rejoined the throng...

The day seemed to be darkening behind the blinds, and was it rain she could hear against the window glass? Her hands and feet felt quite numb now; her circulation had never been good and she remembered how, in those married days after Paphos, he used to massage her toes, her fingers. Would kiss her knees, her thighs and then...

'Heavens above!'

The alarm clock suddenly shrieked its wake-up call, and she turned her head to watch its red light pulsing, pulsing... Another of his pathetic little games, she thought bitterly. If his hordes of mostly women fans only knew. If those devotees of his prose who clogged up his website guest book could see her now.

Well, one day, she told herself, she'd enlighten them all. And him, of course. When the time was right. When she was ready.

Chapter Thirteen

The ravens answer to my call,
They imitate and read my mind,
My brothers all in black so fine,
Are never cruel, always kind.
MJJ 1990

Once Bryn Evans's Defender had scorched away from Ravenstone's drive leaving foul blue diesel fumes hanging in the air, Lucy returned to her car with a major headache in the offing.

She'd left Mark to cool down in Wern Goch, but what the Deacon farmer had said to him still gnawed like a death watch beetle at her curiosity. Nevertheless, she had two calls to make. One to Hellebore's MD to complain, the other to Manda Jeffery herself. But what was the point? she thought, stuffing her mobile back in her bag. What the hell did any of it matter now?

She got out of the Rav, slammed its door and made her way out to what would shortly be one of her fields. Here the ground was at least firm enough to walk on but she could see that between the reeds, the grass blades were rust-coloured near their roots. Silt was clearly not very far away.

Suddenly she spotted Mark emerging from the old barn laden with two armfuls of wooden stakes. She froze, uncertain whether to acknowledge him or pretend not to notice. She'd wanted some time on her own just to take a look round and to ponder on what she'd just heard during the two men's recent altercation. What had Bryn Evans meant by saying the family would always be a curse on the land? And what *exactly* had happened to Mark's mother?

'Just going to peg out your boundaries. OK?' He shouted, heading down towards the river with that loping stride of his.

'Fine. Thanks.' But although she decided to follow him, she kept a few paces behind. Her trust had just taken a fresh beating and was still in Intensive Care, for the forestry worker's mask had slipped to reveal a side dark as the inside of that cauldron in Wern Goch. Dark as, she imagined, it was humanly possible to be. Before any signing of contracts, some questions needed to be answered.

'So, where's this brother of yours, then?' she asked as casually as she could as he began laying out the stakes on the ground in regular intervals. If this query disturbed him, he showed no sign of it. Instead, he pulled a claw hammer from his back pocket and knocked the first stake into place. The noise caused those ewes grazing nearby to scatter in terror and a clutch of previously hidden crows to hit the sky.

'That Evans is a retard and his mother's no better.'

'What on earth do you mean?'

'Inbreeding,' without looking up. 'She's been in and out of Parc-y-Nant's rubber rooms all her life. It's common knowledge round here.' He picked up another stake and took six paces between them.

Bang bang bang.

He placed each blow with consummate skill, but whether it was because the sliding sun had momentarily passed behind a purple cloud or because she could all too easily imagine that same claw hammer landing on her skull, she shivered audibly as he selected another stake.

When that too had gone in the ground, Mark Jones turned round, his face suddenly different out of the sun's light.

'Look, Miss Mitchell, you'll thank me one day. I've just dug you out of a huge fucking hole, excuse my language. Bryn Evans is best kept at arm's length and that's how it's always been here. There are rumours he's fiddling the F&M compensation and my mates down the forestry reckon he was bribed with a diseased ewe's tail to infect his latest flock.'

For a moment she couldn't speak. There'd been months of heart-breaking pictures of tiny lambs crammed into pens waiting for slaughter and mountains of poor beasts on fire. How could someone even *think* of doing that? she asked herself.

'So, it suited us to have the land grazed, but now things are different. You've made it different...'

'Me?' She blinked in surprise at this sudden compliment.

'Yes. Him and his mother should have kept their gobs shut.'

She watched as he returned to his task, observing how his arm muscles below his rolled-up shirt sleeves were like carved and burnished wood. How his sleek black hair shifted with each stroke. Put him on a London pavement, she thought, and he wouldn't be a single for long. But still other less savoury thoughts added to her creeping headache. Who was lying and why? Was a man of the church and his fussing mother any less honest than an intense and clever sawyer? And if there had been or was still a brother called Richard, wasn't it odd that even Hector Jones hadn't mentioned the fact?

She recalled the ex-copper's lie about the Birmingham house-hunters. That had come easily enough, so what else was being kept secret? She frowned, knowing she'd have to keep probing, but hadn't her mother and subsequent school teachers always picked on her for asking too many questions? Warned her that this habit of hers would inevitably lead to trouble? Nevertheless, she moved closer to Mark and took a deep breath.

'You've just said Mrs Evans was mad. If so, how come she used to babysit up here when you two were small?'

Mark slowed up. The hammer in his right hand poised to strike at what, she didn't give herself time to find out. The silence between them felt deadly. Anything could happen out here and she knew for a fact that with the Hall being some distance away, no one would hear her scream...

She began to run.

'Hey! Come back!' he yelled as she made for the track, but suddenly grass had become like moss sucking at her feet. It was as if she was being pulled to the bottom of the world.

'Oh my God...' She was sinking fast with nothing to hold on to. Her hands flayed around pointlessly, because there was nothing. Only the mental picture of her mum and dad in Llanberis. Smiling at each other...

'Don't move! I'm coming!'

She stared in shock as he drew closer, hammer still in hand, while overhead a mass of ravens had gathered, blocking off the last of the dying sun.

He croaked three times, then he shouted 'Now!'

She instinctively shut her eyes, thinking about Irmgard Muller's fate. Even as a kid she'd never hung around the local pet shop's parrots and budgerigars. Instead she'd dragged her dad towards the rabbits. Soft, warm and comforting. And hadn't Cicero been forewarned of his own death by the fluttering of these same birds?

She felt the collar of her denim jacket being dragged upwards. Then both sleeves as the flapping wings generated an overpoweringly oily smell in their effort to keep her upright.

'Grab this,' Mark nudged her with the longest stake and she obeyed. Then, inch by inch, helped by this and the effort from above, she found one foothold then another until she was safe again. 'Brilliant.' He dropped the stake and pulled her towards him. Immediately the ravens relinquished their grip on her jacket, then touched his hair with their thick beaks as a parting gesture, before heading east for the hills.

She heard him breathe a deep sigh of relief as he watched them go. Then he turned to her. 'You were lucky. Even the sheep never go near that spot.'

'Why not?' Her teeth still chattered. She felt as limp and useless as a rag doll, but without the energy or desire to pull away from him.

'It's an old well. And before that...' Here he stopped.

'Go on, seeing as it's my money paying for it.'

'Probably some Druidic site. Water was always very significant for them.'

'Was?' she quizzed, aware of her feet and ankles still weighted by mud. 'I thought they still existed. Doing all that weird stuff with mistletoe and dead animals...'

'You're right. They like to hang out where it's really wild. Where no one can interfere...'

'Like here, you mean?'

He didn't answer because the spongy ground had moved them even closer together. She could feel the forester's warm sap-scented shoulder against her cheek and the surreal stillness of life after near-death. She wanted him to kiss her, to hold her tight, but his eyes seemed too full of shadows. Or was it fear?

'Rhaca would have helped you as well,' he said, gently easing her away from him and bending down to gather the remaining stakes into a neat pile.

'Rhaca?'

'My special right-hand raven. D'you know, he could understand every word I said. He could mimic me too.'

'That's impossible, surely?'

She looked at him. This was no Barnaby Rudge referring to Grip, his own pet raven. This was real and Mark Jones was deadly serious. Surely, she thought, there were no surprises left. Then she remembered what Hector had said about the recent blood on that salting slab. How it had most likely come from an injured bird.

'What's happened to him?' she asked, guessing the worst.

'Gone to Annwn.'

'I don't understand. Who's she?'

A tiny smile reached Mark's mouth. 'It's the Celtic Underworld, or *Other*world as they call it. The strange thing is though, I'd dreamt about him the very night before I found his body. I'd just buried him when you arrived. He was eighteen years old, and only four when ...' Here he stopped himself, but she was still too incredulous to notice.

'Eighteen? Surely not?' Then thought of those earth-covered hands, that same grief as her own mother's, in his eyes.

'Some live to be forty-four in captivity.'

'I don't believe this. And in the wild?'

'Survival of the fittest. Usual story.'

They'd reached the first of the old elms near the Hall and she rubbed each foot in turn against its bark Her trainers looked like red-brown overshoes coated in a viscous mud and spectacularly hard to shift. 'I reckon some bird of prey must have got him,' Mark suggested in a tone she didn't find altogether convincing. 'We get eagles here, you know. And red kites. Nature's greedy, I'm afraid.'

Not only nature, she thought, sensing a flutter of alarm pass through her, because apart from that one piece of window glass at Wern Goch, there was nothing to keep *any* kind of intruder out.

'Look,' she said, thinking of the bird's horrible blood again. I'll need new locks and lockable double-glazed windows first thing. Top priority.' Then she checked herself. Wasn't this Tooting all over again? Keys and more keys?

'I was just about to say the same thing.' He picked up the end of a length of flattened hose which snaked invisibly across the ground. 'Just give me a list of what exactly you want and I'll see to it.'

'Are you sure?'

'Course. My shifts are from six a.m. till two. After that, I'm all yours.'

All yours.

She stared after him as he strode away to an old tap set in the Hall's windowless side wall and immediately a jet of yellow water spewed from the pipe's nozzle. She jumped away from it in surprise as he then directed the flow towards her trainers. She tried to think rationally about the implications of his offer, but that rampant headache was already like a bush fire burning up her reasons for saying no.

'So,' he then trained the hose on to her Rav's wheels. 'Tomorrow's Tuesday. I'll go to Jewsons for you after work.'

'Thanks,' she relented, 'but I can't pay for anything till next Monday.' No way was she revealing the details of her father's legacy to him or anyone else. She watched the red mud slide like thin old blood from her tyres on to the hardcore.

'No problem. We'll arrange an account with them. Settle up at the end of each month.' He went to turn off the tap.

'We?'

'You. Sorry.'

'Look, I'd better go.' She unlocked her car door and opened it. Never had she felt so grateful for its familiar smell and the cheerful dancing figures on its upholstery. 'Thank you for saving me, back there,' she called back to him. 'Those birds were amazing.'

'Pure self-interest, Miss Mitchell,' he smiled again before heading up the Hall's steps and into the gloom beyond the front door. 'By the way,' he added. 'Did you know that ravens possess the biggest brains of all birds and they always mate for life?'

'No, I didn't.'

'According to Roman legend they bear the character of Saturn and were once white as swans. Very picky carnivores too,' he added with a wicked grin which didn't quite work.

'Your father told me they ate Frau Muller when she'd been shot.'

That grin soon changed. Perhaps she should have kept quiet, because obviously she'd upset him. But surely, that tragedy happened a long time ago. Way before he was even born...

She watched him knock on the study door and go in. Shortly afterwards an argument was in full swing, permeating outside through the Hall's old stones as she unlocked her car and secreted *Magical Tales* safely in the glove box. She wondered why the rumpus, and it was only when she'd peeled off her denim jacket that she realised not one fibre of it had been damaged by the ravens' beaks.

Lucy drew breath in the privacy of her own car but its comforts were short-lived as she dwelt on Mark's last odd comments. Maybe he was as mixed up as the Evanses he'd so derided. After all, wasn't his surname like hundreds of others in the local phone book? No, she told herself, aware of her damp feet beginning to smell of the marsh. It was more than that. Further anxieties had spawned like mould in her mind; not least the prospect of returning via that scary narrow lane to Horeb House, but also what else its allegedly barmy proprietor there might have in store for her.

Chapter Fourteen

I am spear that roars for blood
I am a raging boar
I am a stag of seven antlers
I am guilty of love.
I am a wave on the sea.
RFB 1990

Books and more books. Robert had never seen so many in just one small place. Even the State Library off Macquarie Street couldn't match this. Not that he'd been much of a reader – more a doer, his teachers had said – but apart from learning most of Sohrab and Rustam off by heart for his English teacher, he'd been drawn far more to non-fiction tales of *real* life. Conflict and revenge. The sense of justice done. Yes, he thought, finishing breakfast on his second morning at The Bont B&B in Hay-on-Wye, that notion certainly hadn't lost any of its appeal.

He walked away from the guest house feeling as stuffed as a Christmas turkey after what the menu termed "the full English." However, he'd left both slices of black pudding to languish against his plate's decorative border. Why assume he'd enjoy the *taste* of blood? It was bad enough seeing it, and to his relief, the crusty widower who ran the establishment had merely raised his eyebrows when he'd cleared the table. No further questions about this or that or where he was off to next. Something at least to be grateful for.

The sun felt warm through his cotton shirt. Short-sleeved, blue-striped, paired with maize-coloured chinos. Country yet smart. He'd spent time and money getting this balance right, because in Oz, despite the slobs on the TV soaps, appearance was all. Shoes especially, which is why he'd not only invested in natty suede loafers but also discreet mole-coloured lace-ups which went well with most things. And glances of fellow pedestrians told him that in these details he was well ahead of the game.

He'd just stopped by Gervaise Talbot's Antiquarian Bookshop to goggle at some illustrated fairy tales which hadn't been in that window yesterday, and which no kid of his would ever be shown, when a sheila's voice behind him made him spin round.

'That'll cost you an arm and a leg,' she laughed. 'Don't even think of it.'

He took in her cropped cerise-coloured hair, her mini-skirt and matching jacket, the accompanying scent.

Her *scent*…

The stranger's recklessness was catching and he laughed too.

'It's not called Rip-Off on Wye here for nothing,' she added, shielding her hazel eyes from the sun before asking the next question. 'Are you in the book trade?'

'No. Company law. How about you?'

'I write articles for in-flight mags. Not as romantic as it sounds, I'm afraid. Hack work if you want the truth. Have you ever been to the Festival here?'

'I've heard of it, naturally.' He was content to nudge along in this manner because where he came from it was no big deal for the sheila to start up a conversation. But here? Surely here was different?

'My aunt's got some Margaret Tarrant books,' she went on, peering into the shop window at the illustrations from Puss In Boots. 'Used to work for The Connoisseur. Knew exactly where to go hunting.'

'Ditto.'

'Really?' She looked up at him.

'House-hunting. Something near a river. Own mooring, fishing rights. That sort of thing. For vacations.'

'Hey, tell me more.'

She seemed impressed, but it wasn't mutual. He'd seen the way her hair lay damp and dark against her neck. So, she sweated easily, he thought. Black mark number two. He gestured towards The Granary Café.

'It'll do till the pubs open,' he said, pulling out some estate agents' details from his chinos pocket and passing them over to her. 'Then you can tell me which one of these you like best.' Nothing featured was valued at less than £450,000. She looked even more impressed.

'Great.'

They made their way towards the few still unoccupied tables and chairs outside the café, occasionally having to stop close together on the narrow pavement to allow horse riders or some farm vehicle or other to pass. It was then he detected her other smell, as if she wasn't wearing grundies.

'You're Australian, aren't you?' she asked finally, removing her jacket and settling herself in a chair. 'Great place.' She crossed her sturdy bare legs and instead of looking along her thighs, he transferred his gaze to the deep freckled cleavage showing above the neck of her Tee. He saw her nipples, the ribs of her bra. She shouldn't sunbake, he thought.

'S' right. Woollomooloo, in Sydney.'

'You're kidding,' she grinned. 'Who'd dream up a name like that, for God's sake?'

'It's fair dinkum. London's got Park Lane and Mayfair, we've got

Woolloomooloo and King's Cross.'

'Have you read any Noel Ricci? He's from Canberra.'

'*Dark Waters? Cold Coming?*' He rushed the last title which had recently been plastered all over Sydney's bookshops because it was too near the bone.

'Sure. Just missed out on the Booker longlist. Shame. He'll do it one day. Just like Peter Carey.'

A young lad with a white apron tied around his middle emerged from inside the café and Robert ordered two coffees.

'I'm Phil, by the way,' he said to her afterwards. 'And you?'

'Jade.'

'Hey, that's my cousin's name. Got a vineyard near Adelaide. She grows the Grenache.'

'Lucky her. Tell me more.'

'It's bloody hard work, I can tell you. I used to spend Uni vacations helping out there. Yeah, we had some fun too, I s'pose.'

The coffees arrived, and the sunshine helped of course. The young woman relaxed by uncrossing her legs and stretching them out, glancing occasionally at the property sheets in front of her, but much more interested in telling him about her busy job and why she was in Hay-on-Wye in the first place.

'They start planning now for next year's Festival,' she explained. 'Bit of a busman's holiday for me, really, but I'll be on a panel with some of the other journalists I work with. We provide good all year round entertainment for the discerning traveller. Could all do with a bit more exposure, that's all.'

Exposure...

She could do with rather less, he thought, aware of a birthmark like a bruise on her left thigh; her pink knees and how she gulped down the contents of her cup as if all her yabbering had made her thirsty.

'Do you have any family over here? Any friends?' she asked unexpectedly.

'No family, but a couple of mates to call up if I get lonesome. Trouble is, I've only got a fortnight to find a place, so I'm homing in on the Wye until Monday, then off to Gloucester to suss out the Severn.'

'Sounds good, but they do both tend to flood.' She'd found a half-dissolved brown sugar lump in the bottom of her cup and popped it in her mouth. 'You'd need to watch out during the winter.'

'I've considered all that,' he said, checking his watch. 'No probs. So, where are you shacked up?'

'Fulham normally. Got a big interview in London tomorrow.'

'Sheep from the goats, eh?'

'That's life, isn't it?'

''Fraid it is.'

This one liked to talk alright, he thought. In fact, she probably liked to do a lot more with her mouth than that. He didn't usually have to wait too long to be proved right.

'Are you doing anything special right now?' she asked once his cup was also empty. 'Would you like to see Booth's Bookshop?'

'Booth's?' he lied as if he'd never heard of it. He'd got what he wanted from there yesterday.

'The King of Hay, no less. Come on.' She secured her vinyl bag's strap over her shoulder and, after he'd insisted upon paying and leaving a generous tip, they both set off down the hill towards a grey stone building set back behind a parking area. Seeing each of its book-packed windows again renewed his hatred of such places. Even at the best of times. To him the fiction shelves were repositories of every kooky mind under the sun. You only had to read the blurbs on the covers, never mind ingest what was harboured between them.

He followed her into the shop's small foyer. Some consolation at least seeing her solid rear move inside her skirt and wondering if her pubes were also cerise...

'Hi,' she said brightly to the same assistant who'd served him before. 'This guy's new here. From Australia. I'm just showing him round.'

However, the assistant turned to him.

'Sure I saw you yesterday evening. You enjoying that Mabinogion you bought? Nice copy. Worth hanging on to.'

He gulped. He'd never stepped on a landmine before but this was close.

'Mab *what?*' he asked with a major frown, aware that the tart was looking at him.

'The Charlotte Guest translation. You spent long enough finding it.'

He thanked God his tan was hiding the blush.

'You're mistaken, sir,' he said. 'I've never been here in my life.'

'Okay, okay,' the guy raised both hands in a gesture of defeat. 'My mistake.'

With that, they both entered the cave of print and its mix of smells as if the volumes themselves were breathing in and out, filling the whole vast space with madness and confusion. Robert's eyes soon began to feel heavy as she fidgeted her way along the Biography shelves. Whether it was a delayed reaction to the long-haul flight or the subsequent sleepless nights after that Sunday shower, he didn't know, but when she reached CRIME he made his apologies.

'Need to grab some fresh air,' he said. 'I'll wait for you outside. Take your time.'

'I won't be a mo. Say ten minutes?'

'No worries.'

He strode out of the fusty hole without making eye contact with the geek at the desk and once in the bright daylight installed himself on a low wall out of sight of the foyer, to plan his next move. He now wished that, with a little more foresight, he'd thought of a different persona.

Anything. A Cardiff tennis player. A mineralogist. He realised it was too late now to change things here. Which meant no slip-ups. No ends untied...

'Hey, look at this,' she waved a worn looking book at him, fifteen minutes later. 'Dodie Smith. *I Capture the Castle*. D'you know I've never got myself another copy since my mum nicked mine off me when I was a kid.'

'Nice mum,' he said in a way which made her glance up at him. 'Anyway,' she ferreted inside a brown paper bag and produced a slightly grubby paperback. 'This is for you. Only little, mind. A souvenir of today.'

He stared at the title.

'*History of the Kelly Gang*. It's ripper. Thanks.' He grinned at her, and she grinned back. Then he realised that after all the tiresome preamble, the moment had come. 'Look, would you like a drive out to Clifford? Just for an hour? Got a viewing there at midday. Be good to get another angle on the house. Especially a woman's. This could be the one.' He patted his chinos' pocket where the particulars lay then held his breath.

For a nerve-wracking moment she hesitated then checked her watch.

'Where's your car?' she asked at last.

'Up by the B&B. Cusop Road.'

'OK. Do me good I suppose. It *is* lovely round here after London.'

'You're on. Anyway, I've got to seriously move my butt this afternoon. Got another three to look at. It's all go, I'm telling you.'

He was on the ball, doing great, he told himself as they reached the minor road out of town. It had been too long since the last time for him to fuck this up and, dammit, he'd earned it...

'Nice car,' she said, patting the warm spare at the back. 'Black's my favourite colour.'

'Keeps itself clean, that's the main thing.' He disabled the alarm and opened the passenger door for her, relieved all his camping gear and that Mabinogion lay hidden under a tartan rug.

'Whew, it's hot,' she exclaimed, sitting down and arranging her bags on the floor by her feet. Her skirt was right up now. Her smell more intense. 'I came in by bus today from where I'm staying. Just to give it a whirl. There were only two of us on board. Mad, isn't it?'

'Yeah.' He switched on the AC and spread the new Ordnance map over both their laps. It was a kind of unifying thing which she didn't seem to mind. 'But you can't blame folks for wanting the freedom of their own wheels. It's human nature.'

'There's Clifford,' she pointed to the spot with a pearly pink nail. Another black mark as far as he was concerned, mounting up now. One by one. Which was good.

'Nice route, should be easy as opening a tinny,' he grinned again, then sensed her hesitation.

'I just need to make a call,' she said out of the blue, bending forwards to reach her bag.

His pulse was paying tricks. This was totally unplanned.

'Right now?' he asked, starting the ignition and urging her to click in her belt.

'Yeah. I need to let my friend Cass know what I'm doing in case we're held up.' Her tiny silver mobile was already in her hand. It looked like some stupid fish he thought, anger tightening his chest. He hit the throttle and central locking simultaneously.

'This friend, is she some kind of nanny, then?'

'Jesus Christ,' she lurched forwards as the Ford moved off and gripped the top of the dash. The map slid to the floor. 'It's just a precaution. I always do it. Could you please stop this car?'

No chance.

The dial showed seventy not fifty.

He could see her eyeing the handbrake so he steered with one hand to protect the only means of control his passenger had.

'Stop now,' she repeated surprisingly calmly. 'Or I'll call the police.' She punched 9 but got no further, because with a scythe-like movement of his free hand he swept the gadget from her grasp on to the floor near his feet. He was well psyched up now, expecting a fight from her. Every nerve and muscle prepared. But she just sat there, hunched up, clasping her bare knees. And this surrender left him feeling oddly cheated.

'So, Jade, let's hear a bit more about your family,' he encouraged as the road narrowed to a sharp and unexpected bend and she momentarily lost her balance. 'What was it made you want to go round looking like some tart, eh? Was it your mother? Your father? Christ, d'you know, you're all the same? The world's pavements are full of you sluts.

You're like the plague. Fucking everywhere. What hope has the next generation got eh? Answer me that.'

But as Cifford came and went, no answer came. She'd had her chance to take him just a little way into a particular kind of woman's mind. And he'd have been quite prepared to listen. Oh, yes. As a Mature Student of the Female Psyche, he certainly wanted to learn. Gagging for it, in fact. Pity, he thought, shaking his sun-blonde head, because right now her yabbering could be making a big difference.

Instead, he turned off in a north westerly direction towards New Radnor and a far more interesting destination than Clifford. Here the green summer hills became smudged by russet and the darker hues of forestry, which in turn became naked black.

'Your favourite colour,' he announced, taking extra care down the gradient into a gloomy cavernous valley. The Maverick's windows began to mist up. The silence she was maintaining oppressive, and that perfume... Jesus. If he hadn't seen water just then, there was no telling what might have happened.

And seeing was feeling, no doubt about it. As he slowed up, ready to stop, that same flow from the hole marked MEMORY was once more filling his eyes, thinning his blood and bloating his mind.

Chapter Fifteen

Let him magnify the Truth, it will magnify him.
Let him strengthen Truth, it will guard him.
Let him exalt Truth, it will exalt him.
MJJ & Brehan Morann Mac Caibre

Despite the ruination of her jeans and trainers, and yet another unsettling conversation with Mark, Lucy was once more feeling upbeat about
the whole Wern Goch project. She'd be thirty on Saturday and at last
able to access her father's money. Today was Thursday and at least a
start had been made.

Mark had already replaced the house's two ancient locks with new,
and had ordered five sealed double-glazed sash window units to be
delivered there on the 27th. At her insistence, he was to ask 'Simnai'
Williams from Maesybont to sweep the house's chimney.

'Waste of money,' the sawyer had countered with surprising vehemence. 'No one's used that range for years. It'll be as clean as a whistle.
You'll see.'

'Maybe so, but I still can't risk a fire. Anyway,' she'd reminded him,
handing over her mobile for him to ring the number, 'you said yourself
that once it gets chilly I'd need to light it and have an open fire in the
parlour. End of August, you reckoned. And have you forgotten what
you told me about the mists?' How they hang around the Mellte for
days?'

He'd shrugged, then reluctantly dialled. She'd been puzzled by the
oddly short one-sided conversation which had followed. And why had
she shivered just then as if autumn was already upon them, as they'd
both stood there in that bare neglected place? Why too had he insisted
that the salting slab and the cauldron remain in the kitchen at all costs?
She could clean them certainly, he'd said, but to get rid altogether would
bring the Morrigan's curse upon everything. This awesome goddess of
Death would poison her water supply, draw her very air up from the
Underworld's foul depths and woe betide any hopes for restful sleep...

She'd stared at him in disbelief, yet recalling what Mrs Evans had
said, asking herself how could such dark primitive forces be believed as
if they were ever-present in the world? And more worryingly, *his*
world? It was then he'd handed over his poem in a home-made envelope, but neither this nor the gloriously sunny day could purge his
freaky scenarios from her mind as she left Horeb House at 10 a.m., having declined the usual greasy breakfast and the landlady's inevitable
quizzing as to why. She stood in the sun against the B&B's black rail-

ings organising her thoughts. For a start, she had two new calls to make on her mobile – the first to Anna, the second, because she knew this could be the trickiest, her mother.

Dammit.

Enid Evans was on look-out duty. She could tell by the slight movement of the parlour's net curtains. Ever since Tuesday morning when the landlady had handed over Wern Goch's two old keys wrapped up in a filthy torn page from *Tractors Today*, her manner towards her had cooled to the point of rudeness.

'My Bryn'll be taking his ewes off the land sharpish as well, so you can please yourself what you do with it,' she'd muttered, delivering a plate of sausages sealed in a cawl of fat. 'And don't say I didn't tell you.'

'Tell me what?' Recalling Mark's remark about her mental health and not being entirely convinced by it.

'A sin never dies. Remember that.'

Lucy punched Anna's number more forcibly than usual, and waited for her to answer while two teenage girls in riding gear walked past giggling to themselves.

'Hi, you,' she said to the voicemail, disguising her disappointment that her friend hadn't answered. 'It's me, Lucy. Just touching base. Speak soon…'

Then she heard Mrs Evans shout from her front door.

'What time will you back here, then?'

She headed for her car, unlocked it and folded back the sun roof.

'And will you be wanting liver or rabbit tonight?'

Lucy's insides lurched at the prospect of either delicacy.

'I'm meeting a friend,' she lied. 'So I'm not sure. But thanks all the same.' What the woman didn't know was that her getaway tomorrow would be swift and silent. She'd paid up until the Saturday so her conscience was clear, besides, Hector Jones had offered her a spare room at the Hall until completion and Wern Goch's water and electricity had been installed. Strictly business of course, but cheaper than Horeb at £40 per week with the added possibility of finding more out about the Joneses.

She reached for her sunglasses and opened out her AA map on the passenger seat and with Furtado's *Like a Bird* filling the car, proceeded along the A44 towards Kington with an almost full tank of petrol. She needed a change of scene, to enable her to see Wern Goch in a wider context. A chance to think about everything, especially Mark. Why he'd fielded her question about his brother with that innuendo about Mrs Evans. Why he was so uptight around his father and that uncanny relationship he'd got with those ravens. She thought of his poem in her pocket. To be read in just the right place. Suddenly, just beyond the Red Lion pub at Llanfihangel-Nant-Melan , she noticed a bilingual sign which read, WATER BREAK ITS NECK   HALF A MILE ON THE LEFT.

She shuddered. That name again, accompanied by the words PERIGL! and DANGER! in larger red letters. She recalled the boy's story at the Texaco garage on Saturday, and slowed up wondering why just four ordinary words could collectively create such a presentiment of evil. But because they did, she glanced again at her map and made the decision to take a look at this so-called attraction. After all, the weather was summery and there'd probably be other visitors there. So, nothing to fear, she told herself and once the densely fir-covered hills had passed and the countryside opened up, she wondered how, with such beauty ready and waiting, she'd managed to survive those six years in London. She duly turned left and found herself in a single lane bordered by the lushest foliage she'd ever seen and an array of wild flowers she'd forgotten existed, except of course in *Magical Tales* which was still keeping her travel sweets and car service history company in the glove box.

Here was Heaven and now that she had a part of it, nothing or no one was ever going to take that away from her. It was on this high that she knew she must call home as Barbara Mitchell was still after all, her mum.

No reply. Just the faintly crackling answerphone bringing the teacher's breezy professional voice into the car. Lucy felt a sudden stab of longing for those days when they'd looked after each other just after Dad had died. And now that longing became regret that she couldn't personally reassure her that all was well. Nevertheless, she left that very message in the most upbeat way possible, naming Ravenstone Hall as her next billet and leaving the address. Finally she suggested that once things were sorted this end, she must come and stay.

With the call ended, she sat for a moment watching drifts of black-nosed sheep move amongst the surreally green landscape of tumuli and what must have been some vast burial mound. Time to read Mark's poem, she thought, feeling the hot sun on her cheek, embedded in silence, save for the occasional burst of birdsong. She held her breath as she opened the envelope and extracted the single white sheet headed with the Hall's details. Three short lines and how innocuous they looked. How oddly formal, given everything she'd learnt so far about the place.

RAVENSTONE HALL
RHAYADER
RADNORSHIRE

The Celtic prose and verse form of the englynion has its origins in Sanskrit showing how the heroic epic grew from a verse dialogue, with the actual story left to the creative memory of the reciter. You should look up the Red Book of Hergest for the verse dialogue which takes place between Llewarch Hen and his sons Gwen and Maen.

Here anyway, is mine. Purists will argue for the four line, thirty syllable englynion, but since when have I been pure?

Lucy, bringer of Light to my dark world.
As brightest star, you foil the deepest night,
And keep the gloom from gathering in my mind,
Like worms uncurling in the cold red earth.
MJJ 23/8/01

Her skin felt cold as if the sun had suddenly slipped behind a cloud. But there were no clouds, just an overriding taste, like sour milk, filling her mouth. She gathered up spit and pulled a tissue from inside the door to expunge the effect of that last line from her mind. Boy, he'd got some baggage, she thought, looking for any signs of a litter bin. And was she the one to turn his life around? For God's sake, she'd got a derelict house on her hands. She didn't need an emotional cripple as well.

Cruel again? Just like with Jon? 'Fraid so. Thanks, James Benn. Catching, isn't it? And then as she restarted the car came the unwelcome realisation that maybe she was just as screwed up as the sawyer, except that maybe he, Mark Jones, was being more honest about it.

She executed a poor three-point turn back on to the main road, only to be reminded of her father by seeing another more discreet sign, this time for a nearby Crematorium. She thought of his final selfless act towards her, even though he'd been seriously ill after open heart surgery and, noticing a car emerge from that particular turning, wondered if its occupants were also carrying ashes away, just like she and her mother had done. Then for a brief and numbing moment she imagined it was her own plastic casket being clutched by white fingers, its lid unscrewed and all that remained of her scattered over where the ancient dead lie sleeping.

Mark's poem lingered in Lucy's mind as she followed further signs for the waterfall and swung left on to a large parking area which had obviously been recently resurfaced. Soon his words had lodged there indelibly, just like the contents of *Magical Tales*, and threatened to spill like a dark stain over all those other happy associations. She looked up at the sky for some reassuring blue and saw instead a large brown bird of prey bearing a squealing rabbit towards the nearest hills. Ted Hughes would have done something with that, she thought bleakly, but to her, he'd never been a patch on RS Thomas. Now *there* was jaundiced in capital letters. But powerful, nevertheless.

She got out and locked the car, still aware of the rabbit's cries diminishing. The air was fresher here, and she pulled her denim jacket closer around her as she followed a rutted track towards the waterfall, wishing she'd brought her little camera with her. Soon the sound of rushing plummeting water reached her ears, swamping all other sensations. It was awesome, and so deep and steep did the way down to the cascade appear, that she preferred to stand where she was to take it all in. A furtive peep over the barrier was enough, because that sour taste had returned together with a whiff of fear. She spun round but there was no one else. Just her and the noise and the high hot sun.

Suddenly, over the roar of water came what sounded like a scream. It couldn't be anything else, surely? Lucy instinctively looked up, but this hadn't come from some animal. It was definitely human. Definitely a woman.

'Jesus.' There it was again. Just like what she'd heard on Saturday but somehow more real, solid. More penetrating, somehow.

She began to run back to the car park and, to her surprise, she glimpsed a large black vehicle pulling out from behind a clump of bushes to the left. This had got to be too much of a coincidence. And the way the thing sped off with a shriek of tyres told her this was no ordinary picnicker off home. At first she was tempted to follow in the Rav, but when she reached it, just the combined smell of diesel and tarmac remained. She tried her mobile only to find 0 CREDITS flashing up.

Damn. What the hell was she to do? She listened again for that same haunting sound, but this time just the torrent's fury filled the air and her head once more as she made for her Rav. No point in looking at the map, she told herself, deciding to head back towards Llanfihangel-Nant-Melan. There's sure to be a farm or somewhere, or even a public phone.

After a steep hill and a bend in the road, she noticed a sign for home-cured ham as the smell of pigs wafted into the car. Undeterred, she drove in and parked near the gate for a quick exit if need be, before braving the farmyard which was thick with semi-dried slurry, crisp on top, sloppy underneath, plus a trio of Alsatian dogs who circled non-stop around her. In an adjacent grassless paddock a mass of saddleback pigs snuffled at the earth. She sniffed. Here lay the concentrated source of that earlier smell, which now, together with the dogs made her stop and shout her introduction.

Moments later, she saw a stout young woman emerge from a hay barn, call the dogs to heel, then approach the Rav with a defensive look on her face. Lucy held her breath. She still had time to beat a retreat, but decided to stick it out. This stranger could well prove useful.

'Hi,' feeling her nostrils closing. 'I've just heard awful screaming coming from the waterfall over there. It sounds like someone's in trouble.'

'Kids mucking about, most like,' the countrywoman smiled, removing her sleeveless quilted jacket and shaking it free of hay. 'At it all the time they are.'

'This didn't sound like kids. More like a woman.'

'Whereabouts exactly?'

'By the cascade somewhere. I didn't dare look down.'

'It's deep. Don't blame you. Look,' the farmer pointed to a single-storey building behind a hilly copse in the middle distance. 'There's an Outward Bound place up by there. They go abseiling, canoeing, you name it. Why don't you try them? It's a nice walk. We've never closed off the right-of-way.'

'We?'

'Yeah. Me and my partner. We run this outfit together. Though God knows we fancy breeding bloody pigeons after what we've been through. Anyway, ask at the centre. That's what I'd do.'

'Thanks.'

'Sorry I can't help you.' The woman turned to go.

'I ought to call the police. Just as a precaution,' Lucy called after her. 'I couldn't use your phone, could I?'

At this, the other spun round, her demeanour quite different. Far more wary.

'I'm sure there's nothing to worry about. Here's our number,' she scribbled with a Lottery pen on to a scrap of paper from her pocket. 'If you like, I'll pop up there round midday. Got to check the pig wire in the back field anyway.'

'That's great.' Lucy tucked the scrap in her shoulder bag, wondering why the P word had been such a problem for her.

'I'm Mel, by the way,' the farmer said. 'And you?'

'Sonia.' Anna's mother was the first name she could think of.

'Buzz me at one, then.'

'Will do.'

With that, and the blood-curdling screams still ringing in her ears, she swung the Rav round and re-traced her journey back to Rhayader.

Spooked by her recent experience, Lucy stopped outside a small snack bar in Llandegley for a much-needed coffee and a cheese roll. She felt cold even with her denim jacket now on, and the warm drink between her hands made little difference.

'You alright, Miss?' asked a solicitous-looking woman wiping over the pastries counter and who, to her amusement, lifted a blob of piped cream from a doughnut and popped it in her mouth.

'Sort of, thanks.'

'Like that, is it? You from here, then?' Was more automatic than genuinely curious, so Lucy felt she could respond with a question.

'Tell me,' she began. 'Have you ever been to that place called Water Break Its Neck?'

'Only the once. Why d'you want to know?' She rinsed out her cloth in a bowl positioned below the counter and continued wiping.

'I've just been there and heard screaming going on. It was weird.'

The woman stopped her labours and looked at her.

'Well that don't surprise me at all. Let's say I wouldn't let no family of mine go to it, leastways not on their own. Been two deaths there since last March as it is. Now, I'm not saying they was anyone's fault, but when you're talking about a seventy foot drop into what the locals here call The Pit Of Hell, then you'd think twice.'

The Pit of Hell?

'I did.' Lucy felt even colder. She was now entirely convinced that the waterfall was one experience she could have done without. Yet this surely wasn't a rational response, she reasoned, finishing her coffee, wondering whether or not to ask to use the phone. For before meeting Jon hadn't she trekked to the Gorge de Verdun, sailed through the Peloponnese and stood on Beachy Head without the slightest fear?

But Wales was another world. Never mind the native Welsh themselves who seemed to say one thing and do another. She'd also picked up on other not-so-hidden forces at work. For a start, their language used to keep so-called "incomers" in their place. She'd found that scenario in the bank and in the tea rooms but guessed it was pretty widespread. Even her quota of words from the *Magical Tales* glossary didn't add up to much when she needed it. Then there were the sheer numbers of black predatory birds – especially ravens – and, despite Mark's companions having helped to save her life, to her, reared on urban streets, they represented nothing less than a persistent malevolence.

Look, she told herself half an hour later, pulling up a short distance from Horeb house to collect her belongings. Like that farmer had said, there's probably some entirely normal explanation for those noises at the waterfall, and at Wern Goch. Anyway, Hector was an ex-copper. He'd know what to do. She was getting too jumpy. This wasn't the Great Wen for God's sake, where she'd got so used to being wary. Where every young black in a baseball cap was a potential mugger and some stray pervert was lying in wait around every corner.

No, it was best that she think positively and re-acquaint herself with the little house and its urgent renovation. For example, what sort of floor tiles to choose? Which curtain fabric would let in the most light? And, during a thankfully uneventful trip back along the dreaded narrow lane to Ravenstone, with the sun on the hills and huge white clouds motionless in the still air, she felt for the first time that despite all her doubts, the unexplained tensions there, at last she was coming home.

Chapter Sixteen

I invoke the woman of my childhood,
The breasts which fed me, the
breasts of sweet yellow milk as she
sings of love...of love...but not for me.
Anon

Thursday's dying sun had cast the sky over the estate's acres into a liquid gold, threaded by blood-red strands like those severed veins which he'd witnessed fourteen years ago. And now, despite a refreshing shower, Mark stood by his bedroom window at the front of the Hall, fixed by such a devilish Celestial resemblance to that horror, that he relived yet again the dread morning when he'd seen her lying there. His own mother, butchered in a way which made the halal method seem kind, but not only that, abandoned as carrion, just like that other long-ago occupant from Munich.

His stomach turned over, as it always did on these occasions, and he wondered if a day would ever dawn when he'd be free of the constant watchfulness which kept him awake at nights. Free of the black lies poisoning his mouth, when he knew that Truth was the Word and the Word was sacred and divine.

He now trained his eye along the distant hedge bordering the lane, checking for unfamiliar vehicles passing along, musing how, unlike his grief which came and went like a tidal sea, a huge fear had grown and festered in his mind for fourteen years. He closed his eyes tight and mentally exhorted every fibre of his being not to let the unseen enemy steal his fragile sanity, and by doing so, sabotage his one possible chance of happiness.

He saw Lucy's blue 4x4 on the driveway, still stuffed with her belongings from the B&B. She'd be down at the little house, or rather, *her* little house, probably deciding on wall colours and working out what furniture would go where. Everything had happened so quickly, he thought to himself. Like the final moments of human birth, from light into darkness. Between her initial call to Lloyd Griffiths and her arrival, he'd barely had time to consider the implications of her not only occupying such a special place, but also her permanent proximity.

Maybe even his favourite goddess Cerridwen had had a part to play in all this. He liked to think so. Cerridwen, keeper of the Underworld's cauldron. The mother whose two children represent dark and light. And which was he? he asked himself yet again, knowing that like most ancient mythology, nothing was ever that simple. Maybe the

Londoner's presence here was all meant to be, and now, gradually, there'd be time to find out more about her; her previous job at Hellebore, her family – if she had one – and why she'd moved so quickly from the metropolis.

He'd never had much opportunity to fight his apprehension of the opposite sex, and to have asked her these personal questions already would have seemed way too intrusive. A risk he wasn't prepared to take, because from the first moment he'd glimpsed her getting out of her car, he'd realised that here was someone special. And not just physically, even though she was taller than his mother, blonde where she'd been a redhead, and had the most expressive blue eyes he'd ever seen. Not only that, but Lucy Mitchell was following her soul. Determined to live her dream, whatever the cost.

Whatever the cost.

He felt a chill reach under his clothes as those crimson skeins in the sky turned the colour of old meat, and her now-familiar figure trekked towards her car and began disembowelling her possessions. She seemed preoccupied and he wondered if she'd had any more hassle with Bryn Evans or that little rat Hughes on her way to Ravenstone.

He saw her glance up at his window, catching him unawares, then gesture for him to come and join her. He didn't need bidding twice and, in pleasurable anticipation, slipped past his father's study where the old man could be heard laughing to himself. Perhaps there was something funny on TV, he wondered, or, more likely, he was into double figures with the gin. However, he'd not been too pissed to ask Lucy if she'd like to rent one of the Hall's bedrooms until after completion and Wern Goch becoming habitable. In fact, it had even crossed his mind that the cunning old sod might just fancy her himself...

As he reached the front door, he also wondered how he could play Jesus with the near-empty freezer and drum up the loaves and fishes equivalent of an evening meal for the three of them. He'd meant to go shopping straight after work, but Lucy's order for the builders' merchants had taken priority. And so it had been mortar mix instead of mozzarella, and treated hardwood from sustainable forests instead of a pre-packed salad.

No contest, he told himself, seeing her smile at him. No contest at all.

'Thanks for that poem,' she smiled again, then finally closed her boot door and locked it. 'I've never heard of an englynion. It was certainly powerful stuff.'

'That's me,' he bluffed, and she smiled.

'And for getting those windows for me. That sash style will really suit the house.'

'No probs, besides, hardwood will last for ages even with all the damp we get here. Is that why you called me down? I'm not used to gratitude, you know.'

'Yes and no.' Her smile stayed long enough to reassure him, then she grew serious.

She picked up the two heaviest bags stuffed with clothes and started walking towards the Hall.

'No you don't.' He took them all from her as she began to describe her morning's visit and how she'd seen a large black 4x4 race away from near the waterfall.

'Did you see who the driver was?' he ventured.

'No. But he or she was definitely on their own.' She frowned to herself, trying to recall that profile, the shape of the head... 'I'm pretty sure it was a bloke.'

'A bloke?'

'Yes.'

'And the make of car?'

'I don't know. Some Jeep type of thing. An off-roader.'

'Them and vans is ten a penny round here.'

'So I've noticed.'

She'd also noticed how he'd ironed creases into his jeans and his dark hair now cleared his collar instead of straggling over it. All of a sudden, Mark Jones was smartening himself up, and the big question was why? The possible answer brought a sneaking blush to her cheeks. She was glad he was some way ahead of her when she broached her next question.

'Does your dad still have any contacts with the Police Force?'

He stopped in his tracks. His expression made her think of the woman farmer she'd encountered earlier.

'Yeah, but not much. Why?'

'Something's wrong. I can feel it, here.' She pressed an hand to her chest and for a split second saw his eyes on her breasts. 'I'd like to have a word with him,' she went on regardless. 'Might be useful, you never know.'

Mark laughed wrily, setting her bags down on the top step before nudging the front door open with his shoulder. 'All you'll get is alcoholic poisoning by proxy.'

She repressed a smile because now wasn't the time for humour. 'Has he always been a heavy drinker?'

Mark lowered his voice as he held the door open for her. 'No. But like I promised, one day I'll tell you everything.'

'Ah, Romeo and Juliet...' A yet more unshaven Hector Jones beamed at them both from inside his bar. This time a full glass of Burgundy lay to hand and he promptly raised it in the air. 'To the two of you, and may lots of happy little sprouts be following...'

'Cut it out, Dad.' Mark strode towards him, reached over and snatched the glass away, swearing as the wine slopped on to his jeans leaving dull red stains on each thigh. 'If you can't think of anything *useful* to say then shut the fuck up.'

Her lingering blush had deepened in embarrassment. Her plan to ask for Hector's help quickly evaporating.

'Well I can, and you'd better listen,' the ex-copper eyed her as if to ingratiate himself into her good books. 'a), the sweep's just phoned from a job he's just finished in town. He'll be here any minute and b), after midday tomorrow there'll be no sheep on the land. Easily upset is our preacher. When you think what the good Lord suffered. However, thanks to Miss Mitchell here, we'll soon be solvent again, and besides,' he smiled at her benevolently, 'it's too long since we had a pretty woman around the place.'

'*Dad...*'

'I mean it, son,' he said, looking her up and down appreciatively. 'She's a real looker.'

Lucy went up to the bar, cheeks burning. Whether Hector was pissed or not, that compliment was more than Jon had ever managed in front of anybody.

'Thank you, Mr Jones. Only my dad ever said that to me. He was special.'

'Was?' Mark seemed more than curious.

'He died of a heart attack three years ago.'

For a moment no one spoke as if the well of grief there was already full to the brim and words of sympathy had long since swirled in its depths and drowned. Yet she now had Hector's full attention and close-up she noticed how his dark eyes had the same intense expression as his son's. How they were ringed by sadness.

'Mr Jones, I know you're not in the Force any more...' she began.

'Detective Inspector, retired,' he interrupted, not without some pride. 'And call me Hector, please. Yes, I'm out to grass just like those buggers down there.' He indicated the cropping sheep beyond the window. She could have added that her own father had never even reached that stage. That NHS targets had worn him out, but Mark spoke up first.

'They're killing ewes,' he said darkly. 'In a month's time they'll be dog food and that preacher's wallet'll be full to bursting.'

'I wish yours was, son. No good sneering at those who get on in the world.'

'He's had it cheap here for years. On our bloody backs, let's not forget.'

She decided to break the strained silence which followed this outburst. She had to press on and to that end, renewed her eye contact with Hector.

'If you're out somewhere and you hear something suspicious, like a scream,' she began, 'would the police take it seriously? I know people often fool about, but...'

'It depends. There are screams and screams. If it sounds like someone being threatened or assaulted, then it's taken very seriously indeed.' His voice grew more animated as he spoke, and she sensed that here was a man who'd clearly loved his job, loved the work...

'It was at Water Break Its Neck,' volunteered Mark, 'and there was also some jeep keen to get away.'

She shot him a grateful glance, while Hector pondered what he'd heard so far.

'When?'

'Around two o'clock.'

'Why go there, Lucy? It's a danger area, for God's sake.'

'I'm just trying to get my bearings. See a bit more of what's around. Making sure this place is right for me.' She sighed. 'It's a long story.'

'I'm waiting.' Hector came out from his bar and parked himself in one of the shabby unmatching chairs put out for visitors who rarely came. Mark too sat alongside listening intently as she spoke of her time at Hellebore and, careful not to mention her rape and its aftermath, gave the glass ceiling and her dead father's dream for a country life as her reasons for quitting. And of course Anna's offer of editing work. Actually paying her...

'So, what did you do after you'd heard the screams and seen the vehicle leave?' he finally asked, as if despite his apparent attentiveness, it was her first account which really mattered.

'I called in at the nearest farm, just to tell someone.' Then Lucy added how she'd given a false name to the woman there.

'What name was that?'

'Sonia.'

Suddenly the study felt like an ice box. She looked from one stricken man to the other, completely at a loss as to why that particular Christian name should cause such a reaction.

'God's truth.' Hector muttered, then, as if to regain his composure, attacked his stubble, rubbing it this way and that. Mark got up and stood by the window to hide his face. 'That's what my wife was called,' Hector said. 'Mark's mother.'

She wanted the floor to open and swallow her up. Of all the ones to choose...

'I'm so sorry. I never realised...'

'It's okay,' Mark turned to face her. 'How could you have possibly known?' He then looked at his father. 'We've had fourteen years to get used to it.'

'Why give a false name, then?' Hector was businesslike once more and although she'd breathed a sigh of relief, she took a few seconds to collect her thoughts.

'I had to be careful. Anyway, this Mel woman didn't seem too chuffed when I said the word Police.'

Hector smiled.

'Plenty of dodgy farmers out there. Still, she could be useful.' He got out of his chair with unexpected vigour and tapped her gently on the shoulder. 'Would you like me to take a look?'

'Someone ought to. Yes please.'

'What, now?' Mark incredulous. 'How much have you had?'

'Son, mind your own business. Now then, if you'll forgive me, I'll just go and get myself cleaned up a bit...'

Both she and the sawyer stared after him as he lumbered over to the study door ignoring his walking stick which still lay propped up near the bar. She also noticed with a mix of gratitude and pity, the shiny seat of his old black trousers, the back of his hair still ruffled from his pillow.

'Let me give you something for the petrol,' she called out.

'You can try, but I won't take it,' he stalled by the mound of her belongings in the hallway, then half turned towards Mark. 'Why don't you show the young lady to her room and help her get sorted out? And when I get back, a Cornish pasty and mushy peas wouldn't go amiss.'

'The old sod.' Mark hefted the bulkiest of her bags to the first floor landing, then stopped at the sound of a car coming up the drive. 'Might be old Williams. I'll go and see. By the way,' he gestured towards the rear of the landing where two closed doors stood next to each other. 'There's your room,' he said, and she automatically headed for the one with the rose on it.

'This is pretty,' she said, her hand already closed round the door's strange brass handle. A raven's head, its beak cold against her palm.

'No, not that one,' Mark interjected so abruptly that she turned round in surprise. 'It's private. Sorry.'

As his thudding footsteps faded, she could hear sounds of running water coming from a nearby bathroom. Obviously Hector, she thought, which gave her the chance to compare Horeb's overstuffed accommodation with her new quarters' grander proportions, and to puzzle about Mark's sudden reaction to her going near that particular room. Why too weren't there any mementos of those who'd previously inhabited the Hall? Lord Howells and his descendants, for example? Irmgard Muller or the grandparents with their funeral business? Even Sonia Jones and her other son, the so far elusive Richard? It seemed to Lucy that all these lives had, for some reason, been secreted away, just like the dead who lie in drawers within France's marble tombs.

Gradually the late daylight began to change yet again as the spreading sun outside cast the first floor's unadorned walls the colour of egg yolk, exposing even more the cobwebbed cornices, the shabby woodwork, and when she looked down, Lucy noticed the threadbare runner which lay over what she assumed must be the original floorboards.

She turned once more to touch that strange china rose on the door next to hers, wondering what it represented. Something feminine, certainly, and she was just about to try the handle again, to discover what lay beyond, when all at once a voice called out.

'I put that there.'

She spun round to see Hector Jones leaving the bathroom. His face was pink, clean- shaven, and his hair newly combed and still damp against his scalp. 'For my wife. Bought it in Worcester just after we were married. Now then,' he rested a hand on the banister's newel post as if he was about to leave. 'You make yourself at home and if there's anything you need just get that son of mine moving.'

She saw steam creeping from the bathroom and decided that now wasn't the time to ask if she'd be sharing its facilities with the two men of the house. Surely in a place that size there'd be at least an extra shower room?

'I'm sure everything's fine,' she smiled. 'And thanks for letting me stay.'

'Like I said my dear, our pleasure. Right,' he steadied himself, peering down towards the open front door beyond which the sound of voices could be heard. 'I see your sweep's turned up. Don't let him take advantage, mind.'

'What d'you mean?' As she imagined a furtive grope by the kitchen's range.

'Shouldn't cost you no more than twenty quid. So, watch him. It's not London here.'

'I know that,' she said with feeling. 'And I hope you won't be wasting your time with the waterfall business.'

'It'll do me good to get out.' With that, he was gone.

She didn't hang about either. Having done a quick recce of her new room, opened its musty velvet curtains and dumped her holdall on the double bed, she went downstairs to see what was going on outside.

Hector had already left and in his place a hunched-over man in his sixties, who reached no higher than Mark's chest, was opening his smart new van's rear doors. Eschewing the sawyer's help, he pulled out two dismantled brushes and hoisted them over his shoulder. He then stared at her as if he'd never seen a woman before in his life.

'This is Miss Mitchell,' Mark explained. 'She's buying Wern Goch.'

'Is that so?' Those two pinprick eyes switched to Mark. 'Haven't you told her, then?'

'Told her what, man?'

Nevertheless, she saw him tense up. His neck muscles taut, his pulse throbbing.

'About your mam being down there.' He shot a weasly glance in the little house's direction.

She knew Mam was Welsh for mother, but what did he mean by *down there*?

Mark loped towards the track, kicking stones away left right and centre. This was anger management alright. Letting his boots suffer instead, each step removing him from the older man who doggedly followed. But why? she asked herself, desperate to quiz the sweep herself.

'Miss Mitchell hasn't come all this way to hear your gossip,' Mark shouted without turning round. 'And seeing as we're into plain speaking, Mr Williams, she's paying you for your work and not your tongue.'

She waited for the other man's response, sensing that this latest addition to her workforce wasn't going to be deterred so easily. And she was right.

'I never liked coming here before,' he grumbled, 'and I don't like it now. When there's been foul deeds in an 'ouse, I picks up on it, see? That's just the way I am.'

Foul deeds?

She held her breath. How quickly dreams sour, she thought, aware that the sun had now vanished and a cloud of black birds were winging their way towards Wern Goch.

'Do you mean Druids?'

'No, I don't, Missus,' said Williams in a loaded tone. 'Everyone knows what really went on, and I'm telling you for a fact, Wern Goch's no place for a young woman to be living. Husband or no husband. I'll do your chimney – fair do's – but don't you expect me to hang around afterwards. Folks normally give me a cup of tea for my throat but I don't want nothing like that here. I'll be sending on the bill next week.'

Mark glanced back at her, his expression one of utter anguish. She overtook the sweep to catch him up and take his arm. He was trembling, and not for the first time, she felt powerless.

'He's lying, Lucy. You've got to believe me. Apart from Rhaca nothing else has happened there.'

But she shook her head.

'I swear I heard a scream coming from the house. Last Saturday it was, after your dad had showed me round. *He* seems to think these weirdos are somewhere in the area.'

'I'm not denying it. And wherever they are, they're beyond evil.'

'Be careful what you say, sir,' muttered the sweep, who then suddenly tripped up and righted himself. 'No self-respecting Druid would do what was found in that kitchen. I know, because my brother was a bard at the Gorsedd last year, and I've read up on it. Bloody families, it is,' he added, cryptically. 'Why I've stayed a bachelor all my life…'

She let go of Mark, gripped now by a fear so deep, so intense that her legs felt like stone. She couldn't move even if she'd wanted to. All her questions, even any reasoning shrivelled up to nothing, while Mark's anguish had turned to bewilderment.

'Come on,' he whispered as the sweep hustled by like some troll to reach the house first. 'You mustn't listen to him, or any of the other creeps who crawl out of their holes in the ground just to make trouble. They'll say anything for effect. It's the peasant Welsh. The worst kind…'

That Hellebore author had been right again, she thought, and not for the first time.

He reached for her hand and she took it. Warm like his arm had been. Warm and strong.

'Wern Goch needs you. Christ,' he looked at her, dark eyes as if on fire. 'I never thought I'd hear myself saying that. Look,' he pointed to where, as before, a row of ravens were already settled above the scullery door. 'They're saying, welcome.'

'Can't they park somewhere else?' she asked. 'I hate the way they just stare at you.'

'They're my allies,' he replied. 'Just like other people keep guard dogs or whatever, I have these.'

'But supposing I don't want them hanging around once I've moved in? I mean, I have agreed to keep that slab and the cauldron. Why can't they hang around the Hall and poo on that instead?'

Mark clicked his fingers and immediately they all raised themselves, ominously spread their wings, then settled back into position again.

'Simple. Because they like you.'

Even though there'd been no rain since the weekend, that same jet of water continued to spew from the bank adding to the mire around the little house. Lucy tried to keep her replacement trainers out of the worst of the mess as she approached, but a sudden urge to pee made this impossible. The only way to some privacy by the barn was through the worst of the slippery mud. Williams was waiting with Mark when she returned. He looked defeated.

'That'll soon need fixing,' he pointed to the bank. 'If not, then this place'll be floating away.'

'It's all in hand,' Mark gave her a reassuring nod. 'There's nothing like spring water.'

'Never mind spring, man. *Holy* water's what you need here.'

'Please explain,' she said, having counted seventeen ravens in all on the guttering. Each one following the sweep's every move. But the man didn't reply.

'Sad bastard,' whispered Mark to her, yet loud enough for Williams to hear.

'That's *you*, sir, if you don't mind my saying.'

Five minutes later, in an atmosphere of growing hostility, Williams was preparing for his task with all the accoutrements of his trade laid out on the kitchen's stone floor. He'd already donned a baseball cap, which to Lucy's urban eye, looked faintly ridiculous, and had also spread bin liners around the range. He was now assembling the bigger of the two brushes, muttering to himself yet making sure that his audience could hear.

'I don't like the atmosphere in here,' he started up again. 'It's getting right to me bones. Getting to me brain, an' all.' He then placed his small body alongside the range and rammed the brush head up beyond the blackened brick flue. 'Lord knows I've not done the chimney here for fifteen years when you boys were still in short trousers, but to me, it's always been an odd sort of place...'

Boys. Even he'd *said it.*

'Give it a rest, man,' Mark snarled. 'Or I'll shove you up there as well.'

'Don't you threaten me you half-made. Just because you live in the Hall you think you're it, when everyone knows there's not a tuppence to rub together. Why she's buying, isn't it?'

She and Mark stared at his skinny behind as he worked the brush higher and higher. The only sweep for miles, and with most dwellings still reliant upon coal, he could pick and choose his work. And risk causing offence.

'And what about this bloody cauldron, eh?' Williams went on regardless. 'And bloody it was too, so I heard...'

Her fear returned with a vengeance. She could see the thing out of the corner of her eye. Even blacker, suddenly more significant than before. 'What's he saying, Mark?' she begged him. 'I can't take much more of this.'

'Nor can I.'

They listened to the brush scrape repeatedly against the old brick-work, and knew that even if they left him to it and went upstairs, his voice would still follow. It would reach into every crack of old plaster, be drawn into every grain of every beam, tainting the place more than it was already. She was about to press the man further about the cauldron, when all at once his vigorous actions with the brush came to a sudden stop.

'Damn and blast it. Can't go no further.'

She watched Mark squat down next to the swarthy dwarf-like figure and fingered some of the foul mulch which had dropped on to the bin liners.

'It's wet, that's why,' he said, sniffing it. 'Probably compacted further up.'

'Could be leaking brickwork,' she added. 'We had that problem at home once.' Where she'd grown up in Manchester now seemed on the other side of the world. The neatness of it. The colourful garden, even in winter, and just then in this darkening kitchen with people she barely knew, she pictured her mother, on her own with a meal for one in front of her, and felt tears begin to sting.

'Summat's up there, for sure.' Williams broke her reverie. 'I'm going to take a look from outside.' He got to his feet, dusted himself down and retracted the brush. Its spiky head clotted by rotting gunge which smelt of sodden earth and something indefinable but even more unpleasant. 'Got a ladder?' he asked Mark who then led him out to the barn without saying a word.

While they were gone, she held her nose and examined the cauldron more carefully. She'd seen pictures of the famous silver Gunderstrup cauldron with all its mounted warriors being plunged to their deaths before re-birth, but this was totally different. At first she was loathe to touch it, but when she saw a previously unnoticed low-relief modelled head protruding from its belly, she allowed just one finger to trace over its details. She discovered long braided hair, two brow ridges above human eyes, a small chiselled nose...

But what came next made her step backwards in surprise, for beneath that roughened exterior, lay a mouth. Not any ordinary mouth, but one stretched open as if in terror.

No one will hear you scream…

She shivered, recalling last Saturday, then the waterfall. But the reality was here. In Wern Goch. In this very room. Time to exit, to leave that weird receptacle behind for a moment, and as she stood by the scullery door in the gathering dusk, men's voices reached her from the barn. Mark was clearly on the defensive, the other like a terrier with a bone, and when they emerged with the ladder between them, both men looked tense. The anger between them palpable.

Moments later the sweep plus the smaller brush in one hand, had clambered up to the roof. When he reached the chimney and its broken cowl, Mark returned to the kitchen to wait by the range, but when she tried to join him he put up a hand.

'No,' he barked. 'Just in case.'

'In case what?'

'You know, dead birds, stuff like that…'

'I'm not some kid,' she remonstrated. 'And this *is* going to be my house.'

Mark's response was drowned by Williams yelling from above. His voice seemed to come from far away; primordial, echoing and curdling around the range, and before it ended, a bundle of half-burnt rags flopped down on to the existing mess below.

Mark frowned in puzzlement as they both knelt down to examine these partially charred remains of two entirely different fabrics. Plain blue cotton and a more elaborate design of large red roses. Each piece brown and mottled like old skin.

'What are they doing up this chimney, for God's sake?' she asked.

He paused, then took a deep breath as if to mentally steady himself. Everything about his body language said to her, this is serious.

'Look, I'd rather you hear it from me than from anyone else,' he began. 'It's best you know now so you can decide what to do before the exchange of contracts.'

'Know *what* exactly?' She stood up, for the house had grown suddenly dark and cold, and goose bumps prickled her skin as she watched his lips.

'My mother was murdered fourteen years ago…'

'Murdered?' She gulped. That word suddenly uglier than ever, because up to now, it had always related to someone unknown to her. This however, was grimly different. 'Do you mean *here?*'

'No. Of course not,' Mark said too quickly, she thought. 'Up at the Hall. In that room with the rose on the door.'

'You're lying.'

'It's true.'

'I'll ask Mr Williams.'

Mark cupped his hands round his head, his black hair covering his fingers. She could hear the ravens outside growing restless as she waited for the worst.

'OK,' he sighed. 'It was here. Now you'll be changing your mind, won't you?' His tone more desperate than challenging but she barely heard him.

'My God.' She felt that numbness again. Cold sweat erupting under her clothes. She glanced over to the salting slab lying under the back window. It had disturbed her from day one. 'Why?' Was all she could ask.

'Someone had their reasons,' he said bleakly and she noticed his deep dark eyes were now glazed by tears. He placed his hands on her shoulders.

'Who's this *someone*?' She demanded trying not to let the sudden warmth, his very closeness distract her.

'The Dagdans. A kind of Druidic cult.'

'My God. Are they still around, then?'

He gave a shrug which could have meant anything.

She thought of the old well. What Hector had said about the area being Pagan. And yet she couldn't put the sweep's words out of her mind.

'So why did our friend make that remark about families? It sounded pretty significant to me.'

Mark's hands stiffened against her skin. He pulled her towards him.

'He's jealous because he's never had one. Look, all I want is for you to be safe here.'

She stepped back, but he held on, drawing himself even closer.

'But I've never felt safe here, from the moment I walked in and saw your bird's blood all over that salting slab.'

Mark let his mouth rest above her ear and brought it down over her cheek. Her skin seemed to burn under his lips and for the first time since she could remember, a surge of longing for closeness, even love, coursed through her damaged body.

'Look,' he murmured. 'I know my life hasn't exactly been what everyone wants on their CV, but God's truth, since the day your blue Rav arrived, things have been looking up.'

It was hard to ignore his flattery.

'What if I find out?'

'At least it won't have been me who told you.'

'It's *you* who's afraid, isn't it?'

'Hell, I can't handle this,' he said, and she believed him. But before she could extract any more from him, a wad of soot suddenly plopped on to the pile of rags and Mark scrabbled for the buried pieces of cloth. He laid them out almost reverently on top of the range as if it was some kind of altar. How gentle he could be, how tender, she thought, watching his every movement. But what else? Could he somehow be involved in this? Could she, simply by being around and finding herself more and more drawn towards this complex character, be falling into the biggest most dangerous trap possible?

'Are these bits anything to do with what happened here?' she ventured.

'Course not. This was my den, remember? I was always hoarding things, burning stuff. Didn't you used to muck about away from the parental gaze?'

She was too busy thinking to answer.

'What will you do with them?' she asked instead, watching him pick them up one by one and lay them in the palm of his hand. 'Surely your dad and the police should take a look?'

Mark spun round.

'I'm begging you never to mention them to anyone. OK?'

She shrugged, just to be free of that laser-like stare. No wonder he'd not wanted the sweep involved.

'I'll sort it out when I'm good and ready. One day, you'll understand why.'

She heard the ladder scrape against the wall outside as Williams climbed down to the ground, then saw Mark position himself out of sight behind the scullery door and make that odd croaking noise three times.

'Corax...corax...corax...'

And, no sooner had the sweep's watery footsteps faded away up the track, the willing ravens left their perch to follow him.

Chapter Seventeen

𝕳𝔦 𝔂𝔬𝔲,

𝕿𝔥𝔦𝔯𝔡 𝔱𝔦𝔪𝔢 𝔩𝔲𝔠𝔨𝔶 – 𝔣𝔬𝔯 𝔂𝔬𝔲 𝔪𝔞𝔶𝔟𝔢. 𝕸𝔢, 𝕴'𝔪 𝔠𝔞𝔩𝔩𝔢𝔡 '𝔰𝔨𝔦𝔫𝔞𝔫𝔡𝔟𝔬𝔫𝔢' 𝔥𝔢𝔯𝔢.

𝕿𝔥𝔢𝔶'𝔯𝔢 𝔤𝔢𝔱𝔱𝔦𝔫𝔤 𝔴𝔬𝔯𝔯𝔦𝔢𝔡, 𝔴𝔥𝔦𝔠𝔥 𝔦𝔰 𝔴𝔥𝔞𝔱 𝕴 𝔴𝔞𝔫𝔱. 𝕴 𝔰𝔱𝔦𝔩𝔩 𝔠𝔞𝔫'𝔱 𝔰𝔢𝔫𝔡 𝔂𝔬𝔲 𝔪𝔶 𝔞𝔡𝔡𝔯𝔢𝔰𝔰

𝔟𝔲𝔱 𝔞𝔱 𝔩𝔢𝔞𝔰𝔱 𝔂𝔬𝔲 𝔨𝔫𝔬𝔴 𝔴𝔥𝔶 𝕴'𝔪 𝔦𝔫 𝔱𝔥𝔦𝔰 𝔤𝔬𝔡𝔣𝔬𝔯𝔰𝔞𝔨𝔢𝔫 𝔥𝔬𝔩𝔢. 𝔇𝔦𝔡 𝔱𝔥𝔢 𝔦𝔫𝔨 𝔴𝔬𝔯𝔨? 𝕴

𝔴𝔦𝔩𝔩 𝔰𝔢𝔢 𝔶𝔬𝔲 𝔞𝔤𝔞𝔦𝔫.

𝔜𝔬𝔲𝔯 𝔬𝔫𝔢 x

While some 150 miles north west of Burton Minster, 'Simnai' Williams was still nursing his anger at being driven off the Ravenstone estate by a posse of hungry ravens, James Benn sat at his study desk in deep despair watching the typical late Friday afternoon traffic already beginning to clog up the Wimborne Road, heading south to the sea.

People carriers – hideous things, he thought, especially the hearse-like ones with dark tinted glass – jeeps and 4x4's. Then caravans in every permutation of cream and beige. Fucking Kestrels and Rapidos with top speeds of 20 mph, who should be banned from every non- dual carriageway during daylight hours...

All this helped him forget for a few seconds, the freshly edited manuscript which had just arrived by special delivery from Hellebore, but the longer he sat there, the more dispirited he felt. Even though the sunlight was still warm on his desk and his wife had had the good sense to keep a low profile since her protest last Monday, he was looking at a demolition job. So much for his intended dedication to Manda Jeffery as a brilliant editor. The bitch would now be getting nothing.

He lit his third cigar of the day, focusing now on page one, decimated like all the rest. But why, for Christ's sake? What was her problem? Especially when he recalled the same editor's minimal alterations and polite suggestions for *Tribe*. Here instead lay angry circlings in red, the 6B slashings from corner to corner meaning one thing only. That this particular page which had taken him a fortnight to get right, was, in her eyes, utter crap. He stubbed out his cigar prematurely, watching the last of its smoke fade away. Page two was no better, showing stray smears of scarlet nail varnish caught in the mesh of long curving arrows which mutated most of its paragraphs into aerial views of Crewe Station.

He flicked through the remaining 320 pages with growing disbelief. Barely a single word of his was untouched. She was taking the piss, surely? Treating him like an illiterate. Besides, he wondered, contemplating yet another cigar, how could she have possibly wreaked such havoc in just three days? Instead of reaching for the cigar box, he noticed a pink post-it note jutting out from the last page. The same handwriting, but this time, less frenetic, more controlled. He pulled it free, forgetting to breathe.

I was prepared to overlook your shag with Lucy Mitchell, but VT? Oh, please, Major Benn. That's paedophilia, surely? Get a life, eh?

Damn her.

So she'd known about June 15th and never let on. Then must have seen him eyeing up the design assistant, in the sushi bar on longlist day. He'd only cupped Vikki Tate's little arse in his hands for two seconds as they'd hovered in the restaurant doorway. Nothing more. Benn looked at his open cigar box then the lighter. It made short work of the note and he blew the ashes on to the floor.

If he was honest, hadn't he *wanted* Jeffery to see him flirting? To send out a signal she was getting too close, too pushy. And then later, over coffee, he'd reminded her – nicely, of course – that despite one or two moments of weakness, he was still Elizabeth's devoted husband.

That must have done it, he thought, closing his manuscript. Because, as the Hellebore party were returning to the office, she'd held him back to lie about her pressing for a big advance for his next book. The first part of her revenge. The second lay in front of him like a crazy battleground.

He snatched up the phone's receiver and dialled Hellebore's number which of course he knew by heart.

'James Benn here,' he barked at the receptionist when she answered. 'Extension twenty-one for Manda Jeffery.'

'She ain't around. Can I try someone else?' This was clearly the same moron as he'd seen there last Monday.

'It's about my new book. She's my editor.' That last word stuck in his gullet, nevertheless he urged himself to try and be patient.

'Yeah, I know. But she left for New York this morning.'

'New York?'

'Yeah. Business trip. Three weeks.'

He stared out at the creeping traffic beyond his window. So, this was her leaving present? A manuscript he could barely read, and his unique voice totally undermined...

'I want Nick Merrill. Now.'

'Sorry. In a meeting.'

'Don't give me that crap.'

He knew full well that on Fridays, the publisher liked to be installed in his rustic Suffolk retreat in time for an evening's solid and solitary drinking.

'Excuse me?'

'Let me have his private number then.' His fingers drummed on the desk bought by Elizabeth when *Relic* was first published and his future looked bright and certain. 'It's urgent.'

'Can't do that, sir. More than me job's worth.'

'Who's your line manager?'

'Why?'

'How dare you insult one of this country's top authors. It's people like me who pay your damned wages. You're supposed to be a facilitator, not a prevaricator.'

'A what?'

He slammed the phone down, his neck burning with fury. Then he glanced back at his study door – an irrational act since his wife had been left in her recliner in the lounge since 1 p.m. when he'd last escorted her to the lavatory.

'Curse the lot of them,' he snarled turning once more to his manuscript. He took a couple of deep breaths, flicked to the pivotal Chapter ten then gasped. The grainy photo of Preston slums, a bummer to get hold of, had been scored through not just by the usual pencil but a thick black marker pen which made distracting weals on the reverse side of each sheet.

'Tightarsebitch...' he muttered, reaching for his PCs mouse and deleting his specially commissioned screensaver showing a trio of bronzed female butts on some tropical beach. Normally he'd have lingered over their sand-dusted curves, but not now. The 14th *Labour of Hercules* had been delivered so late in the day that he couldn't protest.

He accessed Word and the *Kingdom Come* file with grim determination, scrolled to his original script.

CHAPTER ONE

Could I come near your beauty with my nails
I'd set my ten commandments in your face.
Shakespeare: Henry VI Pt 11. L iiii (1590)

Monday 8.15 a.m. and a punishing sun prevailed with no hint of the usual easterly wind, nor any likely interruption to the blue sky. The only activity on the Meadow Rise development was at number nine where a couple of car valeters hosing down two luxury saloons, left soapy maps on the tarmac.

Louis felt the cool spray of water kiss his cheek as he passed by. Heard REM from the men's radio. His favourite group. He liked their name, their lyrics, especially *Nightswimming*, and that gave him some much-needed credibility with the others in his class, especially Toby Lake.

He'd just re-typed these two paragraphs when his phone suddenly rang. He jumped, pressed something wrong on his keyboard by mistake and watched as his words disappeared.

Error! Your file will be lost unless you save on to A Drive!

He swiftly obeyed instructions then picked up the receiver.

'Who is it?'

'Good day to you, sir,' a cheerful sounding man responded. 'Guy Roper, Features Editor, *Dorset Gazette...*'

Immediately the author brightened. At last, a local paper showing some interest.

'Ah. Is this about the longlist?' he asked.

The other man paused.

'Er...Yes and no.'

He frowned. Why the hesitation? he asked himself, when the big guns, *The Independent* and the *Mail* had come straight to the point with their congratulations.

'What d'you mean, yes and no?'

'We've an interesting little story here and were just wondering if you'd like to tell us more...'

'More? Do please explain.'

'Certainly. Does the name Sarah Dyson of Kingsdown Travel in Shaftesbury ring any bells? Ding dong ding, you know.'

Sarah Dyson. Big milkers. Nifty fingers...

His heart thudded in his chest. So this was the price for fixing up a weekend return to Paris with his editor. Things were getting worse. He tried to calm down. 'What's she been saying about me?'

'Ah, so you're not denying that you know this Miss Dyson?'

'No, I'm not. I was merely buying tickets from her.'

'She's claiming you gave her a lift home and raped her in a field on the way.'

He swallowed hard. Regained his composure.

'Look, there she was, giving *me* the big come-on. If you must know, I was embarrassed. She's young enough to be my daughter, for God's sake. In fact, my own stepdaughter would be about her age. She died ten years ago.'

'That doesn't alter what Miss Dyson's claiming...'

'But Mr Roper,' he began in his most controlled, most patronising voice, 'isn't it sad that the only way a mediocrity like Miss Dyson can get any attention these days, is by spinning such an outrageous lie. And isn't it disappointing that a reputable paper like the *Gazette* should be so easily taken in? Naturally, I'll be contacting my lawyer straight away.'

'I think *we* should talk,' Roper said quietly. 'Before she goes to hers as well.'

James Benn glowered at the wreck which was his MS. If he didn't nip this slander in the bud, all his achievements would slip away faster than his own turds in the Armitage Shanks.

'Where?'

'Let's say The Pilgrim, Dean Street, Wimborne.'

'Hold on,' he covered the receiver as a high-pitched wailing sound was coming from behind his study door. 'Elizabeth?' he yelled, wondering how the hell she'd managed to move herself from the lounge. 'What the hell are you up to?'

He left the receiver on his desk and stumbled towards the door as the wail was now a full-blooded scream, so loud, so hellish it delivered him an instant migraine. When he opened the door his mouth fell open. There was no sign of her, but something else instead. The small white CD player normally kept in the kitchen, was blaring out one of the Horror music tracks he always listened to when writing the first draft of a new work.

The crafty cow…

He kicked the thing out of its socket and returned to the phone where Roper's voice was all too audible.

'What's all that racket?' asked the newspaper man. 'You having a spot of bother down there at the ranch? Sounded like a woman yelling, to me.'

'Just some American rubbish on TV. My wife often nods off with the set on full blast.'

'OK, as I was saying, The Pilgrim. Can you make one o'clock Sunday?'

'I'll try.'

'Mr Benn, if I were you, I'd do rather more than try…'

He slapped the receiver back in its cradle then spun round bellowing out his wife's name and everything else about their relationship that he could dredge up. He found her back in her recliner, his biography between her trembling hands. She didn't look up as he towered over her, casting her whole body in a dark shadow the way a cloud can change a hill.

'No good my saying that next time will be the last time,' he hissed, 'because there won't *be* a fucking next time.' He hit her arm and she flinched. 'Are you listening?'

Elizabeth continued to stare doggedly at the book's pages.

'How the hell did you set all that up, eh? You must have taken that CD from my collection and the player from the kitchen worktop when you're supposed to be...'

'Disabled?' she interrupted. 'With no zimmer frame, no sticks. Go on, say it,' she challenged, her eyes unwavering from his fulsome account of her 'fall.'

'You're obviously up for another stint on the bed. That's all I can say.'

'Whatever you decide.' She calmly closed the book and with all her strength, flung it across the parquet floor. It landed in an ignominious heap under the grand piano and he made no effort to retrieve it. 'Just think of all those trees which have been cut down so your prettily packaged lies can be published for all and sundry.'

'What lies, you dry old fanny?'

'You *pushed* me into that filthy pond. I can still feel where your hands touched me – like bruises on my skin. I know you wanted me out of the way so you could have all the women you want, but isn't it strange,' she taunted, turning her pale eyes on to him at last, 'that however much plotting you do, real life never quite goes according to plan?

Chapter Eighteen

Our doubts will like a cancer spread
And steal our joy, our one rare dream
If tongues don't cease to rumours make
Who will remain to hear the scream?
MJJ 24/8/01

Although the rest of the United Kingdom was bathed in a late summer's warm faintly muggy glow, over mid-Wales, clouds from the west
had merged and thickened to hang brooding above the land. The breeze
too had sharpened and before Lucy left the Hall once more to visit
Jewsons and a plant hire firm with Mark, she swapped her denim jacket for a pink fleece which Jon had bought her last Christmas.

Both Hector and Mark were waiting at the foot of the stairs and it
seemed the ex-copper had something important to say.

'The newsagent over in Llanfihangel-Nant-Melan has just phoned,'
he began. 'You weren't the only one to have heard something odd by
the waterfall. Apparently, a local woman out walking her dog nearby
reckoned there was some kind of row going on – lover's tiff kind of
thing – just after half past one it was…'

'That must have been just before I turned up,' observed Lucy, sensing this wasn't going to go away.

'Didn't want to get involved, mind. Sign of the times, that, I'm
afraid.'

'So, what are the police doing about it?' realising for the first time
since she'd met him that Hector's breath wasn't likely to start a fire.

'Taking a look,' he said, allowing her through. 'That's got to be the
first step.'

'You will tell me if anything comes to light?'

'Course I will. Like I said. Leave it to me. I'll have a sniff round
again on Monday as well if that'll make you feel better. Now then,' he
turned to her as she checked the sky, thinking umbrella. 'You choose
those new roof tiles carefully, eh? We don't want the Council round
here kicking up a stink. In fact,' he added mysteriously,' the less attention we draw to ourselves, the better.'

'But it's not a listed building, surely?' She wondered what he meant
by that.

'No, it isn't,' said Mark. 'Dad's getting a bit paranoid, that's all.
We'll call in on Dai Davies who does real slate from Bettws-y-Coed.'

'He's kosher. Good man is Dai.' Then Hector tapped her shoulder,
adding mischievously, 'pink suits you, don't you agree, son? Just like

your mam.'

At least he can talk about her now, she thought, but Mark had visibly tensed up and made for the front door. Having acknowledged the compliment, she selected the least decrepit umbrella from the stand and tried to press the stiff clasp to open it.

'No, no, don't do that,' Hector suddenly took it from her.

'For God's sake, Dad...'

'Only thinking of Lucy. We don't want any more bad luck, do we?'

Mark didn't reply and as he opened the door she felt the draught of cold air creep under her clothes and for a moment, this unexpected chill seem to slow her heart.

'Jump in,' he told her, 'and thanks for keeping stumm.'

'That's okay,' she hesitated, sniffing the intense smell of sap and sawdust which came from inside the vehicle and noting the mounds of old sandwich wrappers and *Farmers Weekly*s which made the passenger seat invisible.

'Sorry about the mess,' he leant over in front of her, gathered up a heap of junk in his arms and crammed it into the already full wheelie bin. 'I keep meaning to sort it.' She noticed a strip of tanned back where his shirt had risen up above his jeans belt; like the rest of him, it was smooth honed flesh, and at that moment, very touchable.

'The fields seem bare without the sheep,' she observed instead as he reversed out of the drive. 'You never know, I might try rearing a few here myself. I've always loved Jacobs. My dad had a cap made from their wool once – it was his favourite whenever we went out anywhere in the country. Look,' she produced her wallet and withdrew the Llanberis photo. 'That's my mum holding it for him because it was windy.'

Mark glanced down at the image and quickly looked away. He had the narrow track to negotiate after all.

'You look like him,' he said simply as the van lurched over the bumps and potholes.

'Thanks. Receding hair, ears a funny shape...'

'No, I mean his eyes. They're kind but curious. I bet you got on well.'

'We did. He always took my side whenever Mum had a go at me. Used to tell her to be thankful I wasn't like some of the kids he saw on his travels. Nine-year-old addicts, the hard cases he used to treat in some of the Local Authority homes. But she was obviously dishing out to me what she'd had. Convent schools, the puritan bit about not flaunting yourself around and being a useful member of society.'

'And so you are,' he grinned. 'Very useful indeed. Read my poem again if you don't believe me.'

'Or, why not write me another?'

'I'm honoured.'

She watched the river Wye spuming over the rocks below the road-side while a heron lifted itself into the air and cruised over the water's length on outspread wings. Yes, her father would have loved it here, she thought which was why, despite everything, she was going ahead with the strange little house. Using his money with a clear conscience to get herself something he'd never had. The Irish called it *Canan Ara*. She called it nurturing the soul.

'My God, I'm thirty tomorrow,' she announced without thinking. Immediately Mark turned to her.

'Right then,' he said.

'Right then what?'

'We celebrate.'

'How?'

'We find the best digger, the best pipes for a mains supply, the best tiles for your roof and by the end of next week you'll be snug as a bug, able to wash your clothes and, listen to this,' he smirked, 'even have a Jacuzzi...'

She was about to thank him when suddenly huge blobs of rain hit the windscreen, sluicing away the red mud which had gathered in its corners.

Distant thunder next and not so much rain an attack, pummelling the van from all sides, forcing Mark to drop to second gear. It was then, despite the recent laughter that she became truly aware of the reality of her undertaking, and more importantly, having enough funds over to get herself started.

She then asked, 'why have you just mentioned mains? Why not a private water supply like you've suggested all along?'

'D'you really want to be frozen up from December to March and run the risk of someone mucking about with your supply? Blocking it up, whatever?'

'Who on earth would do that?'

'Two people I can think of, for starters,' he said as the first small shops appeared. 'Do you want me to spell out their names?'

She fell silent while the van rumbled over a defunct level crossing and veered into a layby filled by an ever-deepening puddle.

'But mains will cost an arm and a leg, surely? She muttered, slumping down in her seat while a few brave shoppers hurried by, bent against the weather.

'Initially, yes. The supply would come down from the Hall. but at least you'd have peace of mind.'

Peace of mind? That's a joke...

'You should have called those ravens off,' she sat up again to make her next point. It had been on her conscience since yesterday afternoon. 'Supposing they'd had that sweep's eyes out. Then where'd we be?'

Mark shook his head then reached behind his seat for his old parka. He placed it on her lap and the smell of the forest which rose up made her catch her breath.

'Not them. They know just how far to go. A fright's all he had, and serve him bloody right too.'

'What if he'd had a heart attack? I mean, he's not exactly young.' She'd never heard a man yell like that before – even in films – but he'd surely woken all the dead for miles around. And as for Bryn Evans and his seemingly telepathic collie who'd arrived yesterday on the dot of twelve to corral his flock into the massive trailer he'd brought. Would he really interfere with Wern Goch in that way? Or was he, despite being a Deacon, really one of the dreaded Morrigan's cohorts?

'Those sheep could have stayed a bit longer too,' she went on. 'I'm not going to be needing the land till the spring at least.'

'Not the point. I've already explained to you about him.'

'So you have.' She pulled her fleece closer around her body and zipped it up to her chin, suddenly aware of someone standing outside her door blocking out what little light there was. At first, she thought some shopper was taking cover from the rain, but a second glance told her there were two people, one tall, one shorter; and they were staying put.

'Mark, look,' she urged.

'Huh huh. Talk of the Devil.' He ratched up the handbrake, but his eyes now betraying something less lighthearted. 'Sit tight, okay? Leave this to me.' With that, he got out, slammed his door and went round the front of the van to where both Evans and Sion Hughes pressed their wet bodies against the van's near side. Neither moved nor looked him in the eye when he asked what they were doing.

'I'm counting to ten,' he said, drenched already. 'And if you're not on your bikes by then...'

'Then what, freak show?' taunted the nineteen-year-old. 'Going to tell Dada are we? That useless piece of dung.'

'I'll shift you myself.'

By now, four curious female onlookers had gathered. It was clear they formed part of the Deacon's congregation and acknowledged him as if they were outside chapel, not awaiting a possible brawl on some wet street. Lucy prayed nothing more would happen. That the men would just move on, like she had to, because in half an hour Jewsons and everything else would be closed. She held her breath as Mark seemed poised to throw the first punch, but the young farmer kicked him smartly in the groin. He doubled up in obvious agony, giving Evans the chance to push him into the puddle.

It was only when they'd finally gone and the miserable quartet dispersed was she able to open her door and wade through the water to reach him.

Half an hour later, in the Morfa tearooms, she poured Mark his third cup of tea from a big brown teapot. She was ratty and fed up. How dare those two idiots jinx her plans. Besides, Mark still seemed to be in pain and had to scrounge a cushion for his hard wooden chair.

'Bastards,' he muttered yet again, loud enough for one or two customers to look his way.

'And cowards,' she added, putting the last slice of bara brith on his plate. 'Still, a few of his flock saw what happened and word'll get round. Come next Sunday, that Evans will probably have an empty chapel. Not once, but twice.'

'No chance. They're like crows round newborn lambs, that lot. Give them a whiff of trouble and that hooks them in. He'll be a main attraction now. Have you read *Under Milk Wood* by any chance?' he emptied his cup with a single angry gulp. Or shouldn't I ask?'

'Loads of times. It's brilliant. Hellebore's bringing out a new paperback version plus audio tape in September...'

Here she stopped herself. She was going on as if she still worked there. As if this Welsh thing was some weird short break, and next day when the rain had cleared, she'd be heading back...

'Penny for them,' he said, reaching out and covering her hand with his. 'Or is that too cheap?'

She smiled, and as she did so, noticed behind Mark, amongst the herd of anoraked and mackintoshed tea drinkers, someone utterly different. A man of around her age she guessed, with sun-blonde hair above a tanned fine-boned face. His immaculate trench-coat positively glowed against the gloomy throng as he sat at a table for one in the farthest corner of the tea room next to a Welsh dresser full of old plates and knick-knacks.

The moment he caught her eye, she quickly diverted her gaze and made a pretence of looking at the menu. Because her heart was on the move and because Mark might detect her quicker pulse rate, she also gently removed her hand from his.

'Would you like anything else?' she asked him. 'My Auntie Phyll used to make a brilliant carrot cake and you know what carrots are good for.'

He shook his head and droplets of rain showered on to his parka's shoulders. She'd slipped that over him once he'd managed to stand in the puddle, and now, being wet through, it resembled a night-coloured cloak.

'Better go. We don't want the Mellte flooding.'

With a final backward glance at the intriguing stranger, she left the table and waited as Mark paid. He'd insisted, and rashly, in return, she'd offered to rustle something up from the Hall's freezer. According to him there were three steaks plus some onion rings and ice cream.

'Hold me back,' she'd joked, but, given what he'd just endured, it was the least she could do.

'Who were your witnesses?' asked Hector as he ladled yet more dubious-looking mustard over his meat. 'You must have recognised someone for God's sake.'

Lucy watched Mark chewing with difficulty. She suspected the steaks were of the Tyrannosaurus Rex variety. Nevertheless, she'd done her best with a sluggish grill.

'Four women. They didn't want to get involved. Like you said, no one ever does.'

'They addressed him as Deacon Evans, though,' she added. 'As if they knew him from chapel.'

'That's something, I suppose,' Hector took a drink of his bottled water and grimaced at the taste of it. 'Still, don't expect me to go hanging round that bloody place on the off-chance of finding them. Gives me the willies it does. All those black Bibles, those dark pews. No wonder RS Thomas had a problem with it all, and he'd been a bloody minister…'

She pricked up her ears at the name of that illustrious poet who'd been dead for barely a year. Despite his religious calling, none of his work ever spoke of redemption and, as the antithesis of *Magical Tales*, a bleaker view of Welsh life she'd yet to find. However, her dissertation on his uneasy relationship to God had at least helped her gain a First at Warwick. And now, six years later, wasn't it as if she'd just stepped from one of his pages – sitting at a formica table in a draughty kitchen with two relative strangers, blighted by grief? Sure. She could even imagine what the first line might be.

'Never mind him,' Mark snapped. 'I'm going to nail those two before they get even bigger ideas. You try and stop me.'

'The law's the law. You be careful, son.'

'Why? Evans is probably sitting there right now getting a sermon ready for Sunday, or else knobbing that little queen of his…'

'OK. OK. Let's calm down, shall we?' Hector set his knife and fork together and finished his glass of water. 'I've nothing else on this evening, so I'll go and pay a couple of calls…'

To her, this seemed idiotic. Supposing the two men were armed? She knew that most farmers kept guns.

'That's exactly what they'll be hoping for,' she challenged him. 'I wouldn't give them oxygen just yet. Let them think they've got away with it. False sense of security if you like.'

'She's right, Dad,' said Mark, finishing a beer and wiping his mouth with his bare forearm.

But Hector stared at her in a way which made her realise that there'd not been a female voice at the Hall for years. No one to keep him in check. And yet again, she was proved correct.

'With the greatest respect, Lucy, no one tells me what to do.'

He stood up, pulled his napkin from under his chin and made his way out of the kitchen.

'By the way,' he called out as he went. 'Make sure you lock up after me.'

Chapter Nineteen

No,

A poem this time. Didn't old Bowen (remember him with the
dyed tache and eyebrows?) say I'd got something? That was then. Got
nothing now, mind. Down to 8 stone.

I hear songs on the waves in my head,
Her songs, dying.
I see lips that never were so red,
In the grave lying.

X

Mark Jones spent longer than usual in the bathroom next morning, not only because the last Saturday of every month was his day off, but also because it was Lucy's birthday. He'd planned to take her to lunch at the Hotel Metropole in Llandrindod Wells. Home of his Grammar School and somewhere both his grandparents and his parents used to visit before the tensions started. It was kind of in the family – or what was left of it.

He finally emerged, wearing just his briefs, only to be surprised and embarrassed to find Lucy waiting outside, wearing a Yogi Bear T-shirt nightdress and clutching her wash-up bag. However, he needn't have worried about his state of undress. She seemed too deep in thought to notice.

'Sorry,' he stepped aside, holding the door open for her. 'Thought you'd be having some extra kip as it's your birthday.'

She shook her head and with one practised movement pulled her hair from its ponytail where it stayed covering her left cheek. For a tempting moment he wanted to draw it aside to feel the blonde softness under his work-coarsened hand. To touch her nipples which he could see pressing against the cotton fabric.

'I couldn't sleep at all,' she said. 'Not with those awful screams going round and round in my head, and what happened to us last night.' She edged past him into the bathroom and began to close the door.

'Look, don't worry. Dad knows what he's doing and like he said, Monday'll come soon enough. When the old fart makes a promise, he keeps it. OK?'

She nodded, but to him, not convincingly.

'It's Hughes and Evans,' she began. 'I don't trust them any more. How can I? What else are they going to do to intimidate me? Burn the place down? Cast some weird spells?' Her eyes were wide, angry. He felt defeated. Then to make himself feel better, imagined lunch.

'By the way,' he began. 'I've got a treat lined up for you. It's not much but...'

The door shut on him. Tight.

Damn. Damn. Damn.

He stayed to listen as her shower water began to fall and imagined her body glistening under its flow. Every time he came close to her now he just wanted to hold her, to feel those small firm breasts against him, to let his hands follow every contour, every mysterious hollow...

Hold on now. Hold on...

Maybe he shouldn't push it, he thought. Maybe she'd got her own agenda – even a boyfriend somewhere – and all this fixing up things for them to do together, might have the reverse effect. To drive her away.

He was just about to return to his bedroom when a heavy finger tapped his shoulder. He spun round. Always edgy. Hector, nattily dressed in navy slacks and a clean open-necked shirt, was smiling despite a purple bruise above his right eye.

'You okay?' Mark asked him.

'Nothing to what I dished out, son,' he winked, causing his eye to twitch. 'I don't think those two will be troubling us again for a while. Anyhow, breakfast's ready.' He then pointed to the bathroom. 'Lucy in there?'

'Yep.'

'Good. Gives me a few more minutes.'

He watched this changed man go downstairs and along the hallway until the top of his Brylcreemed head bobbed out of sight. He'd not made breakfast for anyone for years.

'What happened last night?' He called after him.

'Tell you later. Don't be long, you two.'

Mam...

His smile flickered and died. That's exactly what she used to say on a typical school morning, just before the grammar school minibus was due at the end of the drive. And he'd never let her down. Not like Richard, who'd spend half an hour simply putting on his socks, checking them for holes or patches of wear. Who'd stand by the hall mirror repeatedly slicking his hair until the driver sounded his impatient horn from too far away...

Then there'd been the Goodbye Kiss. Not from his dada, mind, but *her* while he, Mark had to be content with a mere brush of her red lips on his forehead at bedtime, before she invariably went out.

Richard, ever greedy, would grab her by the neck and plant his mouth on hers, then run away down the Hall steps, his satchel bumping on his back. Richard who could turn into a poisonous snake if he didn't get his own way.

'Hi, have you seen the mist out there?' Lucy appeared on the landing, her hair lay damp against her pinkened face. She looked stunning, he thought. More than just kissable. So why hadn't he expressed these aspects in his poem to her, instead of focusing on what she represented?

He didn't know, because whenever he'd sat down to write in his den, the words had seemed to come not from any conscious thought, but from somewhere far beyond his control. The slough of his past, perhaps? Still, he'd got another chance to put that right. She'd asked for another one, hadn't she?

'It'll clear,' he said, glancing out at the blank whiteness beyond the landing window. 'The September ones are the worst.'

'I didn't mean to be such a grump just now,' she said, making for her door. 'It's the birthday thing as well. Even as a kid I was never that bothered about them. In fact, I hated getting older.'

'Me too,' he said with feeling. Because each year which passed had brought increased strains within his parents' marriage so that by the time he was twelve and a year into the Grammar, his father sulked at home while his mother... His mother...

'Is anyone coming down?' Hector's voice interrupted his recollection. The aroma of frying bacon filled the stairwell. 'Everything'll frizzle up otherwise.'

My God, he thought. The man's actually been near the stove.

Without waiting for Lucy, he leapt down into the hall and jogged into the kitchen where he stopped, his mouth agape at the sight in front of him. For starters, a clean white cloth covered the table and in the middle, amongst a new HP sauce bottle and a sparkling glass cruet stood a vase full of half-open orange lilies. Four coloured envelopes also lay by Lucy's side plate.

Hector was wearing one of his own mother's crossover aprons and looked ridiculous. He was prodding at eggs in the frying pan. What was going on? Mark asked himself.

'Jesus Christ, you,' he said.

'Makes a change, son. Now tell me – it's so long ago I've forgotten – was it you or Richard who always liked sunny side up?'

'Me.'

Me...me...me...

'Wow!' exclaimed Lucy from the doorway, obviously unaware of the sudden painful silence. 'Those lilies are fantastic. How did you know they're my favourites?'

Mark felt as though a little knife labelled jealousy had just pierced his heart as she went over to the cooker to plant a kiss on Hector's cheek. The wound seemed to grow inside him as she then studied the ugly bruise.

'Does that hurt?' she asked him.

'A bit. Still, that kiss of yours'll make it better.' Hector then pulled out three unmatching plates from the oven and added an egg to each triangle of fried bread more tenderly than Mam had ever done, Mark admitted to himself, still hearing his brother's name in his ears. But this was just for Lucy's benefit, surely? As for his mother, she'd loathed cooking as if it got in the way of the fun she could be having instead. So they'd existed on oven meals and more oven meals. Expensive too, and all tasting the same...

'Bon appetit,' said Hector, pointing his knife at the envelopes, then Lucy. 'They're all for you. And there's another present. I nearly forgot.'

'What's that?'

'We're exchanging contracts next Friday. Mr Harries just phoned but you were in the shower. You happy with that?'

'Fine.'

However, Mark saw her mouth tense up as his own pulse quickened. After then she'd be legally bound to proceed. Halfway to being there every day, every night. Like he'd said, his one star in the sky. He watched her study the cards' postmarks as if glad for a diversion, before opening each in turn. She had the most perfect profile he'd ever seen. Everything in proportion. Just like the rest of her...

'That's from me,' Hector proudly as she pulled a vivid Matisse image from its red envelope. 'Thought some sea would make a change from all the fields here.'

'View from Collioure,' she read then looked up. 'It's lovely. Thanks.'

Well, she would say that, wouldn't she? But look what was coming next...

Mark held his breath as her finger slid under the flap of the home-made envelope and he saw her eyes widen as she withdrew his pen-and-ink drawing of a raven. Its feathers had taken him hours to complete and now he devoured every moment of her appreciation. 'Rhaca, by Mark John Jones,' she read then looked up at him with those big blue eyes. 'August 25th, 2001. Hey,' she got up to place her hand over his for a brief but soaring moment. 'I'd no idea you could draw like this. And a poet too.'

'I wanted to go to Art College, remember?' He death-stared his father as she perused the detail in close-up. 'But guess who said that was only for ponces and poufs?'

'Not now, eh?' Hector admonished, stirring his tea. 'It's Lucy's day.'
Anyone's but mine. Yeah. Sure. Whatever you say...

'You still could give it a try,' Lucy said. Those eyes again, not picking up on his boiling resentment. 'Go to College, I mean. They much
prefer mature students. My best mate Anna did her degree when she
was twenty-five. After that she just got lucky being in the right place at
the right time...'

He shook his head. That hadn't been the only dream of his all those
years ago. May 1st 1987 hadn't just brought one death to Ravenstone.

'Now then, what else have you got?' The ex-copper's fork poised
over his burnt sausage.

'Please start both of you,' Lucy said to him. 'After all the trouble
you've gone to.'

And they did, while Mark saw how her expression immediately
changed the minute she picked up the Manchester envelope.

'My mother,' she informed them both, examining the £50 cheque
which had been enclosed with the card. Then she stopped herself in
time from reading out the handwritten message inside it, and he knew
why. Because she still had a mother.

Mark leaned over and sneaked a look.

25th Aug 2001   Happy Birthday to a Special Daughter,
Much Love,
Mum. XXXX
Am so relieved you got in touch. Jon sends his love and I know your
Dad does too.

'Who's Jon?' he asked as that old familiar jealousy returned to linger
like the smoke from a dying fire...

Lucy hid his name with her arm. So, now we know thought Mark.
Someone else *is* sniffing round her.

'My ex, if you must know.'

'Since when?' He couldn't help himself.

'Last Whitsun. OK? Inquisition over?'

'No.'

'Well, tough,' she smiled.

But Hector's laugh was the last straw for him as she slotted the £50
cheque into her jeans pocket. She dabbed her eyes with a tissue and just
then, but for quite a different reason, Mark felt his own begin to sting.

'At least she knows where you are,' his father said just to change the
subject and Mark watched the food churn round in that same mouth
which had once, unbelievably, kissed his mother before the separate

bedrooms, the endless silences. 'But does Mrs Mitchell know the company you're keeping? That's the thing, isn't it?'

Mark saw Lucy smile. If she was any slower, he'd be after her grub as well, and sure enough, she let him take the last piece of her bacon.

Hector tutted in mock annoyance. 'Now what would Mrs Mitchell say to that, eh?' He took his empty plate to the sink and began running a tap into the washing up bowl. The tension was broken, but not for long. There was one unopened envelope left. She examined the postmark.

'Lambourn, Berkshire.' Lucy then pulled out the card from inside, clearly not very impressed and just as quickly stuffed the thing back in its envelope. But not before he'd noticed it too.

SMARTIE TART!
Now you've caught up with me!
See you very soon,
Hugs,
Anna
XXXXXXXX

'That looks fun.' Hector dried his hands on his apron and took a closer look, while Mark puzzled over that choice of card for the most untarty girl he'd ever seen. Why that degrading title? That grungy image of a young woman? He couldn't see why people thought that sort of thing was funny and hoped the card said more about the sender than its recipient.

Hector returned to his chores. 'Anyone for toast? When *you've* finished, of course,' he turned to smile at her. 'Come on now. Get some weight on those bones.'

Bones and blood. Bones and blood...

'You've still not squealed about last night,' Mark reminded him tersely. 'Where exactly did you go?'

'By Caban Coch. Nice and cosy.'

Lucy looked up. 'That's in the Elan Valley,' she said. 'I went there once.'

'Come on, Dad,' he urged his father. He could see Lucy was waiting for news.

'Let's just say I caught them at it.'

'At it? Those two? No way. That's gross.' She stopped eating.

'If Hughes was underage,' Hector went on, 'Evans's career as a preacher would be over. Still,' he added smugly, 'knowing that *I* know should keep 'em in check for a while.' He began stacking wet cutlery on the draining board. 'But it wasn't a pretty sight, I can tell you. And I don't think much of the company they keep.'

'Do you mean Druids?' she asked.

'Yes. Or Dagdans to be more accurate. Like I said. Not very savoury.'

'What were they doing? What were they wearing?'

'What they always do.'

'Surely not?' She looked at Hector then him. He left it to his dad, who nodded. But she didn't seem convinced.

'Hang on,' she began. 'His mother told me he didn't go along with any of that stuff. In fact he called her a Heathen for believing it.'

Mark suppressed a scowl. She was getting just a little too clued up. Asking too many questions. It was time to get the old scumbag spieling the spiel so that life could go on as normal.

'Look Dad. Stop talking in riddles. You saw Evans and Hughes and you told them to lay off, okay?'

His father nodded.

'And the others – you asked them about May '87?'

Hector tipped out the dirty water and refilled the bowl.

'Course I did. And I got this as well for my trouble.' He rolled up his right trouser leg.

The shin he revealed was darkened by dried blood.

'Christ.'

Mark watched Lucy move in for a closer look.

'That needs a proper dressing,' she said. 'Is there any First Aid stuff in the house?'

'Only you,' Hector patted her shoulder and Mark wanted to slap him away. 'It's nothing. Looks worse than it is. Anyhow, what else did I expect?' He covered up his injury and resumed washing up. 'They're probably out and about today again – the caring Deacon, the hard-working farmer – probably planning some new harm or other...' His voice weakened and Mark watched with growing alarm as with wet hands dripping across the tiles, his father found an empty chair and slumped down in it.

His own head begin to heat up like an electric element, reddening, reddening... What was the old git playing at? He knew what he had to say. He *knew* it, off by fucking heart... Everything in the kitchen began to blur. The shelves, the tiles the man at the sink. The lilies, her flesh, her smooth, smooth flesh... He snatched the bread knife from the table. A gasp from somewhere then the man standing up, untying his apron and placing it over the back of his chair.

The knife felt good in his left hand, restoring something to him which he'd lost a long time ago. Power, control. The ex-copper came closer as if daring him to use it.

'Come on then, son,' he goaded. 'What's holding you back?'

His whole body began to shake, but the blade stayed pointing at the man's shirt front.

He heard a woman scream. Like a hundred times before. Then foot-steps fading...

The man's gut now touched the tip of the blade. One tiny move, he thought. That's all it would take. And then in that instant, something inside him snapped. Nothing you could see, of course. But that mental fuse wire – so taut and brittle – which had connected him and his father together all this time, finally broke. Its after-shock made him blink. Made him waver...

'You're right, son,' came the man's voice in his ear, calm and even as the water in Caban Coch itself. 'As Lucy here's a witness. It was you who killed my wife. And I sent the wrong one away.'

Chapter Twenty

Dark seed that made me,
Ripened not by the sun
But shrunk by the shade,
While my one Light's fading...

See now the roses
Twine round that heart,
Fold tight her breasts
Too damp for burning...
MJJ 25/8/01

I sent the wrong one away drummed in Lucy's mind as her wobbly legs bore her up the stairs. She felt sick. She'd heard enough. Seen enough. It was time to exit, to do some hard thinking about this predicament she was in, because if she made the wrong decision about Wern Goch, there'd be her blood too on that salting slab. Friday was looming and still she was lost in a maze of tensions, of seemingly unfinished business. But from now on she would make it *her* business to find out what had really happened that grim year when that Zeebrugge ferry had already taken too many other souls to a watery oblivion. When the hurricane had done its worst.

However, before going to her room to gather up her belongings, she stalled by Mark's bedroom door. Raised voices were still coming from the kitchen down below, giving her time to act, because she had to find whatever she could, including those burnt fragments which had so mysteriously dropped from the chimney yesterday. No wonder he wanted them kept secret. She'd been a fool to believe all his grief, all his false sentimentality.

Now then. Be quick, she told herself, forgetting to breathe, turning the cold raven's head handle. The door was unlocked and made a slight groaning noise as she eased it open just enough for her to slip through.

Mist.

It had insinuated itself through the half-open window and lay like a shroud over the disorder of clothes, books and bedding which was his domain.

She shivered, not knowing where to start, yet trying to think logically. What if *she* was hiding something crucial? That grubby bundle Mark had made in Wern Goch would be too bulky for an average-sized pocket, so she tried the plain brown wardrobe which was oddly empty. Then his parka hanging behind the door. She burrowed into each of its sawdusty depths and, finding nothing there, moved on to his other out-door gear, the bed, the pillows which still smelt of him. The mattress.

She lifted one of its heavy corners then paused at what lay pressed underneath. OK, so he was into porn. Everybody was. Yet from what little she knew of him, it seemed odd somehow to find stuff like that here. Then she remembered being at the convent school and hiding a rude joke about one of the nuns under the insole in her shoe.

Shoes.

There were wellingtons, jungle boots, trainers reeking of stale sweat, all stained by that same red-brown mud, which she was now beginning to hate. But hang on. Here was an oblong cardboard box with *Size 10. Onyx.* written on it. She opened the lid on to some best black shoes. Almost new. The kind seen at weddings and funerals. After all, hadn't the Hall once been an undertakers?

Then her pulse quickened, because tucked inside the left shoe was a tightly bound Spar bag containing two more of the same. However the faintly nauseating smell which snaked out from the final one as she opened it was nothing to do with any Pass the Parcel party game.

She wrinkled her nose in disgust as she stared at the collection of brown morsels, some of which had stuck together at the bottom of the bag. No way were they dog chews, smelling like that, nor some child-hood leftovers of a meal. These were surely the remains of old flesh.

Repressing the need to heave, she stuffed the bags and their con-tents back into the shoe and closed up the box and ran towards the door.

Damn…

Someone else had been there too. It was locked.

She shoved her shoulder against the wood, once twice, three times, but that just hurt. Then she started to kick it. She'd always been nifty at hockey, and now those hours on the Convent's fields were paying off. The noise alone made her feel better.

Bang bang bang…

'Hector?' she yelled at the top of her voice. 'Let me out!' But just then after her next and strongest kick, the door opened inwards, almost toppling her over. Mark's body took up the whole space, blocking out the light from the landing. His eyes seemed darker still, like she'd seen in that cauldron and her scream died in her throat.

He suddenly gripped her shoulders, his fingers pressing deep into muscle. His strength not something she could deal with. This was like James Benn all over again, but she willed herself to wait. To bide her time.

'What the fuck are you doing in my room?' he asked.

'I thought it was mine. I forgot. Sorry.'

'Another liar. My God,' his grip tightened. 'Is there no escape?'

'From you there is.' She kicked out once more, this time catching his ankle.

'Goddamn you, that hurt.' He buckled in pain and in that precious moment, she dived along the landing, into her room and, as if the end of the world was imminent, snatched up her bag and jacket then somehow reached the bottom of the stairs before he recovered. Her heart trampolining in her chest, her mouth dry, she made for the kitchen. All her cards and the lilies were there. But not the man who'd put them there.

'Hector?'

No reply.

What was going on?

Without even trying his study or anywhere else, she was out of the front door within seconds and into the mist. Having fumbled for what seemed like a century for her car keys, she was in and starting the engine. She revved away down the drive, then glanced back in her mirror and saw not only Hector's old truck missing, but a murderer standing on the steps staring after her until he was out of sight.

Where to go? She asked herself, out of breath. Anywhere. Somewhere busy, normal. Lots of people yet amongst that, a private space of her own to think. She pumped the screen wash and switched on her fog lamp, staying in third gear all the way along the lane for fear of damaging the car. She also wondered where Hector had gone to and why.

Nothing made sense any more except that the dependable dumped Jon was growing more appealing by the minute and her mother's kitchen in Rusholme, her home-made cushions and loo-roll doll which Lucy had always despised, now represented the epitome of a safe secure life. She made up her mind to phone her the minute she could reasonably drive with one hand.

The lane seemed to take for ever but thankfully there were no obstructions, and once she'd joined the A44 she pulled into the first layby picked out of the gloom. She then dialled Manchester and waited as six rings came and went.

'Yes? Who's calling?' Barbara Mitchell's voice one of many. It was as if she was in the middle of a football crowd.

'Thanks for my card and my cheque,' Lucy shouted. 'You shouldn't have. It's me who should be getting you something, and I will after Monday.'

'No, you mustn't. I forbid it. Anyway, Happy Birthday. I can't believe it was thirty years ago that I was lying there in the Maternity Ward convinced I was going to die. You were ready for your school uniform the nurses said. And you were ravenous straight away.'

'Ten pounds three ounces?'

'That's right. A big strong girl...'

Normally Lucy would have laughed but she was in reality close to tears. Big and strong was the last thing she felt like now.

'Are you shopping or what?' she managed to ask, yet it was precisely the buzz of other people which was making her feel more alone and vulnerable than ever.

'I'm in Deansgate. It's absolutely crazy here. I'm just trying to get a couple of new skirts for school.'

How normal, thought Lucy as some huge transporter brushed by, making the Rav rock in it wake. For a moment a shaming envy consumed her.

'Anyway, is everything going to plan down there?' her mother asked.

'Yep. Fine. I'm sorting out a water supply in the next few days...' Just saying that sounded surreal. As if it wasn't her at all.

'Sounds like fun, but tell me,' Barbara Mitchell continued as the noise around her increased,' are those people at the Hall trustworthy? I mean, this is a huge commitment for you. Your bag needs to be safe. Especially once your money comes through...'

She'd not thought of that one. Her bag. Such irony.

'Of course they are. And helpful too. Like I told you, Mr Jones used to be a copper. I mean, policeman. Anyway,' she'd noticed with alarm that the mist was thickening to fog. 'I'd better be going. Got loads to do.'

'I'm sure you have. Now look,' her mother paused and Lucy wondered what was coming next. 'I start back on the 5th of September if you'd like me to come down before then. I can always bring Jon. He does keep asking about you.'

She hesitated.

'How is he?'

'Still working too hard. Still missing you.'

Lucy bit her lip. Those tears weren't going away.

'Tell him I'll be in touch when things are more sorted here. OK?'

'I will. He'll be over the moon.'

'And as for anyone coming to stay, it's best to wait till I've got beds, electricity etcetera sorted. Shouldn't be long the way things are going...'

'I'm impressed and I know your dad would be too. Oh, and let me know if you have any problems with the bank there.'

'I will.'

Tears finally moistened her cheeks as the call ended and when she stared through the windscreen, it was as if she was blind.

How the hell could she drive anywhere in these weather conditions? Perhaps she should wait. After all, she told herself, it was still only 9.30 in the morning. She clicked central locking and let the engine idle to activate the heater and Radio 1 where at least people seemingly from a different planet were having a good time. She then looked at the road map, calmer now, and saw that Llandrindod Wells was only ten miles south east. At least there'd be hotels and proper shops, she told herself as to her intense relief, a sly pale sun began to infiltrate the sky.

Having waited until the road markings re-appeared, she moved off, still unable to lodge the implications of Hector's admission from her mind. If he was right, why hadn't Mark been banged up? And where had 'the other one' gone? She couldn't ask Enid Evans any more about them now, but surely Llandrindod possessed a decent library. That would be the deciding factor because no way would she proceed towards even an Exchange of Contracts unless she was sure Mark hadn't been involved in any crime. It would be like living with a wolf outside the door. For who could say if he'd killed once, he wouldn't kill again?

Think of the way he'd held that knife, she told herself. Think of those eyes.

Her mother and Jon would have to wait.

Despite the economic downturn following the foot-and-mouth epidemic, the predominantly red-bricked Spa town seemed busy enough with late summer tourists filling its characterful streets. However, as Lucy drew closer to its town centre she realised something else was going on. The many posters she saw proclaimed a week-long Victorian Fair and sure enough, it wasn't long before ponies and traps bearing people in Victorian dress clattered past her to the sounds of barrrel organs and street vendors selling their wares; sweetmeats, candles and all kids of preserves. There were even children dressed up as urchins begging for coins, as if they'd just stepped from between the covers of *Oliver Twist*. She should find out more about this annual event, but her priority was to find somewhere to stay.

She'd heard about the Metropole, of course, but until Monday her funds wouldn't stretch that far. However, The Larches Hotel situated near Temple Park was cheap and welcoming, but it wasn't until she checked in for two nights that she realised she'd not even brought a toothbrush with her. She soon found a shop with a sale in progress and, for £20, acquired a pair of cropped jeans and a pretty blue T-shirt embroidered with flowers across the chest. Her mother's cheque was still intact, symbolising her indecision. If she was staying, she'd bank it on Monday. If not, it would be sent back.

Then on to a discount store for a Bart Simpson toothbrush and toothpaste, leaving her change from two pounds. This was the easy bit, she thought, making her way across to the park itself, where, in the distance a group of young lads in nineteenth century clothes were kicking footballs around. They looked happy and carefree making the quandary she was in seem even worse.

She bought a Coke from a nearby kiosk and sat down on an empty bench next to a rugged sandstone carving of Owain Glyndwr which was clearly part of an outdoor sculpture show. Unlike her, he'd been prepared to die for his cause.

The cool drink calmed her racing thoughts and as the boys' laughter mingling with the melodic tunes of a passing barrel organ reached her across the grass she asked herself, was she *really* that scared?

Certainly the ten miles to Llandrindod had helped restore some rationality to her thoughts, and with the mist having completely lifted, the sun was now casting everything in a balmy light. Its warmth on her face encouraged her to weigh reason against fear; to drive away the stubborn demons blighting her happiness. Hadn't Mark tried to save her from that old well? Hadn't the way he'd held her close stirred feelings she'd never once had for Jon? And what about the hours he'd clearly spent creating that poem and her birthday card? Finally, wasn't it just possible that Hector had lashed out at him without thinking? Her Dad had sometimes done that after a gruelling day at the Practice. Not much fun to listen to, but for him it had been a safety valve. That eccentric chimney sweep was right. Families…

But surely she'd forgotten something? Indeed she had, and like the darkness on the hills before rain, the contents of that black shoe in Mark's bedroom came to mind. That putrid smell, those revolting morsels…She suddenly shivered as if winter had touched her skin and quickly turned her face back towards the sun.

She sipped from the can once more and closed her eyes as the barrel organ's final tune faded away. Bliss…

When she opened them, however, she blinked in surprise. For there, crossing the grass in front of her was the same dishy blonde-haired man she'd seen in the Morfa tea rooms only yesterday.

What is more hateful than lies? — a love which bleeds.
What is more hurtful than loss? — a loss never to be regained.
Anon

This time the stranger's trenchcoat was slung over one shoulder and when the boys' football came his way he skilfully kicked it back into play.

Part of her willed him to keep walking, but the rest was even more intrigued. As if sensing her curiosity he eyed the bench she was sitting on and came over. Her blush deepened just as it had done on June 15th with James Benn. Would she never learn? she admonished herself. Was she that sad and insecure?

'Hi. Mind if I park alongside you?' he asked. 'This whole Victorian thing's worn me out.'

'Sure.' She removed her shopping bags and placed them by her feet.

In close-up, here was sex on legs and just then, all thoughts of the Joneses, of Wern Goch and its troubled history slipped away. It was her birthday after all and not much of one so far. His blue eyes which exactly matched the sky looked her up and down then turned to the statue.

'Been a fan of Mr Glyndwr here since I was a kid,' he began in an accent she couldn't quite place. Part West country, part something else. 'Meic Bowen, our old prof, was a bit of a Nat. His folks had come from the Rhondda during the Depression and we learnt the lot. Fascinating stuff.'

'Where was this?' Because the way he pronounced Rhondda suggested to her that he was no stranger to Welsh. Unlike the so-called literati at Hellebore.

'Bristol.'

'What a coincidence. My mother studied at the Uni there.'

'Nice place if you can afford it.'

She watched the stranger fold his mac and set it down in the space between them. Then he cupped his chin in both hands and stared at the kids as if, given half a chance he'd go and join them.

'I'm sure I saw you in Rhayader yesterday afternoon,' she ventured, gripping her Coke can to steady her leaping pulse. 'At the Tea Rooms.'

'Yeah. I'm taking a sabbatical. Just to see what old Bowen was on about.'

'And?'

'He was right. Wales is weird. I'm planning on Dolgellau for a bit of climbing tomorrow, then Bardsey Island... Hey,' he turned to her, 'I'm

Paul. Paul Furniss. And you?' Those awesome eyes expectantly on hers. In close up she noticed they weren't just blue. More the colour you'd find *underneath* a wave. The sky and the deep all rolled into one.

'Lucy Mitchell.'

'Nice,' he grinned, beautiful teeth. 'You should write a novel with a name like that.'

'My job's to edit them, not write them.'

'So, you're in publishing?'

She thought of Anna and the manuscripts she'd promised to send on.

'Freelancing for a while. Just to take a breather from London. It's hard going there year in year out…'

'Based in Rhayader?

'For the time being.'

Despite the total ease she felt in his company, Lucy wasn't yet prepared to tell him all her business or that today was her birthday.

'By the way, who was that dark-haired guy you were having tea with?'

This caught her unawares. She thought quickly.

'One of my authors on his way to a Writers' Retreat. He's a bit up his own backside if you must know.'

'Doesn't look your type at all, if you don't mind my saying so.'

'I don't, and I agree. He's strictly business. And what about you' she deflected. 'You could pass for an estate agent.'

He suddenly slapped his thigh and laughed.

'Jesus Christ, Lucy. Why not say I'm a pimp or a money launderer? I'd be more flattered.'

'I'm sorry. OK?'

'Apology accepted. I'm what's called a Research Fellow. Shell are funding me till I take up a senior post after Christmas. I'm into mineralogy. It's the new sex, don't you know?' He bent over to brush a speck of something off one of his moleskin shoes while Lucy blushed again.

She told him about the family treks to Malham Gorge where, having scrambled to the top the three of them would stride out over the vast limestone slabs, where the cracks between seemed to go deep into the bowels of the earth. The stranger also learnt about a boat trip she'd taken inside the dark damp Blue John mines, and how after her panic attack her parents had been forced to turn back. He listened until she'd finished, then checked his Rolex, as if she'd been merely describing a shopping expedition, or a night out with friends.

'Now then,' he added with a beguiling smile. 'I'm starving. Can I get you lunch, or do you have other plans?'

'Lunch would be great, but I'd need to get going around two. Got some scripts to pick up.'

'Fine by me.'

Together they left the park and, having sauntered along Dol-y-Coed Road found Luigi's Ristorante under a green-striped awning, half-buried under a mass of plastic vines. After a leisurely hour over lasagnes – which he didn't finish – and a carafe of Chianti, during which her new acquaintance had been attentiveness itself, he left a huge tip and paid in cash from a bulging Vuitton wallet.

Not bad for a researcher, she thought, idly wondering how she could get in on that particular act, watching every move he made. The way his tanned fingers worked the compartments of that wallet. How he pushed back the hair off his face...

Suddenly that hand was in hers and once outside, he drew her into the wider doorway of insurance brokers closed for the afternoon. He was standing close now. His aftershave, everything, making her feel dizzy.

'I'd like to stay in touch if that's okay with you,' he said.

'Me too. Do you have a mobile?'

For a moment his hand slipped into his chinos' pocket. Then he quickly withdrew it.

'Dammit. Been meaning to get a new one for days. What's your number?'

He clearly wasn't geared up for this kind of thing, she thought, dropping her shopping bags, discovering a pen then tearing a page from her Hellebore diary. Anna would have made mincemeat of him. Probably driven him away. But not her. Each move he made was too hypnotic. Each fresh angle of his face and body more perfect than the last. In fact, he was *beyond* perfection and, in trying to describe him to herself, she realised the inadequacy of words.

'Cheers.' He took both items from her and, having pressed the paper against the brokers' window wrote the numbers as if each one was an effort. 'I'll give you a call sometime,' he smiled again as he returned the pen and folded the scrap into his pocket. 'Maybe we could go and look at some rocks together.'

'Sounds good.'

Sounds good? Is that all you can say? Because a new and exciting virtual reality was kicking in. Who better to go over the hills and far away with? she asked herself. Who better to lie next to in some hidden grassy gulley with just the birds and the sunshine looking on? Here was the man who could turn her life around. A man she now desired more than anything else in the world, and every bone in her confused and lonely body knew it.

She reached up to kiss his stubble cheek and in doing so, felt him stiffen against her as his lips moved to cover her mouth. Warm, urgent, but brief as a dream.

'Good luck with everything,' he said finally, drawing away.

'You too.'

'Keep your phone on, remember?'

'I will.'

Then, moments later, he was gone as other anonymous faces took his place in her field of vision. She searched each in turn but there was none so perfect. How could there be? she asked herself, feeling bereft. Not even the dark and moody Mark Jones could hold a candle to Paul Furniss. He'd not only re-lit the flame so cynically extinguished three months ago, but aroused her. Made her want a man inside her again. Simple as that. And at thirty years old, was that so much to ask?

At first, she was tempted to follow him, to see where he was staying, even the make and number of whatever it was he drove. Because being his shadow was better than being without him altogether. However, she soon realised he'd totally vanished.

Dejected and miserable, she returned to her hotel past shops and more shops, quickening past the bookshop window where James Benn's *Tribe* was being featured. In the privacy of her room she dumped her shopping on the bed and accessed her phone's voicemail.

NO NEW MESSAGES

Stupid cow.

What did she expect? He wouldn't have bought himself a new phone in that short space of time. Give him a chance, she told herself.

She had a quick wash then, while drying her face, pressed two fingers horizontally against her lips. He was there, kissing them again. It didn't take much to imagine, especially when she closed her eyes...

'Are you pathetic or what?' She then shouted at herself in the washbasin's mirror, before going out again into the afternoon sunshine and asking a couple of women dressed in bonnets and shawls for directions to the town's public library. She thanked them and headed for Cefnllys Lane where an imposing white building could be seen amongst trees around the corner from Coleg Powys and the converted church, now St John's Headquarters. However, before entering its inviting foyer, she hesitated. Was she sure about going digging like this? Supposing Mark or Hector found out? She watched people passing by on their way to the well-advertised book sale, keeping the library open beyond its normal one o'clock closing time. Mothers and buggies, teenagers, whole families, bits of families yet all seemed content with life. Reassuringly normal. All the more reason to try and find out more about the Joneses and what lay behind Hector's sudden outburst. To discover what had really happened.

A desk-bound official glanced up expectantly as she approached the Local History section in the main area. Lucy guessed she was around her age.

'I'm looking for two things,' she explained. 'Firstly, any parish records for north-east Rhayader and secondly, whatever local papers you've got for May 1987.'

The young woman gestured towards the entrance.

'Parish records are held at the County Archives just five minutes away. But I'm afraid they're not open on Saturdays.   Anyway, I'd have thought there'd be a problem for that particular part of the world you're looking for.'

'No churches.'

'Right.'

'What about Census returns?'

'Nothing doing after 1901. But County Archives might still be your best bet. And if not them, you could always try The National Archives in Kew. As for any newspapers, we'll need some ID first. Just in case…'

'Just in case of *what*?' Annoyed that at the moment, she was of no fixed address.

'We've had some trouble recently with mischief makers. Information can get into the wrong hands, you know.'

'I'm not a mischief maker. I'm buying a house.' Honesty here might be the best policy, she thought.

'Your solicitor would help you there, I'd have thought. After all, they do searches, don't they?'

'Not the kind of search I need.' She placed her driving licence and Hellebore photo tag which gave her the oddest feeling when she saw it. As if she still had a job to go back to; an identity in the world of publishing. 'Look,' she went on as these items were scrutinised. 'If you were putting money into a property where someone had been murdered, wouldn't you want to find out more?'

That did the trick, and once her details had been taken, the librarian indicated where the old newspapers were stored.

'We do make a charge for any copying,' that same voice called after her. 'The copier's here. Next to me.'

'I bet it is,' Lucy muttered, sensing that earlier dizziness return. If her mother could see her now. Or Mark, or Hector…But she had no choice.

She was familiar with operating fiches and soon accessed both the

Brecon & Radnor Times and the *County Times* for 1987. Here was Gorbachev and glasnost; the Herald of Free Enterprise tragedy and local agricultural news a-plenty scrolled by, but so far, after April and more searching she found nothing on Ravenstone Hall.

'We close in twenty minutes,' the librarian called. 'Our book sale will be over by then. Any luck yet?'

'No.'

'Where's this place you're buying, then?'

Lucy had to think on her feet. So far she'd found nothing, but she didn't know this person from Adam. Was it time to cast suspicion to the winds? She asked herself. And the answer was yes.

'On the Ravenstone Hall estate.'

She heard the scrape of a chair against the floorboards. The click of heels drawing closer.

'Here, let me have a go,' the other woman offered. 'I'm Verity, by the way.'

Lucy sat alongside her as she scrolled past Thatcher's third term re-election and the Tour de France result, until August appeared.

'Surely this is too late?' she said. But the librarian shook her head.

'I remember my friend who attended the Grammar there at the time, saying that the murder there was all pretty well hushed up till after the inquest.'

'When was that?'

'10th August. Look at this.'

Lucy's eyes fixed on the screen as the paragraph and its discreet heading scrolled into view.

RAVENSTONE INQUEST VERDICT

On Monday 6th August, the County Coroner for Radnorshire, Dr Walford Hopkins passed a verdict of Unlawful Killing by a person or persons unknown on Mrs Sonia Marcelle Jones (née Ferris) of Ravenstone Hall, Rhayader. Her badly mutilated body was discovered in another property on the estate known as Wern Goch by her husband Hector Meurig Jones, retired Detective Inspector with Cardiff CID. Dr Hopkins advised the jury that the case is now closed and Mrs Jones's body has been released for burial.

'This friend of yours. Would she know any more?' she asked, feeling deflated and disappointed.

'Rhiannon George?'

'If that's the one, yes.'

'She was in the same class as Richard. She might do.'

Lucy gulped.

'*Richard* Jones?'

'That's right. He never came back for the rest of the summer term. Talk was that he'd gone a bit, you know,' she tapped her forehead. 'Doolally.'

'You mean, a breakdown?'

'Yes.'

'Go on, please.' Thinking what an oddly jolly word for something so serious.

'Apparently his father sent him off somewhere to get back to normal. No one's heard of him since.'

I sent the wrong one away...

'And what about Mark? Was he younger or older than him?'

The other woman looked at her watch, switched off the fiche screen and stood up.

'Younger, I think, though she never said anything about him that I can recall.'

But Lucy's mind was once more on a well-muscled forestry worker banging in those fencing stakes...

Bang bang bang...

'I'm afraid I must shut up shop now.' The woman returned to her desk to lock its drawers.

'Thanks for your help.' Lucy hovered for a moment. Tomorrow was Sunday with nothing planned. At least up to now. 'One more favour,' she began. Have you any idea where this Rhiannon George lives?'

Verity finished locking a nearby filing cabinet, a small frown puckering her forehead.

'She may well be married with kids by now. Unlike me.' She smiled ruefully, Lucy thought. 'We lost touch after leaving school. But I know the family had a smallholding near Crossgates. Gellionnen, if I remember correctly. She used to complain that the other kids called her 'shitty shoes' in English, mind. The Grammar here didn't do much Welsh in those days. Not like my Comp.'

Lucy thanked her again and, having made her way out of the building set off for the hotel car park. The sun felt abnormally hot and just the two glasses of Chianti consumed over an hour ago seemed to dull her faculties just when she needed them most.

She wondered whether or not to roll back the Rav's soft top. Whether to head for New Radnor and check around that waterfall again, or make a trip to Crossgates now instead of tomorrow. Suddenly her mobile beeped into life inside her bag.

Paul…

She grabbed it almost too quickly. Held it hard. It was him. Her pulse changed pace.

'Hi Lucy. It's me.' The voice she'd been waiting for. 'I've just got myself a state of the art Nokia,' he said. 'No picture of you yet, which is a shame, but this is the next best thing.'

'I'm glad you can't see me.'

'Rubbish. You're beautiful. Anyway, are you receiving me loud and clear?'

'Loud and clear.' And that was the trouble. It seemed as if he was next to her once more. His lips moving closer… 'Where are you?' she managed to stay coherent.

'Llangurig. Going north.'

Then she remembered Dolgellau, his destination, which now seemed a world away. 'I won't say break a leg, then.'

'Better not,' he laughed. 'I've not climbed for two years now. Hey,' he added, 'say we take a trip next Thursday when I've been to Bardsey? Unless you're too busy reading novels, that is.'

She smiled and it showed in her voice, until she realised that Thursday was almost a whole week away. 'I do eat and sleep as well, you know.' Then, like the maggots who used to invade her Dad's Cox's apples just when he was about to pick them, she realised that this academic was at the helm with the wind in his hair. Anna would have said, whoa. Steady up. This is a two-way thing, surely? But then, she reflected rather unkindly, that apart from her latest man, none of her editor friend's relationships had survived more than a fortnight. 'Where to?' She asked, trying to keep the excitement out of her voice.

A pause followed which seemed like an hour.

'Since you mentioned your Limestone travels I thought of the crystalline variety near Old Radnor. There's also the volcanic Stanner Rocks which some call The Devil's Garden, but don't let the name put you off.'

'I won't,' she lied, suppressing a brief shiver.

'There's also the Elan Valley,' he went on. 'According to the photos in my guide book, it's really beautiful at this time of year.'

'That's better.'

'So, how about the Clock Tower at 2 p.m.?' he suggested.

'Good idea.' It was the central point in Rhayader with no risk of missing him.

'Whatever the weather, eh?'

It could snow for all she cared, but how could she say that?

'Ciao.'

She listened as he signed off then realised with a sinking feeling that by then, Wern Goch might well be a thing of the past, with the Hall no longer a bed option. She'd probably be back home in Manchester with just Anna's reading matter to keep her company during the day.

Anna. The girl who's got it all...

Except that now, the gap between them in the Luck Stakes was beginning to close. Nevertheless, she decided she wouldn't be going anywhere until she'd made some investigations and if that meant giving the Hall a wide berth then so be it. The Larches would do for the time being. In fact for as long as it took.

Chapter Twenty-Two

What is more hateful than lies? – a pretty woman who tells them.
What is more hurtful than loss? –
when the hunter finds his spear is blunt.
MJJ 25/8/01

It was now 3.30 p.m. and decision time. Which mission to choose?
Lucy again debated with herself. New Radnor or Crossgates? She
unfolded her already crinkly map, realising she could easily kill two
birds with one stone if the traffic wasn't against her. Nevertheless, cow
pats first, she decided, and, having set her sunglasses on her nose,
manoeuvred the Rav out of the car park.

The A483 was almost deserted and within fifteen minutes she'd
reached Crossgates, pulled into its one garage forecourt and was top-
ping up her tank with unleaded behind a filthy Mitsubishi Shogun. Its
driver, whom she guessed was a farmer, was just locking his petrol cap
when Lucy asked if he'd heard of Gellionnen and then for simple directions there.

'Sure I have.' He rubbed his hands on his old trousers. 'But them
Georges don't farm no more. Foot-and-mouth saw to that. It's the
Coedglasson road you want, then a mile on from the phone box you'll
see it signed on the right. Two things,' he eyed her Rav. 'Watch the road
there, and,' he warned, 'they've got dogs.'

Her heart sank.

'What kind of dogs?'

'Not the sort I'd want around, that's for sure.'

She thanked him, feeling daunted already and followed the man's
instructions with an ever increasing pulse. Once the last vestige of
human habitation had disappeared, she felt suddenly not just alone but
frightened. She thought of knives and blood and those gruesome
remains she'd found that morning. It didn't help matters either that the
hills to the east looked oddly misshapen, threatening even, like something from Tolkien's Middle Earth, and when the turning appeared
leading off the main road, it seemed to disappear to nothing.

The gradient was absurd. and she wondered how the hell she'd get
back up it again. Now she knew what the man at the garage had meant.
Never mind dangerous dogs. This was proving to be Mission Bloody
Impossible. For a moment, she stopped the car and glanced in her rear
view mirror where some large black 4x4 was travelling cautiously along
the road she'd just left, as if it too was looking for somewhere.
Something about its shape was familiar, but so were Land Rovers and

the like. Big wheels, high off the road. Radiator grilles with more than a practical function...

It was then she decided to leave the Rav on the grass verge and walk to the smallholding. After all, according to the directions she'd been given, it wasn't far. She wished she'd had a car alarm fitted, then realised no one would hear it anyway.

The downward trek took her over a rough earthen surface embedded with potato-sized stones. There wasn't a soul around but by the time she reached the bottom, a growing panic had replaced any earlier sense of peace. The silence was too deep, too intense. The very air seemed to line her throat. Not the pure blown variety of the hills but a rank distillation of weeds and decay, while overhead, nothing obstructed the glowering sun. She'd always hated those Rupert Bear illustrations of countryside, with their creepy sense of foreboding. The bare hill, the foreground bush hiding unseen terrors.

She listened hard for the slightest sound. Some grazing creature, water even, however, all nature here seemed comatose with only her breathing to prove she was at least alive. Even though this sense of unease made her glance over her shoulder several times, she pressed on, willing herself not to give up, reminding herself what the librarian had said.

Soon, with relief, she came across the expected telephone box, surprised to find its old-fashioned contours encased in fluorescent tape. Closer inspection showed that most of its glass was missing.

Vandals? she thought. Here of all places?

And then she noticed a cracked concrete driveway, and next to it a wooden sign bearing the words GELLI ONNEN CHAMPION FRIESIANS with a faded picture of a black and white cow underneath. Lucy ventured towards a dormer bungalow just visible ahead, and the closer she got, realised that like Wern Goch, the place was uninhabited. Where were the supposed dogs? she asked herself, keeping a wary eye out for them. Where was anybody?

Patches of breezeblock showed through the front wall's rendering and the windows were hung with grey net curtains. She then noticed a satellite dish protruding from one of the chimneys and a line of washing in the waste ground to the side. Children's clothes. All the same size.

She knocked on the front door with her fist and waited, wishing she'd bought some bottled water for a drink because her throat was on fire. Heat and nerves.

'Yes?' called a woman's voice from an opened upstairs widow set in the one gable. Lucy stared up at the dirty glass to see the pale anxious face of someone possibly in her late twenties.

'My name's Lucy Mitchell,' she began. 'I'm buying a property the other side of Rhayader. I just wondered if you'd any info on the people who are selling it. Verity at the library suggested I try here.' That wasn't strictly true. It had been *her* idea, but a week of unsolved mysteries had given her scruples a fresh make-over.

'Which people?'

'I can't shout any more.'

'Wait there.'

In the meantime, she had the distinct impression that she wasn't alone. She stepped back off the mangy door mat and looked around, but no. It was just her and the junk and the washing.

'Are you Rhiannon George?' she asked the frightened young woman who finally opened the door. A rusted chain strained tight, kept them apart.

'Yeah. So?'

'Please, I won't keep you a minute...'

'That's what *he* said. Crafty bastard.'

'Who?'

'I dunno. Some bloke. Sneaked up on me yesterday tea time while I was getting the washing in. Said he wanted to look at my kids...' Here she stopped, still clearly distraught by the incident.

'Why on earth would he want to do that?' Lucy checked her surroundings again, with that same sense of being watched. It was eerie. She wanted to get indoors, even if it turned out to be a rat-infested dump.

'I dunno. Told me I'd once been his girlfriend.'

'Did you recognise him?'

'No.'

'Did he give his name or did you ask who he was?'

'It wasn't like that. I was scared for the kids. They were indoors...'

'Have you told the police?'

'They're crap.'

'Look,' she glanced round yet again. 'Let's talk inside because we might be able to help each other.'

A barefoot Rhiannon George dislodged the chain and she entered a gloomy flag-stoned hallway strewn with children's well-used toys and various discarded garments. The smell of cigarettes and recent meals thickened the already stale air. At least so far, there weren't any rats.

'Here, this'll do,' said the mother, indicating a kitchen whose lime green walls made Lucy blink. In the middle of a tiled floor stood a table covered by a stained waxed tablecloth, and surrounded by an assortment of unmatching chairs. 'I don't bother with the other rooms now, and the kids sleep in the front parlour. At least, that's what it used to be.'

Lucy took in the cobbled-together units, the old Belfast sink and what looked like job-lot crockery. Clearly the recent epidemic had dealt this enterprise a devastating blow and seeing this poverty sent out a warning bell for herself. How risky farming was. If not the weather and the array of possible infestations, then a wipe-out such as the George's had experienced.

The woman brought over a chunky Guinness ashtray and sat opposite her visitor and Lucy saw how she was still pretty, in a fragile way. She was, however, seriously underweight and her man's shirt and leggings bagged off her skinny frame. Her once pink nail varnish showed more nail than varnish on her strangely childlike hands.

'The boys are having a kip now,' she explained. 'Thank God. Twins they are. Four years old.'

'They must be a handful,' Lucy wondered where their father was and couldn't imagine never having known hers.

'Tell me about it.' Rhiannon reached for a cigarette and stuffed it unlit between her lips. 'Anyway, you mentioned Verity. Lucky cow, she is.' She dug in her shirt pocket, produced a cheap lighter and lit up. She aimed the first plume of smoke at the ceiling. 'Nice job, nice town, not stuck out here like me. Grammar School, College, now look.'

'I think she envies you really.'

'Oh yeah?'

'So where are your parents? I was told they were here too.'

'That's them.' Rhiannon pointed to a black and white wedding photograph propped up on the mantelpiece above an old Aga, then withdrew her cigarette to cough. 'Buggered off to Calais to look at a farm there. My dad lost all his herd, see. All the milking...'

'And the dogs?'

'Boom boom.' She imitated gunfire, and immediately Lucy felt a sinuous chill touch her skin. 'Too expensive to keep, see,' Rhiannon went on. 'And me? I'm only here so people can view the dump. It's not with an agent and there's no sign, so it's hard for me to tell who's genuine and who's not. And I'm telling you, him yesterday certainly wasn't.'

Two more hefty pulls on her cigarette before it was squashed into the ashtray.

'Why would he turn up like that. Out of the blue? I don't get it.'

'Neither do I. Been trying to make sense of it ever since.'

'He could have been lying about wanting to see the kids. Maybe he planned to distract you and nick what he could.'

She shrugged her thin shoulders. 'I dunno. Before I met Gary, the kids' father, I'd loads of boyfriends. It was the only way I could get out of here. You know, get dressed up, put some slap on. Into the pubs…'

Shitty shoes…

Lucy looked out beyond the net curtain, held to one side by a piece of faded ribbon. All she could see was the slope of a bare hill against the sky.

'I know what you're thinking,' said Rhiannon suddenly. 'What the hell is there to do in this poxy hole? But you get to know this and that and anyway, I used to sleep over at my friends' houses – the ones who lived in Rhayader, that is. I really envied them, living there. Even though it's hardly bloody London…'

Hardly, thought Lucy, feeling more sorry for her with every minute that passed. And how like herself with James Benn, one false move can change it all…

'And, according to Verity, Richard Jones of Ravenstone Hall was a boyfriend of yours.'

'Is that what she said?'

'Yes.'

Rhiannon seemed to tense up all over and lit another cigarette.

'Please. It's important you tell me whatever you can about him.'

'Why's that then?'

And why so defensive? deciding now to tell her straight.

'I've put an offer in for the house where his mother was murdered. I need to know if I'll be safe…'

'Are you barking?'

'What do you mean?'

'He *loved* his mam. Thought the bloody world of her he did. And he was beautiful. Dark hair. Kind of luminous grey eyes. My God, I could hardly concentrate on my lessons when he was in the same room…'

A wistfulness altered her whole expression. And because she'd met Paul, Lucy understood.

'Go on,' she encouraged her.

'Well, it was this Twmpath Dawns which set it all off. At the start of the summer term it was. To raise money for something or other…'

'What's a Twmpath Dawns?'

'Kind of Barn Dance. Different partners all the way through, but at the end, it was me he chose for the slow dance. I could see the other girls round the edge of the hall, all green-eyed. But I didn't care.'

'And then what?' Lucy suddenly turned towards the open door to the hallway, convinced she'd heard the sound of a car nearby.

'We did go out for about three months and it was great, really great, but he didn't seem to like me showing too much off. He once asked me to wear a polo-neck and Christ knows I hated them. Still do. And then once I didn't wear a bra. He never said anything, but I knew. Never mind,' she killed her second dimp. 'He was the best of the lot. Not that we went all the way. Wish we had, though.'

She saw how Rhiannon's cheeks had flushed, how her hands knotted together until her knuckles showed white through the skin.

'And then,' she went on, 'after the business with his mam, well, I never saw him again. It was as if he'd vanished off the face of the earth.'

'But you don't know where?'

Rhiannon shook her head. 'If I'd known that, I'd have followed him, wouldn't I? At least I'd have been spared Gary with his Friday afternoon-job rubbers.'

'Verity seems to think Richard cracked up after the tragedy.'

'Yeah. Big time so I heard.'

'And what about his brother Mark? Did you have much to do with him?'

Rhiannon pulled a third cigarette from the packet and simply looked at it.

'Not much. He was three years younger. Bit of a cling-on. Usual brother stuff, you know. Always had to join in what Richard and his mates were doing. Copied everything he did. Once though, he got taught a lesson.'

'Why?'

'I guess Richard had had enough. One lunch hour, he stuck his compass right through Mark's hand. He had to have a tetanus, the works. Big fuss at the time, I remember, but after Richard had said sorry and did all his detentions, it kind of faded away.' She returned the cigarette to its box.

'I see,' said Lucy, mentally dwelling on that sudden act of violence. A little black cloud in an otherwise perfect sky. 'And what about Mrs Jones? Did you ever meet her? What was she like?'

Rhiannon got up and walked over to the window, keeping her back to Lucy as she spoke.

'I only saw her the once at the school play. It was in the February. *Gulliver's Travels*, that's it, and Richard was Gulliver. He was amazing. Our drama teacher said he should try for RADA when he'd done his A levels. But he was dead set on Art. Always drawing something or other. Oh, and writing poetry.'

'Was Mr Jones with her at this play?'

'Never clapped eyes on him. No.'

'And Mrs Jones?' She nudged her gently.

'The spit of Marilyn Monroe, I'm not kidding. But with reddish hair, that was the only difference. Nothing like the other mums, no way. And Richard seemed so proud of her, showing her off to everyone afterwards...' Rhiannon turned to look at Lucy. She was frowning. 'Do you think I'm mad saying this, but I felt really jealous of her. God, what am I saying?' She put her head in her hands and shook it from side to side as if to rid it of imagined demons.

'You were young,' said Lucy, thinking back to when she was fifteen. 'I was the same when my Dad treated my pals like princesses. Or the times he'd go on and on about so-and-so in hospital being *so* brave. I actually grew to hate them. Do you know that? What a thing to admit,' her voice tailed away and she bit her lip as if she'd said too much.

But Rhiannon looked relieved. She came and sat down again.

'Hey, about you buying up at Ravenstone,' she said suddenly. 'I'd go for it.'

Lucy's heartbeat quickened. 'Do you really mean that?'

'Course. I know that Mr Jones and the boys were grilled at the time but rumour was some Dagdans or other killed her. Their kind of thing, wasn't it? Poor cow. Even my mam and da used to keep a look-out here. Why we kept guard dogs all those years. There's all sorts of oddballs hanging around.'

'You should have a dog now,' said Lucy, still not entirely at ease so far from civilisation.

'Why? I'm not stopping. I'm pissed off with fitting into everyone else's plans. We're going down to Swansea soon. Least I'll have my own place and the kids'll grow up with some company. Not like here.'

Lucy heard sounds of children waking up as she wrote down her mobile number on yet another page of her Hellebore diary and left it on the table. Then she made a move to go.

'If you remember any more about that Jones family, please give me a ring. Or if you just want to keep in *touch*. It's been good to talk to you. I feel more optimistic about things now.'

And that was true. Not only that, but she'd got a date for Thursday and money soon to spend. However, there was just one unasked question. She took a deep breath. 'This may sound odd,' she began, 'but would you have said Mark Jones was capable of killing anyone?'

Rhiannon whitened, visibly shocked. Her hand gripped her cigarette lighter so tight Lucy thought her knuckles would burst through their skin.

'And I thought *I* was mad?'

She didn't pursue it. The maggot had surely, finally been driven from the apple. Namely, her head. Although Rhiannon George hadn't seen Mark for fourteen years, her reaction had to count for *something*, surely? Then, as they both left the kitchen for the noise of children, she noticed a rifle leaning inside the doorway to the understairs cupboard.

'Is that loaded?' she asked.

'You bet. It's my da's. I must remember to take it upstairs with me next time.'

But Lucy wasn't happy. Gun or no gun, this little family was still vulnerable.

'Look, I've got an idea,' she said. 'I'm renting a room at Ravenstone Hall till things are sorted. Why don't you let me phone there to see if you three could come too? Just to tide you over?'

'No thanks. We'll be OK.'

Had she said that too quickly? she wondered, but just then, a child's scream filled the bungalow. She froze as Rhiannon skidded back down the passage grabbed the rifle and ran towards the front room. Two small boys sat tight together on the bottom mattress of their bunk bed, their eyes wide with terror. They were both wore identical red Welsh Rugby shirts and neither looked as if their curly hair had been combed for days.

'Mam, mam,' yelled the bigger lad pointing at the net curtain in the window. 'There's a bogey man out there. I saw him. I saw him.'

'And me,' chipped in the other. 'I'm scared.'

Rhiannon lifted a corner of the net and peered out. The sun in her eyes. 'Which way did he go?'

'Dunno,' they cried in unison, but he was there. Honest to God.'

Rhiannon glanced back at her, her face white again.

'Is the back door locked?' Lucy asked.

'No.'

'Come on.'

'Right. In the van you two. Now.'

'Where we goin'?'

'Never mind. Just hold hands with Lucy here. She's my friend. Not a word, mind. Shssh.'

Lucy felt their hot little fists tighten in hers as they crept out on to a weedy yard surrounded by empty barns and calf stalls, where yet another clapped-out white van stood amongst empty oil cans and discarded farm machinery.

'What about your shoes?' she reminded her.

'Fuck. Forgot.' Rhiannon threw the van keys at her. 'Get in you lot.' And while she settled the lads on one of the two grimy vinyl benches in the back, trying to ignore pleas for their toys, Lucy glimpsed something moving beyond the van's rear window. It was the top half of a figure hurrying away beyond the brow of the hill.

Whether a man or not she couldn't tell, but the fact that seatbelts were missing or the van was probably unroadworthy were nothing compared to the tangible danger she now felt.

'What are your names?' she asked the two little passengers.

'Not telling.'

'Not a whisper, then. Promise?

'Promise.'

She then slipped round to the right hand side of the bungalow to take another look. To make sure she hadn't been hallucinating, but there was nothing to see. Just the same car engine noise as she'd noticed earlier, but fading fast into the heat.

'What the hell's going on?' she muttered to herself then told Rhiannon her news. The woman shoved the rifle next to the driver's seat then threw coats and a shabby hold-all into the back with the kids. She slammed the van doors shut then looked at her.

'Where's your car?'

'By the main road.'

'God, I wish *we* were.'

'Have you got enough money?'

'Yeah. Thanks.'

After five hair-raising minutes in which the boys could be heard rolling back and forth on their bench, and the van nearly came to a stop half way up the steep gradient, she was deposited by her car. There were no waves, no goodbyes, just the roar of tyres on earth as Rhiannon George slewed her vehicle towards the tarmac and was soon speeding south, out of sight.

She didn't hang around either. There wasn't time to wonder if they'd be alright, nor her, for that matter. She pulled open her door to be met by a wall of boiling air. Then something on the windscreen caught her eye. At first she assumed it was a scrap of litter blown by the wind. Except there was no wind and this wasn't litter. But the carefully torn half of a plain white postcard. She could tell by the fine blue lined square for a stamp on the reverse. However, it was the other side which stopped her breath and turned her stomach over. Two words. That was all.

YOU'RE NEXT

Chapter Twenty-Three

Is the well still there and the chestnut trees?
The river's spray, the heron's lair?
Those hungry lips, that mane of hair?
Once mine, become a fresh nightmare.

Six o'clock and the temperature in the box room situated at the top of Manor House had already reached thirty degrees. Elizabeth Benn, incarcerated there since Guy Roper's call, removed her damp brassiere whose straps had left deep red weals above each of her shoulders, and wiped under each armpit with a fresh travel-wipe reached from on top of the nearby sideboard. The walnut veneer specimen, too big for her parents' retirement bungalow, now seemed gargantuan, leaving her just enough space in the damp and shabby Lloyd Loom chair to stick out her legs and keep her feet moving. There were those same ornate brass handles, the hideous whorls of woodgrain, part of her childhood and adolescence in Oxford. If she was blind she'd know exactly where this veneer had blistered, and be able to trace with her finger the light-coloured scar on the second drawer where James had first thrown a knife at her and missed.

Just one of his many lapses into sudden rage, that one, but this time, she resolved to herself, there'd be no more. After that Friday evening call from Roper and the recorded scream he'd told her to get ready, James had smashed the little CD player to bits and flung the Horror disc at her as if it was a quoit on a beach somewhere. Its sharp edge had caught her left shoulder and the wound was still ripe. Still hurting.

Her breasts stuck to her body, empty and useless. Not that she'd ever fed Katherine herself but in younger days she had conscientiously tried the Bardot uplift technique of interlocking fingers and pressing both palms together – now look at them, she thought. Literally, a waste of skin. Elizabeth slipped on her cotton blouse fastened its dainty buttons then reached for her old wooden sewing box and relic from her grandmother, which lay on the sideboard.

She opened its two lids and peered into the chaos of cotton reels and rusted scissors. A left-over section of name tape bearing KATHERINE LILY HEWITT eight times along its length, some rolls of ribbon she'd never worn and a ball of tired grey elastic, for what use, she wasn't sure. But not so the bodkin which she withdrew from the packet. It was the thickest, longest and sharpest of them all. Excellent in fact.

She pressed its point into the pad of her thumb and flinched, yet the smile which followed as she slipped it under the insole of her left bedroom slipper, more than made up for the past hellish twenty four hours.

Next, and ignoring the pain which followed, she hunted inside her wet knickers for her mobile. Not exactly her lifeline, because she had other more private plans to save herself, but certainly crucial to her purpose. Now that the Dyson girl had got her act together, it was time for the other one to make a decision. Sweat made her fingers slide over the phone's pads and after three wrong numbers she finally made contact and listened as the young woman answered.

'Yes? What d'you want?' Her tone made Elizabeth wonder if now was the right moment to approach her. However, she continued.

'Lucy Mitchell?'

'Who are you?'

More nervy than aggressive, she decided.

'Never mind that. Just listen carefully and you'll see that my proposal will be to your advantage.'

'Look, I've had enough for one bloody day. OK? Just get off my case.'

'I'm offering you two thousand pounds if you're prepared to make your James Benn interlude public...'

'*Interlude? Public?*'

She listened to the stunned silence which followed. Some compensation at least for being holed up without food or water with only dead men's chattels for company. Her velour school hat, her confirmation bible encased in smooth ivory plastic. A corpse colour, she'd always thought. But never would James's blood leave his flesh to that extent. He'd always be the Red Ox, with too many red corpuscles. Too much testosterone. At least Manda Jeffery had introduced the first *bandillera*. Black too, for the coward that he was.

'I'll ring again for your answer in fifteen minutes' time, at seven o'clock exactly,' she went on, aware of a hurting hunger beginning to bite her insides. 'This is no hoax, I can assure you, Miss Mitchell. I've never been more serious in my life.'

Elizabeth waited, knowing her patience would pay off. Hadn't Lance Hewitt taught her that one and a good deal more besides? Except how to deal with grief.

'It's none of your bloody business.'

'But it is. Very much, I'm afraid.'

'How do you know?'

'I saw you and him together at the Chandos Hotel last June. The eleventh, to be precise. He didn't just want a shoulder to cry on or a pretty knee to pat, did he?'

'You're not Manda Jeffery, are you?' the shaken voice accused.

'It doesn't matter who I am. This creature must be brought down to the depths where he belongs.' She nearly said "gutter" but didn't.

She pressed END and stuffed the phone back into her knickers, imagining what the recipient was thinking now. Would she have the courage to call her back? And what of herself?

After Jeffery's revenge and Guy Roper's imminent interview, James wouldn't be doing her too many favours. But she must stay controlled, vigilant, and do whatever she could to stop her body seizing up altogether.

She turned to the sagging bookshelves which filled the wall opposite the sideboard. On top lay a violin case with a stack of sheet music alongside. In those days there'd been music at the Manor House. The regular piano practice, mainly Mozart and Haydn. Before fiction and Sounds of Horror had ruled the roost. Her eyes began to glaze over because here were all Katherine's much-loved books. After her death she'd arranged them in chronological order, beginning with *Anne of Green Gables* and ending with *The Wind in the Willows*. The little boxed sets of Beatrix Potter and the Flower Fairies, of Roald Dahl and Raymond Briggs. Yet another part of her daughter's world which would inevitably end up in some job lot.

She then found herself wondering about Miss Mitchell and *her* life. Where she was now. Had a condom had been used? Because he'd never bothered with her, his wife, nor worried about any possible infection she might have picked up.

'I like to feel a woman properly,' he'd opined once during the usual minimal foreplay, when their honeymoon was just a memory. Before her fall. 'Anyhow, what's wrong with the pill?' Plenty, because her doctor had warned her of a thrombosis risk. Nevertheless, in all the years of unprotected sex in the missionary position, she'd never fallen pregnant again.

Ah, *Flower Fairies of the Autumn*. Her favourite.

She strained to grasp the box and having done so, pulled the book inside free from its companions. It seemed smaller somehow, just like houses revisited and Katherine had drawn some little pictures of her own inside the front cover. They were as fresh as if done yesterday. Just like the grief.

She then found page eighteen where the green and purple Dogwood fairy still stood and in a softer voice than the one she'd used for Miss Mitchell, began to read.

'I was a warrior,
When, long ago,

Arrows of Dogwood
Flew from the bow.
Passers-by, nowadays,
Go up and down,
Not one remembering
My old renown.
Yet when the Autumn sun
Colours the trees,
Should you come searching me,
Know me by these:
Bronze leaves and crimson leaves,
Soon to be shed:
Dark little berries
On stalks turning red.'

Only five minutes to go before her expected call back, and now here she was, with her other weapon snug under her foot. As ready as she could be, in the circumstances, for whatever might happen next.

Chapter Twenty-Four

Like those silver warriors who wait for the fire
Yet who fear not the fire of the burning cauldron,
I will mark my time, mark my time because
Mark is my name. My name...

Having told The Larches Hotel of her sudden change of plan, Lucy left for Rhayader with four unresolved problems hogging her mind. Firstly, she felt guilty at not having returned to the waterfall to check it out again. Secondly, was that same person she'd spotted at Gellionnen now following her? If so, why?

Thirdly, YOU'RE NEXT was still in her jeans pocket burning through to her skin like a disease which she didn't know how to treat. She'd thought of telling the police, but decided that was too knee-jerk and too early. Maybe it was a mistake, meant for someone else. Maybe some kind of joke. Hector could see it when she was ready. And that, she promised herself, would be sooner rather than later.

And finally, there'd been the weird offer of two grand to go public on her rape. Who on earth had that come from? That accentless voice, although definitely female, could have been anyone. However, as Lucy drove at speed back to Rhayader, she cast her mind back to that June evening in Covent Garden. Who had seen her slip away upstairs with the author? Most of Hellebore, if she wanted to be really paranoid. And wouldn't that explain the post-party, newly-cool Manda who'd kept her at more than arm's length? Was this to be her parting shot for whatever reason? Had Benn messed with her too?

But wasn't she forgetting something? Elizabeth Benn. Of course. How could she ever forget the weird way those sharp blue eyes had stared at her while her wine had lain untouched in her glass? Had she actually followed her and Benn to the lift? Listened in the corridor? If so, maybe this kind of revenge was all she could manage. Did the woman really hate him that much? Lucy had only skimmed the biography with gritted teeth, but it seemed to be one long mutual admiration society. A cloying kind of symbiosis...

Nevertheless, whoever had made her this offer, it wasn't enough. Nothing was. Things had changed since that recent afternoon when both Benns had visited the Hellebore office. She now had too much to lose. Not least her mother – the only parent she had left.

At seven o'clock on the dot, as the caller had promised, her mobile rang. This time she calmly said no and clicked END. Then, after organising the Choose to Refuse option of barring the unknown number, felt her lighter heart quicken as she approached Rhayader's Clock Tower.

Thursday. Six hours less.

She switched on the radio for company, only to hear more news of sheep culling on the Brecon Beacons. More tales of woe to match her mood. Like she'd told that recent caller, she'd had enough for one day. As she left the town behind, even the sun had vanished behind the forestry and in the losing light, a white vaporous veil was already rising from the Wye.

What a birthday, she mused. On the one hand she'd met Paul Furniss, a man she couldn't wait to see again; on the other there'd been that disturbing afternoon with the prospect of yet more misunderstandings and strained silences at Ravenstone Hall. However, she wasn't going to lose sight of why she'd left The Larches prematurely. She was going to give Wern Goch one last chance. 'I'd go for it,' was what Rhiannon George had said unequivocally. Hadn't she? Hadn't she..?

Lucy switched on her headlights and fog lamp because when her turning came it was practically invisible. The day had begun and ended in a shroud as if hidden forces were trying to disorientate her; turn her mind away from that one goal of discovering the truth, clearing the way for some chance of happiness. She gripped the steering wheel with renewed determination, because no way was she giving up now. She'd already come too far.

Ever since leaving Crossgates, she'd regularly checked her rearview mirror and been reassured, but now she suddenly drew in her breath. This time there definitely were vehicle lights behind her. She clicked off the radio. The DEFRA countdown to further slaughter wasn't what she needed to hear just then. Her first thought was that Bryn Evans or that little squirt Hughes were up to their tricks again, but if so, why were they keeping so far back, letting the lights fade and reappear at random?

She drove faster. Despite the mist she knew the lane well enough know, and with the following vehicle temporarily out of sight she swung the Rav up the track towards the Hall.

Bang.

All at once she was flung forwards, her belt taut across her chest as the car came to a halt. She could hear the clunk of metal against the front bumper and realised with numb fear that there was no way forward.

Jesus Christ...

She clicked central locking and for a moment gathered her racing thoughts. The first one being had either Mark or Hector deliberately blocked her way back? If so, this was a pretty drastic move, considering she'd still got all her gear in the bedroom there. Maybe the preacher was retaliating after Hector's visit. Or had something genuinely shed its load? What to do? Get out and investigate, or phone the Hall? This last option was surely the only safe one.

She picked up her mobile only to see ZONE UNAVAILABLE appear loud and clear on the little screen. What zone, for Christ's sake? This was Radnorshire not Venus. She slapped the thing against her thigh. It was useless. Time to get a new one when her money came through on Monday.

Damn Damn Damn...

She told herself not to panic, but to wait until that following vehicle had passed by as surely it would. There was nowhere else for it to go. Unless... Supposing it came up behind, trapping her? Then like the snaking mist, the possibility dawned on her that whoever had been snooping around the smallholding earlier on might have tailed her here. After all, the main roads had been busy. Plenty of big stuff to obscure anything with that in mind. But, if so, why choose her?

Why write YOU'RE NEXT? Next for *what* exactly?

She had no answers. Just a vision of the warring Morrigan lurking behind the mist somewhere, biding her time. But neither the salting slab nor the cauldron had been chucked out. She had done nothing wrong and yet, stuck in this silent world with fear instead of blood in her veins she felt singled out for blame. Half an hour passed too slowly and cold moisture began seeping into the car. She switched on the engine for some warmth and waited another five minutes, rubbing her cold fingers together.

She took a deep breath, opened her door and slipped out into the gloom.

'What the hell?' she gasped, because there, in front of her Rav lay a stack of old sheep hurdles. The lane to the Hall was totally blocked. She looked around, but there was nothing and no one. Just her thudding heart. The silence more than silence, just as near Gellionnen. It was as if she'd chanced upon the Underworld itself, half expecting to see Mark's dead, clever raven come wafting by...

Mark...

The bread knife. Those morsels. She shivered, in that instant wishing she was back in her comfortable room in The Larches. Suddenly she heard footsteps approaching, but from which direction she couldn't tell.

'Who's that?' she yelled.

'Me. Mark. What the *fuck's* going on here?'

She recognised his familiar figure as he began picking up the hurdles one by one and stacking them to one side along the hedge. 'Are you

OK?'

'I am, but the car may not. I'd call the police but my phone's playing up.'

She heard him take a sudden breath.

'We don't need to involve those cretins. Let's take a look.'

He squatted down and ran his hands over the radiator and front bumper, checking both lights. It was then she noticed the blue shirt under his usual old leather jacket. The same colour as those bits from the chimney.

'Fucking Evans,' he said. 'I need to sort him out once and for all.' He turned to her. 'Just some minor scratches as far as I can tell,' he straightened, smiling his relief. His teeth impossibly white against his skin. 'You were lucky.'

'I know, but tell me,' she began, still wary, still curious as to where that other mysterious car had gone. 'Is this the only turning off the lane round here?'

'Why do you want to know that?'

'Just curious.'

However, he didn't seem convinced.

'What's happened?'

'Nothing.'

'Well, there *is* an opening for the baler to access our land. It's pretty overgrown now, mind. You wouldn't notice it.'

I'm not thinking about me...

'I sometimes cut through there to the Hall,' he elaborated, drawing closer towards her. His warmth palpable. Equally the faint smell of spirits and aftershave as his eyes fixed on hers. Then he made his move and before she could resist, had enclosed her in his arms.

'You don't honestly believe what my dad said this morning, do you?' The question burned on the skin of her neck. 'Please say you don't. Please. He does stuff like that all the time. Goes way over the top. Says things he doesn't mean...'

'We all do that, but I'm just an outsider here, and...' she hesitated, aware of that strong primal rhythm of his heart on hers. 'I'm only trying to find out the truth.'

'And I'm telling it.'

'Only the part you *want* me to hear. Something's missing. I know it. And what about this junk dumped here? The feeling that I'm being followed everywhere.' She felt anger rising despite Mark's mouth pressed on her hair. 'I'd come back tonight thinking yes. Let's get on with it. I'm not going to find anywhere with three acres for the price. And what happens? All this.'

She could have told him what she'd found in his room, her encounter with the dishy mineralogist, her hour at Gellionnen, but not here. Not now. His heart was one thing, his fragility another.

'It'll be alright. I promise, and you've got to believe me.' his breath hot against her skin. 'I've been worried about you all bloody day. We both have. I couldn't bear it if you left here now. I'd burn the place down. I wouldn't care. Can't you see, Lucy Mitchell,' before his lips found her mouth. 'I love you. I've been dying to tell you that all day.'

Her resistance began to ebb away. Her body pressed closer to his like an iron filing to a magnet.

'Even though I kicked your ankle?' she murmured.

'I deserved it. I'm sorry. Shouldn't have had a go at you like that.'

'And I shouldn't have been nosing around.'

'I love your nose. In fact, every little bit of you.'

His kisses became rough, urgent, as if all his loss, his unhappiness had suddenly found release. But this huge need, this devouring power wasn't enough to drive Paul Furniss from her mind and, if she closed her eyes, could imagine it was his hands gripping her waist, moving down over her hips... And there were still four days to go.

The reek of gloss paint eked out into the misty evening from the Hall's open front door. Hector Jones smiled down at them both from his step ladder. She wondered if her mouth looked bruised, if he could tell what they'd been doing, but his gaze was one of simple benevolence. The same as Jon's father whenever she'd turned up at the house in Stanmore.

No walking stick, she noticed. No unsteadiness. Even the nasty bruise seemed less obvious now. Was this the same man she'd first met a week ago? she thought, dropping her bags by the stairs. Had that bitter and terrible statement he'd uttered about his son been a kind of exorcism? It certainly looked like it.

'My penance,' he said. 'For spoiling your birthday.'

'It's alright,' as she forced a smile. 'Families.'

'I don't know why I said what I did,' he set his brush down across the top of his paint tin. 'I suppose it's years of heartache. Trying to cope. I wouldn't wish this on anyone...'

'I understand. Really.' She detected a tremble in his bottom lip, a slight glazing-over of his eyes. 'By the way, this yellow you've chosen is my favourite colour. It reminds me of sunflowers.'

'Not many of those round here, I'm afraid,' Hector resumed his hearty brushstrokes. 'Still, you never know. You might fancy growing a few.'

'I might indeed.' She caught Mark looking at her with those awesome eyes, and she felt her neck begin to colour. So far he'd not mentioned the dumped hurdles. They were clearly his business not Hector's, she thought, noticing several rust stains scored against his blue shirted chest. Just then her eyelids felt leaden. Her head began to ache. The day had been too long already.

She parked herself on the bottom stair, her eyes following his painting. It was a way of keeping awake. Then she realised she'd not gone to New Radnor again, as originally planned.

'Look, if you can't make it over to the waterfall on Monday, I'll get the police to take a look,' she said suddenly.

Hector wobbled on his step and gripped the picture rail above to steady himself.

'I never break my promises,' he replied in such a strange way that she glanced at Mark who merely shrugged and raised his eyebrows.

'Come on,' he said. 'There's a pizza waiting for us.'

'And a bottle of St. Emilion,' added Hector, working skilfully around the umbrella stand.

'You shouldn't have,' she said.

'We wanted to. Reckon it's just about ready.'

Mark led the way into the kitchen and when the door was closed behind them whispered, 'by the way, I'll get the exact match for those scratches on your car. No one'll notice any different once I've sprayed them over.'

'Thanks.'

'The old man doesn't need to know anything, okay? I'm sorting this one.'

'Fine.'

She slumped down on the most solid looking chair, every bone in her body giving up the ghost. She noticed the lilies had opened even more since the morning but their sickly funereal smell made her push the vase further away to the far side of the table. Her cards were also still there, arranged to form a frieze of colour on the white formica. In this setting, Anna's seemed too large, too loud next to the raven drawing, so she moved it behind Hector's.

'And I meant what I said out there just now.' Mark opened the red wine, filled her glass and brought over another for himself.

'You barely know me. I might be a raving psychopath whose been in the slammer. I might be gay, for God's sake.'

'Shh.' He planted a kiss on her cheek. 'I know you, and so does Cerridwen. She sends you warmest greetings.' He clicked his glass against hers.

'Not the Morrigan, then?'

'Hell, no.'

'Well, that's alright then.'

Next, having missed her sarcasm, he announced his intention to take her to Elan tomorrow morning. There were places to go, people to see. Besides, he needed a witness. He drained his glass in one go, refilled it and held it aloft. 'Here's to success.'

But she felt piqued. And why? Because Paul had also chosen that very same beauty spot. It was going to be *their* special place, not somewhere to have a blistering fight, and for one reckless moment she was tempted to say so. Instead of raising her glass too, she picked at her pizza. 'But your father's already been there, done that, and got a whacking great bruise and a bad leg.' She said. 'Besides, surely Evans and Hughes won't be there again. There's Chapel for a start. He's on twice a day, according to his mother.'

His face looked as if a sudden dark cloud had crossed it. Then he smiled, swiftly resuming his role as host.

'You'll see,' he refilled her glass until she covered it with her hand. 'All will be revealed.'

'I can't wait.'

Her eyes felt heavy. Her strict temperance upbringing had a lot to answer for, because where drink was concerned she was poles apart from Anna who was a veritable sponge. Probably born with the stuff in her veins, she'd often marvelled during their nights out together in London. Now, after a total of five glasses that day she felt sleepy and relaxed to the point of subtle inebriation. Mark settled next to her, his long jeans-clad thigh almost touching hers. On Thursday, she told herself, it would be Paul's. Then her gaze strayed to his left hand, where a small pitted blemish she'd not noticed before, lay between his second and third fingers. That compass stabbing must have caused a painful injury for a young lad, she mused and this prompted her to ask as casually as possible, if he'd known Rhiannon George at the Grammar School.

Mark smiled again, this time to himself, but it seemed forced. For her benefit perhaps?

'Yeah. Skinny little thing,' he said. 'She'd do anything for a packet of M&M's, that one. And I mean anything. How come you've heard of her?'

'We collided in a shop in Llandrindod…'

'What were you doing there? His tone caught her off guard and she had to think quickly. Think up another lie, she told herself, but he beat her to it. 'Oh shit. Sorry,' he slapped a hand against his forehead. 'I didn't mean to sound like an Inquisitor. It's just that I'd planned to take you lunch at the Metropole today.'

The awkward pause which followed was an opportunity for her to back off. But no. There were decisions to make. Friday was the finishing line.

'We could still do that sometime. Thanks. That's really sweet of you.' She reached out and touched his other hand. 'Anyway, back to Ms George. She had two little boys with her.'

'Sure there were only two?' He took another drink and Lucy went on.

'We got chatting as one does…'

'What about? Tell me.'

'Mainly about my plans for here…'

'Mainly?' Mark set down his glass, his dark eyes seeming to turn even darker.

'OK, she mentioned Richard. And the fact she'd been mad about him. She seemed scared too. Apparently some guy had just turned up her at the farm asking to see the kids for some reason, and was still hanging around.'

Mark's facial muscles had frozen. But why? What was Rhiannon George to him? According to her, she'd barely known him. He pushed back his chair and got up to leave. Moments later she heard him exchange a few words with his father, then angry boots on the stairs and a door closing.

Through the open doorway she saw Hector climb down his ladder and dunk his brush in a jam jar of turps. He too seemed pre-occupied and went straight into his study while she busied herself by the sink wishing now that she'd told Mark the truth about her eventful afternoon. About the note left on her windscreen, and how fearful Rhiannon George had seemed.

While she dried the plates and glasses, she puzzled yet again about this mysterious brother who, if Rhiannon was to be believed, had not only some pretty odd hang-ups, but also exerted a powerful effect upon Mark and his father. A brother who, by his continued absence, seemed to becoming more significant in the scheme of things. As long as lips remained sealed on the matter of his whereabouts, so would her imagination attempt to fill the silence.

She reached the landing and chose to shower and wash her hair then rather than in the morning when both men would be around. Hector had plans for a second bathroom to be plumbed in, while Wern Goch was being connected to the mains but in the meantime, during that uneasy stillness, there was no alternative.

She carried her things into the bathroom and, as usual, because the lock no longer worked, shoved the cork-topped stool against the door. This wasn't the first time that her fingers had partially opened the lid whilst moving it, but now she was tempted to peep inside at the unopened First Aid kits, the rolls of bandages and lint, some clearly used, whose faint smell of ether reminded her with a shudder that in days gone by corpses had once been embalmed at the Hall. Made beautiful and acceptable to view in death. But what about the woman who now lay under a makeshift heap by the wall? Had anyone troubled to do the same for her? It seemed unlikely.

She knelt down on the scarred linoleum to take a closer look. There were scissors of every shape and size – all rusted to some degree – and thermometers and then to her surprise, a strange forceps-like instrument with IGM engraved on one of its handles.

Could the I be for Irmgard and the M be for Muller? And if so, what did G represent?

That already faintly remembered surname was now even more familiar, but she still couldn't place where she'd come across it before.

Damn. This forgetfulness, the losing of the marbles, was getting worse. Was some weird gas being driven off by the marsh, or were even the ravens themselves causing it? That wasn't such a fanciful idea because in *Magical Tales* there *was* a story about the beautiful dark-haired Rhiannon and her birds who could lull men to sleep and even wake the dead.

However, she did recall Anna going on about the strange bathroom habits of one of her German authors during the last Frankfurt bookfair. She briefly glanced over at the loo with its inner shelf partly jutting out over the water, then, having returned the tongs to their original place, rummaged further beneath the bandages. Why was she doing this instead of cleaning herself up? She didn't know, but something was driving her on. Something she knew was waiting to be found.

Deeper now, beneath clumps of pink and white cotton wool, which further down grew more discloured, until right at the very bottom, where rust had seemingly liquefied into a thin pool, where nothing had been disturbed for years, she found a small plastic box labelled STRETCH FABRIC PLASTERS.

She peered inside and held her breath. No plasters. Instead, a rolled-up strip of blue cotton, the same as had come from the chimney. It was so heavily spattered with brownish blood that little of the original colour remained and she asked herself what kind of garment it might have come from. A shirt? Pyjamas, even? Then, with a judder she thought of Mark's blue shirt he was wearing now. Just a coincidence, surely? Because like the identical piece from the chimney, this remnant looked old. Fourteen years perhaps? And if so, whose? And why left to rot here? With trembling fingertips she picked up the plastic casing then sniffed its contents. A less putrid version of what she'd found in the Spar bags. Almost like a sweet and sour sauce, making her recent supper start to protest, triggering a moment's indecision.

However, that moment soon passed, because she realised that this discovery was somehow hugely significant, and should be kept not only sealed and secure, but secret. Just like what she'd found in Mark's room.

She stood up and pressed her ear to the door. There were no creaking boards on the landing outside, no sound anything, in fact, so she used her clean dry shower cap from The Larches Hotel to wrap up her find as carefully as if it was the Kohinoor diamond.

She even kept her eye on it while the warm Nocturne-scented water caressed her skin, easing away the day and the strange mix of memories. She thought of strong, urgent Mark. That kiss and the rest, which until that morning would have been all that she'd needed. However, as she later slipped her nightdress over her still-damp head she calculated that there were sixty-five hours to live through before her next meeting with Paul, and another one or two after that at the most before he'd be going one step further than the sawyer and peeling her clothes from her body...

Chapter Twenty-Five

From this hour, this ignominy that you have inflicted upon me will rebound to the shame of each one of you. When a time of oppression falls upon you, each one of you who dwells in this kingdom will be overcome with weakness, as the weakness of a woman in childbirth, and this will remain upon you for as long as you draw breath...
Anon (with apologies to the goddess, Macha)

The reek of gloss paint still filled the Hall as Lucy took her clothes for washing into the morgue-like scullery where the tiny square window revealed yet another misty morning. Neither Hector nor Mark seemed to be around and, as she took a gulp from the first caffeine shot of the day then loaded up the ancient Zanussi, she hoped that his plan for revenge at Elan had merely been a whim and soon forgotten.

The shifting sands she'd been walking on for over a week now were still shifting this way and that, with every hour seeming to deliver some new secret, some unforeseen event. But she'd made up her mind despite everything, it was time to dig in. To drive her own stake into the heart of indecision and get the little house and its land ready as soon as possible, so her own plans could take precedence. This wasn't selfish as no doubt her former nuns would be saying. It was survival.

She'd already worked out a typical day for herself at Wern Goch. Mornings spent out of doors or in the barn, and afternoons working on Anna's manuscripts. What could be more perfect? she asked herself watching her denim jacket and other stuff nudging around in the foam behind the glass. Except that now there was an added bonus. Evenings out with Paul, of course. Discreetly, however, at first, to spare Mark's feelings. But then, evenings could become nights with weekends away and eventually, who knows? Wern Goch might eventually become home to two not one.

'You ready?' came a voice from the kitchen. Lucy spun round to see Mark checking through his wallet. He then looked up at her expectantly.

'What, now?' she said, mentally rustling up an excuse not to go.

'Yeah. Could take a while with this mist hanging around.'

'Look, I've got so much to organise. I need a phonecard and there's still the plant hire the pipes, the...'

'It's Sunday, remember?' he interjected. 'This is Wales.'

Damn.

She had no answer for that. She'd literally forgotten which day of the week it was and, in that moment of hesitation, Mark moved closer and took her hand.

'Come on,' he urged. 'It'll be perfect over there. Besides, we can sort things out once and for all. This is for you and me, don't forget.'

She glanced back at the washing machine and her familiar clothes inside it as if she was about to leave some kind of mooring. A rare normality growing yet more rare by the minute.

'Off out then?' quizzed Hector from the top of the stairs. His bulky old dressing gown made him look like Rodin's statue of Balzac. 'You take care in that mist.'

'Will do.'

'What about those hurdles?' she whispered as her hand closed round that shower cap package in her fleece pocket.

'Sssh.' Mark closed the front door behind her and blinked as if to see better. 'I got up early and dumped them back where they belong. Carreglas Farm.'

'Any sign of the preacher?' she asked.

'What do *you* think?' Then he stopped short and pulled her back towards the Hall steps.

'Something's wrong. I can feel it.'

She felt his hand tense in hers, just like those two little kids' had done yesterday. He led her under the beech tree which loomed like some weird spectral shape in front of him and then around to the side wall where he suddenly let go of her hand to kneel down by a body's length of red-brown soil which she'd never noticed before. A smaller more freshly made mound lay like a pimple at its far end.

'Is this a grave?' she dared to ask, dreading the answer.

'My mam's. And Rhaca's.' He leant forwards then steadied himself. 'Looks like the bastards have been here too,' signalling for her to see more closely what he'd found. A strange hole had been scooped out three quarters of the way down the grave and in it nestled a square of white card, rumpled by the damp. She felt the mist's chill sneaking under her fleece as she thought of the two words in her wallet. Also on white card. And here was more. WHORE.

'My God,' she shivered. 'Why do something like that?' Then she realised that the hole had been specially created over where her sex would be.

'Because they're freaks. That's why.' He sprang up and tore towards the Hall leaving her marooned in a rising sea of apprehension. She stared at this crude memorial to a much-missed mother. It was horrible. At least her father hadn't been left to moulder like this. And why no proper headstone nor even a name with dates? Was it possible that in this family's eyes she didn't deserve one? Lucy recalled Rhiannon George's remark about Marilyn Monroe. Clearly Sonia Jones had loved life. Loved company and attention, but what kind, she wondered, for the Deacon preacher to label her a whore? Suddenly raised voices came from the Hall steps.

'What the hell did you say to them to make them do this?' Mark yelled at his father. 'You cloth-head.'

'Do what?'

'Come and see for yourself.'

Soon Hector still wearing his dressing gown over his pyjamas, was examining the evidence for himself. When he looked up, she saw how his face had whitened around his bruise. How his paint-spattered hands trembled as he held the piece of card.

'I swear to God, son, I just warned them off normal like. Told them to back off. That Miss Mitchell was entitled to peace and privacy.'

Peace and privacy? The last time she'd known that was in her cosy old bedroom looking out over the vegetable garden and, instead of finishing homework, dreaming of that magical Queen of the Faeries on her white horse.

'So, nothing about their private lives eh?' Mark sneered. 'Everyone round here knows you can't hack gays.'

Hector bristled.

'What d'you take me for?'

'Sometimes I don't bloody know. But you don't get knocked about like that for asking the bloody time.'

'It could be a fox,' she suggested, trying to diffuse the situation. But neither men responded.

'Just fill in the hole, son,' Hector said finally. 'And I'll keep hold of this.' He held the piece of card delicately between his thumb and forefinger. 'It was obviously put there during the night sometime. There's at least six hours' damp on it.'

He was on his way back to the Hall when she caught up with him.

'This was on my windscreen yesterday and to me they look similar.'

Both men fixed on her as she extracted the torn fragment from her wallet inside her bag, and turned it over to show the fine blue lines and the letters ARD. 'I bet they match,' she said.

Hector and Mark exchanged a troubled glance then held the two halves together to make the word POSTCARD.

'By Christ. You're right.'

She then revealed the other side and heard both men gasp.

'You're next,' whispered Mark. 'Shit. Where was your car at the time?'

Still unable to mention her Crossgates trip, she simply said, 'Llandrindod town centre. I'd just done some shopping there. I don't understand. Why me, for God's sake? Why her?' indicating the grave.

'Like I said,' Mark stroked her arm and she flinched. 'Freaks.'

Hector squinted at the block capitals and it seemed a look of despair darkened his whole face. 'Can I keep this as well? Tomorrow's going to be my busy day.'

She nodded glad to be rid of it.

'If these *have* come from Evans or Hughes, is there some way we could check their handwriting?'

Father and son exchanged a quick glance.

'First things first, eh?' Hector suggested. 'Was anyone else parked up near you? Anything odd you might have noticed?'

'No.' She gripped the end of the balustrade by the steps. She felt her eyes begin to fill up. She was so bloody tired – no, exhausted more like – by the ups and downs of the past week which only that morning while forcing herself out of bed, had seemed like forever.

'I don't think you're telling us everything,' Hector said with surprising gentleness, 'and we need to know, believe me.'

'OK,' she caught Mark's eye and he nodded encouragement. 'We'd better sit down somewhere. Because this'll take more than a few minutes.'

'For a start, I can't believe you actually went to Rhiannon George's place. And that you believed anything she said. I mean, at school, most kids gave her a wide berth. Except the lads who wanted a quick grope, that is.'

Lucy winced at Mark's harsh appraisal of a woman she'd grown to like, as he drove his van away from the Hall twenty minutes later, with less care than usual. Several times her seatbelt locked across her chest where anger was beginning to ferment.

'I saw someone there too, remember?' she countered. 'Like I've just told you both, it was pretty nervewracking. I'm sure if Rhiannon hadn't got away, she and her boys would have been in some kind of danger.'

Suddenly she spotted an animal hovering by the verge in front of them.

'Evans's dog,' Mark announced. 'Shall we make things quits?'

'What do you mean?' She looked at him in horror.

'Dog jam. Nice little gift for him.'

'Ugh. That's so sick.'

'Only joking.'

But Mark's sudden callousness had unnerved her all the same.

He slowed down to let the collie cross the lane. She watched it lope away and creep under the hedge.

'We beg to differ on the Rhiannon George business, I'm afraid,' he went on. 'More to the point, she could have nicked your credit cards, the lot. Who'd have helped you then?' He turned to her, his eyes dark, demanding an answer. 'And secondly, Christ, I just don't believe you'd pick up a total stranger and agree to see him again. I mean, is that sane?'

'*You* were a stranger to me this time last week, OK?' Her voice rose more than she'd have liked and she nearly added, *you still are.* 'Anyway, I'm thirty now and quite able to make up my own mind, thanks very much. Besides,' she added, glancing at his strong intense profile, 'it's hardly been a barrel of laughs here for the past eight days. I'm used to having a bit of fun occasionally. Letting my hair down.'

She knew that would hurt, just like her dig at Jon during his last phone call, but at the moment, charity wasn't very high on her agenda and the tense silence which followed, was almost a welcome relief. 'Anyhow,' she went on as the town was left behind, 'never mind that I've had a threat, or whatever it is. That doesn't seem to matter to anybody. Or that some car or other was tailing me.'

'That's unfair and you know it. Why are we here then? For a bloody picnic?' Mark steered the van towards signs for Elan Village and a notice that the Bog Snorkelling Championships near Llanwrtyd Wells had been cancelled due to foot-and-mouth. Anna would have laughed her head off at that, she thought. But not in this van. Not in this atmosphere.

He then drove past a cluster of quaint houses where, to her surprise, she noticed that the window surrounds and gable details were identical that of Wern Goch. And seeing these dwellings so well restored and lived in gave her some hope. If these people could do it, so could she. Having left the Elan River's Suspension bridge glinting in the clearing mist with the sunlight brightening the tops of the surrounding hills, Mark pulled into the visitors' car park and hauled up the handbrake.

'Look, I'm sorry,' she turned to him. 'There's been so much happening that's nothing to do with getting Wern Goch habitable. It's as if somehow I'm being drawn into an extra complicated Celtic Knot, with no bloody way out.'

'And all *I*'m saying is that it's dodgy to go out with some guy you barely know. You could be in trouble. I can feel it here, in my heart.' He banged his chest. 'It's crazy.'

'What about me here then?' She looked around at the chiffon blue water and the partly forested bare-crowned hills. 'There's not a soul around.'

'There's yours and mine,' he said, locking up the van. 'And Rhaca's.'

He cast his eyes upwards to the perfect blue, then slipped his arm around her waist as they made for the framed tourist map positioned on the visitor centre's wall. This showed a selection of walks available for the tourist, all of varying degrees of difficulty.

'So, which one are we doing?'

'Just trust me, okay?'

Another shiver. Another twinge of panic. This was Crossgates all over again. Utterly deserted. No cars, nothing. Just the occasional mewing cry of a buzzard somewhere circling over its prey. If she just shut her eyes she could be back in time, before the drowning of the valleys for Birmingham's water supply. Before the dams when Shelley and young Harriet had Nantgwllt Mansion to themselves…

Yes, she'd looked all this up before the sixth form trip and now twelve years later, here she was again, not with an exuberant group of seventeen-year-olds but a man who still remained a mystery…

'I'm not sure about this,' she said, pulling away from him, remembering with a jolt that her phone was still out of action should she need it.

'It's our only chance. Like I said, there are people we need to see. Evans and Hughes included.'

'The Dagdans, right?'

'Sure. About two miles from here. Above the Claerwen reservoir. There's an oak grove that's been used for ages.'

'Your father said he'd been to Caban Coch.'

She sensed Mark stalling.

'They like to keep moving. With the new moon it'll be Claerwen, I'm telling you.'

'What for?' She eyed the quickest way to exit if necessary.

'The Morrigan demand sacrifice.'

She felt her own blood run cold.

'What kind of sacrifice?'

'You'll find out. Come on, let's go.'

'No. I can't.' She could visualise her father's face as if he was right next to her. As if he'd just stepped out from that Llanberis photograph and was holding her back. That smile so imprinted on her mind now faded. He was clearly warning her not to go.

'Why was there no mention of these so-called Dagdans when I last came here with my school?' she queried.

Mark snorted.

'Tourism's big moolah in these parts. Nothing must gobble up this whopping great golden egg. Then or now.'

However, she wasn't convinced. Where *were* the tourists for a start? This was a Sunday morning in late summer and it was just them and the birds. She held her ground.

'Look, I've seen enough crackpots and gruesome stuff to last me a lifetime. And another thing,' she paused to take a deep breath, ready to run if need be. 'Why are you hiding those freaky bits in that black shoe of yours?'

An imperceptible tension tightened his lips.

'You had no business being in that room. It's private stuff there, okay?'

'Tell me.'

'I can't.'

She was now aware of a lone cyclist approaching from the direction of the Suspension bridge and kept the welcome figure in her sights. 'You and your father know all about *me*. I thought trust was a two-way process.'

'This is different.'

'Why? Think of my situation. I'm due to exchange contracts next Friday. Four days to find out the truth.'

Mark hesitated. His eyes closed against the sun.

'Whoever butchered my mother, not only slit her throat, but...'

'Go on, please...'

Lucy forgot to close her mouth as he told her the rest.

'And I'll give you two guesses what was used for the cooking.'

The cauldron. Oh, Jesus.

'So 'Simnai' Williams was right?' She could barely speak.

'Cerridwen, the mother goddess has been defiled. That cauldron was hers.'

'My God.'

There was no breakfast to come up but something else was forcing its way back into Lucy's throat. She ran back to lean against the van's warm side. So, *that's* what he'd kept in that special place. A sick souvenir. But why mustn't anyone know about this or the burnt blue cloth found up the chimney? And what about the blood-stained strip now wrapped up safe inside her pocket?

She could see it all clearly now. It was total bollocks about him being frightened of someone else. Oh yes, he was frightened alright. About being found out. And hadn't Hector let all that slip only yesterday? Almost been relieved to, she thought, edging away from the man who was trying to stop her leaving. She recalled the way he'd held the bread knife. Threatened his father.

Whatever James Benn had done to her was nothing to this unfolding scenario. She had to get out. To get away, or she really would be next.

Chapter Twenty-Six

I have been an axe in the hand,
A pin in a pair of tongs,
I have been dead, I have been alive
Only to keep what is mine.
The kingdom of Blood.
And now She of the Light
Has turned thief of the night,
Like the dark side of the moon.
Anon

Lucy sprinted away from the visitor centre and Mark's protesting shouts, aware of the cyclist who was thankfully female, chaining her bike to a nearby post. But suddenly nausea overcame her and her stomach lurched so hard she crouched down in a patch of high weeds by the roadside and let her body take over.

Afterwards, still feeling queasy, she stood up and looked around. His van was still there but Mark had vanished.

'Are you alright?' asked the cyclist in a very English voice who, upon closer inspection proved to be a gaunt-faced, elderly lady dressed in cord breeches and an old hacking jacket. 'Can I get you anything?'

'I'm fine now, thanks,' she gave her a weak smile as she found the last tissue in her bag and used it to wipe her mouth. 'Not very nice for you to see that. Sorry.'

'Don't worry my dear. My three daughters were always car sick. Now then,' the cyclist re-secured her headscarf under her chin, 'did that young man upset you? I saw you two together just now…'

'He was expecting me to go into the wilds to some oak grove round here to meet the Dagdans, and I'm just not up for it, after what I've heard about them.' She replied, realising how naff that must have sounded. But, if she told her what Mark had just revealed about his mother, the woman might also need first aid. Her companion's sparse eyebrows rose in surprise.

'My my. I've been coming to this special place for years since my husband died, but I can tell you for a start there are no oak groves as such, and that cult hasn't been in the valleys here since, oh, let me see now…' she frowned in concentration, 'the mid-seventies.'

'*Mid-seventies?* Are you quite sure?'

'Of course I'm sure.'

Lucy felt sick again. Suddenly she didn't want this sympathetic stranger to leave her on her own. She was no longer an adult who'd lived an independent life in London with a job and a flat, but a kid again. A kid who needed to be told that she was safe and that everything was going to be alright. She hoped her desperation wasn't too obvious.

'I'm afraid whoever that young man is, he's wrong. This Elan Valley's my second home, especially now my family's grown up and gone. It's heaven on earth to me, and do you think I'd be coming here on my own otherwise? No.' She cast her watery eyes over the surrounding area, which to Lucy just then could have come straight out of *Magical Tales*. 'Admittedly it was different in those days before the army drove them out,' she went on. 'Even the villagers here were wary of straying too far from their homes. Naturally everyone breathed a sigh of relief once they'd gone.'

'Where?' she asked, trying to make sense of everything she'd heard so far.

'Ireland. Right out west, thank goodness. I expect it all fizzled out as the years went by. There's been no mention of them in this region since then and I do make it my business to keep up with all the local news...'

'So why's my friend back there so adamant that they're still around?'

'Is he local?'

'Lives just a few miles away.' She stopped short of saying Ravenstone.

'Then I really don't know. Maybe he just likes making things up. Lots of people do. My eldest especially.' She pushed back her jacket cuff and checked her watch. Lucy saw how the day was slipping away.

'Look,' she said, relieved to see a red hatchback stop in the car park and a normal-looking family of four emerging. 'I need to get back into town. Are there any buses anywhere on a Sunday?'

Again the veteran cyclist consulted her watch.

'If you're nippy, there's the one for Newbridge. It comes to Lower Llanfadog at midday. You seem young and fit enough to make it easily.' She smiled, and Lucy, having thanked her, felt better already.

She'd previously noticed that sign just before the Elan Village, and, with the sun on her face, power-walked along the B4358 until the bus stop with, thankfully, two other people waiting came into view.

So, if this seemingly trustworthy woman was to be believed, Hector had lied to her, Mark had lied. Not once, with a slip of the tongue, a careless remark, but a sustained falsehood because in her opinion Bryn Evans and Sion Hughes were simply peeved locals with a sad agenda. No more Dagdans then, she was Good Queen Bess. But why this collusion between father and son? And was it possible, given this scenario, that Hector had injured himself? If so, who was he protecting over his wife's murder? For that's what it looked like now. And, she asked herself, for how much longer?

Questions spun round in Lucy's mind, just like her clothes had done in that front-loader downstairs. She was now back in her bedroom at the Hall, deciding on her next move, with the door securely locked. Normally, she'd have done a few simple yoga exercises to sort herself out. To clear her head. They'd been a godsend at Uni just before exams, but here wasn't Warwick and it wasn't a simple exam which was vexing her.

The bus from Lower Lanfadog had broken down outside Rhayader and the expensive taxi back from town had crawled along at 20 mph; yet another drain on her depleted mental and physical resources.

Hector had been trimming a hedge with a noisy hedgecutter when she'd finally returned. Not the best time to challenge him about his Druids theory. But when would be? And was it finally time to admit defeat and step off the rollercoaster?

She stared at her bedroom door too wound up, too hungry to think straight. For a start, angry Mark might have a key to her room. Might just push his way in, or even try the window, still fractionally open at the top. She leapt from the bed and jammed it shut, rattling the old panes. The catch didn't quite connect.

Dammit.

She was going mad. Unable to now work anything out logically. And had this place and its people so disorientated her that even if contracts were exchanged on Friday and Anna happened to send her a promised manuscript, would she be able to do any decent editing? She doubted it very much. But there was Barbara Mitchell, three hundred miles away, believing everything was going so well. There was also her dead father who'd never had this chance to live a different life, yet had passed his one big dream on to her. How could she let them both down after so short a while? How could she throw it all away?

She peered out through the curtains at the view beyond. Not the best by any means, where Wern Goch's bank had steepened to form a high wall topped by rough grass and a few scrubby trees. Thus all lower rooms at the back of the Hall were denied their natural light, and seemed from the inside almost subterranean. Part of an Underworld she could see and smell. A repository of lies and secrets, of a tragedy which had eked into her very soul.

However, to muse on this eyesore from her vantage point at least provided a breathing space, enabling her to plan a logical structured Truth Strategy. This would start first thing tomorrow with an unannounced visit to her solicitor, followed by at least two more hopefully useful outings.

Two p.m., and still no sighting of Mark. After a speedy wash and having put on her fleece again, Lucy tried her phone again. It was working. She parked herself halfway up the stairs to keep her eye on the front door, should either Mark or Hector return, then dialled Anna's number.

'Hey, Luce! Happy birthday for yesterday. Did you get my card? I wasn't sure you'd get it in time.'

Lucy smiled just to hear her.

'It's got pride of place,' she lied. 'Thanks.'

'How's it all going, anyway? Are you growing anything yet?'

'Give me a chance. This is a starting from scratch project. What isn't there to do...'

'You sound a bit down. Shall I come over? Bring an extra shovel and so on?'

'It's fine thanks. Crunch time on Friday, mind. Exchange of contracts. The day of no return.'

'What a weird thing to say. It's not as if you're going to the bloody Scrubs. You're in the most enviable part of the UK, for God's sake, with a new life just round the corner, waiting to grab you by the throat...'

A brief pause followed in which Lucy noticed a black shadow of birds pass by the glass panel above the door.

'I'm not arguing with that, it's just that sometimes I lose my nerve about stupid things I should ignore. Things which are probably all fantasy anyhow. I'm sure everything'll be alright,' she forced her tone to brighten and predictably, Anna took up the slack.

'Look, Nick stuck his neck out to get this place of ours two years ago. Massive mortgage, crusty old neighbours whom he had to schmooze to get garage plans through, you name it... But would he swap it now? No chance. And that's what you'll be saying in a few months' time. Trust me.'

'You're right. You always are.'

'Sorry to talk shop, but I see Benn's made the longlist again.'

The sudden mention of that name made Lucy start. She let her friend go on.

'His wife hates him, you know. Someone told me that the other day. Apparently, she had a daughter by her first marriage. Poor kid died of leukaemia and even though she'd lived with them, Benn never even went to the funeral. Off on some tour somewhere. Can you believe it?'

'Nothing would surprise me about him,' said a tense Lucy, expecting Mark at any moment. 'But he's got Hellebore licking out of his hand, that's for sure. It used to make me sick.'

'For how much longer if stuff like that gets out?'

Lucy bit her lip, poised to tell her closely guarded secret and about the phone calls, but not yet. This was neither the time nor the place.

'I'd better get the old washing sorted,' she said instead. 'It's been brilliant to hear you.'

'Same here, and don't forget, hang on in there. It'll all come right.'

'I will.'

Afterwards, she headed for the scullery where Hector had obviously taken her damp clothes out of the machine and left them in a tidy pile by the sink. Ten out of ten for trying, she thought cynically as she found a peg bag embroidered with MAM on the front and then went outside to the rusty wire washing line in the back yard. All in shadow. She shivered, realising then that in just over one week, she'd managed to step not into any light but a deeper and, it would seem, yet more perilous darkness.

While she wiped over the line and pegged out the garments it was Mark's morning story which soon killed off Anna's encouraging words. That black cauldron now lurked in her mind's eye like a giant and ever-present mote.

'You back then?' Hector came through the front door just as she was about to sneak off to Wern Goch to examine the vessel. Bits of hedge lay in his hair and the sun had turned his cheeks pink. 'Where's my boy?'

'We had a row if you must know.'

Hector responded by prising the lid off a paint tin and pouring some of its custard-coloured contents into an old baking tray. He then picked up a clean roller, mounted the step ladder and started on the ceiling over the door, effectively blocking her exit without any excuse or apology. She watched, fighting back memories of her dad doing exactly the same in her bedroom just before she'd left for Warwick – that almost milky smell, the crackly sound of the roller's sponge against plaster – she realised he wanted to talk. But then, so did she.

'About what you said earlier,' he began, beating her to it, dipping the roller once more into the creamy goo. 'This fellow you've just met...'

The question threw her. She'd missed her moment and her planned challenge about the Dagdan theory was vanishing like the mist.

'Yes?'

'Mark's jealous, you know that? It's really upset him.'

'I understand, but, much as I like him...'

'So, you do *like* him at least?'

She hesitated.

'Of course I do. Why shouldn't I? He's been really helpful about

Wern Goch, he saved my life out in the field there, but, as I was about to say, I'm not *married* to him. He's not my husband. We're not even going out together.'

But there *had* been that kiss. The slow burn...

'He's had a lot of hurt. You do understand that, don't you?'

'So have I,' she retorted. 'I had a crap job – knives in the back all day every day – a Booker longlisted author who...'

Shit.

She saw Hector lay his roller in the tray and lower his head to look at her.

'Go on. An author who?' He waited as she cupped her head in her hands. What the hell was she doing? she asked herself. Here was someone who could lie as easily as unpeeling a banana and yet... And yet... There'd been the friendly car salesman in Balham whom she'd told about Jon. Now here was another shoulder to cry on, but this time, old enough to be her father. Not Anna or her mother, someone ready to listen...

'He raped me,' she blurted out. 'Last June if you must know.'

Without speaking, Hector laid down the roller and tray and descended the step ladder. When he reached the bottom rung, she saw paint spots on his eyebrows. There was even a fresh one at the end of his nose. The last thing she registered before his arms went around her. The way her own dad used to hold her if she'd had a bad day at school, or when a boy she'd once liked had gone off with someone else.

'Oh, Lucy Mitchell,' Hector said at last. 'What a shitty old world we live in, eh? What's his name then. This rapist?'

'I can't say.'

'I'll trawl this so-called longlist for you and find out. Don't forget, I've still got friends in the Force...'

'No. Please don't do anything. It's OK. I can handle it now.'

Just then the front door flew open, causing the stepladder to rock alarmingly from side to side and threaten to dislodge the full paint tray. Mark's dishevelled figure stood in stunned disbelief at the couple now separating in front of him.

'Well, just how fucking cosy can you get?' he yelled at them both, then stormed up the stairs before kicking his bedroom door shut with such seismic force that the huge old house seemed for a moment to lose its equilibrium.

Hector let go of her then made his way towards the kitchen.

'I'll make a pot of tea for us all,' he announced with such detachment that her damp eyes blinked in amazement. 'And tomorrow, don't forget, just like I promised, I'm going to find out about what exactly was going on at that waterfall.'

Chapter Twenty-Seven

𝕳i you,
𝕿hought you'd like this as a souvenir. 𝖂hat does
the postmark tell you?

THE GRAMMAR SCHOOL
Llandrindod Wells
REPORT FOR – Summer Term 1987

As Richard's form teacher and Year Head, I have been very concerned
by his total absence from school at a time when his undoubted talents
were truly coming to the fore. Whilst we all appreciate that the tragedy
of losing his mother has clearly had a devastating effect on his well-
being, nevertheless some return to normality, the companionship of others his own age and the chance to further his gifts in acting, art and
poetry would surely help him at this sad time.

M R Bowen. BSc.

As Lucy Mitchell and Hector Jones emptied the teapot between them
in the kitchen of Ravenstone Hall, the elderly congregation at St
Mary's Church in Burton Minster milled around their sidesman James
Benn at the end of morning service, congratulating him on his newly-
published biography.

'How *is* dear Elizabeth?' someone pressed as he finally tried to
leave. 'It's been so long since we've seen her here.'

'She's fine, Mrs Clipper. Just needs a lot of rest at the moment. I'll
tell her you've asked.'

'Yes, please do. We've our monthly supper party next Friday,
remember. It would be so good if she could attend.'

'I'll tell her that as well, of course. Thank you.'

He was aware of the woman's eyes on his back as he made his way
down the path to the road, too preoccupied by what the rest of the day
might have in store to worry about her busybodying.

After cooking his own Sunday lunch without much appetite to eat
it, he changed his cord jacket and cavalry twill slacks for a Savile Row
summer suit, teaming it with a discreetly striped shirt and a Hellebore
tie. He at least had to *look* the successful author, he reasoned, checking
his greying hair for strands which were too white, aware of his stomach
churning beneath his pigskin belt. After all, how could some wretched
local reporter hold a candle to what he'd achieved? A successful army

career with medals to boot plus an appreciative pension. *Tribe* tipped for next month's Booker shortlist, and 'the biography' – because just then he couldn't even think of his wife's name, let alone speak it – currently at no.3 in the non-fiction charts and already snapped up by six foreign publishers.

And yet, as he buttoned up his jacket and inserted a V of handkerchief in its top pocket, he knew that courtesy of Manda Jeffery, his defences were down. Down and bloody out, in fact. He checked the time on his Gucci watch, already his skin sweating under its strap.

Forty minutes to go. His bowels felt heavy, still on the move. He needed the lavatory. Better here than in the pub he thought, locking himself in and settling down to stare at the rave reviews stuck to the inside of the door and which he knew off by heart.

My God, he thought, careful not to strain too hard. This little collection would have been one in the eye for his old folks, had they lived to see it. Father on the railways, mother a char. Here was success in black and white with the adjective 'stupendous' repeated a dozen times... Yes, the Secondary Modern lad from Bournville had confounded the lot of his wretched family and the rest of the lowlife who'd crawled around its mean streets. That back-alley background was his big secret. Even the wife had no idea he'd been born in a flat above a turf accountants. Hardly surprising then, he thought, snatching a length of quilted tissue from the roll, that his fiction possessed veracity. That he gorged on approval like a wolf with a fresh carcass and on too many occasions had let his cock rule his head.

He flushed the chain and having washed his hands, stopped at the foot of the short flight of stairs to the box room. She'd been in there too long, he knew it. Better be careful, he warned himself, listening out for any tell-tale sounds, or smells, for that matter.

Another check of his watch. Twenty minutes to get to Wimborne. Certainly no time to sort her out.

'You stay there till I get back,' he ordered the silence. 'And no more fucking tricks.'

With that, he removed his costly fedora from the hat-stand and pressed it down on to his head. It gave him stature. A suitable degree of mystery, and to him, represented the furthest distance possible from number 521A, North Road, Bournville.

Not a single glance at his now triple-locked study wherein lay his abandoned manuscript and Manda Jeffery's New York number. He'd tried it of course, only to be told by the operator that it no longer existed.

He parked his new Jaguar some hundred yards away from The

Pilgrim and as he walked towards this rendezvous, fancied that several of the townsfolk recognised him. Hardly surprising since photos of his face and *Tribe*'s hardback cover still had pride of place in the county's bookshops. Their nudges and smiles briefly improved his mood, but only until he spotted a short casually dressed young man standing on the pavement outside the pub, and realised with another twist of his bowels that this insignificant-looking jerk represented his ruin.

'Hi. James Benn, yeah?' he asked. 'I'm Guy Roper. Glad you could make it.'

A girlish hand extended in greeting, which Benn declined. The upstart's clothes were a disgrace with oil smears on his shell-suit top and trainers more grey than white. He wasn't going to last five minutes...

The reporter led the way into a gloomy stale-smelling interior where the deserted tables in front of the bar still bore last night's detritus. However, Benn held his ground.

'I'm not going in here,' he announced, fedora still in place on his head. 'It's a junk heap.'

'I don't think *where* is relevant, do you?' The younger man removed a full ashtray and soiled beer mats off a table by a small leaded window, swept his lower arm over its surface and pulled out two wooden chairs. 'All I know is Miss Dyson's a helluvan angry young woman.'

Benn remained standing, his face in shadow under his hat brim, aware of someone washing glasses at the bar stopping her labours to stare.

'Keep your voice down,' he snarled at Roper. 'That peasant's ears are flapping.'

'Be more than hers doing that if you don't give me your side of the story. Sir.' He looked at his watch. Argos probably, Benn thought, finally lowering his big frame into the chair opposite and trying, privately and futilely, he knew, to conjure up some kind of plausible statement. But now, in his hour of need, his usual flair had deserted him.

'Beer?' Roper asked, extracting a small pad and Lottery pen from his jeans pocket. 'I'm having one.'

'I never drink on the Sabbath.' He was surprised not to see a mini laptop instead.

'So, you're a believer?'

'Read my wife's biography.'

'I have. Pretty impressive. Yes, as I recall, you're an official at your local church.' He got up and ordered a pint of bitter at the bar. 'They say nothing's wasted if you're a novelist.'

'I do it because society today is on the point of collapse. It's a lawless free-for-all and I'm telling you that in ten years' time most of middle England will be cluttering up France and South Africa while we'll be full of bloody Kosovans. Instead of church bells, it'll be the muezzin beating us into submission...'

'Pretty strong views there, I'd say,' Roper collected his frothing beer and set it down on the table. Benn eyed it enviously.

'I've never been politically correct. I'm a writer. I concern myself with what's really going on. Especially in Albion.'

'And what about being *personally* correct, sir?' He took a sip which left him a comical white moustache. 'Miss Dyson claimed she underwent an abortion shortly afterwards. She may not be able to have any more children.'

'I told you,' he tried to keep his voice even. 'I'd just settled up for my Paris trip when up she gets from her desk and touches me down there, if you please.' He glanced at his crotch.

'And then?' The reporter took a large gulp of drink as if for fortification.

'She asked if I was in a hurry. Of course I bloody was. I'd got a book to work on, another to edit...

'You made that clear?'

The bugger was writing in shorthand, he noticed.

'Look. I wasn't interested in a little trollop like that. I adore my wife. Why would I want to hurt her?'

Roper stopped writing and looked up. Bum fluff, thought Benn, unnerved nevertheless by the frankness of his gaze.

'You tell me.'

'That's enough from you.' He stood up, nearly knocking his fedora against the one huge ceiling beam which straddled both saloons. 'I don't have to listen to a prick like yourself rubbish me with innuendos... As I informed you on Friday, I'll be contacting my solicitor.'

'Great,' the clever-dick was still scribbling. 'But he'd better get his skates on. This is hot...'

'It's a woman,' Benn corrected him.

'Thought it might be.'

'What's that supposed to mean?'

'Next issue's out on Wednesday.'

Roper returned his writing gear to his pocket and moved his now empty glass in a liquid arc across the table. Rhythmically, backwards and forwards. 'I think we've got a good photo too.'

'Listen,' Benn eyed the distant door to the Gents, wondering when he might need to make a dash for it. 'I'll do a deal. Anything to stop this getting out.'

'Sorry mate. This isn't London. We're clean down here in Dorset.' Roper got up.

'Five grand. Come on.'

'Christ Jesus!' Roper laughed out loud until Benn poked him in his ribby chest.

'Who's put this tart up to it, eh?'

'Wouldn't you like to know?'

'Five C's then? To you. Personally.'

Roper grimaced.

'The adored wife,' he said suddenly.

Benn gulped, steadied himself against the nearest table.

'You mean..?'

'Very smart lady is Mrs Benn. No wonder you hold her in such high esteem.'

He didn't give the runt a chance to finish. Despite his Pulsar X toned legs feeling like jelly, he strode out of the pub's door into the stabbing sunlight. For a moment, in his rage, he turned the wrong way and collided with a crowded pushchair.

'Charming,' shouted the outraged mother at his retreating figure. 'Call yourself an effing toff?'

He reached his hot car and drove over the speed limit to Shaftesbury where he screeched to a halt on double yellow lines outside the Kingsdown Travel Agency in the High Street.

With demand for holiday flights still buoyant, this firm now opened on Sundays until 4 p.m., and sure enough, when he glanced in the poster-stickered window two employees were sitting behind PCs at their desks. Despite a spinning overhead fan, perfumed air met his nose once he'd pushed open the door. He had nothing now to lose. There were no other clients, nor any sign of the girl he wanted.

'Good afternoon ladies,' he doffed his hat and forced a smile on his disappointed mouth. Normally, he'd have carried out a swift appraisal of their breasts but not today. Today was different.

'Miss Dyson's been handling my recent travel arrangements,' he began in his most beguiling voice. 'Is she around by any chance?'

'Your name sir?' one asked.

'Graham Hammond. Wimborne.'

'Is everything alright, sir? I mean, we can check things for you. It's all here.' She tapped the top of her PC as he shook his head.

'No, no, thank you. I just needed to confirm with her some advice she gave me. From the Foreign Office, actually.'

'Oh, right. Well, I'm afraid she's left. Been gone a couple of days now. Bit sudden mind, wasn't it?' she turned to her colleague.

'Yeah, and she seemed really upset.'

'I'm sorry to hear that, but is there somewhere I can contact her?' he asked, then immediately regretted it, because both now seemed suspicious.

'Sorry sir, but where she is is her private business, isn't it, Joely?'

'Yeah.'

He beat a retreat out of the premises, his normally clear analytical mind a scrambled mess. He could try and trace Dyson's family for a pay-off. After all, she'd mentioned parents while he'd been chatting her up, just like Lucy Mitchell had done. But where would that lead? The damage had been done.

Fuck.

He turned on the ignition then noticed a traffic warden beetling up the High Street towards him and before the noxious official reached his car, had executed a nifty U-turn and sped off towards Burton Minster. His fedora askew on his head, his cheeks like hot coals, but that was nothing compared to his hatred for the woman he'd tried to drown all those years ago. The woman who'd survived to watch him now sink without trace.

Chapter Twenty-Eight

Truth is the Word? Bollocks. The main thing is, my spear's
now sharp as a raven's beak...

Without any of the recent misty preamble, Monday the 27th of August dawned fine and clear with just a fuzzy line of clouds out over Cardigan Bay. Anyone microlighting over the Garreg Ddu reservoir in the Elan Valley would have clearly spotted human activity below the woods on its western side. However, only a solitary red kite was winging its way against the blue as Robert Barker boiled up enough water in a billy can over a small primus, not only for shaving off his stubble but to shift the grass stains off his brand new jeans. He could have taken them to a launderette somewhere, but that would have meant hanging around. And hanging around wasn't on his agenda. Especially since meeting Lucy Mitchell.

He'd dumped his Vuitton suitcase with some happy cruds in a Mind charity shop in Builth Wells then purchased these hardware items at a camping store. So far so good, he told himself, so why the sudden shiver even though the sun was up over Corngafallt, the highest peak above Elan Village? Was it because he'd been careless yesterday afternoon? Too impatient to show his hand? Possibly, he thought, watching the bubbles form on the surface of the water. There were always lessons to be learnt and never enough time to learn them.

And what about this camping lark? he asked himself, glancing at the small camouflaged tent which he'd used since Thursday night. He'd loathed those trips with his parents in Howard Springs Nature Park near Darwin. The bogs, the mozzies, all those loose bitzers roaming around. Camping was either for the dumb or the hard-up. But he was neither, so what the hell was he doing here, kipping amonst the ferns and the skinny old jumbucks, losing the battle to keep his gear clean?

He supposed some dipstick New-Ager would have a word for it. A kind of bonding with nature to shift all the shit which others had dumped on him. But that was just more crap. He, Robert Francis Barker, was here through necessity. Quite a different matter. And it wasn't just Liza Docherty who'd triggered him into abandoning one life and re-starting another. Oh no, he thought, dipping his disposable razor into the water. And by Samhain, which, given his circumstances, wasn't an unreasonable deadline, his mission would be accomplished.

As he plied the razor over his stubble, then rinsed out its clogged-up head, he could already imagine how that would feel. The end of looking over his shoulder, of interrupted sleep.

Of knowing that the three who still breathed would no longer be an impediment to his future, but a Threefold Death. Yes, he smiled up at the morning. Fair dinkum, that. His peace of mind, after all he'd suffered, would be no more then he deserved.

Suddenly, as he was about to dry his face in a hand towel nicked from the B&B in Hay, he heard the rustle of bracken and instinctively ducked down to hide.

'Hey, you there!' called out a woman's voice. A crone more like, he thought, taking a peep. He was right. It was some old crud pushing a bike. The one he'd spotted yesterday. She looked the sort who'd snap in two like a dried twig if she wasn't careful. 'Fires aren't allowed anywhere here. It's totally irresponsible of you,' she brayed on. 'I'm afraid I'll have to report this.'

She began to remount her bike to leave, but he was quicker and, before she could utter another word, had placed a strong tanned hand around her throat. That shut her up. Old sticky beak was so rigid with fear that when he pulled down her cord breeches and her baggy grundies so he could touch her grey old muff, she offered no resistance. Nor when he unzipped his jeans and pressed himself close.

He closed his eyes. It wasn't desire driving him on but memory. Before his cop-out with that freckled sheila on Thursday afternoon, and the other times way back when he'd failed to crack a fat. Now there was just the whiff of death. This one wasn't going to tell him how far he could go. *He* was in control this time. He had the power, not like during those two Samhain sessions in that steamy green-tiled bathroom with the hot shower running, disguising the sounds of sex...

Okay, so she wasn't a red-head like the Morrigan. More the old granny, still, she was up for it alright and he could always pretend. His grip on her pulsing neck tightened as he forced himself inside her, feeling so close, so fucking close that after so long, there might finally, be some toothpaste in the tube...

Morrigan Morrigan, into your cauldron here we come...

Suddenly the woman's mouth stretched open and she screamed so hard into the silent morning that his balls contracted, forcing a spasm of such power through from the tops of his thighs.

'Shut your face,' he slapped her while withdrawing, suddenly unsteady on his feet, and in that unguarded moment, the old woman scrambled bare-arsed up the slope away from him. He watched, powerless to follow as she pulled up her clothes, retrieved her bike and careered off along the higher track and into the edge of trees. 'You said yesterday there were no more Dagdans here,' he yelled after her. 'I heard you. Well let me tell you something, I'm no fucking cling-on like the rest of them who used to be here. I'm He. I'm The One.'

That felt better, just *saying* it. But he was sore. He was half-fucking dead. He'd not come for fourteen years and to think he'd broken that torturing fast with some old granny.

Jesus…

'Time to go, old son,' he urged himself, turning off the primus flame and flinging the billy can's hot water into the foliage. If she'd ended up as a stiff, she'd have gone in the sleeping bag and then into the nice deep water. No worries. But she'd got away, hadn't she? Would soon be meeting up with someone and that dry old mouth of hers would start yabbing…

His breath came in short gasps as he lugged his camping bundle further down the slope to where the Maverick lay not far form the shore. But there was no time to muse on such a sacred place where wisdom, knowledge and poetry are always revealed, because every second spent there was a second too long. Within five minutes he was driving towards the one exit – which of course Lucy Mitchell and her companion had also used – too preoccupied to notice that the promising expanse of new sky had been encroached upon by a widening belt of black cloud which changed half the land around him into darkness.

He switched on the car radio to Radio Cymru and the tail-end of the 7.30 a.m. news of a thirty-year-old woman and two small boys from Crossgates in Radnorshire, whose Bedford Rascal van had apparently plunged off the Black Mountain road above Brynamman in Carmarthenshire yesterday evening.

Christ Almighty…

The Maverick suddenly swerved, hitting one soft verge then the other. Nothing to do with me, he told himself, trying to right the off-roader and push a series of shock waves to the back of his mind. Yet he switched off the radio with one thought uppermost. Had she obeyed his instructions? No way could he show his face at the farm to find out, because Lucy Mitchell had been there too. And how much did she know? Was it only the librarian who'd given her the nod? Or was someone else trying to find out if he was around? Someone who wanted him dead?

As he continued along the quiet B road trying not to dwell on his former girlfriend's death and those of the kids who might at some point in future time, have been his, he felt as if a yawning hole had suddenly opened up in his life. The possibilities which he'd so carefully nurtured in his mind for his future suddenly gone and in their place, were problems with the present. Such as, where he'd be kippng tonight. And what to do about the Ford Maverick? It was a big black giveaway and he was now regretting his too-hasty purchase. Better to have gone for a tin-pot van like Rhiannon George's which were ten-a-penny in this neck of the woods. Would have saved him some dough too. And thinking of her, he should have tailed her wherever she was going, persevered with his plan to ask her to marry him. Then who knows? But now he'd other fish to fry and time was running out.

Out of Rhayader and up the Wye Valley on the road which sent a shiver of déjà vu through his whole frame. However, instead of heading directly for Aberystwyth and its resident hillbillies, he turned off left for Devil's Bridge and the plundering all-consuming River Rheidol.

Given the time of year, the place was strangely free of rubbernecks. Nice and shaded too, he thought, with plenty of din from the cascades and surf just like he remembered. Robert found an overgrown track leading off this minor road which ended further along the gorge. As he parked on the very edge he couldn't resist murmuring some of Frost's poem to himself…

'The woods are lovely dark and deep

And I have miles to go before I sleep…'

One of his favourites, along with Arnold's 'The Scholar Gypsy' and 'Thyrsis'. And here they were, just for him, in all their damp green flesh.

He emptied the vehicle of all his belongings, careful not to leave anything incriminating behind. He even checked both headrests for hairs, and not just his, because DNA testing was now the main problem facing all those trying to turn their lives around.

It didn't take him long to secrete all his camping gear away behind a nearby beech hedge. There was nothing here to betray his identity should the items be found and, thus reassured, he returned to the Maverick and slipped his arm inside the open front passenger window. Once he'd released the handbrake, he pushed his body against the off-roader's boot until centimetre by centimetre its front wheels moved over the edge.

With one final shove, the black steel hulk tumbled once, then twice, over and over down towards the swollen flow until it hit the water, gurgling air as it sank. He didn't stay for the final echoing sounds of submersion and, having rubbed some earth into his sunstreaked hair to disguise the lighter bits, and made the decision to keep the new brown contacts in, he was off. Walking like any normal visitor to the area, heading for Aberystwyth and anywhere with white vans for sale.

At Capel Gors, he was relieved to find a Murco garage wedged between the end of a line of run-down cottages and a sawmills, and noticed an overalled man he assumed was the owner, lugging blue gas cylinders over to a rack near the air pressure gauge. The drag of steel on concrete set his teeth on edge. He just wanted the fucker to stop and the moment he saw him, he did.

'Sunday's not Sunday any more,' the man grumbled, wiping over his sweaty forehead with his oily cuff. 'But it's not down to me, is it? Murco's my lord and bloody master...'

Normally, he'd have indulged the cretin in his griping, but he had to get back to his gear. It was five miles, after all.

'You got any vans for sale?' he asked in the best Scottish accent he could muster. There was a wired-off area alongside the shop which, from where he stood, seemed to house some promising-looking crates. 'I'm cash. Can give top whack.'

'There's vans and vans...'

'Just a runabout will do me.'

'Got one. Came in yesterday. Gone round the clock twice and I can't offer no guarantees on it.' He waddled over to the compound, unlocked the huge padlock on the wire door and held it open for him to follow.

If only he himself could adopt that neat little homily, Robert thought, eyeing up the possibilities in front of him and beginning to lose heart as the man singled out a maroon Transit for his inspection.

'Nothing in white then?' he asked, glancing at the ranks of wrecks by the far fence. 'Say a five hundredweight?'

The man scratched his dirty chin and moved away towards the junk on wheels.

'Try this one,' he suggested. 'My son wanted something a bit more classy to pull in the birds, if you get my meaning.'

'Yeah, course.' He eyed the van's dented offside wheel hub, its general decrepitude. Whatever its faults, it would certainly fit in. It was also a Renault. And that was key.

'Taxed till November. MOT due end of October. Tyres will do another month and all.'

'Great.'

The other man drew closer then looked round furtively. Robert recoiled. He smelt like those Abos back at Redfern.

'As far as insurance goes, just stick to the back roads, eh?'

Robert didn't respond. Hadn't he been doing the very same with the Maverick? And no tax disc either?

'Say thirty. Cash, remember?' he said.

The man hesitated and Robert began to move off. Always a good ploy.

'You're on. I'll get the keys and you'll need fuel. Unleaded, remember.'

'No worries.'

'So, where you from then?' The man tucked the money deep in his overalls as if he'd just sold a wad of crack.

'Chester. I'm a Scot in this play we're doing. Practice makes perfect, eh?'

'You could have fooled me.' The man replaced the petrol nozzle against the pump and screwed up the van's tank cap. 'On holiday, then?'

'Kind of, yeah.'

'Well,' he patted the bird-shit bonnet. 'She's sure to get you where you want to go.'

'Cheers.'

He steered the heap out into the road and returned without incident to where his stuff still lay intact. Once the van was packed up, he peered down at where the Maverick had once been. It had totally gone. There were no bits of bodywork showing, no chrome, not one piece of the chassis' skeleton and, as if to celebrate his latest achievement, he pulled out a snazzy silver mobile from his jeans pocket.

He'd heard the last two voicemail messages to the tart on it enough times and now, while overhead, the rain clouds also swelled until they could swell no more, turning the vale below to night before releasing their own burdens, he threw the thing high into the air over the water.

The final voicemail was still running as it dropped down down down...

'Jade, it's Cass again. Sunday. 2 p.m. I'm getting worried now. Are you okay? For God's sake just buzz me when you've got a mo. Promise?'

Whoever Cass was, she had every reason to be worried.

Giant raindrops hit his head as he climbed back into the van. But he was smiling. And why not? He felt good. Ready for anything in fact. Just now had been the business, but only by filling the old granny's cauldron earlier on, he'd finally brought himself, the one true Dagda, from the unjust darkness into perpetual light.

Chapter Twenty-Nine

Hi you, I really dig this. No more for a while now.

x

I am the captain of my soul
The Master of my Fate.
WE Henley 1849-1903

Mark had gone to work, and Hector to New Radnor. In their absence, Ravenstone Hall was eerily quiet as Lucy sat in front of the old-fashioned dressing table in her room, repeatedly brushing out her hair and thinking about what style to wear it in on Thursday. She also thought about the sawyer's childish outburst over her and Hector, and how he'd spent the previous evening in a sulk on his own. However *she* should be the one taking umbrage. Hadn't she lost her nerve to even step into Wern Goch to look at the cauldron? Hadn't those ravens there been just too attentive as she'd hovered outside? Even now she kept her eye on the landing through her open door. The words on that cryptic note which Hector had taken to scrutinise further had seeped into her psyche, making her forever watchful and wary. Shortening her sleep.

Yet she had to take the initiative. To find out what was really going on, and that would mean not just a busy morning but however long it took...

She used both hands to create a smooth French pleat at the back of her head. A more formal style for her imminent visit to her bank and her solicitor. The kind she'd used at the London Book Fair or signings she'd been graciously allowed to attend. And, as she set the amber-coloured comb in place, felt a lump form in her throat. The world of books – who was writing what, auctions and advances – all seemed to have drifted away, to be replaced by something utterly different; as if some ancient carapace of land and water now sealed in her world, excluding her past, the person she'd once been, the people she'd loved and trusted, bringing only death and drownings into this guide-book paradise.

She shivered and closed the window on the strange two-tone sky outside, wondering briefly about calling Anna again. But another predictably optimistic response wasn't the answer. It would be going too much against the gloomy grain. In short, it was too easy.

Before going downstairs, however, Lucy tried the handle of the adjoining room with the rose on the door. The raven's head handle felt like ice, but to her surprise, it moved then turned, allowing her a glimpse of what lay beyond, because if this *had* once been Sonia Jones's room, then there might be more of that same rose-printed cotton which had fallen from Wern Goch's chimney. Other clues as well, maybe, but first impressions weren't promising. For a start, it seemed as if everything to do with her had been airbrushed away. As if the woman had never even existed.

She held her breath as she tiptoed across the bare floorboards to the two utility-style wardrobes. Her own aunt still kept hers from just after the war – as plain and functional as the name suggested. Unlike in Mark's room, both were jammed with coats, macs and dresses of every description. One for each day of the week it seemed, and as she probed without success for anything which resembled that striking rose pattern a familiar smell met her nose. She sniffed, then stifled a sneeze on the perfume and dust. Nothing but death and decay…

She made her way down into Hector's study again and having left fifty pence on the bar for her call, dug out her little address book and found the number she wanted. She glanced out at the surreal sky as she dialled 141 first then waited for someone to answer.

'Yes? Who's there?' The sharpness of the man's voice caught her by surprise. He also sounded wary, on his guard.

'Mr Williams?'

'It is.'

'Lucy Mitchell here. Ravenstone Hall. Sorry to disturb you, and I'm also sorry those birds went for you the other day, but I wondered if you could help me. Could we possibly meet up sometime? This afternoon, perhaps? We really need to talk.'

The silence which followed loomed into her ear.

'Mr Williams?' she prodded.

'Look, Missy. I got a good job, my own place…'

'I don't understand…'

'I've no wish to be next. That's all. Bore da to you…'

YOU'RE NEXT.

She looked at the receiver and shivered. Never had a dialling tone sounded so bleak, so ominous and even though the study was the stuffiest room at the Hall, it felt as if that dark slab of sky outside had somehow invaded the thick stone walls and drawn her into its very heart. As if she'd entered another realm beyond this one. A cold and bitter place where all things living wither and die. And as she left the room, having checked his address in Yellow Pages, it took all of her resolve to stick to her agenda. In other words, the appropriately titled TRUTH STRATEGY.

Mark's van was there by the Hall after all. Lucy frowned to herself as she drove away, still puzzled not only by the sweep's reaction, but also by the fact that if Mark had been indoors all along, he'd not made the slightest sound. Maybe he was out in the fields doing something or other.

And although she couldn't actually see him anywhere, it was more reassuring to think that was the reason for his silence.

Having first checked at Barclays that her father's money was indeed now in her current savings account, she added her mother's cheque, sent her one in turn for £500, then repaid the loan.

Finally, she made her way to Church Street and her solicitor's newly-rendered premises. There were two other clients in the equally immaculate waiting room, whispering about MAFF, DEFRA and a road accident somewhere, but as she'd not made an appointment, she was prepared to stick it out.

At last, at ten o'clock, having re-read the single copy of Horse and Hound six times, she was shown into Martyn Harries's office and was immediately struck by the difference in his whole demeanor from their last meeting. A week ago this man in his mid-fifties had been the helpful professional that she'd needed. Now *he* looked like the one needing help and she, rather than wishing to tax him further, retreated to the door.

'No, please,' he said, indicating a chair in front of his desk, still warm from the last occupant. 'Let's hope you've some pleasant news, Miss Mitchell, because I've had enough of the other kind to last till the good Lord finally takes me.'

'Why? What's happened?'

'If I did any other kind of job, I could tell you.' His tired eyes rested briefly on a black and white wedding photograph which she vaguely recognised, propped up in one of his bookcases.

'It's not news, Mr Harries but questions I need to ask you. I know I should have made an appointment but...'

'We're hardly Lincoln's Inn here,' a weak smile appeared on his lips. 'So, how can I help?'

She focused again on that wedding couple.

'As you know, I'm hoping to exchange contracts with Mr Jones on Friday.'

'Yes, yes. Everything's in order. The Deeds to Wern Goch are now with me and you'll be receiving a copy of my search tomorrow. I can assure you there are neither proposed or pending plans for development on any adjoining land or ancient or current Rights-of-Way affecting the property. I've also...'

'Look,' she interrupted him. 'That's not the reason I'm here. I want you to tell me the truth, if you can, about Mrs Jones's murder.'

She was aware of the lawyer's unblinking stillness as she spoke.

'I know it was a vile business, but if I'm to go ahead with buying, I need to feel, you know...' she faltered for a moment. 'Safe.'

Martyn Harries leaned forwards.

'My dear Lucy. May I call you that?'

She nodded.

'If I had any information about Wern Goch which I felt might affect your future well-being there, believe me, I would have passed it on to you.' He spread both white hands out on his papers and looked at her with a determined expression in his pale blue eyes. 'It would not be in my interests to do otherwise. Do you understand that?'

'I do. But I've heard so many conflicting stories, innuendos, I honestly don't know who or what to believe. And, until I get the truth, I'm afraid the sale might be off. Even though we've started fencing, and I've already got new locks fitted and new windows ready, it just feels like my dream's ebbing away.'

'I quite understand your feelings, believe me. But, as you can imagine, the Radnorshire Constabulary left no stone unturned in their hunt for Mrs Jones's killer. They even fingerprinted and interrogated her remaining family for days...'

'But no DNA testing then, of course?'

'No. And I'm afraid the CID team which was brought in from Hereford may have been somewhat over-zealous. Mind you, nothing incriminating was ever found.'

She thought of what lay in her fleece pocket, the burnt fragments, the bits of boiled flesh in Mark's shoe, and decided, against her better judgement, to honour her pledge to him. But not for much longer, she told herself. Friday was the deadline.

'I've heard about the older son Richard not coping very well,' she said instead.

'I fear that's an understatement. He went totally off the rails after the tragedy. I remember seeing Mr Jones, or Detective Inspector Jones as he'd once been, in utter despair over it. Apparently Richard also said some pretty harsh things to his father at the time. Things he just couldn't live with.'

So the present tensions at Ravenstone were probably minute compared to those days, thought Lucy to herself without much comfort.

'In the end,' said Martyn Harries, 'and this is something you shouldn't know, so please bear this in mind...'

'Of course.' Wondering what was coming next.

'In the end because he couldn't forgive him, his father changed his Will and banished the lad to distant relatives somewhere.'

'Where?'

'Darwin. Australia.'

That couldn't be further away, she thought before asking, 'did he know about this change of Will?'

'He was told, apparently.'

'My God.' She tried to collect her thoughts. That must have been a double shot across the bows for him. 'So who's the main beneficiary now?'

'Mark.'

She frowned.

'Do either of them know that?'

'I can't say. Mind you, I have advised Mr Jones that this isn't a very satisfactory situation if anything were to happen to him. That he should play fair either way and treat both sons the same.'

'Exactly. And what's his response?'

'He's waiting.'

'What on earth for?'

'Who knows?'

A brief silence fell between them in which she suddenly wanted to be outside, even though the weather seemed to be changing for the worst.

'What kind of things had Richard said? Can you tell me?'

'That his mother was...' The lawyer stalled and shifted his gaze from her. 'A whore.'

She felt her empty stomach go into freefall as the room grew darker, affected by the blue-black sky beyond the blinds.

'Look, I have to tell *you* something,' she said, trying to keep her voice calm. 'Yesterday morning, Mark and I discovered that someone had dug a little hole in a significant place on her grave, and left a note in it.'

'What do you mean by significant?'

'Below her stomach. Where her sex would be.'

If the lawyer was shocked, he didn't show it.

'I see. And?'

'This note said whore as well.'

Another potent silence, broken by a discreet knock on the door.

'Yes?' Harries snapped.

'Would you be wanting coffee?' asked a pale drawn woman who might have been his wife.

'No thank you Marion. Not just yet.'

'By the way, there's just Mr Powell waiting.'

'Fine. Tell him ten minutes.'

'So, it looks like Richard's back?' Lucy asked once the door was closed again.

'I wouldn't necessarily jump to that conclusion,' Harries replied. 'That sort of prank is easy for anyone to do.'

Anyone?

She puzzled over this for a moment then asked, 'but why would Richard say that about his mother? It's a terrible accusation to make.'

'It was. But to a fifteen-year-old it must have seemed that way. You see, Sonia Jones led quite a life. Dressing up to the nines, out till all hours. At first, Mr Jones would accompany her wherever she was singing...'

'Singing?'

No wonder there was none of that any more at the Hall, she mused to herself. Only grief's silence.

'Yes. She had a wonderful voice. Could really have done something with it, in my opinion.'

But she did, thought Lucy. She screamed for her life...

'Such a dreadful waste. Even now, whenever we go to Cardiff or London to see some show or other, I can't help thinking that's what she should have aimed for. Instead of just pubs and clubs...'

'You seem to have liked her?' she ventured.

Martyn Harries glanced round at the door as if he might be interrupted again.

'Oh yes. She was stunning. And how many women can you say that about round here, eh?' A full smile now changed his whole face.

'Someone I met the other day compared her to Marilyn Monroe.'

'Oh, she was more interesting than that, I'd say. Her colouring for a start. Lovely grey eyes as I recall, and always that haunting scent... Which makes what happened all the more diabolical. I do mean it was the work of the Devil.'

His sudden vehemence took her by surprise and she wondered if this solicitor had once had a thing for her.

'I often suggested to Hector Jones that he erect a gate at the end of their track,' he went on. 'But no. He never did. That must still be on his conscience, poor man.'

She thought of that other hidden entrance from the lane. How the whole estate was vulnerable.

'So, do you believe some kind of Druid did it?'

'Who else? Unless there was a jealous lover somewhere who's never been traced...'

'Not impossible, given her lifestyle.'

'Indeed not.'

'But surely these Druids or Dagdas whatever, left the area in the mid-seventies?'

'I see you've done your homework, but it was never that simple. Like any organisation, you get offshoots, loners with their own agendas. Certainly Detective Superintendent Davies and his team at the time, attached great significance to the fact that the murder had taken place at Beltane. The first of May and when they found the remains of a fire in the range they knew this had all the hallmarks of a Druidic sacrifice.'

'A fire? Why?' Thinking again of those fragments and wondering about the possible blue shirt.

'To mark the return of the sun and the rising of the Pleiades. All very symbolic in Celtic terms.'

'I realise you've another client waiting,' Lucy began, 'but what would this or these Druids have worn?'

'Now you've got me. I'm really no expert on this kind of thing.'

'But hardly shirt and trousers?'

'Goodness no,' he shot her a look of surprise. 'They love their paraphernalia. The dressing up bit, just like Mrs Jones did, I suppose. Feathers, fleeces, leather...I'd say a tunic and belt, definitely a cloak of some sort and their hair like a monk's tonsure. Mind you, the god Dagda himself was supposed to have worn something so short that it showed his buttocks.'

Neither smiled.

She thanked him for that information, but suddenly felt cold. It was simply stretching things too far to imagine mother's boy Bryn Evans and Sion Hughes got up like that. 'You'll think I've cracked up too, asking this,' she said, 'but is Bryn Evans the preacher or Hughes, that young farmer friend of his connected to this cult? You've got to tell me.'

'Whose been telling you that, then? The Joneses?'

She hung her head.

'Well, they ought to be careful. There is such a thing as slander.'

'What do you mean?'

'I know neither character is the sort I'd invite over to share our table with, but both are serious farmers. Not only has foot-and-mouth dealt them a bad blow, but some years back, on October 31st, which is Samhain of course in the Celtic year, a huge Wicker Man was built in secret up by Abbey Cwm Hir.'

'A Wicker Man?' Lucy had heard of the film, but nothing more.

'Yes. Apparently, stock was rustled from both their farms and sacrificed to the flames in it while still alive...'

'My God.'

'So you see, they hate them. And with good reason.'

'And what about 'Simnai' Williams, the sweep? Is he to be trusted?'
Martyn Harries gave her a wry little smile.

'Used to be fly-half for Wales in the good old days. Salt of the earth, that one. Speaks his mind too, which some folks don't always appreciate.'

He moved over to switch on his desk light and then to a tightly packed bookcase which took up the wall behind his chair. 'Remember what you've come into here, Lucy. It's different for me. I was born in mid-Wales. My family are all local...' Here he broke off as if the rest might be too painful for him to mention, and moved the wedding photograph to his desk.

She waited, still reeling inside, as he pulled out a small brown book from between its crowded neighbours. Even from where she was sitting she could tell it was old. 'I'd like you to have this. Waldo Humphreys' *Celtic Deities*,' he continued, giving her no chance to protest. She turned to the frontespiece and noticed that the Garn Press had published it in 1887. Exactly a hundred years before the events at Ravenstone.

'Please read it as soon as you can and remember that to the Celts, time is measured by nights, not days. Not by the sun, but the moon. Now that,' he added, handing the little volume over to her, 'should explain everything.'

Chapter Thirty

I am Fear which blinks a doe's eye.
I am Storm which blackens the hill.
I am Hatred which kills.
I am Fire which devours all Love.
MJJ 26/8/01

Martyn Harries's last words hammered in Lucy's head as she consulted her crumpled OS map in the car outside his office. It was night now, never mind midday, with storm water lashing her windscreen, filling the nearby gutter to overflowing and bearing a motley collection of litter along on its tide.

But this turmoil outside was nothing compared to what the man had revealed about Hector Jones and his two sons. How Richard had not only been banished to the other side of the world but also disinherited. How it now seemed quite possible that in a moment of insanity he'd killed his own mother and subjected her body to a terrible post-mortem violation. And yet, if Mark knew he was the sole inheritor of Ravenstone Hall why was he so judgemental, no, rude was a better word, towards his father? In fact, she'd seen very little gratitude on his part so far.

Perhaps he knew nothing about it, she decided as she started the engine. After all, hadn't the lawyer just said that for whatever reason, Hector Jones was waiting?

Well, *she* damned well wasn't. Friday's exchange of contracts was looming and despite the atrocious weather conditions, Bwlch Ddu farm would have to be her next port of call.

The B road towards Pantgwyn and the source of the Mellte made a welcome change from that to Ravenstone, even though it was five extra miles. Here the smooth shining tarmac was edged by trimmed hedges giving good visibility around the many circuitous bends. Trees had been lopped to avoid the problem of falling branches, gates newly painted and the few dwellings set back in their own land seemed proudly cared for. Loved even, instead of what lay less than half a mile away.

This impression lasted as she followed the first farm sign which led upwards to higher ground bearing north into the hide-coloured hills whose craggy profiles melded against the gunmetal sky. There wasn't one rainy picture in *Magical Tales*, she thought, glancing at the glove box where it still lay in safety. How easy it is to lie...

Smart post-and-rail fencing now led to an already open five-barred gate at the side of which stood a large professional-looking placard announcing:

S. T. HUGHES
BWLCH DDU SUFFOLKS

As far as she could tell, no one had been tailing her. She was totally alone and here she stalled, expecting dogs or worse, but it was as if the weather had driven everything indoors. Even that dreaded yellow harvester had been secreted away.

She drove on to the most immaculate empty yard she'd ever seen, which was enclosed on three sides by various low whitewashed buildings of which any one could have been the actual dwelling house, and despite there being no car or other means of transport visible, she felt nevertheless that someone was around.

Having locked the Rav, she lifted her fleece hood over her already damp hair then stopped to sniff the wet air. No amount of rain could disguise the odd smell which seemed to be coming from the end building on the right. She racked her brains to think where she'd smelt that before and then remembered a holiday visit to a blacksmith near Caernarfon where a huge Welsh cob was being shod. The sizzle of red-hot iron on its hooves had left a strange lingering taste in her mouth. This was similar, except that this time she was sure it wasn't bone being heated, but flesh.

 As she walked towards it she was aware of a front window curtain moving in the adjoining block. Ignoring this she made for a big black door. There was no handle so she shoved it with her shoulder. No joy.

'Mr Hughes?' she shouted, for some reason feeling far less frightened here than at Gellionnen. It was determination, she told herself as she waited for a reply. Because, as she'd soon learnt at Hellebore, there was nothing like a deadline.' Are you there?'

She pressed her ear to the wet door and winced as successive blasts of fiery noise reached her ears. Was this some blowtorch being used? If so, for what? And then the smell intensified. Sheep wool and burning meat.

A moment's hesitation, but too late. The noise had stopped and in the silence she heard a key grinding in the door's lock on the other side. It opened enough to let a rancid stench hit her nose and at the same time reveal a young man's face, red and perspiring. His rodent-like eyes seemed not to recognise her.

'Yes?'

'Lucy Mitchell. I'm buying Wern Goch.'

'Shit.'

That was enough. The door began to close against her, but she'd not come all this way to give up without a fight. Her fleece hood felt sodden, her whole body saturated, but she stood her ground.

'I need your help,' she began. 'I couldn't think who else to turn to. It's urgent, believe me…'

He was only nineteen, she knew that. Clearly a hot-head, but surely raising and caring for animals must have endowed him with some heart? She certainly wanted to think so, and waited in the minimal shelter of her car. To her relief the barn door reopened and Sion Hughes slipped outside then relocked it. He pointed towards the adjoining building leaving her to follow in his scented wake, giving her the chance to see bloodstains on the back of his shirt and the heels of his boots buried in dark green faeces.

'In here,' as he pushed open the front door on to a dark narrow hallway past a front parlour studded with rosettes where a middle-aged woman who seemed completely unaware of either her or her companion, sat near the window staring out through the net curtain. 'Me mam,' he explained. 'She's not been right since the foot-and-mouth, since we buried my da, but I try and keep her spirits up. Got some good new stock now, see. Suffolks is the best. Plenty of meat. Quick and easy it comes too.'

'Are they inside somewhere?'

'Oh, they're inside, alright.' He threw a glance back the way they'd come. 'In the barn. Smokies now, mind.'

'Smokies?'

'Special treat for the London wogs. I torch the lot to a nice golden brown, just how they like 'em. All the bits an' bobs as well, mind. They're not fussy.' He then shot her a warning glance from his small sharp eye before she could react, and it was then she realised he had false teeth. Bright acrylic ones, upper and lower, almost too big for his mouth. As if he'd been fitted with the wrong set. She watched his every move. 'You tell anyone and you're a gonner too. OK?' He ran a grimy finger across his throat, which made her still delicate stomach freeze up as she nodded. 'Not even the preacher. He's getting on my tits at the moment, if you must know.'

'Oh?' Although no apology seemed forthcoming for hounding her on the road to Ravenstone or knocking Mark to the ground last Thursday, any friction between the two men might well be useful to her cause.

'I think he's jealous of my buying Wern Goch,' she said, shamelessly lighting the blue touch paper, watching for the slightest reaction and seeing those eyes narrow even further. 'I've heard he's trying to acquire more land.'

'He is that. Been leaning on me for some acres for a while now. But there's more to it than what you think.' He moved from the end of the hallway into a back room where an old-fashioned tiled fireplace and two worn armchairs in front of it were almost lost in other junk. Bulging suitcases, stacks of books, farming magazines and weathered old clothes as if someone had thought about selling up then changed their mind. Nothing to suggest that Sion Hughes belonged to any cult. Nothing at all. Even the two framed watercolours hanging lop-sided along one wall, showed innocuous enough views of Cader Idris, not some oak grove or men in feathers. 'It was when the rumours started.'

'What rumours?' She'd have liked to sit down somewhere, even slip her sogging fleece off her back, but Sion Hughes wasn't into courtesies. Besides, he clearly had things on his mind.

'That we were some kind of Druids,' he went on and a sour laugh followed, in which his prominent Adam's apple jerked around in his throat. 'Even after what happened up by Abbey Cwm Hir. Oh, and guess what? That we were fucking gay. As if...'

'Who started all this?'

'That Mark Jones twat. And his father.'

So contemptuous was his tone that she flinched. He was genuine alright and she felt more than just damp and miserable. She felt defeated as Hughes gave her another mini death stare.

'Then getting Bryn to shift his stock was the last sodding straw.'

'That wasn't my fault.'

'You could have stopped it happening. Anyway, he was so boiled up about you having the place he paid me to give you a fright. Make you leave. End of story.'

'It wasn't funny. I could have been killed.'

'I'm not laughing.' For a second, he hung his wet blonde head. Drips from his jeans lay in a pool around his feet, darkening the floor tiles. 'Since me da topped himself it's been hard to keep going, what with me mam the way she is. The dough was useful, see.'

'I do, and I'm sorry about your dad and everything, but for God's sake, I've only been here just over a week and I could fill a book with what's happened already.'

'Yeah?' He was curious. The Welsh have always loved stories she thought, but right now it was answers she wanted.

'Were you tailing me near Ravenstone Hall on Sat around 4 p.m., having dumped sheep hurdles in the Hall's driveway to block me in?'

'Don't be daft. Me and Bryn were out at the Show. Stayed on for the terrier racing till gone seven. Then we hit the beer tent. Ask anyone.'

'Okay, and what about my nice little note and the one on Mrs Jones's grave? Mine says, you're next, and hers had whore on it.'

He paled. 'You're kidding?'

'I'm not, I assure you. Mr Jones is supposed to be looking into it.'

'Him?'

'I know what you think of the man. But I'm just trying to find things out.'

'About them notes. I don't do stuff like that.'

'What do you mean?'

'Can't write see. And Bryn Evans, well, he's got God to answer to, hasn't he?'

'So, why did he say to Mark that both he and his brother were a curse on the land? That's pretty shocking isn't it? What did he mean?'

'D'you fancy one of 'em, then?'

'Don't be ridiculous. Anyway, I've already got a boyfriend.'

Hughes shrugged, unimpressed. 'Our Bryn's a Bible puncher, isn't he? Kind of words he uses. Mind you, it's what folk round here think.'

Lucy glanced out at the rain and the empty fields stretching upwards to the leaden sky and the sustained shiver which followed wasn't simply because of her soaking clothes.

'So they both killed their mother, right? Look, I've got to know, because after Friday, I'm legally committed to buying the place. Just think if I was your girlfriend...'

He ignored that remark, but she could see he was beginning to bite. 'Is that what you meant by urgent?'

'Yes.'

Hughes glanced at the door. He seemed uncomfortable. His ruddy complexion now even paler. His eyes shifty. What was he frightened of? Why were his blackened fists clenching and unclenching?

'Look,' she began. 'If it'll help, I won't breathe a word of this conversation to anyone. That's a promise. No one knows I've been here. No one needs to know.'

'Don't bank on it. Anyway, it's that Richard dickhead you've got to watch out for. He's off his fucking tree, I'm telling you. If he ever came back...'

He was interrupted by a sudden noise from the front room and Lucy cursed inwardly at this interruption. Hughes had flinched, was already on his way.

'Tell me, is Mrs Evans a nutter?' she persisted as he reached the open doorway. 'Has she ever, you know, been in a mental home?'

'Get off. Sharp as a new hoof-pick she is. More than you can say for the preacher. Why? Whose been spreading shite like that?'

'Just gossip, that's all.' She tapped his shoulder to restrain him from going any further and he spun round as if his whole life was lived on a high tension wire.

'I know it's a lot of questions,' she began, 'but I wouldn't be here if I didn't think you could help. Please.'

He stalled, leaning against the door frame. He was far too thin, she thought, and those teeth... He'd probably had to have all his real ones out in one go to save trips to the dentist. Mrs Evans had told her it often happened. Even now, in 2001.

'Did Hector ever call round to either of you last Friday evening, after that incident in Rhayader?' she asked.

He hooted his derision and the top row of teeth moved.

'Fuck no. He's a right wuss, him. Can't even look at himself in the mirror.'

'So you didn't see him at Caban Coch?'

Just then, a second noise from the parlour, more urgent this time and Hughes left his post an ran up the passageway.

'What's up, Mam?' he shouted. 'Someone out there?'

Lucy couldn't hear what the poor woman mumbled but her son had already flung open the front door and stood, legs apart surveying the yard where the rain had now turned to hail.

'You've just said no one saw you come here,' he snapped without turning round. 'Lying Saesneg.'

'What d'you mean?' She saw the woman's stricken face, the hands locked on to the arms of her chair.

'Some white van's been in, turned round and fucked off.'

Her heart seemed to stop beating.

'Maybe someone's got lost, made a mistake. It's easily done round here.'

'*You're* the one making a mistake. If I was you. I'd get the hell out, back to wherever you came from.'

A threat and a warning all rolled into one. Each harsh syllable stung far worse than anything the sky had on offer as she pushed past him and headed for her car. When she looked up from unlocking it with a shaking hand he was still there, guarding his territory. Then she remembered that scream near Wern Goch. It was now or never.

'Do you ever use a whistle when you're getting the sheep in?' she yelled over to him.

'What sort of crap question's that, eh?' he stepped from the house and made for the barn once more. 'If I used a whistle with my dog, she'd have me leg. And the rest. Hates the things...'

With that, he unlocked the black door and slammed it shut behind him, leaving her staring after him, in a pall of singed flesh.

Chapter Thirty-One

𝕳𝔦 𝔂𝔬𝔲,
𝕴 𝔣𝔬𝔯𝔤𝔬𝔱. 𝕿𝔥𝔦𝔰 𝔦𝔰 𝔣𝔬𝔯 𝔂𝔬𝔲 𝔞𝔰 𝔴𝔢𝔩𝔩. 𝕭𝔦𝔱 𝔬𝔣 𝔞 𝔣𝔦𝔫𝔡, 𝔠𝔬𝔫𝔰𝔦𝔡𝔢𝔯𝔦𝔫𝔤.

THE GRAMMAR SCHOOL
Llandrindod Wells
REPORT FOR – Summer Term 1987

As Mark's Pastoral Tutor and in the absence of his form Teacher/Year Head, Mr D Roberts, it behoves me to add what I can to the comments of Mark's specialist teachers in an effort to secure for him the psychological help he so clearly needs.

When first a pupil last September, he displayed undoubted aptitude in a wide variety of subjects, without excelling in any one in particular. He seemed eager to learn and to emulate his brother who until 1st May, showed unflagging application and enthusiasm. However, this term's progress has shown us a boy clearly unable to deal with the recent family tragedy. He has started to bully other pupils in a way which is completely unacceptable, showing a degree of cruelty towards them which, in a school such as this cannot be tolerated. Therefore, the Head's request for him to leave is the only option open to him. I will send you details of appropriate agencies to contact in the hope that Mark will be helped.

SV Briers BA

Although he'd slept fitfully and not heard Hector leave, Mark had listened to every sound of Lucy's movements. Getting ready, nosing around his mother's room just as he'd expected she would. A call from the study to the sweep, then a trip to the scullery. He could have intercepted her to apologise, so why not? Because she was stepping out of line. Each of her footsteps, each shut of a door had said to him 'Sod you, I've got my own agenda'. Besides, he wasn't putting himself up for yet another rebuff.

Saturday and that kiss, that declaration of love had been embarrassing enough. He had some self-respect after all. But as far as courage was concerned, it was as if it had suddenly bottomed out of his system altogether, replaced by a growing fear of what this coming week would bring. What had she been looking for? What was she up to? This fear was affecting his head. Up to now, he'd been able to use it to change things, like ballsing up her car or that Birmingham car's brakes. But not any more.

His special gift was being slowly destroyed because, apart from her snooping, Richard was around. He must have sneaked up to the Hall in the overnight mist. This was fact, and he'd known it the moment he'd seen that disgusting note on his mother's grave. Also the note on Lucy's windscreen. The screw was being tightened alright. He could feel it in every nerve of his body, every blood vessel in his head which now seemed engorged with more than fear. Why he'd phoned in sick today. The most honest excuse he'd ever made in all his seven years as a sawyer.

However, this fear wasn't just for himself, but all three of them at the Hall. And what was there to defend them from the Prodigal's return? he asked himself while slipping his T-shirt over his head. Even that brief darkness brought a frisson of panic, and he almost ripped the thing in his haste to see daylight again. The fucker should be in the army now, with the proper licence to kill. Getting it out of his rotten system. But come eighteen, he'd probably been a draft dodger. Yeah, that sounded about right. Par for the course.

OK, so he'd once idolised him. Trod in his footsteps wherever he could. Slept with his old PE shirt on his pillow. Sad bastard, you, Mark Jones... Until the stabbing. Part one of a modern crucifixion, he'd said. After that, nothing was the same again.

He ran downstairs and bolted the front door as pricks of lightning lit up the sky to the north, followed by thunder so deep, so resonant that he wondered if the Underworld could hear it.

Having secured the scullery door and checked all the windows – at least those whose sash mechanism was still working – he realised that Lucy's room was the only one which could be levered up from the outside.

Lucy...

Out there somewhere. God knew where, doing God only knew what and it was all his fucking fault for being so careless. He suddenly charged back up the stairs and into the bathroom they'd been sharing. Here at least, was something he could do. He knew what he was looking for and surely amongst his and his father's drab gear the metallic midnight blue of her Nocturne gel and spray would be obvious. But no. Her toiletries weren't there. Nothing for it but to try her bedroom. It was conveniently unlocked. Just like her big sash window.

He went in and recovered what seemed like the whole product range in her waterproof bag. He had no choice but to take them, thinking RISK more appropriate than NOCTURNE. He squirted a little of the scent on his hand and sniffed it.

My God. No...

He clamped his hand to his head as the past fast forwarded so that it was that last Saturday in April all over again. Sonia Jones had a gig booked up in Newtown for the opening of some new pub or other, and before setting off she'd looked, well, not thirty-five for a start and certainly not old enough to be a mother of two teenagers. She'd also worn her hair up that night, styled like a woman in a painting from some art history book he'd once seen at school. The name Fragonard seemed to ring a bell at the time.

Anyway, Richard had begged to go with her but she'd argued what could he possibly do? Sit in the bloody car for three hours? He was too young to be allowed in the pub and too young for drinking. He was best off keeping his da and Mark company, she'd said.

Well, he recalled as he sniffed his mother's favourite scent again. That had done it. He'd called her all sorts, hadn't he? Not whore, not then, but fairly close. By Jesus, he'd kept out of his way then. Just like he should be doing now.

He unscrewed the shower gel and the scent bottle and tipped both down the lavatory. Next, after pulling the chain he tore off two joined pieces of loo roll, wrote the words R'S BACK and took it into his father's room to lie unmistakeably on his still-dented pillow. Then down into the cellar where, so he'd been told, Irmgard Muller had hidden herself before being taken to the Abbey and where his special hole in the west wall lay behind a big loose stone.

He counted twelve up, and twenty-six along from the corner, then extracted the stone. Here he hid the spray can along with the contents of his shoe and the pieces of burnt fabric. Nothing was safe upstairs any more he thought, replacing the stone to look like all the rest. He'd have to substitute her things too, of course, with something less evocative. Less tricky.

The storm now seemed to be targeting the Hall and straightaway he unplugged the aerial in the study, noting as he did so that the Yellow Pages lay open on the CHIMNEY SWEEPS page. He then crammed his feet into his trainers and forgot to tie up the laces, but took more care than usual in locking the front door behind him, feeling the stinging rain, almost hail, slide down his neck. Once ensconced in the Renault, two anxieties surfaced in his mind. The risk of being waylaid, and someone from work recognising the van.

He held his breath all the way along the single track road to the A44, past Evans's farm with the sheep hurdles still exactly where he'd dumped them. Maybe the resentful so-called Christian had finally got the message. Maybe he'd now lie low.

Chapter Thirty-Two

𝔐𝔶 tuigen will be black as my soul is black.
It will warm my blood. Strengthen my purpose.
What is his was mine and will be mine again.
I am here. That is enough.

If I was you, I'd get the hell out...

No way. Not now, even if the sky did seem to be falling in. Even if the catalogue of lies from Ravenstone Hall seemed to be multiplying, and the truth she needed seemed further away than ever, because there was still *one* person who could tell her what had really happened. And that person, according to the Yellow Pages she'd consulted, lived fifteen miles away to the north. In the rural hamlet of Maesybont.

Lucy left Bwlch Ddu Farm behind and, having repeatedly checked her rear view mirror, rejoined the original B road signed Llanidloes, driving too fast she knew but not fast enough to get there before anyone else could tail her. It was surely too much of a coincidence that a white van had turned up at the last farm for no apparent reason – unless Mrs Hughes was hallucinating or her son's vile "smokies" business had been rumbled. If not, who'd gone to the trouble on such a wet morning? And why?

For the first time since buying her car, she regretted its vivid blue metallic colour which had caught her eye amongst all the other makes and models at the dealership. Better she'd gone for grey or black as Jon would have surely done, then it would be blending in perfectly with the drab, saturated conditions.

As she neared her destination and the rain eased to a steady drizzle, the word "families" stayed in her mind. Three syllables, that was all, but the most significant she'd heard so far. And the next half hour could well reveal all. Thirty minutes in which at least she would know which way to turn. She was prepared to believe Rhiannon's view of Richard, but if the sweep were to hint that he'd been guilty, she still might proceed with the purchase, because to all intents and purposes, he was still on the other side of the world. However, if he said Mark, then she'd be packing her bags that very afternoon...

An *Arafwch Nawr* sign preceded that of the hamlet and the road suddenly narrowed to a single car's width. She slowed to second gear as a humped-back bridge came into view, where a caped fisherman was casting his line into the water beneath. He turned briefly her way when the act was done then focused once more on his sport.

She slowed up and lowered her window. Her father had once told her that fish can be scared off by the slightest sound so not wishing to upset him, she whispered, 'Excuse me, but I'm looking for Mr Williams, the sweep.'

'Pantyfynnon it is,' he replied without looking. 'Turn left by here, then it's the second bungalow on the right.'

'Thanks.' She was about to navigate round him when he continued.

'He's poorly, mind. Not been at work since Thursday last. Thinking of retiring, he is. Then where'd we all be?' He wound his reel as he spoke and cast again into the flow while she parked up on the wet high verge beyond the bridge rather than venture down any more poky lanes. Was it possible that ravens attack at Wern Goch had been the last straw? He'd sounded pretty uptight on the phone. Scared even. Hadn't he said, 'I don't want to be next?' What the hell had that meant? Then her own special note surfaced into her consciousness making her keep a wary eye out as she locked the Rav. She shoved in both wing mirrors and checked the plasters box was still in her pocket. It was. Safe and dry, but not her. Not by a long chalk.

She sneezed twice as water slewed away downhill under her trainers and gathered in a dark pool outside the gate to the second bungalow. The already familiar new van was parked in front of one of the bay windows on a cindery patch of ground, but, apart from the simple logo along its side, there was outwardly no sign of this being home to a chimney sweep. In fact, the place didn't look like a home to anybody.

She stopped to take in the place which had now accrued so much significance in her mind.

A kind of Delphic Oracle, and one she should have consulted three days ago straight after his visit. Here too, like the other places she'd visited, an uncanny stillness prevailed, added to by the drawn curtains, the total lack of anything else living or breathing wherever she looked. She felt like a trespasser. As if here, someone's very private, self-contained domain didn't welcome strangers, least of all, anyone from Ravenstone Hall.

So, instead of going straight to the front door, she made her way round the back of the bungalow. Here again more curtains were drawn against the dark midday and the damp drenched air, in which clumps of lilies and dahlias in the busy garden had keeled over under the weight of water. Here were new PVC windows and guttering. Money well spent, she thought. A brand new chimneyless roof too, she noticed, judging by the even rows of Welsh slate the colour of Hector's bruise. 'Simnai' Williams hadn't lied. Business had clearly been going well until...until...

Mark would have to know about the consequences of his actions, she decided. The old man had obviously been badly affected by the birds' attack. In fact, if the sweep saw her, he might suddenly snap. Might even have a gun, and leap upon her like the little gnome he was. Instinctively, she looked behind her and to her surprise saw that same fisherman standing in the road. A dark, conical shape with his rod protruding like a mast against the sky.

'Haven't you tried the front yet?' he asked in a gruff Welsh voice. 'He never answers the back door.'

'Course I have,' she lied. 'But there's no reply.'

'Try again, then. He sleeps like a dog.'

'OK.' But her confidence wavered as she approached the porch, aware of the stranger's gaze on her every move. He was local, that was obvious. In his sixties she guessed, and proprietorial too. She pressed the doorbell.

'What's your business with him, anyhow?' he challenged her.

'I've got a bird's nest in my chimney. I'm not sure how to deal with it.'

'Nesting season's over. No harm in lighting a fire now. Where you from?'

She thought quickly. Tried to remember the signs passed along the way. 'Llanmadog.'

'Saesneg are you?'

'Welsh mother. Born in Cardiff.' She felt like adding, if that's alright with you.

'That's not Wales,' he said. 'And as for that Assembly. Blair's bloody puppets, the lot of them.'

The wait was too long. She tried the bell again, aware that now he was joining her, nudging the door with his black-cloaked arm.

'It's open,' he said, then whistled to himself. 'Du du. This isn't like old 'Simnai.' He's fussy about security, specially since his tools got nicked last year.'

She saw the sweep's baseball cap hanging next to five red rugby caps on a mahogany wall unit alongside photos of him as a young player. There was also one of a bearded man in white whom she assumed must be the Bard brother he'd mentioned. She stared at the poet's benign features which bore no resemblance to what she'd heard about Dagdans.

She held back as the fisherman went further inside, dripping the morning from his cape hem on to what looked like a new carpet. Normally she'd have accompanied him, but not now. Not after her visit to Bwlch Ddu. This guy could be anybody, and perhaps somewhere not so very far away, a white van was lurking...

He called out the sweep's name then reached the kitchen. Here he stopped and seemed to falter.

'Jesus Christ. My God, man,' he burbled.

Her blood had chilled. Her pulse slowed up.

'What's the matter?' she breathed, but she knew the question was futile. She only had to inhale that sickly sweet smell of death.

'Call the police, Godammit. Christ Jesus. Hurry now. Call the police.'

She snatched up the receiver in the hall but it was dead. Just like its owner.

'It's kaput. I'll use my mine.'

'Where is it?'

'In my car.'

'He's had it anyway. Tell them that.'

She heard him groan then lurch as she ran from the bungalow, her legs feeling like bendy rubber. Her head spinning. She punched 999 and her words which followed were almost incoherent. So was her promise to wait with the stranger until the police and an ambulance had arrived at the scene.

Chapter Thirty-Three

How come that blood on the point of your knife
My son come and tell to me?
Oh it is the blood of a whispering mouth
That would not silent be.
That would not silent be.
MJJ 27/8/01 After trad.

Rhayader was full of people come down from the hills braving the storm for their weekly supplies. The car park was also full but eventually Mark found a gap alongside some recycling bins and immediately began looking round for Lucy's Rav.

His heart quickened as he suddenly spotted it between a camper van and a Jeep Cherokee and when he peered in saw her sunglasses case on the passenger seat. So, where the hell was she?

He loped out of the car park sensing he was being watched, but he too was watching the bustling pavements for a man of almost thirty who would surely be tanned and possess the unmistakeably grey eyes of his mother.

More drops from the sagging shop awnings found their way to his skin as he progressed past huddles of farmers clogging up the many doorways, still moaning like Bryn Evans about paltry compensation and how some had been forced to leave lambs in phone boxes. He understood enough to know that bitterness would blight their lives for a long time and a few he'd heard of had already topped themselves, leaving widows and children to face the coming year alone.

He dived into Siop y Dic and bought a copy of the local rag, without fully registering the banner headline on the front page. It was the middle ones he wanted. For jobs. Because if something better came up where he could still hang on at the Hall he'd go for it. But only if Richard wasn't around. Today however, the Situations Vacant section made dismal reading.

Apart from a part-time butcher needed at Griffiths Meat Processing and a Betterware catalogue distributor, there was nothing. However, as he re-folded the paper in that busy damp-smelling newsagents, the headline now hit him between the eyes.

LOCAL FAMILY IN TRAGIC ACCIDENT

The body of Rhiannon George of Gellionnen, Crossgates, and those of her two four-year-old twin sons, Ben and Rhys, were discovered yesterday evening in their partially burnt-out vehicle at the foot of a ravine below a notorious bend on the A4069 to Brynamman, Carms. Although the remains of a loaded air rifle were found in the wreckage, a police spokesman said there were so far no suspicious circumstances. Meanwhile, further tests are being carried out and Rhiannon's grieving parents Eira and Iwan who suffered badly in the foot-and-mouth crisis are already on their way back from a trip to France.

Mr MH Harries, Senior Partner in Tomkins & Harries Solicitors, and Mrs George's brother, is quoted as saying, 'This is a needless loss of three young lives and I will press for a full investigation as to why my niece and her family were ever in that area at all...'

He ran from the shop, slipping the rolled-up paper inside his parka as he went. When he reached the local police station, his head began to throb again. He didn't want to see another active copper as long as he lived, and yet here he was, even *thinking* of brown-nosing a fucking uniform. Putting them off the scent...

He was just about to cross the road towards the stone-built Victorian building when he spotted a familiar figure wearing a pink fleece and carrying a Spar bag emerge from its double doors. Her face, paler than usual, with eyes fixed straight ahead. Her wet hair scooped up into a ponytail. His heart began thudding against his ribs. What the hell had she been doing in there?

'Lucy, please,' he begged her. 'Don't walk off. I've got to talk to you.'

'You've had your chance,' she turned to him, her blue eyes fierce in a way he'd not seen before. 'I've got things to do, if you don't mind and I'm certainly not wasting any more of my time with liars.'

'Liars?' His stomach took a dive.

'Yes. You and that father of yours.' She increased her distance between them and when he tried to pull her back towards him, she elbowed him away. 'Making out that Bryn Evans and Sion Hughes were one of those weirdos. Blaming the cult for killing your mother. Dagdans do *not* wear blue shirts, okay? And the rest.'

'What do mean, the rest?'

'You know damned well.'

He stared at her as if the intervening years had suddenly unfurled and she was Sonia Jones all over again with that beautiful white neck and those tiny blue veins like strands of cobalt oxide he'd once seen on pebbles in Cardigan Bay... And when he looked again he saw a crimson line below her chin. A line which seemed to widen in a mocking hideous smile... Then he remembered the bread knife still under the passenger mat in his van.

'We only wanted to protect you.'

'To protect *yourselves,* you mean. You're despicable. Anyway,' she checked her watch and began to move off again, 'I've given myself until Friday to find out who left me that threat and who killed your mother in the house which I had hoped to buy. Now, leave me alone.'

'*Had* hoped?' His voice barely more than a whisper.

'You heard.'

Nothing to lose, then.

'What made you go in there?' he gestured at the police station, at the same time attracting the locals' usual curious stares. She looked around as if unsure where to start and while he waited, felt his blood run cold.

'I'd been to see that poor sweep, if you must know,' she began. 'To apologise for what your ravens did to him last Thursday. After all, if I'm to go ahead with Wern Goch, I'll need the chimney swept regularly...'

'I don't believe I'm hearing this,' he tried to keep anger out of his voice. 'The man's a trouble-maker. A number one shit-stirrer. I wasn't going to let him get away with what he'd been implying. I was concerned for you. Anyway,' he pulled his Parka hood off his head and swept stray hair from his eyes, 'why the cops?'

'He's dead.'

'Oh my God.' He looked away at the shuffling shoppers moving up and down East street, his stomach playing tricks, his mind on fire.

'I must have just turned up after it had happened. It's terrible. Whoever did it,' she fixed her blue eyes on his, 'must be truly, deeply evil.'

He put a comforting hand on her wet arm.

'It's OK.'

'No it's not.'

'Someone hated him big time, then?'

'That's what the police assumed. Apparently he'd fallen out with people in town last Thursday morning. They'd accused him of overcharging and it got nasty. Came to blows, they said.'

'That would explain his foul mood when he turned up at our place,' he suggested, disguising the freezing fear which had griped his vocal chords. 'By the way, you didn't mention the ravens business, did you?' He watched like a hawk as she shook her head. 'Good, because I don't fancy another stint in Parc-y-Nant just yet.'

'Another?' her eyebrows raised. 'What do you mean?'

Shit.

'Sorry. Was thinking about Enid Evans.'

She threw him such an odd glance that to swiftly change the subject he pulled out his rolled-up newspaper and pointed to the headline.

'Have you seen this?'

'Yes. It's awful.' Her eyes squeezed shut for a moment as if holding back tears. His hand moved to her shoulder and he drew her closer, smelling a trace of his mother's scent.

'I can't fucking believe this either. What is going on, eh?'

'I don't know, but I had to tell the police I thought Rhiannon was being stalked. That's why she got out… Those dear little boys. Oh Jesus…'

His stomach felt worse than hollow. Was more proof needed that his brother was around? Back to rock the fucking boat. Fucking great… And here she was jumping in with both feet as well…

'It's all my fault.' She interrupted his thoughts. 'I did think about bringing the three of them back to the Hall for the time being, at least until her parents got back. I should have trusted my instincts. What's the bloody matter with me?' She came to a halt, her wet shoulders beginning to heave. He took her hand again and this time it felt as cold as winter. Then he noticed his wrist and withdrew it, to rub it clean against his Parka.

'What's the matter?'

She'd noticed it too. Christ, she didn't miss a trick.

'Nothing. Come on, we'll find somewhere warm and dry and I'll get you a drink.' He guided her over the road to the crowded Coffee Bean Café and a table at the back of the shop away from possible prying eyes. He ordered two mugs of coffee at the counter and carried them over to where she sat as if in a daze. It was time to find out more about her trip to the can because as always, forewarned is forearmed. 'By the way,' as he set both mugs down then helped lift her fleece from her shoulders. 'Did you tell the plods she used to fancy my brother?'

'Yes, but they were far more interested in the boys' father. Apparently he's a real loose canon. Wanted for burglary and intimidation. Drugs money, they reckon.'

'Sounds like a good dad.' He tried not to let his relief show, because if they came sniffing round Ravenstone again it wouldn't just be the ravens croaking. 'Let's hope the plods will re-invent themselves and snap him up pretty quickly.'

'But he's got a red Sierra and the latest news is that someone herding sheep for a cull saw two white vans on that mountain road. One seemed to be chasing the other.'

His coffee tilted in his mug as he lifted it to his lips. 'Plenty of white vans around,' he said. 'Probably yobs up from the valleys.'

'And the hills…'

'What's that supposed to mean?'

'Just thinking of some RS Thomas poem. Anyway, I told them that as far as everyone was concerned, your Richard was over the other side of the world in Darwin.'

My Richard…

'How did you know that?'

'Mr Harries mentioned it.' She pulled out her hair clasp then gathered up the damp strands of her original pleat into a ponytail. 'No wonder he seemed so upset this morning. I'd got no idea till I'd seen the newspapers.' He noticed her eyes glaze over again. He didn't want to overdo the interrogation, for fear of her clamming up, but he had to find out what she knew.

'You have been a busy bee. What else did Mr Perfect have to say?'

She didn't like that one bit. Bad move, he thought, inwardly cursing his stupidity.

'At least he's straight,' she glared at him

'Unlike me, eh?'

She sighed. A signal if ever there was for him to watch his step.

'I was about to say that according to Mr Harries, the three of you were completely cleared of any involvement in your mother's death, and in his opinion, it was either some left-over cult weirdo or someone totally infatuated with her.'

'Clever man.' He gulped down the last of his coffee. It was time to change the subject again, and he was on just poised to quiz her about her planned meeting with this other guy next Thursday when suddenly his mouth fell open, empty of words, because there outside the misted-up window was a figure he'd know anywhere. A figure whose name wasn't only Richard Ferris Jones, but Certain Death.

He leapt from his chair and hurtled towards the door, almost toppling an elderly woman and her companion as he went. His heart seemed on fire, his fists coiled, bloodless as he searched from left to right. Right to left, at strangers who eyed him with alarm and edged away.

'Mark?' Lucy was calling him. He glanced back into the café.

'What's up?' she asked as he rejoined her. 'You look terrible.'

'Thought it was the foreman from work, that's all. Shall we go?'

He waited while she gathered up her bags and slipped her arms back into her fleece.

'I need to buy a lock for my bedroom window, at least for the time being,' she announced, and once they'd left the crush of wet coats behind, she set off towards the Brynberth industrial estate and its DIY retailer which was some half a mile away. As she walked on ahead, he realised how in just two days she seemed to have imperceptibly changed. The extra-glowing skin, the subtle touches of make-up, and now, in close-up he saw wayward tendrils of dark blonde hair curled against her neck. He thought of that Smartie Tart birthday card her friend had sent and maybe now he knew why.

'This guy you're seeing,' he began as the crowds thinned out along the pavement. 'What's he like?'

'Why?' She didn't turn round.

'Just curious.'

Nevertheless he felt he might elicit more if he lightened up a bit. The question was painful enough for him as it was, and he braced himself for the answer.

'Where to start. That's the trouble...'

'OK. His voice. How does he speak?'

'Sort of West Country I suppose. He's from Bristol.'

'We went there once,' he said. His mother had done a gig near the Arnolfini one Saturday night and Hector had taken them all in the car. He also remembered the harbour. The way she walked along the quayside with her arm round Richard. The lapping oily water...

'He's a research Fellow at the University there.'

'Researching what?'

'Minerals.'

'So why's he in this neck of the woods?'

'Looking at rocks. More research, I suppose.'

'Another clever man, then,' he couldn't resist. 'You seem to go for those.'

'For God's sake, Mark. He's just good company.'

But he'd detected a blush rising above her fleece collar and in that moment, emptiness seemed to spread its tentacles around his heart.

'And I'm not?'

'That's really childish.' She turned round, glass-bead raindrops on her skin. 'He's a bloke I met quite by accident. Is having coffee together a deadly sin? Look,' she stuck out her left hand. 'See. Nothing on that fourth finger, okay? I've got to compare, haven't I?' she added.

'So how am I doing so far?'

'I'll tell you on Thursday evening.'

'I can't wait.' And he also told himself that if secretly being with her at the rendezvous meant him taking another day off work, so be it. 'Look, I know what you're thinking,' he said. 'I'm thirty. I've got my own life. I can please myself, yeah, yeah, yeah... Right?' This passable imitation brought a rare smile to her face and she playfully smacked his outstretched hand. He kept it there, as if in a trance, all the while scouring his surroundings for the man who'd just changed the blood in his veins to ice.

'I've also a confession to make,' he added.

'Now what?'

'I've got rid of all your Nocturne stuff.'

'You went into my room?' That same glare again.

'I had to. You mustn't use it any more, okay?'

'Why on earth not?'

'It reminds me too much of my mam. One sniff and everything comes back. I mean, everything. I just had a mad moment, that's all...' His pleading look seemed to work. She was softening.

'Seems like it. They weren't off the back of a lorry you know. It's the coolest perfume around in London at the moment, revived from the seventies. The spray was actually a present from Anna. It's her favourite.'

'Sorry. Look, I'll get you something else just as nice once we've sorted out a window lock.'

'That's not the point. They were mine.'

They proceeded in silence, turning off the main road until Parry & Sons DIY store came into view. Its glazed entrance doors offering an inviting glimpse into the man-made world of lighting, furniture and bathroom ware, contrasting with the dark wet hills which reared up behind the building and its busy forecourt.

He soon located what was needed and noticed that for the first time she wasn't peering at taps, or showing any interest in those artefacts which would make Wern Goch a home. She was keeping to her word, then. Keeping her project on hold until Friday 1st September. Calling all the shots.

As she rummaged in her shoulder bag for her purse at the checkout, he noticed a small brown book slide from it on to the moving rubber belt. He turned it over in his rough hands then smelt the pages.

'Hey, this is pretty ancient,' he said as she handed over a clutch of coins. '*Celtic Deities*, eh?'

'Mr Harries gave it to me, would you believe. Recommended reading, he said.'

'Oh yeah? Then he'll quietly rip you off like the rest of them. He's just got himself a brand new Daimler, did you know?'

'All *I* know is, he's lost his niece and her twins.'

'OK. So I'm a heartless bastard.' He moved over to a nearby ledge and re-opened the book on a new chapter entitled Omens and Portents.

He noticed her eyes on his fingers as he scanned the various paragraphs. How a scream will bring a death, how white feathers on a raven spell good luck. Nothing he didn't already know. He shut the book quickly. 'My brother was into all this stuff,' he found himself saying.

'So are you, it seems.'

He shook his head and handed it back to her.

'I mean, ob*sessed.*'

'Right.'

In the pause which followed, Lucy made her way to the store's exit. Here she paused and took a deep breath as if she was about to ask a question. He was right and made an effort to look normal.

'I know it's none of my business,' she began, 'but I'm just curious, okay?'

'Fire away.'

'Supposing something happened to Hector...'

'Yeah, so?'

'Who'd inherit Ravenstone?'

This was a bolt out of the blue. He blinked in surprise.

'What's the old man been telling you?'

'Nothing. Why would he?'

'The Truth is the Word, Lucy. It's the one who was sent away.'

'Richard?'

'Yup.'

She frowned. It didn't suit her. Then a funny little laugh followed. He didn't like that either.

'Given what happened, that's ridiculous, surely?'

'Like I said, Truth is the Word and the Word is sacred and divine. Why I write what I do. And why my next poem for you will knock the air out of your lungs.'

She edged away still frowning.

'It's stopped raining now,' was all she said.

And so it had. Outside, a slash of brightness pierced the penumbral sky and made them both shade their eyes. A split second of blindness in which the tall brown-eyed man who'd been observing every move, slipped away unnoticed and headed for the town's main car park.

Chapter Thirty-Four

All this beauty
and all this pain
of beholding it emptied
of those not deserving.
It is the morning of a world
become suddenly evening.
MJJ   27/8/01 (with apologies once more to RST)

So, either Mark, or worse, Martyn Harries had lied. But why? She was-
n't too befuddled to realise that the Ravenstone inheritance was an
issue and probably a complex one. Whatever, she must find out, and
told Mark she had to make a call to London.

'OK, I'll wait then you can drive back behind me. It'll be foul out of
the town.'

'Thanks.' She then punched in the lawyer's number, only to hear a
recorded message saying the office would be closed until Monday the
3rd of September.

Damn.

Hardly surprising, she thought, feeling suddenly drained by the
day's events. Her stints at the bungalow and the police station had been
demanding enough, and although DC Pugh and his team had been
grateful for both her prompt action at Maesybont and her contribution
to the Rhiannon George case, there'd been far too much paper to fill in.
Too many questions she'd been unable to answer.

On the other hand, Iolo Thomas the fisherman knew everything
about everyone with theories to match. He'd divulged how the bachelor's post-Rugby life had been blistered by disputes and grudges which,
in that part of the world never healed. So, she thought, seeing the
sawyer's reversing lights come on, small wonder Williams had said to
her he didn't want to be next. Mark was right. However, no one on this
earth deserved that kind of savagery. Neither a ratty little tradesman or
a glamorous mother of two.

Yet why had Mark been so edgy when he'd met her outside the
police station? What didn't he want the police to know? And why had
he kept looking around like a meerkat all the time? This was Rhayader
not some dodgy part of Moscow. And why that slip about Parc-y-
Nant, the local mental hospital? A quick enquiry there wouldn't do any
harm, she decided. Just to make sure.

These questions preoccupied her as he waved at her then set off out
of the car park and along the still busy main street leading to the Clock

Tower. She glanced at it, fast-forwarding to Thursday. Just then, its glistening stonework seemed to represent the one beacon of hope she so desperately needed.

Mark's head showed darkly silhouetted against his windscreen. A man she could have loved, would willingly have shared her new life with, but he was a man she couldn't fathom. Whose past and his way of coping with what had happened fourteen years ago, had already taken her way out of her depth. Like that bay just north of Caernarfon where her family had rented a holiday caravan. Where the sloping shelf of sand, suddenly sucks you down, down into the sea's grey-green womb. It had happened to her once, when she was twelve and proudly wearing a new yellow swimming costume. Her mother was busy reading on the beach, her father examining shells with his usual curiosity.

She'd waved to him, like Mark had just done to her, then felt her ankles gripped by the sand. One heavy step to free herself, then another, until to her horror, the cold salty sea had reached her mouth, her lungs, filling her up so her scream was drowned. She'd vomited water then screamed again, feeling nothing under her feet, until a hand fastened on hers. A strong, pulling hand dragging her to safe dry sand.

Yes, her father had saved her life. Just like she knew he would again, before it was too late. So, had those screams she'd heard at Wern Goch and the waterfall been some kind of echo from her past? A warning, even? She told herself no. That sort of notion was more Mark's domain – the cyclical world of the Celts. A world she was growing more and more reluctant to enter.

He waved yet again and sounded his horn. She replied, observing how the whole region seemed to have sunk in upon itself by the sheer force of the morning's rain, and that normal daylight wasn't going to be resumed.

She continued in tandem behind him as far as the Coed-y-Bryn Forestry on her way back to the Hall, then watched his white van take the rough track off the main road and disappear among the firs. He gave a further series of toots on the horn as he went which sent a coven of back birds into the sky. He'd planned to offer himself for the number 4 shift which would mean a late return that evening, however, thirty quid's pay was thirty quid he'd said, smiling, especially as he'd just stumped up the same amount for Chanel No.5 eau de toilette and body spray.

To keep herself sane, she thought about Thursday. At least she'd bought herself another new T-shirt – pink, this time – which would go well with her River Island skirt. Six mother-of-pearl beads lay beneath the low neckline and, considering it had come from Dorothy's Dresses, whose archaic window display was hidden behind a shroud of yellow cellophane, not bad at all. Anna would certainly have approved.

Flirty, feisty Anna who'd made the step up to editor two years ago and for whom, just the once, on the day of her appointment, Lucy had felt a moment's jealousy. However, Anna had never flaunted her success, often telling her friend that her time would soon come. And before freelancing, hadn't she on more than one social function with drink in hand, nobbled Hellebore about their lack of foresight in not promoting her? Yes, good old Anna. Her one true mate. Yet surely there'd been plenty of other birthday cards to choose from? And talk about pot calling the kettle black, she thought meanly.

Maybe she was over-reacting, guilty about her imminent date with a relative stranger. Maybe after her busy, horrendous morning, she was simply going mad.

She stepped on the gas and by the time she'd manoeuvred the Rav on to the Hall's driveway had convinced herself that somehow, by divine intervention with the guardians of both herself and the sacred land fully activated, the only way, surely, was up.

To her surprise the Hall's front door was locked and for a few seconds she tussled with the hideous handle wondering why if Hector was around, he'd done that. Maybe he was out on the estate somewhere. Maybe down at Wern Goch. She wanted to ask him why he'd lied about Hughes and Evans. In a nutshell, to tell him to stop taking the piss.

She used her own key, and sneezed repeatedly in the bright yellow hallway, praying that full-blown flu wasn't on its way. She unpacked her shopping and left the Persil and fabric conditioner in the scullery. So far no sign of the man who'd promised to go to Llanfihangel-Nant-Melan, and even the usually cluttered kitchen table was ominously bare.

She unwrapped one of the cereal bars she'd bought and jammed half of it in her mouth as she made her way back down the hallway to his study. She listened outside the door but her chewing was the only sound she could hear. When she turned the handle she realised that this too, was locked.

'Hector?' she said. 'It's me, Lucy.' Sensing that earlier optimism slipping away and unsure where to try next. If he'd been outside somewhere, surely he'd have heard her car and come to see her. This was very odd, she decided. Very odd indeed, when all she wanted to know was if he'd managed to find anything more about what she'd heard at Water Break Its Neck.

She poked her head round the dining room door which was next to the kitchen. A room where the curtains were still drawn and the smell of damp from that nearby soil bank pervaded. Rarely used, she guessed and because it wasn't somewhere she wanted to linger. She was about to close the door when, to her horror, she noticed a dark shape slumped in the farthest dining chair at the end of the long oval table.

'Who's that?' she called out, ready to run if necessary, then slowly recognised the familiar shape of a head, shoulders and body as Hector Jones began to raise himself from the chair. 'I didn't mean to disturb you,' she blurted as a deep shiver made her teeth tap-tap together. 'I was just wondering how you got on in…'

Here she stopped, because this dishevelled man who was advancing ever closer, none too steadily on his feet, looked as if he'd just risen from that very grave outside.

'My God. What's the matter? What's wrong?' She felt the door press into her back and for a split second realised that here she was, alone in a huge old house with someone she barely knew and who was now clearly disturbed.

No one will hear you scream…

But scream she did. Then with her shoulder bag clutched to her damp fleecy chest, she fled the Hall. Within ten seconds she was in her car, heading full tilt back to the Coed-y-Bryn Forestry. She had no choice. How else could she reach Mark to persuade him to get back home? If he'd been truly part of the twenty-first century, he'd have possessed a mobile. But no. Not him. And as the overgrown hawthorn hedges brushed the Rav's sides, she was vaguely aware of some white van behind her. She tried to pick out the driver's features, even the shape of the head, but in the poor light it was impossible. She cursed the sawyer's almost primitive insularity at being phoneless, and wondered yet again if she'd been hearing things as she'd pelted down those Hall steps.

'Come back, Lucy. For Christ's sake. Come back…'

The white van slowed up behind her then continued on its way after she turned right on to that same unmade track down which Mark had driven only forty minutes earlier. It was therefore impossible to read its numberplate, or to identify the make, and she wished she'd pulled over to let it overtake. Could it be the same one shown up at Sion Hughes's farm? How on earth could she know? And if it was the same vehicle, who was keeping tabs on her and why?

Her ponytail suddenly fell loose around her face as she entered the sombre daylight of the plantation and followed signs for OFFICE over a wide stone bridge. Yet again, Martyn Harries's comment about Celtic nights came to mind as the day's gloom deepened and the Wye stormed in turmoil beneath the bridge's old stone parapets, its din even through the glass, blasting what was left of her brain.

She saw at close hand how the rocks, despite their size and number, were treated with contempt by this river's powerful flow. The only concession to their presence being flimsy bursts of spray which vapourised as quickly as they'd appeared, and to her just then, this watery chaos seemed to symbolise everything she'd so far experienced in this strange unpredictable country.

She opened her window a fraction just to hear for herself the roar which seemed to devour not just her but the whole universe, then quickly closed it, amazed that this racket hadn't made Mark deaf.

To her relief she soon reached a Portakabin fronted by a dirt yard where two lorries were being loaded up with timber. Here a different bedlam assailed her the moment she got out of the car. A tinnitus-inducing whine of saws coming from an adjacent open barn, drowning the drivers' wolf whistles as she jogged over to the office's main door.

'Is Mark Jones anywhere here?' she asked the young lad who sat with a ledger and thermos in front of him on a trestle table. 'He's a sawyer. About my age.' The din was only marginally less inside and she could barely make out his reply.

'I dunno. Just standing in till me mam gets back.'

'He must have arrived half an hour ago,' she persisted. 'He's got a white Renault van, for God's sake. He's tall, dark, wearing jeans and a dark green parka…' Not so long ago she'd have added attractive, hunky, just like Ewan McGregor… But not now. That was Paul, unencumbered, uncomplicated.

'If he's on the saws, he'll be down The Cwm.'

'The Cwm? Where on earth's that?' Minutes were ticking by. She had to get Mark home as soon as possible.

'It means valley.'

'So?'

''Bout a mile from here, I reckon.'

'Is there any way you can get hold of him for me?' She looked around the office in vain for any signs of a mobile or two-way radio. 'It's urgent.'

'You'll get to it easy enough. Just follow the blue markers down past the nursery slopes. You should see him there.'

She ran back towards her car, acutely aware that with such lax security, anybody could just wander in and out at will. This wasn't a reassuring thought as the trees now seemed closer together, usurping the few remaining fragments of grey sky. She strained to catch sight of the blue markers, wondering why the hell they weren't yellow instead, and as soon as the ill-defined route, criss-crossed by mountain bike tracks dropped downwards, an almost total darkness encased her.

'Damn.' She narrowly missed a group of firs and just as she was praying for some evidence of forestry work, some legitimate human company, her left wing mirror showed a white vehicle threading its way between the more sparsely planted younger-looking pines. Was it a car or a van? She couldn't tell. Then when it was sideways on, she knew, and panic followed. Surely if it was Mark and he'd seen her Rav, he'd have made a beeline for it. So who could it be?

She was distracted by the track suddenly widening to a clearing and a group of men about to set off into an older plantation of broad-leaved trees, their saws slung over their bodies like the weapons they were.

Mark seemed to freeze when he saw her.

'It's your dad,' she shouted through her half-open window, allowing that familiar sap smell to fill her car. 'Hurry.'

'Something's come up, boys,' he yelled to the rest of the team as he pulled off his protective gear and his saw then disappeared round the back of a makeshift shed. 'I'll be in at 6 a.m.. Tell the boss if you see her, eh?' Within seconds his van appeared from behind it and he led the way back through the secretive darkness, his red tail lights intermittent between the trees.

Of that other van there was no sign, but her immediate anxieties centred on what was awaiting them at the Hall, and why Hector Jones had seemed like a man who was losing his mind.

'Open up, you pain in the arse!' Mark repeatedly banged the solid brass knocker because neither his keys nor hers could unlock bolts. While they waited for a response, she glanced down at Wern Goch's one chimney which had once naively represented a hoped-for peace and independence. Fat chance of that now, she thought bleakly. For a start this afternoon had been completely sabotaged and her TRUTH STRATEGY lost in a mire of imponderables. Yet now wasn't the time to let on she'd been to Bwlch Ddu. The two inhabitants of Ravenstone Hall weren't the only ones who could lie.

'Who is it?' Hector called out.

'Mark and Lucy, you old fuckwit.'

'Move to the right where I can see you both.'

'Shit, he's losing it this time,' muttered Mark, placing himself directly in front of the study window and beckoning her over.

She caught sight of Hector's face staring out. More a death mask than anything living. He suddenly banged on the glass. 'You've not been playing tricks have you? You didn't turn up about an hour ago and just circle round and round out there?'

'Don't be daft.' Mark turned to her, perplexed. 'I've been at work...'

'So who was it?'

'God knows.'

'There was just the one person inside, I'm sure of that.' Hector moved away from the study window, slid the front door's bolts and pulled it open. 'But when I took a proper look from the door here, the thing had gone.'

'Did you see the plates?'

'No. Covered in mud they were. But I'd swear it was a Renault.'

'Look,' said Mark his eyes roaming around the drive and surrounding marshland. 'It could have been anybody. I mean think who's got white vans round here? The fish, the papers, the fruit...'

'We've not had fucking fruit for years.'

'OK. You know what I mean, and by the way,' he added, letting her in through the door first. 'If you'd been behaving like a rational human being just now, she wouldn't have had to drive all the way to Coed-y-Bryn and I could be back there earning some dough.'

Without replying Hector re-bolted the door behind them both. Then he prodded Mark's shoulder.

'Don't you lecture to me about being rational, son. Just cast your mind back fourteen years ago...'

Mark tore off his parka still with the newspaper jutting from its pocket and slung it over the coat rack.

'Yeah? And?'

'I wouldn't have described *you* as being exactly normal.'

'For God's sake,' she stepped in. 'This slanging match isn't going to get us anywhere. We've had this awful news about poor Rhiannon George and her kids, and now the sweep...'

'What?' Hector's face blanched. 'You don't mean old 'Simnai'?'

'Chop chop,' smiled Mark. 'Not very tidy either, according to Lucy here.'

Hector looked at her for some explanation.

'I called to see him this morning. No big deal,' she shrugged. She'd been interrogated enough and putting two detailed statements together had almost squeezed the lemon dry.

'Apologising about the ravens if you please.'

'Fair enough, son. Fair enough.' He returned to his study. 'Could have got us in a spot of bother that little episode. We're not in the line of fire are we?'

'No. Our plods are fingering Llew Bevan, or so I heard down the Cwm. Doesn't surprise me, mind. Nasty piece of work, he is.'

Hector's colour returned to normal but his eyes, she noticed, seemed on fresh alert, focused now for some reason on the field to the left of the driveway.

'Four people dead, and why? That's what I'd like to know,' he muttered.

'Any news about the waterfall?' she judged it a good moment to ask him, since the Rhayader Constabulary had clearly had no luck so far.

'I have been busy, I can assure you,' Hector said, making for the bar and considering the bottles on offer. 'My trip was well worth while, and all I can say at this stage is that wheels are in motion. When we know more, then that information will be passed on to you.'

To her, this sudden formality was alarming and she noticed how Mark too had paled.

'We? What do you mean?' he demanded.

Hector poured himself a hefty dose of gin and not much tonic. In three gulps it was gone.

'I still have friends, remember? Good friends who can help. Now, that's all I'm prepared to say, except that given what we know you, Lucy, were lucky to leave that unsafe place with your life.'

'My God.'

She slumped into one of the worn old chairs. It wasn't just hunger making her legs weak, but a creeping sense that something horrendous was determined to turn her world upside down. A world which, against all the odds, she'd struggled to rebuild. Now it seemed that dreamy book which through her childhood years had brought her and her father so close together, was nothing more than sugary icing on a mouldy cake. In fact, all deception.

She looked over towards Mark for support but for some reason he'd buried his head in his hands. What could have upset him? Surely any help to find what had happened there was a bonus? Then the disquieting thought niggled in her mind that maybe, for him, the police were bad news. She only had to remember his face that very morning as she'd left the police station. And what about the grilling she'd been subjected to later?

Hector meanwhile, fingered the gin bottle, obviously contemplating another drink. He then turned to her and Mark, looking older, frightened.

'I would urge you not to mention anything about what you heard at the waterfall to anyone. And I mean anyone. Understood? This is low-key, at the moment, and we don't want information reaching the wrong ears. Now then sir,' he looked across at his son. 'What's up?'

'You.'

She bit her lip again as Mark got up and walked out. He slammed the door behind him and left a relieved silence in his wake.

'Damned boy.'

'Look, what about that note I had?' she asked, to divert attention from the floorboards juddering overhead.

'I still need to keep it for the time being. It's quite safe, believe me. And I'm sorry if I gave you a scare, earlier on,' he said, 'but I don't get the wind up easily.'

'I'd be lying if I said it's OK. I *was* scared stiff if you must know.' She could hear the noise of doors banging upstairs. Of drawers being opened and closed. But surely, Mark's room was next to hers. 'Is that his bedroom?' she asked as evenly as she could.

'Yes. And he's a noisy fucker. Always has been.'

'So, whose is the room the other side of your wife's?'

'His brother's. Why?'

'No reason at all.'

And yet this was where that shoe box and its grisly contents lay. Could this be a room full of other secrets, she asked herself, with Mark as its zealous caretaker?

Chapter Thirty-Five

And what will you do when your father comes to know
My son come and tell to me?
Oh I'll set foot in a bottomless boat
And sail and sail across the sea
And sail across the sea.
The Brothers. Irish Trad.

While a badly bruised Jade Gregory lay unconscious on the riverbed's wet stones near the edge of the Pit of Hell, Elizabeth Benn heard her husband leave the house, knowing he was on his way to the local newsagent in Burton Minster to collect a copy of the *Dorset Gazette*. Immediately she heard the front door click shut behind him, she transferred the bodkin from inside her slipper to her nightdress sleeve and reminded herself that from now on she must keep that right arm straight.

He'd not slept at all, she could tell by the protesting sighs of what had once been their mattress under his restless weight. And now at 6.45 a.m. back in her own bedroom, she could hear him getting up, using the lavatory and then the buzzing whine of his electric shaver. She hated that sound more than anything, because she could imagine the shaver's head on his skin, smoothly caressing, just as her foolish fingers had done so long ago.

Now she longed to hear a gasp of pain, to know that he'd nicked those jowly flaps which during recent years of excess, had so altered his looks. But James was far too careful with himself for that. Except for *Conquests 2001*, which anyone but the blind could easily have discovered. Unless he'd wanted her to find it, of course. To drum home that, as his wife she was literally bottom of his fucking heap.

She felt numb with exhaustion. The last few days almost beyond endurance but she'd felt Katherine had been with her, willing her to survive his cunning cruelty. The disorientation games he'd learnt in the army. Even the fact that Lucy Mitchell had declined her offer of money hadn't depressed her as much as she'd imagined. After all, she told herself, hearing the front door slam behind him, it would only take one and the rest would follow.

She propped herself up higher in her bed and reached over to lift up the nearest venetian blind. She'd need a little light – not too much – and where sunlight would have been inappropriate, so this dull grey strip of morning was perfect. She heard the phone ring in his study, not just once, but twice and then again. She smiled to herself, despite her hunger pangs. So, the news was out. The bush telegraph clearly in full swing. All she must do, knowing that Guy Roper was on her side, was compose herself, raise her will over her bodily failings in readiness for what the next hour might bring.

The sound of his key in the front door came first. Next, it closing. Once upon a time this was an event she'd looked forward to, but never Katherine, even as a youngster, and he'd resented this until the day she died. He'd crave attention from a cockroach, would James Benn, she thought bitterly, listening now to his every move. She recalled how he'd never attended any school concerts where his violin-playing step-daughter, not he, was centre stage.

What now? She angled her head towards the bedroom door, puzzled by the unexpected silence. Was he shoeless to confuse her? Or had he gone out again, perhaps to the garage or garden, leaving a door ajar?

With the greatest effort and the worst pain ever in all her joints, she moved her legs sideways until both bare feet touched the floorboards. The wood felt cold against her skin, but at least sitting there, actually facing the only point of entry made her feel less vulnerable against the inevitable…

Eight a.m.. An hour gone already, but the dull light from outside stayed resolutely unchanged. Her stomach rumbled on emptiness as she blinked repeatedly to stay awake, because even one second's dozing off would give him the advantage. He'd already snatched her mobile before handing her something disgusting called a Pot Noodle at five o'clock yesterday, with no means of eating it except with her fingers. The smell of it still lingered. Chicken and mushroom, now that *was* pure fiction, with bits of yellow noodles dried on to her nightdress. She eyed the empty plastic carton on her beside table. Its glossy unopened sauce packet lurking inside…

She saw neither the door open nor his beige socks. When she did, she gasped in fear. He was smiling with no teeth showing. The most dreaded expression in his repertoire.

'Well, Elizabeth, my dear,' he produced a folded newspaper from behind his back and presented it to her with the heavy black banner headline facing her way. 'Take a look at this.'

TOP DORSET AUTHOR ACCUSED OF RAPE

'Someone's been having fun.'

'I don't understand,' she tried to make her frown convincing as she read Guy Roper's damning report. 'This really is terrible. It can't be true, so why's this…this creature saying it is?'

Benn sat next to her, immediately causing her to tilt towards him.
And still he smiled.

'You tell me.'

In close up, his shaved skin resembled that of sunburnt pigs she'd
once seen in Spain. His eyes the hardest she'd ever seen, but when he
suddenly hit her, they became a multitude.

'No. It's preposterous,' she blurted. 'Even about the screaming he
says he heard when he spoke to you.'

Benn snorted spittle into her face. 'That's the fucking least of it. So
why did Roper tell me you'd stitched it up, by offering money to the
tart?' He leaned closer so she could smell him and when her normal
vision returned, the capillaries in his cheeks were the rivers of hell. His
wet mouth an adulterer's cave...

So, she thought. Thank you for that, Guy Roper. So much for
trust...

'He's making this up. He's got to be. I've never heard of the man.'

But Benn wasn't listening any more. She could tell. Instead he
pulled her mobile out of his inside pocket and waved it in front of her
face.

'I should have found this on you sooner. Do you realise, woman,
this could finish me? All my years of writing and re-writing, the
research, the fucking degrading creeping and crawling to get myself
noticed...' He then flung it to the floor where it splintered and died and
all the while Elizabeth could feel his thigh against hers where her nightdress had rucked up to expose it.

'You've planned this all along. Blow by fucking blow...' His fist connected with her cheek and the spasm of hurt made her bladder release
hot pee down her legs on to the floor. 'You filthy lying bitch.'

This time, her mouth took the third hit and immediately she felt her
teeth loosen and float in a thick coppery stew. Her left hand began to
move as if to check the damage, but instead rested near her nightdress's
other sleeve. It would be so easy. He was as close as he'd ever been during the past five years. As close as he would ever be again, and she was
thankful that his clothes, minus the usual vest, were lightweight. Her
weapon lay firm, invisible against her palm. She would be quick and
accurate. Something for which Lance Hewitt had always praised her.
And now this was for herself, and Katherine.

Her husband made no sound as the bodkin's length pierced his
heart, just a rather strange gurgling sigh from the depths of his open
throat, before he keeled over behind her. She checked his pulse above
his flaccid freckled hand. It had gone.

She turned her head to see a crimson trickle appear from the corner of his mouth and added to it by spitting out a mix of blood and teeth on to his upturned face. She then slid away from him and on to her knees. After half an hour she'd crawled from this ground floor bedroom to his study, surprisingly unlocked, and managed to reach the telephone.

Guy Roper wasn't available, so she left her brief toothless thanks to await his return. Then she eased James's signed hardbacks and paperbacks off the lower shelves, slewing them one by one across the hall's parquet floor. *Elizabeth* the heaviest of all, then *Tribe, Fellow Bones* and *Stark Light Rising* - the rotten fruit of all his lies...

She had to keep spitting out blood, but that didn't matter now because once she'd formed a sizeable pile of volumes in the middle of the floor and found his cigar lighter handily near the edge of his desk, it only took a click of its lid to produce a compact little flame. Blue and hungry.

'I couldn't destroy the garden, dearest Katherine,' she said, letting its bright tongue nudge against the first book he'd ever had published. 'Because that was your special place. The only spot on this earth where you were truly happy. And now soon, at last, I'll be joining you...'

She felt a comforting warmth already begin to reach her punished body and watched dispassionately as the pages of her eponymous book crumpled and browned with startling ease. Those sombre photographs of her life soon devoured, together with all previous plans to save herself.

As the heat increased and the flames began to lick the chandelier above, she heard the phone ring then the answerphone with Guy Roper returning her call. Elizabeth smiled once more, recalling that Flower Fairy poem as the hem of her nylon nightdress which lay closest to the blaze, began to melt...

> '*I was a warrior*
> *When, long ago,*
> *Arrows of Dogwood*
> *Flew from the bough...*'

It wasn't until 9.45 a.m. that a perturbed Nick Merrill, who'd been trying to contact his author since the news broke, called the Dorset police. At ten o'clock, against a backdrop of church bells tolling out the hour on that dismal morning, two officers from the Blandford Constabulary arrived at the Manor House but could get no further than the gate.

Chapter Thirty-Six

Ständige Nacht, Köningreich der Morrigan, Phantomköningin, dessen Sexgeruch dieses
Nichts verdebt, während des Eisatems von ihrer Kehle kein mitbringt, nur Todesschrein. Wie
viel Leiden kann sie noch zufügen? Wie viel mehr irdischen Tod? Der kahlköpfige Rabe ver-
liert nie meine Seite, doch ich habe mehr Angst vor seinem Schnabel, als vor dem, welch er
von meinem Verstand stehlt, da ich weiss, was so eine Waffe tun kann. Und was ist mit
meinen Lügen? Meinen überspannten Konfekten, die zu viele geködert haben, in meiner
Dunkelheit zu teilen? Verzeih' mir.

IGM   No time

At 10.30 a.m. as the Manor House in Burton Minster smouldered like the
last of some huge bonfire, and the Benn's charred remains were being
transferred to Dorchester in a flurry of flashing lights, Lucy took a thank
you call from DC Pugh about the incident at Water Break Its Neck. She'd
been planning to make herself some toast from a new loaf she'd bought
yesterday, but after just two minutes had something far less pleasurable
to think about. She knew for a fact that Hector Jones hadn't gone anywhere near any newsagents in Llanfihangel-Nant-Melan on Monday
morning, or contacted any of his so-called "friends" in the force.

In fact, the officer had seemed puzzled she'd even mentioned him in
connection with the affair, and his tone also slyly suggested that the ex-
Cardiff copper wasn't fully compos mentis. So, why had Hector lied
about even that? Why the exhortation for secrecy? she asked herself as
she stared at the uncut loaf with suddenly no desire to eat. These questions persisted as the DC continued.

'The young woman we located there is, unfortunately, in a coma.
It's touch-and-go at the moment, I'm afraid.'

'My God. So it *was* a young woman's scream she'd heard. Her gut
instincts had been right after all.

'What happened to her?'

'We can't be sure yet. But she certainly fell a long way.'

'Is there anything else I can do? Has she any family?' she asked,
because just then, any kind of normal supportive family seemed the
most precious commodity in the world.

'That's very kind of you, Miss Mitchell, but her parents are already
on their way from London.'

London... What a strange word already...

'That's something then,' she said bleakly, keeping a wary eye on the
open kitchen door as she sat at the table with her Wern Goch file and
the lilies' foul odour for company.

'We've also spoken to staff at The Granary Café,' he went on. 'At

around half-past eleven the lad serving there saw a young female matching her description with a man who had a definite Australian accent.'

'Australian?'

'That's right.'

Something was niggling at her again; to do with that typical Aussie
expression "no worries" which Paul had used on Saturday. No, she
berated herself. That was totally and utterly crazy, everyone uses
Aussie slang these days. It's a universal language. And so busy was she
with these new thoughts that she missed the beginning of DC Pugh's
response.

'...and very personable he was too, according to the young waiter
and an assistant at Booth's bookshop who remembers him well.
Apparently, on Wednesday evening he'd purchased a copy of the
Mabinogion.'

'That's odd.'

'We're also investigating a brutal rape which took place above the
Garreg Ddu reservoir in the Elan Valley in the early hours of Monday
morning...'

She forgot to breathe. Both her hands gripping the table edge.

'You don't think this rapist is connected to that woman as well? I
mean...' she couldn't finish.

'We're keeping an open mind at this stage, but certainly wouldn't
rule out a connection. The rape victim also claims her assailant might be
Australian. In both cases a black 4x4 has been seen in the vicinity.'

Again.

There was no time to offer her sympathy, because Mark was coming
downstairs. She immediately made for the scullery where the officer
continued.

'We'll keep you informed, and thank you again for your help and
vigilance. We'll be contacting you later.'

'Later?' she whispered from behind the door, aware of Mark's footsteps in the hall.

'When's that?'

'As I'm sure you understand, Mr Williams is our priority at the
moment. I can't say too much, obviously, but an arrest is imminent. It's
good people like yourself and Mr Thomas who enable us to enjoy the
success rate we have in solving crime.'

Enjoy? And what about May 1987?

She shoved the phone back in her pocket and sat down again in
front of the file. The word Darwin suddenly like a tic on her brain.

Her stomach rumbled and she thought of toast again, so she got up
to pull open the cutlery drawer beneath the old worktop. Where the

bread knife had been was just an empty space.

Don't panic.

But where on earth was it? She'd have to ask someone, because there was nothing else to use apart from a small worn-down vegetable knife. She checked the sink and the other drawers without success then gave up on the idea altogether because when she glanced out of the kitchen door, Mark was carting an array of full carrier bags and assorted hold-alls to the front door. His face a mask of grim determination.

She followed him, surprised not only to see him wearing a black leather jacket and matching jeans but also the fact that by wearing these clothes, he clearly wasn't going to work. And now wasn't the best time to ask for his help.

However, once he was safely outside, she ran upstairs to what she now knew had been Richard's room. Apart from the knife, she had to find those black shoes. This time the bed was strewn with various items, as if waiting to be either binned or sorted, including, and here she held her breath – a half-empty pack of white postcards, nestling under a paperback on Dürer's art with **Rf Jones** scrawled on its flyleaf. Nothing remotely like the writing style of those two poisonous messages.

YOU'RE NEXT and WHORE was all she could think of as she searched for the familiar onyx shoe box, and when she'd discovered it under the bed, breathed a huge sigh of relief. She lifted off its lid. So far so good. Both black shoes still lay inside it. However, they them-selves were empty and the collection of Spar bags and their contents nowhere to be seen.

For God's sake, where to look now? she wondered, wishing she'd snatched the lot while she'd had the chance on Saturday. Now the police would never find them. Nor was there time to look anywhere else, or even work out whose postcards they were. Or indeed if they were significant.

And what about the knife..?

No time to dwell on that. She had to get out of the room pronto, and as the door into the green-tiled bathroom was conveniently wide open, she ducked inside and leant her weight against it, not daring to breathe. While he returned for yet more belongings, she noticed Mark's facecloth and toothpaste had gone, and also more oddly, the lid of the cork-topped stool was open. Had someone been looking for what she'd already found in that plasters box? she asked herself, more than puzzled by what had triggered off his show of leaving. He'd said he'd loved her, hadn't he? She'd never forget that pleading look in his lustrous eyes as long as she lived. That need to be some part of her life. So why was he presumably finding somewhere else to live? Or was this all because she was seeing Paul tomorrow?

As a kid, she'd done what he was doing. Twice round the block and back home for a sound telling-off from her mother. So much for freedom. The great escape. And then she remembered his ever-present fear. Was something or some*one* driving him away?

As Mark repeated his journeys to and from his own and his brother's room, she kept track of him, and sure enough, from her vantage point by the umbrella stand, saw him load up his van in the drizzle. She went out to join him but he was patently ignoring her.

'What's all this about?' she tapped him gently on the shoulder. 'Where are you off to?'

For a moment he flinched, then glanced at her long enough for her to notice that between his thick black eyelashes lay droplets of tears. He looked the saddest man on the planet, and she was tempted to reach out and stop any more of his loading up. To ask him to stay, to write her more of his strange poetry. To be a friend. Instead she thought of the kitchen drawer.

'You've not seen the bread knife anywhere, have you?' was as bland as she could make it. 'I wanted to cut some toast.'

He in turn, barely reacted.

'It's in the van. I need it for cutting baler twine. OK?'

'Sorry I spoke,' she muttered to herself, feeling somewhat stupid as he retrieved it from the front somewhere and waved it in the air before returning it to the car.

'You can have your toast when I've finished.'

'Fine. Not.'

Then, just as she'd turned towards the Hall again, wondering where Hector was, his voice suddenly boomed out from inside his truck, making her jump.

'That's enough, Mark John Jones. Stop right there.' He pushed open his driver's door and charged over to his son before expertly locking his arms behind his back. 'I've been watching you,' he grunted. 'And where do you think you're going eh? Deserting the fucking sinking ship, is that right?'

Sinking ship? What on earth did that mean..?

Too confused to fully absorb the implications of what he'd just said, she didn't know whether to stay and watch the proceedings, or go to Mark's aid. She felt the shower cap safe in her pocket. A time bomb maybe, but now wasn't the time to reveal it to anyone because tomorrow was for pleasure. The first she'd known since she'd arrived in Wales, and nothing was going to stand in her way. Friday – deadline day – would come soon enough.

'Leave me alone, you poxy old turd.' Mark wrestled in his father's grip until suddenly Hector kneed him in the back and brought him down.

She couldn't bear to watch any more. She'd left the mean streets of London for a better quality of life, and here she was in the middle of peaceful Radnorshire with a serious and to her, unecessary, brawl on her hands. She went over to where Hector who now straddled his croaking son on the wet muddy ground.

'Corax...corax...corax...'

Time to act. To show she meant business. She took a deep breath. It was now or never time. As if everything she'd heard so far had curdled into that river mist. As if reason and logic were just useless words, with even her own father egging her on.

'OK,' she addressed them both, seeing Mark's dark eyes focused up on her in a way that was impossible to ignore. 'Whatever's been done, whatever's been said is history and it must be put back in the past where it all belongs. The fact is, I'm going to need you both. I realise you've strung me a load of lies like some kind of weird double-act and my pro-ject's been derailed from day one, but,' she looked away towards Wern Goch not noticing the steadily advancing cloak of ravens overhead. 'I've given up everything to come here. I mean everything. And look what *you've* got, for God's sake. I've seen decent people through no fault of their own shacked up in cardboard boxes. Women and kids scavenging round the bins for food... You take a trip under Waterloo Bridge sometime. That would make you bloody grateful. There's this place for a start,' she gestured towards the building behind her, 'which could be a stunning home; you've got the landscape, the skies, the whole natural world on your doorstep...'

But her rousing monologue was cut short by the ravens' sudden presence, as if from nowhere. They were advancing even closer towards her, their white-tipped beaks open in attack mode, and suddenly she screamed as Hector let go of his grip on Mark and staggered towards the Hall. He gamely fought them off and cursed non-stop as he pushed her up the steps and into safety.

An uneasy truce reigned throughout that dank and dismal morning, with neither man referring to the incident either to each other or to her. While Mark changed back into his old gear, unpacked his van, and left in surly mode as though for the forestry, she overheard Hector receive several calls, getting more and more agitated as each one ended. When she finally went into his study, she found him hunched inside his bar in surly silence, and upon asking for both her items back, received no reply. It was as if she'd never been in Ravenstone Hall and triggered that hopeful change in him. Now he looked like a man awaiting the gallows.

She then binned her stinking birthday lilies and finally, with her half of that postcard safe in her bag, she went up to her room holding a welcome mug of coffee between her hands. She placed it on the floor while she tried the door of Richard's room to hunt again for those morsels. It was locked.

Damn. What else did she expect? Now there was no way anyone would believe those bits had ever existed, and that thought filled her with such panic that she delayed going down to blitz Wern Goch. Better to try and chill for a few moments with her drink and Mr Harries's little book, she told herself. She needed to calm down. To try and think straight.

She sat at the dressing table amongst her make-up bits and pieces, the new window lock still hermetically sealed in the Parry & Sons DIY pack and the new Chanel companions. Anna would have gone ape at Mark's interference over that. However, seeing these replacements which had cost him a day's wages, hit home to her how traumatised he still must be. Traumatised enough to sustain what were clearly now untruths, and lead her up so many convoluted garden paths? Possibly. And hadn't her Christian upbringing rammed forgiveness down her throat since day one?

Maybe that's what she had to do, now that iconic *Magical Tales from Magical Wales* was so obviously wide of the mark. Her mother would approve; her father too. She actually felt better believing that yes, she could forgive. Forget? No way, but at least that particular Commandment might help her see a way forward. Because now, more than ever before, that's what she needed.

She now turned her attention to the musty little volume whose pages almost seemed to part on their own to reveal a pen and ink study of a giant male figure, who, with his wheeled club, dwarfed the surrounding landscape. She stared at the face – full of glowering menace, of hatred even. Nothing remotely like the decorative picture in *Magical Tales.* She suppressed a shiver then began to read the accompanying caption…

THE DAGDA

The most illustrious of the Celtic gods who was specifically associated with Druidism. His is a deity of great power and two of the most potent symbols of this power are the Club or Staff, and the Cauldron. These, according to Druidic tradition, were both primal and pagan implements, providing both spiritual and physical nourishment.

By controlling the Cauldron, the Dagda shows himself to be the god of abundance and fertility, while his club brings life with one end and death with the other…

So, the Dagda overrides Cerridwen...

She stared at the text's unsettling symbolism, but read on, unaware of time passing. However it wasn't until she reached the next section which detailed several other well-known legends, that the shiver had become an inexplicable chill invading her whole body. But why? There was no draught from her door or the window which was wholly shut. Nevertheless, as she read further, she had the strangest feeling that maybe at least a small part of Ravenstone's puzzle might just be falling into place...

> *On the eve of Samhain, the turning point of the Celtic year, the Dagda makes love to the Morrigan, the fiery red-haired goddess of death.*
>
> *He mates with her while she stands astride the river Unius in Connaught, for she is the death goddess, washing the dead of an imminent battle which he will win.*
>
> *The Morrigan (see also page 27) otherwise known as the Phantom Queen, possesses other forms known as Nemhain and Badhbh, meaning 'frenzy' and *'raven.' Therefore, good readers, here is a god of life conjoining with a goddess of death – symbolising the great universal forces which affect mankind...*

> **Ravens are deeply significant in Celtic mythology. It is widely believed they can induce memory loss, even death, but so far, research into these phenomena is unproven.*

Lucy stared at the page, feeling the blood leave her face. Was it possible that those creatures out there were casting some kind of spell over her own memory? Hadn't she been waking up too early recently, having to crank up her brain to function? Weren't things she'd seen and heard beginning to blur and lose their significance, to form part of that vaporous veil of mist which now hovers over the Mellte for most of the day, spreading its milky fingers over the marsh?

She closed the book and blinked hard to return to reality. She had tomorrow to think about. Her one big chance and she mustn't blow it. Everything must be perfect. She gathered up her new T-shirt and skirt then took them downstairs to the scullery to be re-ironed. But, just as she was setting up the ironing board her mobile rang from inside her bag. At first she thought police or even her mother saying her cheque had arrived safely, but no.

It was Anna.

Lucy clamped the phone to her ear in relief at hearing again her friend's happy-go-lucky voice. And why shouldn't she be happy? Nick seemed a good guy and Lambourn was a lovely place to live. She deserved it.

'So, how's old Luce getting on in the midst of woolly Wales, or daren't I ask?'

'Less of the old, for a start, and yeah, it's okay.'

'Okay?' Anna challenged. 'For an assistant editor, shortly to be a freelance for Sayer Price, that's hardly an in-depth response. So, come on. Tell me...'

'Are you serious? About the freelancing?'

'Course. I had a word yesterday.'

'Do they know I got the sack?'

'Look, you showed an independent pro-active response. In other words, spunk.'

Lucy winced at her unfortunate choice of word and hesitated. It sounded as if Nick was with her friend, tickling her. Having fun. She suddenly felt more alone than ever, aware of how abandoned her clothes for tomorrow looked, heaped up on the ironing board.

'We heard about that girl and her two kids going off the road near the Beacons,' Anna went on. 'And that old chimney sweep. Hell, Luce, I thought Wales was all milk and honey, with those lovely Biblical names, all that singing...'

'It should be. Oh, Jesus. I mean, I'm not sure of anything any more. A lot's happened since I got here.'

'I'll hazard a guess. It's man trouble. Go on. I'm listening.'

Lucy heard her tell Nick to back off so she could concentrate. Salty tears began to sting behind her eyes and she turned her back to the kitchen door lest Hector catch sight of her in that state.

'Men plural, if you must know. Are you on your own?' she asked.

'I am now. Nick does as he's told.'

'Look, Anna. D'you know why I came here in the first place? The real reason?'

'You didn't get that last interview for the new editor's job and because you found some slapper and palmed her off with part of your slush pile, Merrill gave you the push. Oh, and growing stuff in Wales was something your dad always wanted to do. Correct?'

'Not quite. There's something I've never told you. But once I have, you'll know why my need to make a go of things here has been, well, almost maniacal. At the expense of pretty well everything...'

'I'm all ears.'

'Remember those shoes? 15th June?'

'Course I do. I bet you looked a million dollars in them.'

'I did, and that's not being immodest.'

Lucy then glanced back at the door and perched upon one of the chairs by the table to begin her story of the rape. When she'd finished, the silence which enveloped her seemed to come from another world.

'You are kidding,' Anna finally murmured. 'Did our friend use a rubber?'

'Yes.'

'I hope you told the police.'

'How could I? I still had my precious job to hang on to.'

'Well, *I* can start dishing some dirt now, don't worry. I'll be glad to.'

'I think his wife has plans in that direction too. She tried to bribe me to shop him. At least, I'm sure it was her.'

'Who needs fiction?'

'Exactly.'

'Hey, I just want to give you a great big hug. So hug yourself and pretend it's me, okay?'

Lucy managed a tiny smile as Anna went on.

'Now I come to think of it, when you brought those shoes back you didn't hang about. In fact, you looked washed out.'

'Thanks.'

'No wonder your little house on the prairie's a bit special. It would do for me if a toad like that had slobbered all over me, and the rest. You should stick with it. It'll be brilliant. I've got really good vibes about it. Can you send me some pix?'

'Do you really mean that?'

'What?'

'About sticking with it.'

'Look, when I told people at SP the other day what you were doing, they all turned green. Honestly. God's truth.'

'I'm meeting someone tomorrow, actually,' Lucy lowered her voice. 'Paul. From Bristol. He's nice.' She felt herself blush.

'Nicer than Jon?'

Damn. Did she have to?

Typical Anna.

'Different. Anyway, will keep you posted.'

'You do that. And remember what this wise *young* bird said? Up and at it, girl, and when you've got a bed ready, I'll be the first one in it. Let me grab my diary...'

While Lucy waited, she felt as if the sun had moved away from the massive cloud which had so far smothered her day. Somehow now, there was nothing she couldn't handle and nothing was going to stand in the way of success. Like she'd said on the driveway only hours ago. The past was the past.

'Say the 28th September. Then we'll have the whole weekend to catch up.'

'Just you and me, OK? No men.'

'No men, and it'll be like a little palace by then. You'll see.'

'I'll bring some manuscripts to keep you out of mischief.'

'Cheers you.'

'And good luck with Paul.'

Yes, Anna had given her hope. In fact all the hope she needed and a goal to aim for. Immediately Lucy made a short list, not a Truth List any more, but of jobs to be done. She couldn't just sit around and let the grass grow. Not now, and as she extracted her old Hellebore diary and began to write, She felt once again that William Mitchell was right alongside her.

Blitz WG

Elec. Board quote

Ironing

Eyebrows

And just to gather together old cleaning cloths, bin liners and the litre carton of bleach she'd bought on Monday, restored the sense of purpose she'd lost.

However, as she lugged the clobber down the hallway, Hector stepped out of his study. His face, already pale, reflected the bright yellow of the new wall paint. He looked ill.

'Are you crazy, girl?' He placed his body between her and the front door. Gin filled the air between them. 'You stay here.'

'You succeeded in stopping Mark but you can't stop me. Sorry.'

'You don't understand...'

'I think I do.'

'You've just said you needed us.'

Damn.

She paused, wishing she was hard enough to deny it.

'Why don't you and Mark just sort your problems out and leave me to mine? I've done bugger-all of what I'd planned. I'm like a hamster on a wheel here. Round and round and bloody round. Now, if you don't mind, I'd like to get on with something positive.'

'Give me a ring here in half an hour.'

'What on earth for?

'Just to say all's well down there. That's not asking for the world, is it?'

She dragged her cleaning gear even closer to the door. *He* could say all he liked. Nothing was going to hold her back.

'I'm only glad I never had a daughter,' Hector finally stood aside to let her by.

'Why's that then?' as she unbolted the front door.

'Because I'm a coward, see. I couldn't bear to lose her...'

For a moment she was stuck for words and once she'd stepped out-

side, turned to see tears beginning to well up in his eyes. Then Richard
came to mind.

'But you lost a son, and nobody says a dicky bird about what's happened to *him* on the other side of the world...'

Suddenly behind her, the door slammed hard against its frame –
loud enough to scare a solitary raven from the nearby beech tree. Loud
enough to remind her, as if she needed reminding, that she'd hit a raw
nerve and those shifting sands she'd felt under her feet from day one,
were in fact still alive and well.

And just then, as she struggled down towards Wern Goch with the
broom dragging along behind on the stones, the sneaking drizzle
turned to rain.

Having scrubbed and dried the gruesome salting slab, without managing to remove the stains, she sat down on it to draw breath, suddenly not caring what had lain there before. For a start, there was nowhere
else to park her bum in this gloomy kitchen, and secondly, that slam of
the Hall's front door symbolised a powerful full stop to all the ifs and
buts she'd endured for long enough. Mark had gone to work, and she
was doing the same with Anna's encouragement still ringing in her ears.

She rolled up her sleeves, because this is exactly what her friend
would be doing. 'Up and at it, girl,' she'd said, and here she was, obey-
ing, because deep down she believed she was right. Apart from the
numerous sheep droppings everywhere, the filthy area around the range
and beneath the old brick flue would be a good place to start next, and
that meant a shovel which she'd spotted in the barn twelve days ago.

She sloshed her way through the standing water outside and, upon
reaching the old building and pushing open its unwilling door, stood
stock still in amazement. Someone had cleared out all the junk and now
there was heaps of room for plants and possibly animals to be housed.
Even a sizeable office space.

Her heart leapt at these possibilities while she paced around the old
lime-washed walls, touching the solid ancient stones beneath as she
went. Mark must have worked his butt off to do this, she thought, finding a stack of cleaned implements in the far corner next to the five double-glazed windows. She reached for a square-headed shovel, feeling
gratitude mingled with shame that she'd taken him too much for grant-
ed, and that if tomorrow with Paul turned out to be a no-no, then who
knows? Before leaving, she took a final look round at the transforma-
tion. 'I want you to stay', it seemed to say to her. 'Please, for me...'

She was poised to make her way outside again when suddenly, she
detected another noise which appeared to come from the left side of the
barn where the reedy grasses began. It was nothing to do with rain,

more as if the skin of mud out there was catching on the soles of someone's boots...one...two...three...four...followed by the defensive croak of ravens.

'Who's there?' she edged forwards, shovel at the ready. But when she stepped beyond the doorway there was nothing to be seen. No human, no birds. Just the rain and that perpetual fount of water from which she'd earlier filled her bucket, curving from the bank.

'That's bloody odd,' she muttered, looking towards the Hall, the river and the empty fields. Unless there was some other explanation – that she was cracking up.

Nevertheless, once again in Wern Goch's kitchen, and still unwilling to inspect the cauldron, she began to sift great mounds of compacted soot from around the range, making sure that at all times she could at least see the scullery door. Having filled four bin liners with the vile-smelling stuff she paused for a breather and decided, after all, to give Hector a ring as he'd suggested.

'There is a fault with the line. There is a fault with the line...' replied a computerised voice.

Another odd thing, she thought, returning the phone to her bag. Perhaps he'd not noticed anything amiss and yet he'd been making calls earlier.

She soon refocused on the job in hand until gradually, and to her great surprise, the shovel's end scraped away the muck of ages to reveal a block of terracotta tiles surrounding the range. She knelt down for her damp cleaning cloth to finally expose their beautiful rich colour. She ran a hand over the smooth cool surface, aware of a deep joy filling her heart.

But little did she know two hours later, as she made her way back to the Hall to shower and change, that the watcher from the chestnut trees' damp shelter was noting her every move.

Hector's van was still there, so he must be around, Lucy reasoned as she let herself in and left the front door unbolted for his return. She was minging, as Anna would say, and a hot cleansing shower couldn't come too soon. Her hair and skin were filthy, while her fleece was now more grey than pink. It went in with her to the bathroom as no way was she letting it out of her sight for even one second.

Once undressed and inside the frosted glass cubicle, Wern Goch's grime sluiced down her arms to her feet and when she freed her ponytail, yet more of the same appeared. What she didn't notice however, as she turned round to train the shower on to her head, was the bathroom door slowly begin to open.

Chapter Thirty-Seven

The fiery red-head is raising her hand, sniffing the air which smells to me like a stale sea... Her chant of a Threefold Death to come rises like some evil echo, snaking into what's left of my soul, strangling, strangling...

My embalming skills aren't needed here of course, for the dead float naked and lost until the promised Re-Birth. I never believed in that sort of hocus-pocus before and I don't believe it now, because why are Lord Howells and his grandson still here? And why has my Mary given up...?

Well, well, well. Here's the meddler at last. I had to see her, didn't I? On my terms only, of course...

The voyeur with rain in his hair was less than two metres away from the one who held his future in her hands. Her body tantalisingly visible – *sfumato* style – behind the steamed-up semi-opaque glass as if Leonardo da Vinci himself had painted her in that pose. It was a word he'd learnt in school once while the class had been studying the Mona Lisa.

This time, the work of art was Mona *Lucy*, her flesh softly pink, her nipples pinker still. Her sex, her buttocks all there for him to gaze at. And to hate. But not for too long. He had to be careful. Especially now. It had been bad enough climbing up to her dodgy window and prising it open. Bad enough too that a piece of broken guttering had cut his right hand.

He found the shower cap and its contents inside her fleece pocket and then exited as silently as he'd arrived before creeping along the landing and downstairs to the hallway and the cellar.

Mission accomplished. In part, he reminded himself. *Don't get too cocky eh?* Because there was still one vital item missing. His old hunting knife.

He squeezed his way out through the one opening window which lay just above the wet back yard. Forget your clothes, he told himself. They'd soon dry off once he'd finished, and on his way back to his wheels he scooped up a handful of earth from the whore's nearby grave and with one swift movement, deposited it on the middle step leading up to the Hall's front door.

Pathetic little copy-cat, thought the one who'd seen everything. *Even after all these years...*

Chapter Thirty-Eight

I could murder that woman making passes at my husband. Poor fool. So easily flattered, he is. Always has been a sucker for red-heads has John.

John… John Thomas… I'd not seen his for years, mind, before we came to this place. Now I have to laugh because it looks so stupid, sticking out like that. But he can't hear me or see me, because this is her Hell, and already I've forgotten all my prayers. Forgotten everything…

Still no sign of Hector, just a faint musty smell which seemed to linger in the stairwell. However, after her shower, and despite the new more pungent gel, Lucy felt human again. She changed into clean jeans and a blue sweatshirt, went down to the scullery to deal with her health-hazard fleece. Having checked its washing instructions – 40 degrees with a warm iron later – she was just about to load it into the machine when she suddenly remembered what was in the pocket.

Dammit. How could I ever have forgotten? Her hand groped for the shower cap in first the right then the left one. *Dammit again*. Her heart started playing tricks, her throat suddenly dry. Where the hell had that gone? She'd guarded it with her life, for God's sake. Could Hector have taken it? Or Mark? Whoever it was, must have seen her in the shower. Seen everything…

She checked again. Nothing doing. Anger made her shove the fleece into the machine for a hot wash, any wash. She didn't care.

'Hector?' she shouted, then moved out into the hallway. 'Are you there?' She stared up at the stairwell and the dark cobwebs looped in its high ceiling corners. There wasn't a sound. Not a floorboard creaking or a loo chain flushing, even the familiar clink of a glass from his study. Hector had disappeared. So had his van, she noticed. With Mark gone too, she was on her own, with her pulse thudding in her neck.

With no time to waste, she hurried to the scullery then pulled her mobile from her bag. She had three calls to make. All vital. The first, via Directory Enquiries was to Parc-y-Nant Mental Hospital to find out if Mark had ever been a patient there. However, when a BT answerphone replied, she punched END and swore in frustration. Next, she tried reaching his female boss at the forestry who, to her surprise, confirmed he'd not been to work at all.

What the hell..?

With her stomach churning, she then phoned the police in Rhayader.

'It's Lucy Mitchell here. Ravenstone Hall. I need to speak to DC Pugh urgently please,' she kept her eye on the kitchen door. 'The fact is, I'm scared.'

'I'll put you through to his mobile. One moment.' In fact it took ten for her to mentally sort everything into some kind of order, so that when Pugh finally answered, her story tumbled out like the Wye in full flood, sweeping away her resolve to let sleeping dogs lie and to even forgive them. Her time had come. She was no longer the trusting novice buyer, prepared to give her fellow human beings the benefit of the doubt. She had finally turned betrayer. To save her life.

She could tell the detective was recording it all, from Mark making the ravens attack Simnai Williams last Thursday – and how frightened the man had seemed to be when she'd phoned him – right up to the bread knife in Mark's van and her being aware of someone lurking around Wern Goch. Finally, details of the bloodied fabric in the plasters box, stolen from her fleece while she'd been taking a shower ten minutes ago...

'We'll have someone over there within the hour,' he reassured her.

'An *hour*? For God's sake...'

'We're doing our best, believe me. Like I said, all our resources are tied up with the Williams case for the moment.'

Her sigh must have been audible because his tone brightened. Trying to help her stay positive, she thought. But all too late. 'By the way, Miss Mitchell, I shouldn't be telling you this, but, seeing as how you've been very helpful to us, I've got some good news for you.'

'Good news?'

'Yes, but just between you and me. Is that clear?'

'Of course.'

He was used to this, she thought. Keeping the informer sweet, so don't get too excited. Nevertheless, her heart joined her stomach in turmoil. 'Go on, please.'

'Our young lady from the waterfall has come out of her coma. She's been speaking to one of our WPCs. Very interesting I must say, even if somewhat cryptic.'

'And?' realising she was now trembling. Feeling sick. Being a turn-coat had no rewards at all.

'Apparently her abductor, someone called Phil, claiming to be a lawyer, told her to pass on the fact that someone called Richard has landed and wants revenge,' Pugh went on, 'whatever that means.'

Richard? Revenge? Whatever that means? She stared at the open kitchen door, a certain grim mantra hammering in her head.

YOU'RE NEXT...YOU'RE NEXT...

Then she understood. That name he'd just mentioned was no mere coincidence.

'Are you still there?' the officer asked, clearly disconcerted by her silence.

'Yes.'

'Now then,' he added in an even firmer tone. 'Stay calm. Do nothing to attract attention. Go to your car now, lock yourself in, lie low and wait for us. Understood?'

But there was no reply.

Her legs bore her unsteadily along the hall, where that wet clothes smell still hung in the air. Familiar enough from those days when she'd attended author events with the public coming in off rainy streets... Maybe it originated from her sooty gear bundled up in the Dorothy's Dresses bag ready for the next time. If there was a next time...

She grabbed one of Hector's old coats off the stand, noticing that his duffle was still there. Automatically, she searched all its pockets but fluff and more fluff was all she found, until something more solid met her fingertips. A pink ball of toilet paper. Carefully she unravelled the two joined sheets and recognised not only that it was the same as from the bathroom but the few handwritten letters were identical to those on the postcard pieces.

R'S BACK.

She recognised the writing as the same on that postcard. But it couldn't be. Could it? And if R did mean Richard, then where was he? What did he look like? And crucially, would she recognise him if he showed up?

She held her breath, her thoughts racing, then instinctively glanced behind her. The Hall was suddenly too silent and, once on its top step, she checked the drive and distant fields for any signs of life. There were none and her nerves kicked in big time. This wasn't just Crossgates and Elan all over again, but all the other menacingly silent places she'd been to.

The drizzle put everything in soft focus, muffling all sounds of the outdoors, even an aeroplane heading west overhead. There was no breeze, no stray leaf falling from the nearby beech tree and the alders along the Mellte stood as still as a distant waiting army.

Anything could happen.

Besides, where was Mark if he wasn't at work? And why did that short walk to the Rav feel like so many tense scenes she'd seen in those Westerns Jon liked? Or more specifically, the final scene of *High Noon*? Her legs felt boneless and her churning stomach suddenly leaden as she recalled DC Pugh's instructions. The police knew what they were doing, didn't they?

Well, here goes.

With car keys ready, Lucy gripped her shoulder bag as if it wasn't just a piece of BHS mock leather but also a lifebelt. However, just as she reached the middle step, she spotted a pile of red-brown earth lying there, just like before. Instead of sidestepping it, she kicked the soil with her trainer toe and scattered it wherever it fell. That small act of defiance made her feel much better.

Then something which almost made her miss her footing on the bottom step. A group of ravens were perched on her car's fabric roof, just as they'd done on Wern Goch the first time she'd been shown round. Her first reaction was to send them packing by yelling and clapping her hands but she remembered Pugh's advice. Besides, the way their avian eyes stared at her put them fully in control.

As she stared back at them, at least six more arrived and faced her way. Of course, she reasoned to herself, Mark had willed them there to protect her. That in the midst of all this open land and an apparently vengeful brother on the loose, lay a place of safety. Thankfully the rain had eased off as she slotted her key into the driver's door lock. But she needn't have bothered, because to her consternation, the Rav was already open and when she opened the driver's door, a smell, entirely different from the one she'd noticed at the Hall eked out. She thought of that first time she'd seen the salting slab. This was bird blood, alright.
Ugh.

She hesitated, trying not to breathe in. After that forestry trip, she'd forgotten to do that one thing which her pernickety landlord Mr Shah had banged on and on about in Albany Villa. Namely, lock up or else. She covered her nose with one hand as she settled in her seat. Was some dead raven inside the car? Rotting even? Where the hell was that smell coming from? She didn't dare get out again to look in the car's other areas; instead she checked the rubber-matted floor around her and the glovebox, but all seemed normal. To distract herself from retching, she switched on the radio. Company at least until the police arrived. She then watched helplessly as yet more birds settled on the bonnet. Bringing fear not comfort.

Three p.m. and the regular hourly news bulletin from Radio 4 came on air. She barely listened to details of yet more farmer suicides in Cumberland, so terrified was she in the way the birds seemed to be following her every move though the glass. However, when a report of the Burton Minster fire which had just claimed the lives of famous author James Benn and his wife filled the car, she gulped in disbelief.

'My God,' was all she could say as further gruesome details were added, and while Nick Merrill was offering his own fulsome tribute, she suddenly had the overpowering feeling that she wasn't alone.
Jesus Christ...

She turned round and screamed like she'd never screamed before. Louder than when drowning in the sea that time; louder than anything she'd heard since. Because someone with a head full of black and bloodied feathers was now sitting right behind her.

Chapter Thirty-Nine

Why my breasts are tingling, swelling up like they did all those nights ago before each birth? I don't know. Then I had too much milk which went to other new-borns. (So you see, I was a giver, not the Taker they claimed I was.) The ugly and the beautiful I had. Who'd have thought my two could be so different from the same womb? But now, when I try to sing a lullaby for them, my throat closes and the silence of this place drowns me, drowns me…

'You say my God, but *I'm* the only God round here,' came a muffled yet not unfamiliar voice. 'I'm The Dagda, you see. All powerful, all-seeing. Representing life and death. Or rather, my life. Your death.'

YOU'RE NEXT…

'Who the hell *are* you?'

Lucy tried to get out, but the intruder had somehow jammed central locking into lock mode and it wouldn't budge. Then she angled her rear view mirror with shaking fingers, to see who exactly was sharing her space, bringing with him that unmistakeable smell, and when she saw the two brown eyes focused on her from between the feathers, she screamed again. Mark had brown eyes. Most likely Richard too. Except that Rhiannon George had said grey.

'Shut the fuck up,' it said. 'Or you'll get this.'

A hunting knife whose blade glowed dully in a black-gloved hand. A blade which moved nearer her neck. Her breath barely there. She remembered her yoga but so what? Nothing could stop this terror. Never mind her mother her dead father or Anna or Jon, her mates from Uni, even Mark and Hector… No one could help her. Only herself.

The ravens were pecking at the windscreen now. Their beaks opening and closing, their swollen bodies black as the sky moving in from the west. Meanwhile, the stench inside the Rav had worsened.

'The police are on their way,' she tried to sound strong, aware of that knife poised behind her. 'Go while you've got a chance.'

'My chance is yet to come. Anyway, they can't get through.'

'What d'you mean?'

'We're all blocked in. Nice and snug.'

'Jesus.'

She tried the door handle again, because no way could she risk using her phone.

'They'll only kill you if you go outside,' the voice said. 'Look at them.'

Tap…tap…tap…

'Can't you get rid of them?'

'They don't listen to me any more.'

'I don't believe you.'

'You'd better.'

Several birds were now pecking the steel strip above the windscreen. Their weight pressing down the soft top, their noise making her head spin, all logic and reason now in a land of no recall. If she had nothing to lose, so be it.

'You're Richard, aren't you? Out for revenge, that's what that poor woman said. Revenge for what, you sad bastard? And why me now? Go on, say something. Or haven't you got it in you?'

'Hey, hey, you fucking little gold-digger. D'you realise that's the worst possible thing you could say to me?'

'Gold-digger?'

'Getting your feet under the table here. I've seen you at it. Crafty cow. So, it's payback time,' said the man, waving the knife so she could see it. 'Now drive.'

'Where?'

'Where do you think? To my place. Down there.'

My place? Mark again... It had to be... Yet hasn't he just said the ravens don't listen to him any more? That can't be right...

She started the engine as an update on Iris Carr's rape at Elan Valley made the tail-end of the local news. The hunt was now on for an Australian camper driving a black Ford Maverick.

'Turn that crap off,' barked her captor. 'Now. I've something better for you. So concentrate.'

She obeyed, suddenly thinking of her date tomorrow. How unless a miracle happened, there wouldn't be one.

'In the cellar at the Hall. Stone number ten up. Fifty across. East wall. Got it?'

'I don't understand.'

'You will. Now, move.'

She crashed reverse gear then with the ravens still in place, began the journey down the familiar watery track until Wern Goch came into view. She'd read that victims who'd survived abduction had got their captors' talking, formed some kind of rapport but her teeth had locked together, her dry lips sealed in fear. All she wanted was for the nightmare to end.

But night had come early to the Ravenstone acres and fresh rain had begun to fall.

'Faster,' came the voice. 'Or else.'

Her precious car. She'd never driven down this dreadful track before, but even that didn't matter now, scattering stones, slipping, sliding down towards that pool of red mud.

Suddenly the ravens moved from the bonnet and were joined by those from the roof to fly in strict formation towards the scullery door. Then, as before, they arranged themselves along the guttering.

'Let my armies be the rocks and the sea, and the birds in the sky...' the man in the back muttered to himself. 'Charlemagne said that. Neat, eh? Just about sums it all up.'

Her heart was hurting. Where the hell were the police? And not for the first time realised that this spot she'd chosen for peace and quiet, for a new life, was nothing less than a death trap.

No one will hear you scream...

She stalled. The engine cut out.

Mum? Dad..?

And in those few silent moments which followed, she said goodbye to them.

'Leave the keys where they are and get out.'

The sharp click of central locking being released, made her jump again. Nevertheless she grabbed her bag and pulled it across both front seats as she stumbled from the car into the mud. Fearing its possible loss, she placed the strap over her body in anti-mugging mode and turned to see the bare-legged man push her driver's seat forwards with a bang, then leap out.

Before she could run, a black woollen arm had hooked itself in an iron grip around her throat, dragging her towards the scullery door. The smell of stale blood was stronger now, clogging her nose, invading her whole body. Her shrieks were smothered by lanolin fleece as she kicked and struggled futilely against this almost superhuman strength which surely she'd felt once before.

Bang...bang...bang...This had to be Mark. Who else? But why this weird gear...?

Now in grisly close-up, she saw what covered his head. A black balaclava with ravens' feathers sewn into the fabric, congealed together by lumps of old blood. It was then she realised she'd left the scullery door unlocked.

'I thought you loved me,' she managed to say as they reached the kitchen and its lumpy floor. She glimpsed the shining orange-coloured tiles she'd only just cleaned. All that effort seemed a lifetime away...

'I loved *her. Her...*'

Her?

Nothing was making sense. By turning her head a fraction she saw how those brown eyes had narrowed. Suddenly the little knife was against her right thigh. One false move and she'd be cut.

'Through there. We have to wait for someone.' His hissing breath was followed by its blade now jabbing in the direction of the parlour. The darkest room in the house. She remembered the same way Mark had held that bread knife so close to Hector.

She stalled, registering the kitchen window's lack of glass. If she could only break free and reach it. If only... Suddenly, she heard the sound of another car engine outside. The squeal of brakes. A white Renault van she recognised.

Thank you God. Thank you...

For a moment the grip around her neck loosened. The chance she needed. She ducked out of her captor's grip and hurled herself towards the window.

'Help! Help!'

'OK, I'm coming,' a familiar voice reassured her. 'Hang on there.'

Her knees, her hands bruised against the old wood but at least she was outside, melting in relief against the sawyer's warm body.

Mark slipped a protective arm around her waist and pushed her hair off her ashen face. 'What the hell's been going on? You're all cut up. You look terrified. Shit, Lucy, I should have been here for you...' His smell was different. Not sap from the forestry, but that same dampness she'd noticed in the Hall.

'How did you get through?' she asked. 'That madman who made me drive here said everywhere's blocked off.'

'What madman?'

'Someone parading as the Dagda. He's got a knife.'

'Leave it to me, okay? I can handle it. Now then, let's get you inside out of this piss.'

'No! He's in there!' She felt faint, her trainers sticking to the mud. Her heart on hold.

'Let's take a look, eh?' he nudged her nearer the door where the wet ravens waited, their hunting eyes missing nothing. Her struggle subsided as his grip strengthened, forcing her back into hell. This time there was no scream, because what greeted them inside the parlour knocked the air out of her lungs. Two men were waiting motionless in the shadows. Not a balaclava in sight.

She blinked. Something was seriously wrong. For a start, Hector was slumped against the far wall, gagged by a length of rose-printed cloth – identical to those fragments from the chimney – while his hands and ankles were bound by orange baler twine. His self-inflicted bruise had darkened to a liverish purple around his eye and someone had removed his boots and the soles of his bare white feet were filthy. She noticed too how his lap was littered with bloodied ravens' feathers. His eyes full of resignation.

'My God, Hector. Who did this to you?' She tried to reach him, but Mark restrained her with an iron grip, this time around her wrist while the man with tanned and booted legs next to him bent down and untied the former policeman's gag.

'Leave him be,' Mark ordered. 'And put that back on. I brought him here to listen.'

'You?' she gasped, then remembered what he'd said about the bread knife to cut twine.

'Tough,' said the other, standing up to face him, as Hector licked his dry lips. 'I want to fucking hear him.'

'Well, well, well. So it's happy families time again,' interrupted Hector, glancing from Mark to the man she now recognised as the mineralogist from Bristol. Although his flattened hair seemed more brown, cut into a monkish tonsure style, and the eyes weren't blue, there was no mistaking that even-featured face, that tan, just the way he stood there. The reason she'd desired him more than anyone she'd ever met before. But happy *families*? What on earth could Hector mean? This was Paul, surely?

'If you *are* Paul,' she demanded, 'why the hell were you in the car with me just now saying I was a gold-digger? Scaring me to death?' But the man merely looked at her with a blank expression, as if he'd never met her in his life before. As if they'd never shared that meal. Never kissed. However, when the ex-copper finally caught Lucy's eye, everything about him said sorry.

'I really didn't mean to frighten you up at the Hall,' he explained, 'but I banked on you getting Mark from work and bringing him to where we can all be together again. I knew Richard had come back, you see. I knew he was hanging around. And now,' he nodded his head to the man on his left, 'I'm paying the price for interfering.' He glanced up at the taller man next to him. ' This *is* Richard, my eldest son, by the way...'

She shook her head. 'He can't be.'

R'S BACK...

'He is, I assure you,' Hector went on. 'And Mark of course, you've already met. Now then, son, let go of her please.'

'No. She belongs to me.' He gave her the weirdest look she'd ever seen, and she turned away.

'And *you're* her author who's up his own backside? Fun, eh?' snarled Richard. 'Do what the old geezer says. There's a good chap.'

'Fuck you.'

Nevertheless, Mark eased his grip, but Lucy's growing panic rooted her to the spot. She thought of her car out there in the mud; its little dancing figures on the upholstery; its welcoming interior. How even that had been violated. However, she could still be out of all this in minutes, leaving them to it. But two against one wasn't much of a bet. There really was no escape.

She also thought of her lowly flat in Albany Villa with a degree of love which just then was overpowering. Her one window on to that busy street. The nearness of ordinary things. The life she'd tried to live, whereas all that was near in this receptacle of horror, was imminent slaughter. Why? Because Mark Jones had just pulled the bread knife from inside his jacket. It glinted, rigid in his left hand.

'That's not going to get you very far, son,' Hector observed, unflinching. 'I suggest you put it away.' His voice now persuasion plus something less pleasant. He must have been a good cop after all, she thought. An iron fist in a velvet glove and all that. Then she wondered how she could possibly untie him now.

'And *I* suggest that for once in your stupid unproductive life, you listen. That so-called son of yours there, dressed up like God-knows-what, is a rapist and a killer. I parked my van out of sight and sneaked back in to hear you take those calls from Sydney. Liza Docherty eh?' he taunted. 'Poor cow. He couldn't resist, could he? And what about me? What have I got to show for fourteen bloody years. Tell me? Watching you drink yourself stupid. Night after night. Day after day. That's where our money's gone. And what about my head eh?' He tapped it with his knife. 'All screwed up, that's what. Thanks.'

Hector flinched. She felt Mark's hot breath on her skin – the only warmth in that damp old space which wasn't big enough for all this. She'd heard him deride his father often enough before now, but nothing like these accusations spoken in such a chilling way. And was this true? Were they the root cause of all the misery at Ravenstone? Whatever the answer, she knew then, that like his brother standing silently opposite, Mark Jones wasn't the man she'd believed him to be. Yes, she'd had her doubts, huge doubts, which had often outweighed her gratitude to him, but here, now, with that weapon fixed in his grasp, death was surely waiting in the wings.

'Put it *away*,' Hector growled.

'It's all I've got.'

She thought of Anna. She thought balls. Then took a deep breath, looking from one man to the next.

'So who's been following me? Who wrote that YOU'RE NEXT note?' She dug in the duffle coat pocket and held out the crumpled pink tissue. 'I recognised this writing as yours, Mark. But I'd like to think it could easily have been copied. And which sicko murdered the sweep and carved away his mouth?'

Hector grunted, shaking his head until Richard spoke at last, catching her by surprise. 'Try asking that blowie.' He pointed his hunting knife at his brother. 'You were probably making him nervous.'

'Prove it, you liar.'

'It doesn't matter what any of you say any more. After our mam was killed and I'd gone away, I wrote every bit of the truth down and sent it to someone. Someone else outside the family who had to know what really happened here.'

'Who was that, son?' Asked Hector, an alarmed expression on his haggard face.

'You'll find out soon enough.'

'And what *is* the truth?' Lucy interrupted, thinking that maybe, just maybe, major carnage could be avoided. She remembered the tales her mother told about the school playground. How in a dispute, she'd listen to the kids. Hear all sides of the story. The trouble was that here, it wasn't skipping ropes and Pokémon cards which lay to hand, but two lethal weapons.

'Mam was a tart. You both knew that,' Richard said scornfully to both Mark and Hector.

'She was a Taker, was our Tina Twilight,' his father said abruptly. 'Just like the Morrigan. And you, son, encouraged her.'

Lucy shivered as Richard's mouth became a coy smile.

'Yeah. I guess I did. But she never said no. Twice we had a naughty...'

Hector tried to move to silence him.

'That's *enough*!'. He looked worse than ill.

'No it wasn't. Because when I was up for it again, to try and go one better, she went all prim and proper on me. Just like the first time. So far and no further. Like she'd never...never let me, well, you know...'

'Stop it!' Hector roared, writhing futilely to prevent any more being said.

'Was that here, in Wern Goch?' Lucy asked, her voice wavering.

'Fuck no. She wouldn't have slummed in this dump. In the bathroom up there, it was,' he jerked his head in the direction of the Hall. 'Both times. Plenty of steam, fluffy white towels. It had a lock on the door then. Nice and private, till you removed it, you slimy perv.' He glowered at Mark who was rubbing his knife blade back and fore against his black leather sleeve before repositioning it. 'You see, she knew I loved her. And she loved me. While you,' he snorted. 'You jealous little runt, thought you could have the same. But you couldn't, could you? Tough, eh? Instead, you went and told Dada.'

'Rot in hell,' Mark snarled, while Hector vainly attempted to roll himself away from the wall.

'So,' Lucy dared, 'what *did* happen in this kitchen on May 1st 1987?'

'It was Beltane, the no-time dividing winter and summer, in case you weren't aware of the significance,' Richard now stared accusingly at his brother. 'The time between one world and the next. Like the fontanelle on a baby's head, if any of you half-wits know where that is. It's the weakest part of the year, when dark forces gain control. Anyway, Marko'd done these crap charcoal drawings of his ravens. He'd nicked the paper from school – great big sheets they were...'

Hector scowled in pain. Or was it something else? If only she could get to him, undo the twine and get him on his feet. It was shocking to see him so helpless. What had he done to deserve this treatment? And where were the useless police all this time? An hour, DC Pugh had said, yet it seemed like forever. She sneaked a look through the one window to the front and felt despair leach into her soul.

'He was copying me as usual, wasn't he?' Richard went on. 'I'd just been doing stuff like that for my Art coursework...'

'And then?' She persevered, trying to shut out the fact that two knives were on tense alert. Aware too, that if she shut her eyes, and regressed for fourteen years, these two men could be two warring teenagers all over again.

'Then Marko gets her down here. To *my* den. I was doing some homework in here and I heard them both laughing about something, coming in the door over there.'

But Hector wasn't laughing. Instead he fixed his weary gaze on Lucy while Richard continued.

'We both had identical hunting knives, remember? Dada here bought us them for Christmas in 1986. Mam kicked up a right fuss at the time. Little did she know, eh? Little did she know. But I kept mine,' he announced, waving it for all to see. 'And I'd hardly do that if I'd something to hide now, would I? So, where's yours eh, Marko? Got rid pretty quick, I bet.'

'Like my Nocturne stuff,' she said.

'I've told you already. Having it in the house was too dangerous. But how could I tell you that?'

'Dangerous? Why?'

'Ask him down there.'

'I don't understand.' She saw Hector's pleading eyes. His creased grey skin.

'I can't take much more, Lucy,' he suddenly murmured. 'I've had fourteen bloody years to live with all this acrimony, my lies, perjuring myself with the law, pretending with Mark here it was the Druids who'd killed her, and that Hughes and Evans were now part of their cult. Fourteen years of realising how my wife's behaviour had affected her sons, yet never quite knowing which one was guilty of taking her from me forever.'

He took a deep breath, transferring his gaze to Mark then Richard. 'I've tried to *protect* you both, can't you see? But it's destroyed me, I'm telling you. Then Lucy arrives and hears that woman screaming. What else could I do except pretend to go looking for her? How the hell could I go near any police station, or see any coppers, knowing what I know? But just when things begin to improve,' he fixed Richard with an accusing stare, 'back you come.'

'You liar. I fucking had to,' Richard protested. 'Being The Dagda I'd got the power at last to sort out the wrong I'd suffered. I've had to get my life back too.'

Hector had given up trying to move. Only his mouth kept busy.

'So The Dagda rapes the Morrigan for victory in battle?' he mocked. 'Is that why you went for that old biddy on Monday morning?'

'If you like. Yeah. What's wrong with that? After what I've been through.'

'Jesus.' Mark snorted derision. 'Time for the men in white coats, say I.'

'You should know all about that, you smug bastard,' Richard glowered, then stopped as his father began to speak again while Lucy thought of Parc-y-Nant.

'By the way, both of you. There's something you need to know. I rang Martyn Harries with new instructions for my Will, before whoever it was kindly severed the line connection to my study.'

She remembered with a shiver, the so-called fault when she'd tried to call him...

'And?' Mark in a sinister tone of voice, suddenly producing Hector's bunch of keys and dangling them in front of him. 'Do tell.'

'You'll be contacted in due course through the proper channels. That's my last word on the matter except to say that Richard isn't the only one I've disinherited.'

'What d'you mean?' Mark had whitened.

'I've just done the same to you, son. How could I not? I took legal advice and, as on previous occasions, was advised to be fair.'

'*Fair*? You bastard.'

The keys to all the Hall's hiding rooms dropped from his hand and fell to the floor where they lay splayed out like some strange multi-fingered hand. Her mouth fell open. She watched helpless as Mark let go of her and lunged towards his stricken father, his knife aimed at Hector's throat.

Before she could intervene, the blade had scythed from left to right through the old man's fleshy neck. Hector's dentures loosened and hung free of his lips as two jets of dark blood spurted from both carotids and his bellowing, dying cry sent the waiting ravens flapping away in fright. But Lucy knew they'd soon be back, because Mark's mouth was already open.

'Corax...corax...corax...' he croaked as his father's life flooded over the nearby flagstones and she retched air into her hands.

Suddenly, before either she or Richard could reach any door, the ravens reappeared, storming into the scullery dropping rain off their wings, aiming first for Hector's eyes then hers.

'Call them off!' she screamed to Mark. 'For Christ's sake!'

'Not this time, sweetheart. Sorry. They're looking after me, because no one else ever has.'

'*You're* the sicko, remember? You wait...' From the corner of her eye she saw what the birds had done to Hector's face, and she retched yet again.

'Oh, I will. I will because Dicky boy killed Rhaca. And tore out his feathers.'

'I had to do something. Can't you see? And now, at last, this is mine.'

Richard ran from the parlour into the kitchen and as he did so, snatched the cauldron from over the range before moving towards the scullery.

'Corax...corax...corax...' Mark croaked, and suddenly half the ravens turned on his brother, pulling his hair into spiky tufts then probing his ears as he charged out into the rain.

She saw him flaying the cauldron trying to beat them off, while she too, with Hector's old coat over her head, ran from the house.

She imagined herself back on the school hockey field again, haring down the wing. New rain stung her eyes as her trainers met the sodden ground where once Bryn Evans's sheep had grazed. Meanwhile Richard's shouts grew more indistinct as he travelled westwards. With a supreme effort she managed to narrow the distance between them, aware that Mark was closing on them both.

When she glanced round, she saw his bloodied knife held aloft. She screamed again, then slowed up because Richard was yelling something out, and she was close enough to pick up the gist of his unbelievable story.

'I fucking loved my mam,' he panted as if he was a kid all over again. 'You've got to believe that. Even though she messed me about so I wasn't able to come properly. Even though that tart in Bondi said I'd no toothpaste in the tube. Can you imagine what that does to a guy? And then I found that old granny with her bike... That was the first time in fourteen fucking years... But I still loved my mam. I still loved my mam...'

'So why harm that woman at the waterfall?' Lucy shrieked after him. 'Why?'

'I didn't. I couldn't. She just fell. I was too scared to go after her. It was *you* I wanted to get rid of, because *he'd* got you. He'd got fucking everything and I thought you and him would inherit it all here. It's my home too and I had nothing, except Rhiannon. I expect he followed her over to Brynamman once he'd seen me at her place. Frightened of what she might know. I'd have been a good Dad to her kids. I would...'

Lucy felt a sharp peck on her ear then on the backs of her legs. A stray bird had followed her and now it lifted away into the black sky. Was sick Mark enjoying this? she wondered, stumbling now, losing her breath and worst of all, seeing Richard and the hideous black vessel head straight for where the sheep never grazed. He'd forgotten. He'd been away too long.

'No! Don't go there!' she screamed as he totally ignored her, more intent upon finishing his tale of woe...

'I just loved Mam too much,' he repeated, 'and him back there was pig-sick jealous of every single fucking thing I did. He copied my clothes, what I ate, what I didn't eat. My art, my fucking poetry. He can lie to everyone. He even lies to himself. Jesus... But then he's had to, hasn't he? He's had to live *here* with knowing. Shit scared someone would one day find out. And then where'd he have been?'

'Find out what, for God's sake?' But now, after everything that had happened, she really didn't want to know. There was only so much one could take.

'Let him tell you. Unless he kills you first.'

She looked round to see Mark making headway, his black eyes huge in his head, his hair lifting like wings on either side despite the rain. The knife still poised. Suddenly the whole place seemed to freeze in a pall of silence, and a strange calm enveloped her as she watched her death approach in mesmerising slow-motion. After all, according to Richard, he'd written that note telling her she was next. And here she was, like a beast in the slaughterhouse, ready and waiting with nothing left to say or do, except close her eyes and pray.

When she finally opened them, still alive, soaked through, Mark had overtaken her, splashing, panting. She'd felt his hot breath touch her face and for one terrible moment now threw her a glance she would never ever forget. Then suddenly, catching her unawares, he stopped, turned round and headed back to her, his boots throwing up mud.

'Anyway,' he edged closer, the knife still in his left hand. 'Giving up that Nocturne muck at least gave you a pulse for a few more days. It was a problem for me especially. You never knew that, did you?'

'But you've just said it was Hector who...'

'Sure. Why not?'

He clapped for the remaining birds to scatter then, without taking his eyes off her, laid down the knife in the reeds. Clearly preferring to use his bare hands, she thought, watching them with an almost out-of-body detachment. It was then she noticed a red gash on the palm of his right hand. There wasn't time to ask how it got there, because it suddenly slapped her cheek. But what was the point of screaming any more? Better to use her last moments to fight back.

'I should have realised while I was still in London. You're barking mad.'

'Whatever you say.'

Then before she could struggle free, both rough wet hands were round her throat.

'I can't breathe,' she gurgled, seeing her father's smiling face as if for the last time.

'That's the idea,' he hissed. 'The moment you started snooping around, that's when I started going off you. You're next, or have you forgotten?'

No point in reacting to that now, she told herself. What little breath she had must be saved.

'You were hoping to stitch Richard up, weren't you?' she whispered instead. ' That's a nice brotherly thing to do, I must say.' Those hands were tightening. She saw the sky turn purple overhead.

'I must have had a screw loose to tell you what those bits in the shoe were. And then you go and help yourself to that stuff in the bathroom stool. Again that was very private. Still,' he went on, 'all these goodies are tucked away nicely where no one will ever find them. A chap has to have some souvenirs, don't you think?'

Ten stones up, fifty across, east wall...

'So it was you who sneaked into the bathroom while I was having a shower?'

'Needs must. To stop your games. To keep the plods away.'

For a split second he lost concentration and this time Lucy wasted no time in wriggling free. Despite slipping several times on the wet grass, she managed to whip round, back the way she'd come. Then she noticed a scrap of paper fall from his hand as he resumed the chase for his brother.

'Your second poem,' he shouted back at her. 'Says it all.'

'Mark?' She called out after him but he didn't even slow up. There was no stopping him because bare-legged Richard was still on the move, keeping up the pace, still yelling. She herself dared go no further into the bog to pick up that piece of paper. She could only watch and listen as the powering rain dulled the impact of his words.

'That's right. Tell her, go on Marko. Truth is the Word, remember? How our dada was waiting in the barn. How he'd got his old copper's gun. We had to watch our mam struggle and we couldn't help her. He made you slit her throat with your knife then me to cut out her sex and boil it up in this cauldron. Can you imagine seeing that? Can you? While he just stood there laughing, saying it served me right and served *her* right. Evil bastard. Still, I cut his wrist, didn't I? That made me feel better, but not much. He told the cops he'd done it on some corrugated sheeting, the liar. Then – and this is the icing on the cake – I had to get my Rhaca and the others to finish her off...'

'*Your* Rhaca?' Lucy aghast.

'Yeah, he was mine originally, but like everything else, Marko had to have him. To control the way he wanted. In the end he quite enjoyed telling them all what to do. Didn't you? You freak show.' he shrieked. 'Just like he'd enjoyed slitting her throat.'

'I can't believe this. You're lying.'

'Truth is the Word. *My* Word, okay? Then Dada swore he'd kill us if we told anyone. Now do you see why I begged him to send me away?'

'You *begged*?' She stopped running, still flapping the dead man's coat sleeves, ignoring the blood dripping down her legs. 'Oh my God.'

'We had to live with that murder. *Him* protecting *us*?' Richard snorted. 'Bollocks to that. I kept my mouth shut for fourteen fucking years even though I knew he'd cut me off. And you Marko, you thought by hanging on, by keeping him sweet and everything ticking over at the Hall that you'd pick up in the end... Fat chance now eh?'

This was unreal. Worse than terrible. No wonder Mark hadn't wanted her to buy Wern Goch in the first place. No wonder he'd got the wind up when she'd started snooping. But maybe that wasn't the whole story. Maybe she'd never know...

'Whatever happened to Mark's hunting knife after the killing?' she yelled.

'I told you ... the cellar wall...' his voice disintegrating into the drizzly air.

'Where?' Mark rasped.

'You'll have to catch me first.'

'Come back!' she yelled at them both. 'Come back. It's not worth it. You'll drown!' Then the words ten up, fifty across dying on her lips. It made no difference. No one heard her except those few ravens who'd deserted the parlour and were winging their way laboriously towards the two brothers now locked in a frenzied final embrace as the marsh began to drag them and the cauldron down with a gloating, sucking sound.

'Corax...corax...corax...' she called out in vain, for the birds weren't only too late, there were too few to help a pair of fully-grown men to safety. Besides they seemed too lethargic, too replete to be of any use now.

She scrabbled in her bag for her mobile but the moment it was in her hand, an oncoming bird unseen by her swooped low and snatched it out of reach into the air.

'Jesus Christ. Damn you...' She swore at it then blinked through her tears over to where the two who had so fiercely and at such cost, protected evil, were now sinking into the Druids' starless well. But just before both heads, one dark, one lighter finally disappeared, she could have sworn she heard a voice, choking, choking. Mark's she was sure, and it seemed to be saying, 'I loved you, Lucy. I really loved you...'

She stared at the reedy spot where nothing now remained, praying that the singer's tortured sons might somehow reappear from that Otherworld's stinking depths. Praying this nightmare would end. Suddenly she heard a siren stab-stabbing the eerie silence, and as the rain eased and the wind began to rise, stirring the alders along the Mellte, she saw at last, a line of police begin to swarm towards her over the marshy field.

Chapter Forty

And when will you be coming back again,
My sons come and tell to me?
When Moon and Sun dance in yonder hill
And that will never be be be
And that will never be.
The Brothers. Trad

'Larkin was right, you know.' Anna gave Lucy a brief knowing smile as she set the kitchen table for dinner. 'They fuck you up, your mum and dad.'

'Easy to say that now,' Lucy refilled her wine glass as her friend had suggested, trying to keep blame out of her voice. 'I was all for jacking it in, but you did say hang on in there...'

'Oh, come on, Luce. You wanted it all badly enough. I was only picking up the vibes.'

'True. But I should have listened to what that sweep had said, then gone to see him straight away after he'd done the chimney. In fact, I should never have let him out of my bloody sight.'

'And then what? Back to London for more hassle?'

'I honestly don't know.'

Anna picked up her own glass and raised it in the air.

'Anyway, to the Lady of the Manor. Or will it be B&Bs plus evening meal and a few tasty locals thrown in?'

'Not funny.'

'Sorry.'

The smell of horses pervaded the Berkshire cottage which she'd shared with her vet for the past six months, and as dusk began to fall beyond its mullioned windows, a line of thoroughbreds could be seen returning to their stables which nestled deep in the valley below.

Lucy watched this perfect scene with her glass of chilled wine against her cheek, and if she half-closed her eyes, could imagine herself back at Wern Goch with her dreams intact, at peace with that once-sacred land and its ancient guardians. She wished she could have added a witty reply to Anna's quip about the Hall, but it was too soon for jokes. Way too soon. Because just three days had elapsed in which, besides fighting off reporters, she'd spent the first long morning after with the CID; arranged Hector's funeral in Cardiff to follow the Inquest at the end of next week; and organised the closure of the whole Wern Goch project. Even though Hector Jones had left the estate to her in his brand new Will, no way would she ever set foot near the place again.

Meanwhile, Iwan George at Gellionnen had found Richard Jones's letters and poetry to his daughter. Some items even arriving after her death. Mark Jones's cleaned-up hunting knife and all his other morbid memorabilia had been unearthed in the Hall's cellar wall. Ten stones up, fifty across, just as his brother had said. But he'd not had time to be so careful at Maesybont, and his prints found in the kitchen of 'Simnai' Williams's bungalow matched those on the weapon used to silence the troublesome little man for ever. The bread knife abandoned in Wern Goch's field.

DNA tests carried out on the strip of blue shirt found in the plasters box, stored in the wall, proved that the saturated fibres contained blood from two wounds, His and Hers, fourteen years old. Cold bad blood. The start of a life in hell.

'So, is it Mauritius or Goa for us, then?' Anna grinned, pouring herself a glass. 'Nick says he'll be glad to get rid of me for a week and, apart from my Brazilian which is itching like crazy, I've got a bikini waiting to be worn.'

'I'll have to think about it, okay?'

An easy silence fell between them and Anna's gaze fell on the cat sprawled out asleep on the shelf above the Aga. Lucy gladly would have joined it as she'd lain awake most nights since that terrible Wednesday afternoon, re-living Hector's last moments and seeing those two drowning heads. Images she knew would blight her for the rest of her life.

Her mother had rung immediately the news had broken in the press and on TV and radio, and had insisted upon coming down to Wales, but Lucy had said no. She'd be back in Manchester with her dad's money and job-hunting soon enough. The Ravenstone legacy would be her secret for the time being because, right now, like that Chandos Hotel night in June it represented a certain kind of death.

'From what I've heard and read, I don't think he was entirely mad, you know,' Anna rolled up three linen napkins and slotted them into matching earthenware rings.

'Who?'

'Richard?'

And Paul...

How could she ever tell Anna what she'd once felt for him? How he'd seemed the answer to her every longing? And as she watched the tops of the trees beyond the window sway their heavy green crowns against the sky, she felt nothing but hatred for the beautiful, wilful Sonia Jones and the terrible wreckage she'd left behind. She'd loved one son too much. The other not enough.

Families...

'I actually feel sorry for the guy, do you know that?' Anna went on.

'Seems like he'd had a bum time, living with people he hated in the back of beyond. He hated his father too, for making him stay silent. My God, can you imagine that?'

'I can. Yes.' She set down her glass and went over to the Belfast sink where she stuck her head under the cold tap for a drink. She then wiped her mouth with the nearby roller towel, aware of Anna looking at her as if she too might have caught some of the madness.

'So he never tried a Benn on you, then?' she ventured.

'No.'

'Two weeks ago you'd have laughed at that.'

But two weeks ago was another world. Besides, hearing that man's name again, even though he was now dead, was bad enough, and the word rape too would probably be off-limits for ever.' I wonder if she killed him,' Anna mused as she tore open a pack of bread rolls and emptied them into a rustic woven bowl. 'Forensics are saying it's arson. That's the latest, anyway.'

Lucy watched as another string of horses came and went, this time leaving behind a cloud of brown dust.

Dust and ashes...

She'd not had a moment to follow the news of the fire even if she'd wanted to. But just then, in her mind's eye came that small pale face which had on those two occasions 'at the Chandos and at Hellebore, stared so hard at her. Jealousy wasn't the right word. More a longing. Poor Elizabeth Benn...

'So, what *did* he do?'

The question made her jump. Her wine nearly spilt from the glass.

'Who?'

'Paul, of course.'

'Just a kiss, that's all.'

Just a kiss...

'And what about Mark? I got the message you fancied him a bit too.'

'I did, at first, till I twigged he was covering something up. I tell you, Anna, he had these amazing eyes. They were, I don't know,' she hesitated. 'Kind of like the night. Like the inside of that horrible cauldron.'

She put down her glass and withdrew a carefully folded piece of paper from her bag. 'This was the first poem he wrote for me. The second got trampled on by the police at the end, and I never found it. Please don't look at me while I read,' she added, because already her own eyes were beginning to sting.

'OK.'

And although she took a deep breath, her voice when it came, still trembled.

'Lucy, bringer of Light to my dark world,
As brightest star, you foil the deepest night,
And keep the gloom from gathering in my mind,
Like worms uncurling in the cold red earth.
MJJ   23rd August 2001.'

'Weird. Specially that last line. 'Anna gave her another sideways glance as Lucy returned the poem to her bag, fighting back tears. Her fortnight in that bleak mystical universe, replaying yet again in her mind. How Richard and Mark had ended up hating her. How both he and Hector had lied to her from the start, and still she'd been sad enough to see the drunk as some kind of father figure. Gullible enough to tell him something she'd dared not even reveal to her own mother. 'What a shitty old world we live in, eh?' she added, wiping her wet eyes with her sleeve, knowing that perhaps this was the only truth he'd spoken.

Anna refilled her glass and returned the bottle to the fridge. 'The papers imply Richard had this hang-up about tarts. That he was wanted by the Oz police for a murder out there. They've just done an Inquest on the girl. Have you seen it?' She went over to the pile of newspapers and magazines on the dresser.

'Sorry, but I can't look at any more.'

'Don't blame you.' Anna stopped and patted her shoulder instead. 'Still, you've got your name in lights. One way of doing it, I suppose.'

'Great.' Lucy looked up at her. 'But don't you ever go there, promise me?'

'Where do you mean?'

'Wales.'

'What? Not any part of it?'

'No.'

'That's a bit OTT, isn't it?' Anna checked her watch and tutted. She opened the oven door, eyed the pasta bake inside and closed it again. The appetising smell which emerged made Lucy realise she'd not eaten all day.

'One of the Hellebore authors warned me it was a another world there. But she should really have said *under*world. Land of the Dead. The damned... It's nothing like what's in that thing. Nothing at all. Take a look.' She pointed to a carrier bag she'd left on one of the chairs.

Anna wiped her hands on the roller towel and duly extracted *Magical Tales from Magical Wales* and as she turned it over, then examined the frontispiece, her eyes widened in surprise and pleasure.

'My God. This is bizarre. It's yours, yes?'

'I've had it since I was so high. My bible.'

Anna sat down to study the book more closely and without looking up asked,' do you know the author?'

'Not now. It's so old.'

'And the illustrator?'

Lucy shook her head. It was odd seeing that rainbow cover in Anna's hands. It looked nothing special now, just a drab little book. The kind you get in jumble sales, given away at the end.

'They're one and the same,' Anna went on. 'Sayer Price Childrens are bringing out a new version next year. It was originally published by Aderyn, a small outfit in Wales in 1943.'

'A little black bird with its tail in the air?' How could she ever have forgotten?

'That's right. Managed to keep going till they folded in the early fifties. Anyway, have you ever heard of Gritta Muller?' she asked.

I G Muller...

'Gritta, you said?'

'Yes. She always used her middle name for her books.'

'Of *course...*' Now after all these years, she remembered. Now she knew.

Ten minutes later came the sound of car tyres on gravel. Both friends glanced out of the window but the drive was just out of sight for them to see who was arriving.

'That's Nick. About bloody time too.' Anna went outside, clearly glad for this distraction after what she'd just listened to, while Lucy, still feeling chilled, watched the door into the hallway with a certain wariness. She'd never met the vet before now and, after her recent experience, strange men in any shape or form were going to be a problem for some time.

Except that the person who entered, carrying a bunch of white roses, was no stranger. He smiled and came over, and as he did so, the knot of pain inside her unravelled to be replaced by a surge of happiness. He looked the same, even smelt the same, as if time had stood still since their last meeting.

'Your fridge magnet man,' Anna announced as Jon blushed and handed over the flowers.

Lucy smiled her gratitude. And just then, to do that was enough.